This book should be returned to any Lancashire
County Council Library on or before the date shown

ncashire County Council Library Service,
unty Hall Complex,
d floor Christ Church Precinct,
eston, PR1 0LD

www.lancashire.gov.uk/libraries

Lancashire
County
Council

D1407271   07 1

Discover more at millsandboon.co.uk

WITNESS SECURITY BREACH

JUNO RUSHDAN

COLTON 911: AGENT BY HER SIDE

DEBORAH FLETCHER MELLO

MILLS & BOON

First Published in Great Britain 2020
by Mills & Boon, an imprint of HarperCollins*Publishers*
1 London Bridge Street, London, SE1 9GF

Witness Security Breach © 2020 Juno Rushdan
Colton 911: Agent By Her Side © 2020 Harlequin Books S.A.

Special thanks and acknowledgement are given to Deborah Fletcher Mello for her contribution to the *Colton 911: Grand Rapids* series.

ISBN: 978-0-263-28051-7

1020

MIX
Paper from
responsible sources
FSC™ C007454

This book is produced from independently certified FSC™ paper to ensure responsible forest management.

For more information visit: www.harpercollins.co.uk/green

Printed and bound in Spain
by CPI, Barcelona

WITNESS SECURITY BREACH

JUNO RUSHDAN

For those who fear love.

Chapter One

The next four words to leave his mouth would obliterate a life. Four words every US marshal hated saying. Four words every person in the witness security program dreaded hearing.

"You're in imminent danger," Aiden Yazzie said, closing the last set of kitchen blinds, muting the bright April sun. He turned and met Eugene Potter's terrified face.

The urgency of the situation was spelled out in big, bold letters across the bulletproof vests of Aiden's four-man special operations team, the CAR-15 rifles strapped across their backs and the tactical, turbo-charged vehicle with blacked-out windows parked in front of the suburban Palisades home. When the US Marshals Service identified a need for extraordinary measures, it was the Special Operations Group— SOG—that answered the call.

The sixty-two-year-old man staggered back and sat on a stool at the counter. "But how?" He ran a shaking hand through his thinning gray hair. "I've been so careful. How was I blown?"

Aiden exchanged a glance with his partner and best friend, Charlotte "Charlie" Killinger. The answer to Eugene's question had the entire Justice Department in an uproar, had tarnished the impeccable reputation of their San Diego field office and sent the SOG scrambling.

Eugene had a right to know, along with the other unsuspecting individuals in the program that'd been compromised in the Pacific Coast region, but the reason was classified.

In typical Killinger fashion, Charlie redirected. "If you want to live, we have to relocate you again. Immediately."

"I—I can't." Eugene's mouth hung open, and his eyes blinked rapidly. "My wife is at work."

Aiden stepped up beside the trembling man. "We're prepared to pick her up before we head to the Safe Site and Protection Center. At the SSPC, you'll both be briefed." He put a hand on the older man's shoulder. Tension coursed through Aiden. Each minute they spent in the house endangered Potter. "We should leave now."

"You don't understand." Eugene shook his head. "We've only been married six months. I followed procedure. Sharon doesn't know who I really am or the things I've done." Despite the air-conditioning that matched the temperate SoCal weather, a sweat broke out on his brow. Propping an elbow on the counter, he wiped his forehead with the heel of his palm.

"It's good you followed protocol. Smart," Charlie said in a clipped tone, flicking a look at her watch. "I'll explain why you couldn't have disclosed the details."

Those in WITSEC left everything behind, buried the old version of themselves and were instructed never to share the truth or their past with anyone. Not even a new spouse.

In the event of an ugly divorce, the secret could be divulged out of revenge.

Starting a marriage based on lies was brutal. But not as brutal as a bullet to the head.

Following the rules kept people alive and no witness who'd done so had ever been killed. It was Aiden and Charlie's job to make sure that didn't change.

"She'll know I lied to her!" Eugene's face snapped up. "She'll question everything. My love. Our marriage." His gaze flew to the photo gallery above the breakfast nook. Family memories featuring young children adorned the wall.

"Sharon will never leave San Diego. Her four kids are here, six grandbabies. Cindy, her youngest, is pregnant with her first. I thought I'd be here for the rest of my life. It's the reason I married her, allowed myself to become part of the family. You people promised that after I testified and got settled, I'd be fine." His features twisted in pain, his eyes brimming with tears. "I'm going to be sick." He jumped to his feet and ran into the hallway bathroom, shutting the door behind him.

"What's taking so long?" Johnny Torres asked over the comms device in their ears.

He and Dale Banks were the other two tactical marshals assigned to the high-priority detail. They were covering the front and rear of the house.

"The *dynamic duo* should've had this wrapped up by now," Dale said, his tone caustic.

Aiden rolled his eyes. He and Charlie were indeed dynamic together. They were the best SOG operators in the unit. Smack talk came with the territory. Under normal circumstances he would've enjoyed it, but after taking a wrecking ball to a man's life, he wasn't in the mood.

Charlie met his gaze. Those sapphire-blue eyes of hers were hard as gemstones. Held an incisive gleam that never dulled. With blond hair cut in a sleek bob, her fair skin and icy veneer, she was stunningly good-looking, and called the snow queen by the other guys.

To Aiden, she was more of a Viking warrior ready for battle. She was simply spectacular.

She toggled her earpiece. "If we want your opinions, we'll give it to you. Torres, start the car. We're leaving the wife behind and heading straight to the SSPC." She disconnected.

After Torres gave a curt acknowledgment over comms, Aiden asked her, "Isn't that premature? Mr. Potter might want to try to convince his wife to go with him."

"Did you take a gander at that?" Charlie hooked her thumbs in her gun belt and inclined her head toward the picture-perfect wall of photos. "Each person is an anchor, weighting his new bride to her old life. He never should've been foolish enough to fall in love and buy into some fairy-tale ending. A clean break is best."

"It takes courage to love." Aiden strode up to her, bringing them face-to-face. Their eyes locked. "Don't knock it until you're brave enough to try it."

Charlie slinked closer, sexy as sin, and hoisted her chin like a gladiator, quickening his pulse. They would've been nose to nose if he didn't have a good six inches on her.

"What you call bravery, I see as delusion." Her voice was low and cold but heated his skin.

For a second, he was tempted to lower his head and kiss her. Melt her glacial facade with all the red-hot passion burning in his veins that wasn't professional or platonic, but restraint bred from lots and lots of practice had become one of his virtues.

When he made his move, it had to be the right time and place. He didn't want to be one of Charlie's lovers who had the shelf life of bread. He wanted to be the love of her life.

"Leaving Mrs. Potter behind with a clean break isn't our decision to make," he said.

"Nevertheless, Tweedledee and Tweedledum outside have a point. This is taking too long. We agreed that we'd be in and out in ten minutes."

Aiden didn't need to check his watch to instinctively know they'd been inside for six. Already his gut agreed with Charlie. They'd been there too long.

"You still have that bad feeling?" she asked, her hand resting on the gun on her hip.

The moment they'd pulled up, it was as if a clammy finger had been dragged down his spine.

He wished he could chalk it up to nerves over keeping his big news from Charlie. Telling her that this might be their last assignment together if he accepted the coveted position as an

SOG instructor at Camp Beauregard in Louisiana. It was a conversation he wanted to have about as much as he wanted to get a root canal without Novocain. But *this* wasn't nerves.

Aiden stepped away, scrubbing a palm over his jaw. "Yeah, I still have it."

"You might be in denial about your sixth sense, but I'm not. I've learned the hard way never to ignore your gift."

Denial couldn't be further from the truth. If experience was any indication, the prickly tingle warned that someone was going to die today.

Was it a *gift* to know when death was going to come calling? Felt more like a curse.

"We can't wait for Eugene to pull it together." Charlie shifted her weight from one foot to the other. Crossed her arms over her chest. "We need to go."

No bad feeling necessary to realize that was an understatement.

There was a high price on Eugene's head. His personal information had been sold on the dark web. At least one hit man that they were aware of had been contracted, prompting the urgent relocation. It was possible others might come slithering out of the gutter to try to collect.

A toilet flushed and water ran.

Eugene stumbled out of the bathroom, looking peaked and more devastated than before. "I need to talk to Sharon, say goodbye at the very least. Tell her I'm sorry. I owe her that."

Aiden threw Charlie an I-told-you-so look, which she returned with a conciliatory nod.

"Let me grab something first," Eugene said, "and then we can go."

"There's no time for you to pack anything." Aiden sidestepped, blocking his path. "All the essentials will be at the SSPC, just like last time."

"It'll only take a second. I won't leave without it." Eugene pivoted, scurrying around him to the open shelving beside the stove, which was lined with cookbooks, dishes and knickknacks. He took down a display of wine corks in a tall glass vase, dumped them onto the counter and fished out one from the pile. A relieved look washed over him. "Okay. Now we can g—"

The kitchen window shattered with a pop.

"Get down!" Aiden was already in motion as the words left his mouth.

He lunged for Eugene. At the same time, Charlie drew her 9 mm, taking a defensive posture.

Aiden shoved Eugene hard to the floor as the vase on the counter shattered, spraying glass over them. More bullets buzzed through the air and punched holes in the cabinets, sending jagged plywood shards in all directions.

They had one big problem. The rifle trained on them.

Covering his head with his hands, Eugene shrieked but had the sense to stay pinned in the chaos of the fusillade.

Aiden tightened his hold on him, ensuring Eugene was shielded. No bullet would reach Eugene unless it went through Aiden first.

Charlie? Her name was on his tongue when she came crawling around the kitchen island with her STI Staccato-P, locked and loaded, in hand. Only SOG carried the STI rather than the Glock 22 that rank-and-file marshals were issued. What elite operator didn't want a gun that held twenty-one rounds, shot superfast and never failed in accuracy?

Another volley of gunfire tore through the room.

Distance. Aiden needed distance from the scene.

He pushed back mentally, slowed down the external factors along with his breathing and the rush of blood through his ears. His soul quieted.

His mind brought everything into razor-sharp focus, discarding every distraction in seconds.

From the sound, the rifle being used was suppressed.

Based on the I-want-to-blow-off-your-head-sized holes in the cupboards, it was also high-powered.

The impossibly rapid gunfire was controlled, calculated. Bullets whizzed way too close for Aiden's comfort. The shooter's accuracy indicated that he or she was well trained, stationary, and had a good, if not spot-on, idea of where they were despite the drawn blinds. Aiden had got Eugene behind cover—but apparently they weren't concealed. Which left only one explanation.

Their sniper had a precision-guided smart scope that could track targets behind walls. "Shooter is using LIDAR or ultrasonic technology," Aiden said to Charlie.

"Must be military grade."

If they didn't want to ingest lead, sitting there wasn't an option.

"We've got to move," Aiden said. "Now!" Not waiting for Eugene to react, he grabbed the older man by the collar and hauled him up to his knees.

Bullets peppered the spot where they'd been.

They shuffled forward. Aiden used his own body as cover. Glass crunched beneath them.

A maelstrom of rounds strafed the kitchen all around, riddling the drywall with holes. A hot slug sliced past their heads.

Too close. One centimeter closer and Aiden would've been toast.

Eugene fumbled, a panicked flush on his cheeks. The wine cork slipped from his grasp.

"I need it!" He had the reckless gall to resist moving and reached back for the cork. A piece of glass sliced open his palm, drawing blood.

Eugene yelped from the small cut like he'd been shot.

Aiden pushed him lower and grabbed the wine cork. Rather than handing it over, he held on to it and forced Eugene toward the refrigerator.

The fridge was one of those massive units, a sixty-four-inch side-by-side fridge-and-freezer set.

Aiden opened the fridge and tucked Eugene behind the door.

"Give it to me!" Eugene tried to wrest the cork from Aiden's hand.

If he was more concerned with a piece of bark than taking a bullet, no way in hell was Aiden giving it to him.

Eugene snatched hold of one end of the wine cork and pulled on it, separating it in half, revealing a concealed flash drive.

"What is this?" Aiden asked, holding tight to the drive.

"I need it!" Eugene clawed at Aiden's fingers like his life depended on getting it back.

Aiden shoved him against the interior of the fridge before he waved Charlie over to take the other side. There was only space for two behind the doors.

"Torres, Banks," Charlie said over comms, her voice like steel as she made her way to the refrigerator, "we're taking gunfire. What's your status?"

"I left the vehicle. I'm headed inside to help get Potter out," Torres responded.

Any assassin worth his weight in salt would have both exits covered. Taking Eugene outside would only increase his exposure. They'd never get him to the car alive.

Aiden tapped his earpiece. "Torres, don't. Track where the gunfire is coming from and lay down suppressive fire to give me a chance to move. We've got to kill the sniper first."

"On it."

"Banks?" Aiden waited for the next reply that didn't come. "Dale, come in."

"I think he's down," Charlie said, echoing his thoughts.

If that were the case, the sniper did have a line of sight to the backyard, kitchen, most likely the front, too, and had taken out Banks before unleashing a torrent of slugs on them.

"Protect Potter," Aiden said to Charlie. "The fridge door will make better cover and take the brunt of the gunfire."

He guessed the rifle was a .50 cal. The thick stainless-steel doors wouldn't hold up indefinitely under the heavy fire-power, but they should withstand the onslaught long enough for Aiden to take care of the shooter.

"You stay," Charlie said, her eyes bright and shining, her voice too eager. "I'll go——"

"No. It's an order." Aiden only played the I-outrank-you card when necessary. It wasn't that Charlie couldn't handle the sniper—she was more than capable, but she was drawn to danger like a moth to a flame, and he'd do anything to prevent her from getting burned.

Coming up on one knee, he drew his gun and then moved without hesitation toward the door leading to the yard. He'd be easy pickings once outside. Since Banks had taken the back, Aiden didn't know if there was anything out there that he could use for cover besides a couple of stone pillars.

A grill. He recalled noticing a gas grill on the patio as he'd lowered the blinds, but the propane tank made it more of a hazard than potential cover.

Going outside was a dicey move, but necessary. Eliminating the threat required two people. One as bait to draw fire while the other went in and neutralized the enemy.

Aiden stopped before reaching the doors and stood with his back to the double-wall ovens in a pocket of space protected from gunfire. "Torres, you got a bead on our sniper?" Aiden asked, slipping the thumb drive into his pocket.

"Yep. He's on the roof of the house on the west side."

The location made perfect sense based on the lines of sight, and would put the sun at the shooter's back, but the gunman hadn't been out in the open when they'd arrived at the exact same time Eugene had been pulling into the drive-way, returning from errands. The sniper must've set up while Aiden and Charlie had been indoors explaining things to Eugene. Risked pulling off the hit in broad daylight rather than taking the chance of losing his target.

"I need a distraction so I can move," Aiden said.

"Got it. Be ready on my mark."

Aiden glanced at Charlie.

The fridge doors were doing a good job of absorbing the bullets. Charlie would make sure Potter didn't lose his head, literally or figuratively.

Aiden braced for what was to come, for what he had to do next.

An icy stillness stole over him. His heart pounded, but he grew utterly calm. Resolved. Focused on nothing except the plan forming with brutal clarity. Warfare meditation.

"Go now," Torres said in his ear.

Gunshots from a handgun rang out. As expected, the suppressed rifle fire refocused.

Aiden dashed through the dining area, slipped outside and shut the door.

In the grass, Dale Banks was down on his back. Blood pooled from a hole in what was left of his head. Aiden's gut clenched at the thought of Dale's pregnant wife and how there wouldn't be an open casket.

Aiden pressed his spine hard against a stone column, ensuring he wasn't in the line of fire. Then he drew on honed professional detachment.

Low pops from the big rifle whizzed in the direction where Torres must've taken position on the side of Potter's house.

This was Aiden's chance. It wouldn't last long.

He took two deep breaths and bolted toward the fence, racing across the spacious yard before the shooter spotted him. He scaled the six-foot wooden barrier with little effort while Torres played decoy.

Making his way around the adjacent ranch-style house, Aiden crossed the short distance to the far side of the home. He had to sneak up on the sniper's rear and deal with him quickly.

A trash bin had been propped against a section of the stucco wall alongside an AC unit. The shooter must've used it to get up to the second floor, where there was a broken window.

No time to go through the house to get to the roof. Besides, the plastic receptacle might make unwanted noise or buckle under his weight, giving him away.

He searched for a better option.

Fragrant honeysuckle climbed a trellis that screened either side of the back porch.

The wooden lattice might be perfect. Provided it was sturdy enough.

A quick shake after putting his full weight on two bottom rungs showed it to be a durable frame that'd been built to last.

Aiden holstered his firearm and scaled the privacy trellis. He climbed smoothly, moving from one handhold to another. At the top, he hoisted himself up onto the patio roof and landed softly, straining not to make a sound.

The sniper was clad in all black and in a prone position only several feet away, cheek pressed against the stock, trying to put holes in Torres.

Aiden crept forward. Slipped his sidearm from the holster on his hip. "Freeze! Or I'll blow your head off."

The semiautomatic gunfire stopped. The shooter stilled.

"Hands up off the rifle. Now!" Aiden stepped closer, aiming for the shoulder. If he had to shoot, he'd prefer to wound him so they could question him and find out exactly who'd taken out the contract on Eugene.

Slowly, the man with a buzz cut complied, raising his gloved hands to ear level, staying down on his belly.

Aiden unhooked handcuffs from his gun belt and tossed them over to the guy. They clattered next to his left elbow. "Cuff yourself. Hands behind your back. Take it nice and slow."

"Please, don't shoot," the sniper said with a heavy twang

that came from somewhere below the Mason-Dixon line. "I'm just going for the handcuffs."

Dixie reached across his body with his right hand toward the cuffs, posture tightening, muscles shifting gradually. No sudden moves. Fingers dipped out of sight in front of his chest.

Then a lot of things happened in a flash.

The killer rotated lightning quick, flipping onto his back.

In the same heartbeat, Aiden squeezed the trigger. Missed by a hair and hit a roof shingle because the assassin had been anticipating it, prepared for it.

Steel glinted in the sun. Fast, so fast, Aiden almost didn't see the fracture of light as the hit man threw a knife.

If Aiden had blinked, he would've been dead.

He ducked, narrowly avoiding a tactical blade to the throat. But the gunman launched himself up to his feet while throwing a second knife in one smooth motion.

The four-inch combat knife struck Aiden in the bicep, destabilizing his firing arm.

Dixie rushed him, two hundred pounds of desperate muscle charging.

Aiden used the nanoseconds he had and lowered his own center of mass, grounding his body weight for the impact.

The blow was harder than expected. Aiden used momentum, sending his enemy up from the ground and overhead.

But Dixie grabbed hold of Aiden and ensured they both went down.

They tumbled. Pure kinetic energy propelled two conflicting forces. They rolled and rolled right over the edge, plummeted, falling.

Aiden threw a knee into the other man's gut and twisted, positioning himself on top.

The ground rushed up to greet them.

Dixie's head smacked against the AC unit with a nauseating crunch.

Aiden slammed down hard, his bones jarred, the breath forced from his lungs, the blade knocked from his arm, but the hit man's body had helped cushion the fall.

He rolled off the body. The contract killer's head lay at an unnatural angle, his neck snapped. That was when Aiden spotted it.

A wireless, flesh-colored comms device tucked in the dead man's ear.

The sniper wasn't alone.

Chapter Two

Dead silence.

Aiden must've stopped the sniper. Of course he had. Whenever her partner set his mind to a task, he accomplished it no matter what.

Charlie clasped Eugene's shoulder and gave him a quick once-over, making sure he wasn't injured.

Eugene let out a ragged breath he'd been holding. Other than a bloody palm, he was fine.

The kitchen looked like a war zone. The sniper had turned the cabinets into Swiss cheese and every breakable item that had been in Eugene's vicinity had been shattered.

They were lucky not to have been torn to pieces.

Charlie rose, finger on the trigger of her 9 mm, and stepped out from behind the fridge door, then stopped cold.

A prickle of alarm streaked up her nape, tightening every hair on her scalp. The back door was ajar. Aiden had closed it behind him when he left. She was certain of it.

Charlie raised her palm, urging Eugene to stay put and keep quiet. He clung tighter to a shelf inside the fridge, understanding the silent warning.

Nothing stood out. No overt sign of lingering danger caught her attention.

But that open door was wrong.

Her intuition wasn't nearly as razor-sharp as Aiden's, but her situational awareness—the instinct that flared if you were walking down a dark alley or found a door open that should've been closed—was finely tuned and had kept her alive after four years in tactical operations.

Charlie remained perfectly still and listened.

There. Not a breath. Not movement. *A presence.* Someone else in the room with them.

Then the whisper-soft slide of footsteps across the wood floor.

Her blood ran cold. She dropped to a low crouch behind the kitchen island with her gun leveled. Had the sniper taken out Torres, too, evaded Aiden and got into the house?

The prospect of Aiden being hurt or worse was unconscionable.

Another subtle scrape across the hardwood. Glass crunched underfoot and it wasn't hers.

"Charlie," Aiden said in a ragged groan over comms in her ear. "The sniper isn't alone."

His little news flash was thirty seconds late. Aiden's timing sucked, but she breathed an inward sigh of relief that he was alive. *Thank God.*

"Charlie? Are you all right?" Aiden's usual smooth, carefree voice sounded rough-edged, more than winded. He must've been really hurting. "Come in."

Responding or calling for backup would've only given away her exact position. That was the absolute worst thing she could do.

Shifting the angle of her body, she peered through the holes of the cabinets.

Movement on the other side of the island. A shuffle. Rustle of debris.

Pressure already on the trigger of her gun, as soon as she glimpsed a shadow, Charlie squeezed, sending a bullet into the silhouette.

With an audible grunt, the person changed course. Charlie adjusted likewise.

Instead of tracking the shadow as training had taught her, getting sucked into a game of cat and mouse while uncertain who was higher on the food chain, she did the unexpected. She leaped up and slid across the countertop to the other side of the island, landing at the back of a man shrouded in black.

She was about to fire, but he pivoted and threw a leg sweep, moving with a speed and grace that defied his great bulk. The maneuver caught her behind the Achilles, launching her feet out from under her.

Charlie's primary weapon left her grasp and went skittering across the floor as she hit the hardwood flat on her back. Landed right on top of her CAR-15 and secondary firearm that was lodged against her spinal column.

Agony exploded through her lumbar and skull. Scorching pain spasmed in every nerve along her spine. She gasped for air and swallowed the scream rising in her throat.

Through watering eyes, she spied the hit man's injury.

Charlie had shot the thick, wide bruiser in the side.

Dark red blood seeped between his gloved fingers where he applied pressure to the wound.

She fought through the haze of pain and kicked him in the gut, using both feet and all her might.

He doubled over, pressing harder to his injured side. His face stretched wide in a grimace. The tattoo on his neck of an alligator's head with a skull in its open mouth looked like it was melting.

This guy was big, skilled enough to get close without her knowing, had a high tolerance for pain since he was still standing, and was *armed*.

The gun locked in his hand was the biggest immediate threat.

Charlie threw a boot heel to his groin, redirecting his focus away from aiming and putting a bullet in her head. Another precise kick to his knee, over and over, until she heard the sharp, cracking noise of the kneecap shattering. A howl of anguish tore from his lips.

A well-aimed kick was a woman's ultimate defense.

She didn't stop there and rammed the heel of her foot up into his face, crushing his nose.

He stumbled backward, his arms windmilling in a hopeless struggle for balance that he'd never regain. Blood gushed from his nostrils.

Seizing the momentary advantage, she rolled onto her side, pulled her backup Glock 27 subcompact from the holster at the small of her back, aimed center mass and blew a hole in her attacker.

The force of the bullet wasn't enough to knock the big guy down. He stood motionless, hovering in animated death for an instant, and then tipped forward face-first.

Charlie rolled out of the way.

He hit the floor with a nauseating thud. She looked at his face, stared in his vacant eyes.

She'd killed a man. He'd been trying to kill her and a witness. Extensive training had fortified her for this, but nothing truly prepared her for the stark reality.

Next thing she knew, Torres came in hot through the front, making a beeline for Potter.

Aiden hustled inside through the back door, coming to her side. "Are you all right?" he asked, his proximity sending a rush of warmth through her. He proffered a hand.

Charlie accepted the assistance up and onto her feet, shaking off the vestiges of pain. She took in Aiden's mussed black hair and his deep brown eyes. He looked uncharacteristically weary, and his softer brown complexion that spoke of his Native American heritage was pallid. A nick marred his cheek, but there was a nastier gash on his arm.

Her breath hitched, her chest tightening. "You're hurt."

The deep cut was below the sleeve of his tight black T-shirt. Blood ran in rivulets down his muscular arm and dripped from his fingers.

This was the first time he'd ever been injured on the job in six years and she'd borne witness during the past four that they'd been partners. Not so much as a scratch.

An impressive SOG record that made him a figure of near-mythic proportion in their elite ranks.

"We've got to stop the bleeding, bandage it." She hated the sound of fear that leaked into her voice. Pushing hair behind her ear, she summoned her composure. "You might need stitches."

"It has to wait," Aiden said. "I'll bandage it in the car and worry about stitches after we get to the SSPC."

Always self-sacrificing. Always a pillar of strength. Always so darn hard to resist.

Aiden crouched next to the dead body and reached for something she'd completely missed. A black nylon belt bag on the dead man's waist.

"What about the sniper?" Charlie asked.

Aiden unzipped the utility pouch and dumped the contents. Two loaded magazines and a cell phone fell out. He picked up the mobile device. "We took a tumble off the roof. He hit an AC unit. Neck snapped."

Tumble? She tamped down the watery, sick feeling welling up inside and retrieved her STI Staccato-P from the floor. "Let's go."

The sooner they got Aiden's wound to stop bleeding and Potter out of danger the better.

Torres took point and led the way out through the front.

Charlie and Aiden waited for Torres to give the all clear and start the SUV before they brought Eugene outside and ushered him quickly toward the vehicle.

A few neighbors gawked at them through their windows as they made their way to the curb.

She put a hand on top of Eugene's head, ensuring he didn't

bump it on the frame, and helped him scramble into the third row. After putting the seat back in place, Charlie hopped into the second row.

Aiden grabbed the medical kit from one of their bags stuffed with gear. As soon as he sat beside her, Torres thrust the SUV into gear and sped off, tires screeching.

"Oh my God. Oh my God." Eugene crouched low into a ball on the seat, his teeth chattering between his words. "Do you know how close I came to getting my head blown off? I almost died."

But he hadn't. He was alive and well.

Unlike Dale Banks, whose eight-month-pregnant wife was going to have to bury him.

And Aiden had got injured in the process of protecting Eugene.

Charlie snatched the medical kit from Aiden. No way was she going to let him treat himself. Not when she was there to help. She took out gauze and pressed it to the wound. He gave a small wince and quickly washed the expression from his face.

Risking one's life was part of the job that she had got used to quickly, but one thing rubbed her wrong and she'd never get used to it. Ninety-five percent of witnesses in the program were like Eugene—not innocent bystanders but rather criminals looking to be absolved of their illegal actions and to save their own neck. Snitches who were angry, bitter and had a sense of entitlement. Like the government owed them more.

Few had the common courtesy to even say thank-you.

"Where's my Jumpdrive?" Eugene sat up. Then he looked over his shoulder and ducked back down as if at any moment the bulletproof window might explode. "You got it, didn't you?"

No *thank you*. Only entitlement. Charlie shook her head in disgust.

"As a matter of fact, I did. What is this?" Aiden asked, holding up the drive.

"My insurance policy," Eugene said.

Was he holding on to evidence he'd never turned over to the US attorney's office?

"What's on it?" Charlie inspected Aiden's wound.

His cut was still bleeding in earnest and not slowing down fast enough. Charlie wasn't very good with blood and there was a surprising amount of it, not to mention the sharp metallic scent, but she could handle it. For Aiden. She pressed down, trying not to hurt him, and watched as he looked through the hit man's phone. It wasn't password protected.

Aiden's profile was strong and all male, given his chiseled bone structure and sensual mouth. His hair was the richest shade of black and he had long lashes most women would envy. Damn, he was gorgeous. More beautiful than any man had a right to be.

"I told you what's on it," Eugene said. "Give the drive back to me. It's mine, damn it. I need it."

"No, you didn't tell us." Aiden frowned at something on the phone. "I want details. Right now. Did you know that you can be kicked out of the program for withholding evidence? It's called obstruction of justice."

"Protecting myself isn't the same as obstructing justice." Eugene started to straighten in his seat but seemed to think better of it. "You don't have the right to confiscate my personal property."

"What property?" Charlie asked. "I don't have the faintest idea what you're talking about. Do you, Aiden?"

He shook his head. "Nope."

"You can't do this." Eugene peeked up over the seat. "Marshal, uh, you, the one driving. You can't let them do this."

"Sorry, sir. Wish I could help." Torres lifted a nonchalant hand and checked his mirrors. "But I wasn't privy to the conversation in the house. If they say they didn't take your property, then they didn't."

"Feel free to jog our memories, Eugene," Charlie said. "Start by sharing what's on this *alleged* thumb drive."

"This is so unfair. I'm the victim in all this." Eugene sniveled until he realized there was no wiggling out of telling them. "Fine. Information on a few organizations. I kept it instead of turning it over in case I needed it someday to get out of trouble."

"Well, it seems to have gotten you into more trouble rather than saving you from it," Aiden said.

The gauze on Aiden's arm was soaked through. Charlie removed it and inspected the gash.

He looked down at the deep cut. The wound swelled with more blood and seemed as if it might never stop bleeding. He glanced up at her. "It's not that bad."

Granted, it wasn't a bullet hole. The blade had missed the brachial artery, and she didn't think the knife had struck bone, but the cut was an inch long, at least half an inch deep in muscle, and was gushing.

This was the definition of *bad*.

"I got lucky," he whispered to her as he leaned in. "Could've been my throat instead of my arm."

Her heart lurched. That was so not reassuring. At all.

"Do you know who put the hit out on you?" Aiden asked Eugene.

"Not for certain. There are mobsters in Texas, Louisiana and Mississippi who'd be happy to see me dead."

That was true. Eugene Potter was in fact Edgar Plinski, aka the Money Magician. An accountant for various organized crime outfits from Houston to Biloxi. The people he'd helped send to prison might've put the hit out on him.

Then again, it could be someone on the drive whom he still had incriminating evidence on.

"You must have some idea," Aiden pressed. "Your life

depends on this. Take a guess. Who has the biggest ax to grind with you?"

Eugene's eyes flared wide as if the answer had dawned on him, but he shook his head. "I don't know! Instead of interrogating me, isn't it your job to calm me down? Put me at ease?"

He was hiding something, perhaps protecting someone. In her gut, Charlie was certain of it.

She took out a packet of hemostatic powder from the kit and poured the brown granules into the angry wound on Aiden's arm, really getting it in there good. On contact with the blood, the tiny pellets swelled, forming a soft gel to clot the cut. It'd form a quick scab that would hold until he got stitches.

After peeling open a package of self-adhesive gauze, she applied the pad. As she gave the wound a little more pressure to help the powder set faster, she caught Eugene's eye. "The only way you'll ever truly be safe is if the people on this drive are behind bars."

Eugene, or rather Edgar, had worked for more than a handful of mobsters but had only turned state's evidence on two, claiming he didn't have anything incriminating on the others.

"The marshals at the SSPC are going to look at the contents on this drive," Aiden said. "They're going to find out whatever you're hiding. You may as well tell us, if you have any idea who might've put the hit out on you."

"It's complicated." Eugene sat up, keeping his head low. "Let's just say that someone back home had a lot invested in me. After I testified, I'm pretty sure he blew a gasket. I'm talking off the Richter scale. Okay. Satisfied? Can I have the drive now?"

"Nope," Aiden and Charlie said in unison.

"Come on," Eugene snapped.

Torres called the field office on the wireless comms to update their self-righteous, self-important leader, Will Draper, on the situation. Charlie was thankful not to hear how the loss of a good marshal was going to reflect poorly on Draper. It sure would've been nice to have a boss who cared more about his people than his career.

Inevitably, Draper would spin this, play pin-the-blame-on-someone, anyone, to keep his spotless hands clean. How on earth he'd managed to avoid the chopping block after the debacle with the breach of their WITSEC list that had occurred on his watch was anyone's guess. What happened to crap rolling uphill?

Eugene slunk down, muttering curses under his breath, protesting that he was the victim, complaining about injustice, while she finished patching up Aiden's arm and wiped blood from his skin.

The cut was deep, needed stitches and would leave a scar. Dear God, to think it could've been his throat.

Her stomach bottomed out at the idea. It took everything in Charlie not to deck ungrateful Eugene.

She poured antiseptic on a fresh piece of gauze and cleaned the cut on Aiden's face.

What would she do if she ever lost him?

Sure, they faced danger on a regular basis, and heck, the job was more fun when bullets were flying and they were kicking in doors together and slapping on handcuffs.

But today was different.

Today, hit men had got the drop on them.

Today, Aiden had fallen off a roof where *his* neck could've been the one broken. If the contract killer's blade had found its mark—Aiden's jugular instead of his arm...

She pressed a palm to his cheek, caressed his chiseled jawline.

The intimate gesture sent an electric charge up her arm, making her nerve endings stand at attention. His expression, his piercing stare that bored straight to her soul, was just as intimate.

Perhaps more so because she knew he saw the fissures in

her carefully constructed walls. When they were together, it was the only time she didn't feel alone in the world.

"I wasn't worried." She blurted out the defensive comment, having no idea where it came from.

She dropped her hand, clenching it into a fist in her lap, and forced a pretense of indifference.

Way to go, Killinger, stepping over the professional line.

But Aiden had a way of obscuring the line until she forgot it existed.

The intensity of his focus didn't waver, making the car cabin seem too small, with not enough space between them.

He covered her fist with his hand, his fingers engulfing hers. The scorching touch of his palm was hot as a brand on her skin.

"Biyooch'idi," he said. *Liar* in Navajo. The low, sensual rumble of his voice sent unbidden heat rushing to her cheeks.

She'd wanted to learn the language after going home with him, surrounded by his large family in the heart of the Navajo reservation—a sovereign territory roughly the size of West Virginia—to bury his mother. It'd been a strange trip for her, considering she no longer spoke to her own mother, but if their roles had been reversed, he would've been at her side. Aiden was eager to teach her, to share himself like turning on a faucet and letting her drink until she slaked her thirst, but Charlie was more of the sipping kind. From a disposable bottle.

What passed between them now, unspoken, reflected their bond.

One of the things she admired about Aiden was that he never called Charlie out on her BS or razzed her in front of the others, at least not in a language they understood. He'd never divulge her secrets, never betray her trust.

That was just between them, only for them—the real intimacy she treasured. And the only kind she needed. The depth of their friendship ran deeper than blood ties and she'd never do anything to jeopardize it, especially something as reckless as date him.

"Prove it." She cocked her head to the side in challenge.

"Trust me, I intend to." He gifted her with a devastating smile, flashing his annoyingly attractive dimples.

It was a punch to the gut...to her heart and, unfortunately, to her libido.

Pull yourself together. She averted her gaze and moved her hand from his, tossing the bloody gauze in a disposable motion-sickness bag.

"Did you find anything on the cell phone?" Charlie threw a glance at the device in his hand.

"Looks like a burner. With texts from only one number. Apparently, Eugene is worth two million dollars, if he's killed. An extra four million if he's brought in breathing so he can be tortured."

"Jesus, Bill," Eugene muttered low, but Charlie caught it. He knew who was after him all right.

"That's a first," she said. "You're worth more *alive* than *dead*."

"And if any sensitive information in his possession is recovered...it's worth another four million," Aiden said.

Torres let out a low whistle. "Wow. Ten million. There's a whopper of a bull's-eye painted on your forehead," he said to Eugene. "Let's hope it's smooth sailing picking up Mrs. Potter and getting them to the SSPC."

Eugene's eyes bulged from his head as he clutched his stomach.

Charlie handed him a sick bag and turned to Aiden. "Please, tell me your *bad feeling* has gone away." Two assassins and one darn good deputy marshal were already dead. Not to mention close calls for the rest of them. That had to be the end of it. Right?

"I wish." Aiden lowered his eyes. "The feeling has only gotten worse."

Great. Why did she have to ask?

Chapter Three

William "Big Bill" Walsh was a creature of habit.

Every afternoon he sat down behind his desk to have lunch in his office at Avido's, his James Beard Award–winning restaurant on Bourbon Street.

The place was quiet at this time of day, before they opened later in the afternoon and welcomed customers until 3:00 a.m. Unlike the Windfall, the 24/7 casino he co-owned, which stayed hopping around the clock.

Overseeing operations, ensuring the sex trafficking ring ran without a hitch and the drugs flowed smoothly, and keeping a close eye on his business partner, Vincenzo Romero, demanded his attention the rest of his waking hours.

This was his one respite. From work. From his hostile partner, Enzo. From his clingy mistress.

In here, he could hear himself think.

He looked up from his computer as Colette, the hostess, strutted in carrying a tray with his lunch. A medium-rare rib eye and a side salad that he'd ordered in place of his regular fully loaded baked potato. He was trying to cut back calories lately. Slim down the waistline that'd only grown more robust with stress eating.

Colette had been there three years. Easy on the eyes with a tight hourglass figure. She minded her business and earned extra by selling his drugs at the eleven universities in the area. A true hustler who never missed a day of work. He liked her.

She took the plate from the tray and set it down in front of him, along with ceramic salt and pepper shakers and utensils rolled up in a napkin.

He nodded his thanks.

"Can I get you anything else, Big Bill?" she asked in a tone that straddled the line between sweet and flirty.

He licked his lips as he undressed her in his mind. "A beer, sugar."

"Tommy is pouring it."

Even though Bill was cutting back and could forgo all the fixings, he wasn't giving up his Baltic porter. There were many things in this world he was capable of doing. Abstaining from sex and alcohol wasn't among them.

Colette flashed a small smile, tucked the tray under her arm and headed for the door. He loved watching her leave. Her body-hugging black dress fit her like a second skin, skimming all her curves, framing her nicely.

His gaze fell to his plate. Damn if that steak didn't smell delicious, but Bill had no appetite for it. The only thing he hungered for, the one thing that'd satisfy him, was Edgar Plinski's head on a silver platter.

Correction. Torturing that traitor for hours, *no, no, for days*, if they could keep him alive that long through the punishment Bill was going to mete out, *then* see his head on a platter.

Tommy Guillory, his right-hand man and his late sister Irene's eldest, walked in with the beer. His nephew's demeanor was low-key but could quickly shift to menacing, like flipping a switch. A good attribute for a gangster.

"Yo, yo, here you go." Tommy set the pint of dark, frothy porter beside the plate.

Bill shook his head. Today's youth had a flagrant disregard for old-school decorum. His nephew might be a classless millennial, but he loved the kid like a son. One day Tommy would run the organization.

"The game has begun," Tommy said, with the enthusiasm of a kickoff on Super Bowl Sunday, referring to the hunt for Edgar.

The news gave Bill a much-needed jolt of hope. "It's about time."

"D checked in." Frank Devlin was in charge of the secondary team. The fail-safe. "You were right, Uncle Bill. You won the bet." He reached into his pocket, pulled out a rolled-up wad of hundred-dollar bills and set it on the desk. "Those two Cajuns bit the dust."

The hit men brothers from the bayou were dead. They'd looked sharp enough, seemed capable and had an excellent reputation for specializing in Colombian necktie executions, but Bill had suspected that it'd take more than two backwater contract killers to get the job done.

Edgar was a slippery sucker, tougher to wrangle than an alligator and harder to hold on to than an eel in the dark.

But he wouldn't slip out of Devlin's snare.

Bill tugged on a self-assured smile. He was always right. Tommy was a fool to have doubted him in the first place and an even bigger fool to have taken the bet and staked his money on those bayou boys.

In his gut, Bill knew this would come down to the A-Team. "Nothing wrong with outsourcing, but this is why it's important to have a contingency. Our local fellas will get the job done and collect the fee."

Ignoring the steak, he picked up the cash and tossed the roll in his desk drawer. Later tonight he'd give it to his little lady. He'd learned after two failed marriages to stick with a mistress who was young, had perky breasts, a firm backside and took more interest in shopping and staying pretty than in where his money came from.

That kind of curiosity could be used against him. The feds would jump on any weak link around him and crawl even further down his throat. They were already so deep in his gullet he was choking on their surveillance. Wiretaps on the phones. Spies in the casino. Bugs on the gaming floor and in the Windfall's offices. His every move watched by hawkeyed stalkers.

Besides his house, Avido's was the only other safe space where he could talk freely.

Tommy had the restaurant swept for surveillance devices *daily* before Bill set foot inside.

All Big Bill's men were absolute in their loyalty. Still, the only one he ever fully trusted was Tommy, since he was family.

"But it was good initiative on your part," Bill said, appreciating his nephew's gumption, "for thinking outside the box and contacting those Cajun *housepainters*." A euphemism for hit men who offed someone in their home. Quite acceptable to use around the little lady or in polite company without raising suspicion.

Tommy plopped down in a leather chair across from his desk, rested a booted ankle on the opposite knee and rubbed his bald head. Tall and thickset, the twenty-six-year-old kept his head clean-shaven to spare himself from getting the receding hairline that Bill had.

At fifty, Bill was too old and busy to fret over his lack of hair that emphasized the smooth cliff of his forehead and abundance of wrinkles.

"Do you think they'll bring him in alive or dead?" Tommy asked.

Bill wasn't a religious man and believed in no higher power than himself. Nonetheless, he was praying for alive.

His mouth watered to sink his teeth into Edgar. Literally. He wanted to rip off a body part Edgar would miss. Bill just hadn't decided which one first.

The depth of Edgar's betrayal was despicable. Unfathomable. What he had done was absolutely beyond the pale. Thinking of it, as Bill had endlessly done for the past two years, made his blood pressure skyrocket to the point his eye sockets ached.

It was a wonder he hadn't had a stroke.

Edgar had had a gambling problem and been in the hole up to his eyeballs. Two hundred and fifty thousand dollars. Edgar offered to work it off, using everything he knew about accounting, bookkeeping and tax laws. The proposal had possibilities, so Bill had taken him up on it. Recognized Edgar's true talent for balancing the books and hiding illegitimate activities under legitimate umbrellas without raising any red flags with the feds. Struck a gold mine. Introduced Edgar to some other outfits. Vouched for him as one of Bill's own. Claimed a sweet finder's fee. Had a really great thing going for everybody, especially for Edgar.

Then the weasel had got nervous about heat from the feds, jumped the gun and cut a deal.

But *the way* he'd left tore at Bill's heart every day... *Irene*.

The fallout was never-ending. If Edgar had evidence on two outfits, it was reasonable to assume that he had the goods on all of them.

Now every gangster Edgar had dimed out and every mafioso he'd done business with blamed Big Bill *big-time*. And each one of them wanted their pound of flesh.

Well, no way in hell was it going to come from him. *No sirree!*

Bill felt the vein in his temple bulge.

Money bought many things. Silence. Loyalty. But there was no amount in the world that'd buy a pardon for Edgar.

Or Bill. He'd tried and lost half of the Windfall. There was only one way out of this mess.

The vultures were circling, particularly Enzo, who wanted the entire casino, and Edgar Plinski would be on the menu.

He ground his back molars together so hard his ears rang. "Tell D and the boys, if they can bring him in alive, I'll throw in an extra mil."

"They're going to love the sound of that." Tommy clapped his hands, rubbing his palms together. "They expect to have him within the hour."

Restraining his excitement, Bill simply quirked a brow. "Pretty specific. Pretty damn confident, too."

"D wasn't pleased to hear about the bayou boys getting first dibs. Understandably so. But I think he was planning to let them do the hard part, then kill them and still collect the fee all along."

Nodding, Bill agreed. Sounded exactly like a stunt Devlin would pull. Tommy wasn't ever going to make it into Mensa, but he was sharp as a tack, had solid street sense.

"He took point on the traitor's house," Tommy continued, "to scope out the situation and had the others hang back. Well, those housepainters may have failed, but they set our home team up for success. According to D, the marshals assigned are some tactical special operators. Anyway, one of them is dead as a doornail."

"Really?" Bill picked up his glass and took a long pull on his beer. A small hum of appreciation slipped out at the creamy mouthfeel, decadent notes of coffee and chocolate, and the roasted malt finish. Delicious.

"That's not all." A wicked grin spread across Tommy's mouth, sort of diabolical, like that of a child tearing wings off flies. Without a doubt, Tommy had torn off wings and done far crueler things as a youngster. "You wanna hear the best part?"

Rather than respond, Bill shot him a scathing scowl. Rhetorical questions irritated him worse than sand in his sensitive parts. His patience was already threadbare, and this situation wasn't helping his volatile temper. He heaved a calming breath.

Tommy leaned forward, bringing closer a face only a mother could love—*God rest Irene's soul*. "The Cajuns caused such a ruckus that the marshals left their vehicle un-attended long enough."

Okay, Bill would bite. "Long enough for what?"

"For D to do what he does best. Set the trap."

Bill's appetite flared up something fierce. He draped the napkin across his lap, grabbed the utensils and cut into his steak.

Good old Devlin. One of the Four Horsemen of the Apocalypse…and Bill's personal favorite.

War.

Chapter Four

What was so awful about a clean break when the alternative was to turn someone's life upside down?

Charlie wished Eugene hadn't felt compelled to talk to Sharon face-to-face and simply decided to leave. It would have been faster, easier and, yes, cleaner for everyone.

Sharon oversaw administration and personnel for the logistics services company her first husband started and ran until he died. The business managed the flow of goods and materials between points of origin and end-use destination, handling shipping, inventory and warehousing.

It also meant the company needed a lot of space at a reasonable price, which explained why it was located in the hills sandwiched between Tierra Santa and Mission Trails Regional Park.

In the middle of nowhere.

The good news was the traffic was sparse, making their travel time less than twenty minutes from the Palisades.

They passed the San Diego River and a few minutes later turned right off Mission Gorge Road into a parking lot. Torres brought the vehicle to a stop horizontally across a handicapped parking spot in front of the double doors that had the name Sullivan Logistics written on them.

"I've got this. Keep it running," Charlie said and hopped out.

She pulled open the front door and marched into the stark

air-conditioned lobby up to the receptionist's desk. "Hello. I'm from the US Marshals Service. I need to speak with Mrs. Sharon Potter. It's extremely urgent."

After Charlie held up the badge that was prominently displayed from a chain around her neck, the twentysomething woman said, "FYI, she never changed her name from Sullivan to Potter."

One more anchor for Sharon.

Charlie's temperature rose. This trip was only going to eat up precious time.

In the end, Sharon wouldn't choose Eugene… Edgar Plinski over everything and everyone else in her life.

The receptionist picked up the phone and dialed. "Mrs. Sullivan, you're needed up front. A US marshal is here to speak with you. There's some kind of emergency." The young woman paused as she listened. "Okay." Then she hung up and looked at Charlie. "She's on her way."

Charlie nodded, stepping away from the desk, and put her hands behind her back. The at-ease position was an old Marine Corps habit that came naturally to her.

After serving eight years as a military police officer, living in the culture of extreme violence of the corps, doing merry-go-round deployments to Iraq and Afghanistan, she'd needed a change. Something different but still inside her wheelhouse. She considered working as a contractor or local law enforcement.

A chance encounter in a nightclub that'd turned into a two-night stand steered her in a new direction.

The guy was interesting, intelligent, noticed things most civilian guys missed, had a killer bod and carried a gun. He was a US marshal. In those earlier days, Charlie wasn't good with filler small talk after sex. Truth be told, she still wasn't. Fortunately, the marshal was. He didn't mind chatting about his job and had given her an inside perspective. She was hooked.

Once he discovered Charlie's hard-charging attitude and affinity for the grind of the Marines and military police, he'd suggested not only applying to the USMS, but also setting her sights on the Special Operations Group.

Now she had a job she loved.

Charlie glanced at the tactical black SUV, itching to leave. Rather than tap her foot impatiently, she paced around the wide lobby.

The sound of sensible pumps click-clacking across the tile floor snagged her attention.

An elegant, athletic-looking brunette in her early sixties, with bright eyes and gray at the temples, entered the lobby. She wore a silk blouse with a long, fancy scarf tied around her neck and slacks. "Excuse me, I'm Sharon Sullivan. Can I help you?"

"Mrs. Sullivan, I'm Deputy Marshal Killinger. I need you to come with me. Right now."

They'd already been attacked at the house. No way were they going to play sitting ducks twice in one day. Any talking would have to happen in the car and at the SSPC.

If Sharon later decided that erasing her past and forging a new life with Eugene wasn't what she wanted, the marshals would allow her to leave. But that discussion wasn't going to happen here at Sullivan Logistics out in the boonies.

"What is this about?" Sharon asked.

"Your husband. Eugene."

Her eyes grew wide and her hand flew to her chest. "Has something happened to him? Is he all right?"

"Mrs. Sullivan, is it okay if I call you Sharon?" The conversation in the car was going to be awkward. Calling her Mrs. Sullivan in front of Eugene would only compound things.

She nodded. "Yes."

"If you'll come with me, Sharon, I'll explain everything

in the car." Charlie extended a hand toward the door, but the older woman stayed planted, as if rooted in shock.

"Please, tell me, what's going on?"

Charlie put a hand on her shoulder and gently coaxed her to start walking. "As soon as we're in the car."

The receptionist stood behind the desk. "Mrs. Sullivan, what should I tell everyone?"

"I'm not really sure," Sharon said. She stopped and looked from the receptionist to Charlie.

"Tell them there was an emergency. She'll check in with you later." Charlie held the door open. "This way, please."

Sharon walked across the threshold.

Charlie put a hand on her back, shepherded her the ten steps to the vehicle and ushered her into the third row.

"Honey, what's happening?" Sharon asked, confusion stamped on her face.

Eugene reached for her and helped her sit. "I'm so sorry. I hate that you're being blindsided like this. I never thought this day would come."

Charlie climbed into the front seat, since Aiden's wound was bandaged. Torres whipped the car around into a U-turn and headed out of the lot.

"Blindside me with what?" Sharon asked. "Why are marshals here?"

"Sweetheart." Eugene kissed her hands. "I don't know what to say, where to begin."

"Sharon, your husband is in the federal witness protection program," Charlie said, cutting to the quick of it. If left up to Eugene, he might hem and haw all the way to the SSPC.

"What is she talking about, honey?" Sharon turned to Eugene. "How could you be in witness protection?"

"It's come to our attention that his life is in danger," Charlie continued.

"In danger? Oh, God. This is all so much. I don't understand. I thought witness protection made people disappear so they couldn't be found."

"That's correct, ma'am," Aiden said.

"Then how did someone find him?" Sharon asked.

"Yeah, I'd like to know that, too," Eugene demanded.

A fellow deputy in their field office had compromised the US Marshals Service. He'd accepted a bribe and handed over a classified Department of Justice laptop to the Los Chacales cartel. In turn, the cartel used the laptop to breach the Pacific Coast WITSEC list, along with the personal information of every marshal in California.

The ultimate betrayal of a colleague.

Justice was being served to the traitor, but the ripples of his treason spread far and wide and deep. The cartel was now selling the sensitive information piecemeal.

Edgar Plinski wasn't the first with a bounty on his head and he wouldn't be the last. If the truth got out, panic and turmoil would infect every witness in the program like a disease.

Containing the news of the breach was crucial.

"The most important thing at the moment, Sharon, is the decision you're facing," Charlie said, doing her best to spin their attention in a different direction. "Very dangerous men know where your husband lives and about his current life. Which means they know about you, too. The only way we're authorized to protect you is if you choose to relocate with him, start over. New name. New history. No further contact with anyone that you know now."

Sharon gasped.

"We're taking you both to the Safe Site and Protection Center," Aiden said, "where you two will be able to talk and think in a safe environment. If you decide not to relocate with your husband, we'll take you to a relative's where you can stay, but you need to understand that unless you're in the program, we can't protect you."

Tension edged with fear radiated from the third row. The

silence was agonizing because it was temporary. Charlie had never faced this particular scenario, where a witness had to be relocated a second time after marrying someone who had no clue he was in the program, but she guessed that any minute now there'd be weeping or screaming or both.

"What have you gotten me into?" Sharon's voice was brittle. Pained. "How could you put me in danger?"

"I was supposed to be safe and so were you." Her husband ran his palms down her arms. "I'd never do anything to hurt you."

"Oh, Eugene." Sharon sobbed. "Is that even your real name?" she asked in a sorrowful whisper.

A crease formed between his eyes. He looked down, silent for several seconds. "It feels like my real name, but no, sweetheart."

"Who are you?"

"Edgar Plinski."

"Why are you in witness protection? Did you see a murder or some other crime?"

His shoulders slumped. "Something like that."

"You know how the program works," Aiden said, turning in his seat and facing the couple. "At the SSPC, the marshals are required to let her read your file. She has to know the truth so she can make an informed decision. That's how it works. Total honesty about who you really are and the things you did when a spouse is considering relocation. It's the only way to have a successful transition for all parties, whether you stay together or go down separate paths, where you never see each other again."

Brutal truth delivered in an environment where witnesses were on strict lockdown in forced proximity sounded like a recipe for murder, in Charlie's book. But managing the messy emotions of others wasn't her forte.

She barely dealt with her own. Better to tamp it all down, keep people at a distance.

Even Aiden. The one person in the world she was closest to.

"Eugene, were you some kind of criminal?" Sharon asked. "Or should I call you Edgar?"

"I prefer Eugene." He raised his head. His throat bobbed on a nervous swallow. "I was an accountant. I didn't set out to be a criminal. I got roped into a bad situation. One thing led to another and I found myself getting deeper and deeper, until I felt like there was no way out. At least not alive."

A situation where he was complicit in tax fraud, sex trafficking, drug dealing, racketeering. The sordid laundry list was long, and Sharon would see every dirty detail at the SSPC.

"You lied to me. About everything," Sharon said. "Were any of the stories you told me about your past even true? Do you love me? Or were you using me to create your new identity?"

Eugene gaped at her and then snapped his mouth closed. He cleared his throat, a strangled noise that sounded as though he was choking on the answers.

Oh, hell. Not that Charlie had sympathy for criminals, but this predicament wasn't Eugene's fault. "He had to lie," Charlie said, throwing him a lifeline, hoping to defuse this inconvenient distraction. "It's part of the program. He wasn't allowed to tell you."

The tension started to deflate, and Charlie swallowed a sigh of relief, turning her focus on the road. No cars ahead in either direction. In the side mirror, the stretch of road behind them was clear to the bend, where she lost visibility farther back.

This full disclosure couple's session was making it difficult to concentrate on doing the primary job. Getting them to the SSPC was the priority. Not counseling them through this unmitigated disaster.

There were marshals with specialized training for that.

Sharon turned to her husband. "But I have no idea who you really are, Edgar, who I married." Her voice was soft and forlorn.

"Yes, you do. You know me, sweetheart," Edgar pleaded. "We met in church because I became a born-again Christian. We fell in love because we share the same passions. Charity work and dancing and visiting vineyards and trying new wines. I love you. I love your kids. And the grandchildren."

Sharon burst into tears again. "Oh, the grandbabies. How can I leave them behind? And Cindy. She's due next month. I'm supposed to be there for them. They mean everything to me," she said, her voicing breaking. "My children are my life." She buried her face in her hands and sobbed.

A sudden stab of envy hit a sore spot in Charlie that she kept buried. There was an emptiness in her, a terrible aching void that'd never be filled. She'd never experienced what Sharon offered her family—the unconditional love of a mother.

Charlie's mom was a heroin addict, loved her next fix more than her children. Charlie and her sister, Britney, were shuffled in and out of foster care. Sometimes placed with different families. Sometimes in group homes.

Growing up that way had left her with a longing, a hunger and a pervasive fear of love.

As soon as Charlie was legal, she'd enlisted in the military branch that'd take her the soonest. She'd never gone back to Roanoke, Virginia. While Britney had never left. She became a stripper and married the first drunk loser to propose.

The only time Charlie heard from Brit was when her ball and chain was fired from another job and they needed money.

"I'm so sorry." Edgar wrapped his arms around his wife. "If I'd thought it was possible for this to happen…" He dropped his head along with his voice.

No one in the DOJ thought it possible. Why would Edgar?

It was one thing when a person entered the program, preparing to testify. All newbies understood the risks and gambled that the government would protect them, since the alternative was far worse.

Edgar's story was a cruel anomaly. He'd crossed the threshold into a brand-new life, spent the past two years establishing roots and had finally stopped looking over his shoulder.

Believed he was safe only to find that he had to start all over again.

"I can't bear the thought of never seeing my family again," Sharon said, tears flowing down her cheeks. "My children. My grandchildren."

Family. Children. Grandchildren. Charlie's heart ached at the phantom pang inside her body. After suffering from endometriosis and failed rounds of medication therapy, she'd found herself unable to take the agony anymore. She'd been recommended a full hysterectomy by the doctor.

When Charlie woke up in the recovery room, she'd been surprised to find her mother had made the five-hour drive to the Naval Medical Center at Camp Lejeune in North Carolina. Charlie had been even more surprised at how glad she'd been to see her, clean and sober at her side.

Then her mother spoke, and the little miracle turned into a nightmare. "The doctor says you're going to be fine. Surgery went well. I can't believe you let them take out your lady bits. You should've held out until you had children. Now you'll never be a real woman."

The bruising reality of those callous words had seared Charlie's heart like acid, scarred her soul in a way that she had never recovered from.

What Sharon had, four children, six grandkids, the love and warmth and security of a big, happy family, Charlie never would.

The unhealed wound she carried inside had grown bigger, deeper over the years as she tried to fill the emptiness with her career and ambition. With SOG. A unit that demanded the very best from her and the ability to drop everything and respond in six hours.

Old pain, still very sharp, sliced through Charlie. She gritted her teeth, cursing this assignment.

Being shot at and almost killed was part of the professional package, and she could handle it. But facing her personal demons was the worst torture. She'd choose waterboarding over this, no contest.

"You still haven't given me an explanation about how my new identity was blown," Edgar said, keeping an arm wrapped around Sharon. "I have a right to know."

"I'm afraid that's classified," Aiden said. "We're not authorized to share specifics."

"Then what guarantee do I have that it won't happen again?" Edgar asked.

Giving reassurances while holding their hand wasn't in their lane. At the SSPC, the other marshals would make it clear that he'd be relocated to a region in the program that was still *secure* and should never have to look over his shoulder again. More or less.

"You'll be briefed at the—"

Pop! Pop! Pop! Pop! The jarring sounds came from under the car. Tires exploding. A deep rumble. The slapping thud of rubber as the vehicle swerved. The shriek of metal grinding against asphalt.

Torres swung the car on the wide shoulder of the road near the river and brought the SUV to a stop.

Charlie's pulse skyrocketed as she gained her bearings. One *flat* tire might be an ill-timed accident. Two, possibly shot. But not all four decimated down to the rims.

Two black vans raced up to the shoulder. Ground to a screeching halt in front and behind them, bracketing the SUV, kicking dust in the air.

They were blocked in, sitting on rims, with nowhere to go besides the river.

Charlie pulled her 9 mm. Torres and Aiden did likewise. The Potters' panicked cries filled the cabin.

"Stay quiet!" Charlie said. The more noise they made, the more they were adding to the chaos and inadvertently helping their attackers.

The front doors of both vans opened. Four men wearing dark utility uniforms, bulletproof vests, balaclavas with skull faces, tinted goggles and tactical helmets jumped out. Each had a gun with a suppressor in their left hand. In their right hand was something else.

Something she never would've expected in a million years. Her brain cramped to make sense of it.

They surrounded the SUV, holding up paint sprayers. Cordless and high-powered. Ones you could easily pick up at any large home improvement store.

At the exact same time, all four men began spraying the bulletproof windows pitch-black, obscuring their vision. Blinding them. They couldn't even shoot out the windows.

Paint fumes flooded the car.

The Potters clung to each other. Edgar hyperventilated.

Sharon was hyperventilating. "God! We're going to die!"

The men had worked fast in a fluid, coordinated effort like they jacked marshals on the side of the road all the time as a hobby.

If it hadn't chilled her to the marrow of her bone, she would've been impressed.

The windows and both windshields were completely blacked out except for a four-by-eight-inch space on Edgar's windowpane. Where they taped something brick-shaped, covered in plastic wrap and attached to a timer.

"A bomb! Plastic explosives!" Edgar said, driving Sharon's screams to a fever pitch.

The countdown was at one minute.

They had to get out of the vehicle. There was no choice

about that, but if they didn't go as a synchronized unit through the same exit point, firing simultaneously, they'd be hosed.

Everything transpired in only seconds. Gut-wrenching, terrifying seconds that made adrenaline course through her veins. In her mind, it all unfolded in slow motion.

Torres grabbed his door handle and pulled.

"Wait!" Charlie reached to stop him, but it was too late.

The driver's door opened. Torres hopped out and fired.

A flurry of gunshots from weapons with suppressors pinged. Torres caught a bullet in the throat and dropped.

Charlie trained her gun on the opening, not letting panic poison her. Air punched from her lungs. Her heart pounded in her throat. But she stayed sharp. Laser-focused. Ready for someone to shove the barrel inside, while keeping out of range and taking a potshot.

A loud champagne-cork sound echoed, and something was launched into the car, landing on the driver's seat. The door was kicked shut.

It was a familiar-looking canister. "Smoke grenade!"

Charlie dived into the back seat while Aiden leaped into action, climbing past Sharon and Edgar into the trunk.

"Sinaloa," he said, referring to a dicey mission in Mexico, where they had apprehended a fugitive. The circumstances had been much different, but a tactic they'd used would work for them now.

They were on the same wavelength. A single exit point for them both, but his idea was better. Smarter. She cracked a grin.

He was the best partner. The best outside-the-box thinker. The best friend.

The best everything.

"Stay put," Charlie said to the Potters, following Aiden into the rear of the vehicle.

"No!" Edgar grabbed hold of her leg as she maneuvered over the seat, and she had to knock his hands off.

The timer hit thirty seconds when the ballistic smoke grenade went off.

She held her breath, pressed up against Aiden in the sixteen cubic feet of space.

Red smoke suffused the tight quarters.

"Don't leave us!" Edgar coughed out the words.

Aiden hit the emergency latch, opening the trunk door. They rolled out, landing low on their feet. Smoke billowed around them, providing perfect camouflage to conceal their movements. Staying crouched low, Aiden broke to the left and Charlie went right.

As expected, each of the four gunmen was trained on one of the four doors, anticipating someone to leave from there. Not the trunk.

Charlie and Aiden had to press hard and fast to get the Potters safely out of the car and clear from the explosion within the next fifteen seconds.

Then the driver's-side rear door burst open.

Edgar jumped out and it all went to hell in a handbasket.

Chapter Five

Frank Devlin's plan was working without a hitch. Better than expected.

Eugene Potter, formerly known as Edgar Plinski, or *The Package*—as Devlin's team simply referred to him, removing the element of humanity—jumped out of the car, choking and gasping, right within arm's reach.

Thick red smoke blew from the trunk and rear door. No one had a clear, clean line of sight—most important, not the marshals.

Devlin didn't need one. He had The Package by the back of his shirt collar, holding him in front of himself like a shield with his Beretta 92FS against the base of the captive's skull.

But just because you didn't need something, it didn't mean you wouldn't be better off with it. Devlin and his team seized every advantage available, flipping down the thermal monocular strapped to their helmets, which allowed them to see through the smoke.

The wife stumbled out of the vehicle next, falling to the ground on her hands and knees. Tate, his buddy behind him, grabbed her and hauled her up onto her feet.

Devlin considered putting a bullet in The Package now and collecting two million dollars, split four ways, but why settle for two when you could have eleven? And at such a close range, it would make one hell of a mess all over him.

"We've got to move!" Edgar said, his arms flailing. "The bomb. Five seconds."

Devlin smiled behind his mask, so pleased with himself. "Three. Two. One."

Edgar covered his head with his hands, cowering, but there was no explosion.

Instead of using an expensive, volatile brick of C-4—that quite frankly wasn't so easy to come by—Devlin had covered basic silicone putty in colored plastic wrap. The timer sold the gambit. Made it imperative for the marshals to leave the vehicle. The smoke dialed up the pressure, fueled the chaos, stoked the panic.

"Package secure," Devlin said over the wireless communications devices his guys wore, keeping his gun pressed to The Package's head and his full attention on the blonde female marshal.

She was holding her position, using the rear of the vehicle as cover, gun raised. There was little else she could do, given the situation.

Layers of smoke rolling through the air obscured essential details, offering only glimpses. The Package was in his grasp. The wife was frosting on the cake.

Neither marshal would risk the shot.

The two others on his team came around the front of the SUV, their weapons aimed in the direction of the male marshal.

A silent, single tap on his shoulder told him his team had formed up and they were ready to move.

They backed away from the SUV toward the vans, quickly but steadily, sure-footedly, out of the protection of the smoke.

A random passing police cruiser switched on flashing red and blue lights. Whipped around and stopped.

Without a word, Devlin's team changed their formation. They went from a horizontal line, trained only on the marshals, and shifted back-to-back, moving in a circle as one efficient unit. All the threats were covered before the patrol officer even left the car. It was second nature to them.

One of his guys popped more smoke toward the police car to cover their retreat.

"Freeze!" the cop said, crouched behind the door, his side-arm drawn.

The marshals hung back, using the cover of the SUV, but the smoke still put them at a huge disadvantage, clouding their field of view.

"Stop! Release the hostages," the officer said. "Lower your weapons and put your hands in the air!"

Devlin saw where this was going. Instinctively, he knew his guys did, as well. This wasn't their first rodeo.

"Stop!" the cop yelled again. "Or I'll shoot."

Unlike the marshals—highly trained, tactically skilled and wise enough to use a bulletproof vehicle for cover—the patrol officer was going to make a bad judgment call and would indeed shoot.

So one of his guys fired first.

A single bullet blew out the cruiser window and took the cop out of the game.

They reached the vans that they'd left running and peeled off into two groups. Devlin opened the sliding door and backed into the bed of the lead van with The Package while Tate did the same at the other van with the wife.

Nothing like a solid day's work to energize Devlin. A mission like this always got the blood flowing.

The vans sped off, heading to the theme park. It was a twenty-minute drive or less from most parts of the city, making it a good spot to pinpoint in advance. From this part of town, it was less than fifteen minutes. They'd dump the vans and have their pick of vehicles to choose from, and it wouldn't be reported stolen for hours.

Devlin lowered to a knee beside Edgar. "You're going to die. Slowly. Painfully. There's nothing you can do about that."

"Please, no, no. Please."

He hated it when they begged. It never changed anything. Why not die with a little dignity?

"What you do have control over," Devlin said, "is whether or not you have to watch your wife get tortured first."

"Oh, God! She didn't do anything. She doesn't know anything."

"Like I said. Her fate is in your hands."

"What do you want?"

"Big Bill is under the impression you have incriminating evidence on him and his associates that you didn't turn over to the Department of Justice."

"Yes." The Package nodded emphatically. "Yes, on a flash drive. I protected Big Bill. I didn't rat him out. Please, don't hurt Sharon."

"Bill wants it." More like needed it. The noose was tightening around Bill's throat. It was the only thing that could save him from Enzo and the others. Maybe Devlin would sell it for double to the competition. It was the golden ticket. "Where is the drive?"

"If I tell you where it is, do you promise not to hurt Sharon?"

"How about this? I promise that if you *don't* tell me, I guaran-damn-tee I *will* kill her. Where is it?"

"I don't have it." The Package lowered his head and wept like a baby. "The marshal, uh, the big guy with the bandage on his arm, took it. He's got it."

Devlin cursed and slammed his fist against the side of the van near The Package's head, making him cringe.

They had to turn around and go back. It was worth too much to leave the flash drive behind. They could pop more smoke, surround them and take them out.

"Hey, D," Tate said over comms. "We've got a serious problem."

Make that two problems. "What is it?"

"Those two marshals are following us in the cop car. Lights flashing."

Then the siren started blaring.

Fury pooled in Devlin's gut. It burned him to the bone that those two were in possession of the flash drive and would soon have every cop in the city chasing after them. With that kind of heat, they'd never make it out of San Diego.

They needed to find an alternate place to ditch the vans sooner than planned. In five minutes, SDPD would have a helicopter in the air and over their position.

First, he'd take care of those marshals. Teach them both a lesson they'd never forget.

"T, we no longer need the wife," Devlin said. "Injure her. Make it critical and toss her."

The Package's eyes flared wide in horror. "No! You can't. You promised you wouldn't kill her."

Devlin sighed. "I told him to wound her, didn't I? Not kill her."

Chapter Six

"Nice touch with the siren," Aiden said to Charlie.

He was kicking himself about losing two colleagues, plus Edgar and his wife, but it wasn't over. Not yet.

Charlie had been the first to make a beeline to the cruiser. When others might buckle and concede defeat, she bucked up and dug in for the fight.

She was relentless.

God, he loved her. Always had. Always would.

After they checked the patrol officer and saw he was dead, they took off in pursuit. Charlie had radioed in the incident to the police, giving the make and model of the vans, but there were no license plates. The cops' response would be faster and more widespread than the Marshals'—hot and heavy with one of their own gunned down. No mercy would be shown.

Aiden was closing the distance up to the rear van.

Only a few hundred yards separated them.

The sliding door slashed open. A face covered in a skull mask peered out, and then the man threw Sharon from the van.

Panic seized Aiden as her body slammed to the blacktop, bounced violently several times and rolled to a stop on her back.

Those heartless bastards.

Aiden stomped on the brakes in front of the woman.

They both hustled out of the car and to her side. There were scrapes and bruises all over her, but her left thigh was covered in blood.

It didn't look like it had been caused by the fall out of the van.

Aiden peeled back the fabric where her pants had been torn. A fountain of blood spurted.

Jeez. The femoral artery had been sliced. This wasn't like the cut on his arm, something within their power to control. In three to five minutes she would bleed out. It could take that long or longer for an ambulance to reach them.

If they didn't get her medical help right away, she'd die here on this road.

That was what those men were counting on. Marshals giving up the chase to save a life.

"We've got to get her to a hospital or she's as good as dead," Aiden said.

He swore under his breath as they lifted Sharon up and carried her to the squad car.

"I think the closest hospital is off I-8," Charlie said. "Maybe ten minutes away."

That was the nearest hospital, but Aiden recalled seeing a smaller medical center on the map when they were going to get Sharon.

"There's one closer." Possibly five minutes. He hoped not any longer than that.

Gently, they got Sharon into the back of the vehicle.

Aiden took off south down Mission Gorge Road. Prayed his memory didn't fail him and he could navigate them there.

Charlie tore the sleeve from Sharon's blouse. Applied direct pressure on the artery.

"Tourniquet," Aiden said.

She nodded. "Okay. Yeah." Charlie took the scarf tied around Sharon's neck and wrapped it above the injury.

Good choice of material. For some reason on TV shows

and in movies, people always used a belt. But a belt was too rigid, and you'd never get it tight enough to stop the arterial flow in the real world.

"I need a windlass."

A tourniquet without a windlass was a constricting band at best. Anything from a chopstick to a pocketknife could be used. Aiden pulled a carabiner from his utility belt and handed it to her.

Charlie worked deftly. She held the tourniquet tight and kept up the pressure on the wound. "She's so pale. Hurry, Aiden."

He was going as fast as possible, taking bends in the road harder than he should.

"They didn't have to do this to her," Charlie said, her voice low.

No, they didn't, but it had worked. They'd known marshals would never abandon a wounded innocent. Aiden clenched his jaw and swallowed back the surge of white-hot anger.

They had to be close to the medical center. Sharon's life was literally draining away with each passing minute.

There. Set back off the main road about where he remembered from the map.

He saw a sign for the medical center that he'd overlooked before and took the turn. Followed the road and raced up to the emergency entrance, stopping in the ambulance parking area by a separate door.

Aiden flew out of the car and inside, grabbing the first attendants he spotted. "Help! There's a woman bleeding out. Cut to her femoral artery."

The orderlies got a stretcher and ran outside. Aiden helped them load her onto the gurney.

So much blood.

Charlie stayed at Sharon's side, going with them. Aiden killed the siren, lights and engine, and he sprinted to catch up to them.

By the time he did, after passing the treatment bay with curtains, Sharon was in a room for severe cases. A doctor and nurses swarmed around her, every medical person taking a specific action, each knowing exactly what job to do.

It reminded Aiden of the team that had attacked them. Precise. Prepared. Executed with ruthless efficiency.

"Excuse me," a nurse said to them. "We're going to need you to step out of the room." She ushered them into the hall and to the nurses' desk. "I need you to fill out some forms." The nurse reached behind the desk and proffered a clipboard.

Charlie looked down at the blood covering her hands and ballistic vest. The nurse directed her to the bathroom.

Aiden took the clipboard with a heavy heart.

"Also, her next of kin should be called," the nurse said.

"She's going to make it, isn't she?"

"We're doing everything we can for her."

Aiden called Sullivan Logistics and passed on the tragic news to the receptionist, who assured him that she'd call her children immediately. Then he filled out what he could on the forms and returned them. "Her children are on the way. They'll have the rest of her information."

He paced in front of Sharon's room, watching the medical staff work on her.

Once the frenetic energy simmered down inside, the doctor stepped into the hall as Charlie came back from the bathroom.

"I'm Dr. Patel," the woman wearing green scrubs said.

"How is she?" Aiden asked.

"We've finally got her stabilized. The bleeding from the femoral artery is under control. She also suffered a severe head injury and has some broken ribs. I understand she was thrown from a moving vehicle at high speed?"

"Yes," Charlie said, her hands clenching to fists at her sides.

"She has swelling on her brain. The major head trauma has put her in a coma."

Aiden swallowed hard, his anger swelling.

"Is she going to recover?" Charlie asked, her expression tight.

"She's no longer in critical condition, but there's no way of telling how long the coma will last or if she'll wake up. We're going to send her for an MRI. Her family should get here as soon as possible. Excuse me." The doctor left.

One vicious act of cruelty and Sharon with her kind face, earnest eyes and fierce love for her family might never wake up. It was beyond unfair.

Two years ago, Aiden's mother had died after a painful battle with cancer. Where his father was the backbone of their large family, his mother had been the heart. With five kids, she always made each of them feel special and loved. Her last wish had been to die outside, under the sky. Not to be mourned, but to be honored, and for her children to live a full life.

Losing a parent wasn't easy, but to have them taken away by violence was unspeakable.

They'd failed to protect Sharon. This was their burden to bear, but that strike team had been a formidable force. Charlie tended to carry around guilt like sandbags. He didn't want that for her.

Aiden put a hand on her shoulder.

Charlie pulled away from his touch, pounding her fists against her thighs. "Bad things shouldn't happen to good people. I want to kill those men." She stalked off down the hall, storming through a set of double doors.

They'd get back out there, find Edgar and make those men pay for what they'd done. With any luck, the police already had them in custody.

Aiden went after Charlie, pushing through the doors. He walked down another hall, past vending machines and through another set of doors into the waiting room near the main entrance. The handful of people seated inside gave them a once-over, dismissing their weapons after noticing their badges.

Charlie stood still as stone, staring at the television mounted on the wall. He followed her gaze to the screen. Both of their pictures were featured on the breaking news.

"Two US marshals aided and abetted gunmen," the anchorwoman said, "in kidnapping a high-profile witness. In the process, they shot and killed a fellow marshal as well as a local police officer."

The bulletin was a punch to the throat.

Charlie muttered a curse. "This isn't good."

"That's the understatement of the century." Aiden grimaced at the television. "But I don't understand. We haven't done anything wrong."

"Not according to that." Charlie gestured to the screen.

"US Marshals Killinger and Yazzie," the anchorwoman said, "should be considered armed and dangerous."

What was happening?

Painful shock made Aiden's legs feel wooden. To have their names and faces splashed across the news was a gross violation of protocol.

The media could've only learned their identities from one person.

"We need to find out what's going on." Charlie gave a furtive glance around, prompting him to do likewise. "And why the police think we killed Torres and a cop."

"I'm sure our favorite person, Mr. Wonderful, would love to tell us." Will Draper.

Charlie groaned.

A little girl about ten years old was looking straight at them. Her gaze bounced to the television and then back to them. She turned to her mother, seated next to her with her face buried in a magazine, and tugged on her sleeve. The mother leaned closer, gaze glued to the article she was reading, and said something.

The little girl whispered in her ear as she pointed to the television.

"We can't hang around here unless we want to leave handcuffed in the back of a squad car." Charlie nudged Aiden, guiding him through the double doors to the emergency room and around the corner out of sight.

Everything boiled down to two responses for Charlie—fight or flight. There was a time and a place for each, but if they weren't careful, they'd make a bad situation much worse.

This was a misunderstanding. It had to be the result of a breakdown in communication. "Before we make a rash decision that we might regret and run off half-cocked, we need to understand what we're dealing with first. Let me call Draper."

"Whatever he has to say, I'm sure it'll make my head want to explode." She drew in a deep breath. After a brief moment of hesitation, she nodded. "You're right. We need to know what's going on, but make it quick."

Aiden toggled his earpiece and dialed Draper's direct line. Unlike headquarters in Arlington, Virginia, and larger field offices, the San Diego office didn't have secretarial gatekeepers.

"US Marshal Draper," their boss said, answering his own phone.

"Sir, Aiden Yazzie here." He stared at Charlie as she tapped her Bluetooth comms device, conferencing in.

"Aiden?" There was a muffled sound and a quiet exchange as if the mouthpiece had been covered while Draper spoke to someone else in the room. "What were you and Killinger thinking?"

No mention of the witness or Torres. Not a good sign of how the conversation was going to go.

"Sir, we were about to call with an update when we heard there was an all-points bulletin out on us. What's going on?"

"I could ask you the same question. What happened out there? Did you two snap? Or are you doing it for the money?"

Charlie squeezed her eyes shut, frustration stretching tight across her face.

"We were doing our jobs. We had Albatross," Aiden said, using Edgar Plinski's code name, "and had just picked up the wife when we were ambushed on Mission Gorge Road. Torres was killed, along with a police officer that stopped to assist. Albatross was abducted and the wife was injured. She's in critical condition and the doctors aren't sure she'll pull through. But we had nothing to do with it, Draper."

"Nice touch on your part, trying to save the wife and calling in. It'd be enough to give me reasonable doubt about you two, if it weren't for the damning evidence against you."

Aiden's heart stuttered. "What evidence? We would never kill an innocent person, especially not a colleague or a police officer. You know us. You have to believe me."

"I believe money makes people do horrible things that they otherwise wouldn't. Before today, I would've thought you and your partner were the best marshals I had, but you wouldn't be the first ones in this office to sell their soul."

"Doesn't that say more about you than it does us?" Charlie snapped.

"Killinger." Draper sighed. "With a chip the size of an iceberg on your shoulder, perhaps I shouldn't be too surprised about you."

Charlie barely suppressed a snort.

Draper had some nerve, standing on his self-righteous soapbox, spewing whatever garbage was going to help him sleep at night. There was absolutely no love lost for the man. Still, Aiden narrowed his eyes at Charlie. A silent warning not to get sidetracked.

"We're not traitors or murderers," Aiden said. "Why is there an APB out on us? Why do you think we killed Torres?"

"There was an eyewitness who saw it all and called 911."

Eyewitness?

Aiden sucked in a shallow breath, the taste somehow acrid, making his eyes burn.

Charlie slipped her hair behind her ear, her expression giving away nothing.

The bombshell unnerved her, too, although no one else would've been able to tell. Her Rock-of-Gibraltar demeanor appeared unflappable to the untrained eye, but Aiden knew better. Knew her well. The little hair tuck, a seemingly insignificant gesture, betrayed her emotions.

In that moment, she was feeling just as vulnerable as he was, even though she wanted the world to believe she kept her heart frozen in a block of ice. But when Charlie Killinger felt threatened, watch out. She became dangerous with a capital *D*. Went into take-no-prisoners attack mode, illustrating why a person should never corner a feral beast.

"That's impossible," Aiden said. His vision tunneled. "There were no witnesses."

"I guess you two weren't as careful about covering your tracks as you thought." The bitter accusation in Draper's tone was thick as ipecac syrup.

Aiden wanted to vomit. "Other than the police officer who stopped to help us, there was only a group of four guys who attacked us. There were no other cars on the road. No one else around." A strange numbness seeped through him.

Even if there had been someone, how could they have seen anything clearly through all the smoke from the grenades?

"Unfortunately for you two, that's not the case. Yazzie, you and Killinger disgust me. You should be ashamed of yourselves. As if this office didn't have a big enough mess to deal with, now you dump this in my lap. There's no way I can clean up this kind of nuclear fallout."

A tide of fury rose in Aiden, washing out his anxiety over being railroaded. Only someone as self-absorbed as Draper could turn this around and make it about himself.

"We called the police when we were tracking the men

who abducted Albatross," Aiden said, "before they threw his wife out of a moving vehicle. Have the cops located the two black vans we reported?"

"There's no sign of those supposed vans. The chief of police is ticked that you had them spinning their wheels on a wild-goose chase when they should've been looking for you the entire time. Listen to me. Stay put at Mission Medical. Surrender your weapons to security. Cooperate with the police and go with them willingly. Don't endanger any more civilians."

The GPS trackers in their phones pinpointed their exact location. There was no doubt in Aiden's mind that as soon as Draper had been notified by the police, their boss had given them up without hesitation.

Not as if they'd been trying to hide. They'd taken the police cruiser of the dead cop to the medical center.

Charlie's gaze pinned him. Her cool, stony expression didn't waver, but he caught the flicker of fear in her piercing blue eyes as she took out her cell phone, removed the battery and smashed the screen against the wall.

A second later, she'd chucked it in the trash.

She was preparing to run.

There has to be another way out of this.

Charlie pointed to her watch, reminding him not to waste precious time if they wanted to avoid incarceration, and peeked around the corner. Whatever she saw, she must not have liked. Her index finger went up behind her back and she twirled it vigorously. The signal to wrap up, now, end the call.

"Draper, this doesn't add up." It didn't make any sense why anyone would falsely accuse them. "We're not guilty of this, and the real shame here is your utter lack of support."

There has to be another way out of this.

"I got an update right before you called. The eyewitness just arrived at the police station. He's seen pictures of you that I emailed after the chief of police notified me what was happening. The witness is swearing out an affidavit as we speak, identifying you and Killinger as cold-blooded murderers."

If there was another way out, Aiden couldn't think of it.

Chapter Seven

Two police officers entered the medical center through the main entrance and looked around the waiting room.

Charlie stepped back out of sight around the corner. "We have to get out of here."

Aiden hung up. "The dead cop was wearing a body camera on his torso. The footage should exonerate us. It'll show that we didn't kill him."

"We don't know what it'll show. There was a lot of smoke and he was hunched down behind his door. But they will have clear footage of me checking to see if he was dead. On the remote chance that it did clear us of his murder, it doesn't help us with Torres. Any time we spend in handcuffs, answering questions, is time lost to find Albatross before it's too late."

Aiden popped out the battery on his cell and tossed the phone in the trash bin. "We won't get far." He gestured to their vests and rifles.

They stood out like sore thumbs.

"Yes, we will." Determination fired through her veins. Surrender was not an option.

They'd been ambushed on an isolated strip of road where there hadn't been any CCTV. The two black vans had disappeared. There was an alleged eyewitness accusing Charlie and Aiden of collaboration and murder.

Only two people could clear their names. One was in a coma. The other was alive, but not for much longer.

They had to save Edgar. But first, they needed to get out of the medical center.

"Find the employee locker room and get us something to blend in," she said to Aiden, her pulse quickening. "Then meet me at the employee entrance."

No questions asked. No hesitation. He just nodded and took off.

That level of complete trust he had in her, and she in him, she'd never known with another soul, and she cherished it.

She went down a different hall back to the emergency room. When Sharon had been brought in, one of the nurses had run from the treatment room in the direction she was headed in now and returned with medication.

Another squad car with flashing lights pulled up to the ambulance entrance and parked behind the police vehicle they'd left. Officers rushed inside.

The emergency room buzzed with activity.

Staying close to the wall, she looked for the room she needed.

The officers were working their way in her direction, searching the emergency ward, pulling back curtains in the bay area. An infuriated nurse jumped in their path and read them the riot act about patient privacy.

The first room was no good—a janitorial closet. Neither was the second room. Nor the third.

One cop with a beard strode around the nurse and moved in the direction of the treatment rooms, with his head on a swivel.

Her chest tightened. Any second, he'd spot her. As his head turned toward her, his hand on the hilt of his weapon, a large orderly stepped into his line of sight.

Charlie turned the next knob, opening the fourth door, and ducked inside. She breathed a sigh of relief. Finally, it was the one she wanted.

There were two refrigerators. Through the clear doors she

saw vials of medication. Moving past the regulated drugs, she hurried to the shelving unit with medical supplies.

She quickly rifled through things and grabbed what she needed. Sterile gloves, gauze, saline solution, antibiotic ointment, topical anesthetic spray and a suture kit. Aiden's wound still needed stitches. They'd left all their supplies back in the SUV.

Once they had a moment to catch their breath, she'd patch him up properly and make sure it didn't get infected.

She went to the door and pulled it open.

On the other side stood the bearded cop. He drew his sidearm.

Charlie shuffled back into the room, forcing him to follow her inside.

The officer stepped across the threshold, the gun leveled at her head, and let the door close.

A mistake. On his part.

"Hands in the air!" the cop said.

She dropped the supplies and did as instructed. Her small gesture of compliance emboldened him, made him think her arrest was in the bag.

"Turn around and put your hands on the back of your head," he said.

She didn't move. Didn't breathe. Didn't blink.

"Now!" His second mistake was getting close enough to touch her. He put his hand on her shoulder and tried to force her to turn around.

Charlie moved fast.

She snapped her hand up, catching the body of the pistol while shoving the muzzle sideways to keep her head out of the line of fire in case he pulled the trigger. Then she twisted the gun hard, not enough to break his wrist, just the right amount to sprain it badly.

The gun dropped to the floor.

The cop yelped, clutching his wrist.

Charlie kicked the gun, sent it sailing into a corner and threw her elbow into the side of the officer's head. A follow-up punch to the side of his neck and he fell into a boneless sprawl.

The neck was a vulnerable spot; you could crush a larynx or, as she'd done, deliver a sharp strike to the vagus nerve. At a minimum, it would cause disorientation. In the case of the cop, unconsciousness.

The emergency ward was crawling with police. For Charlie to get out, she needed to make herself less conspicuous.

Taking off her rifle, she grabbed two hospital gowns from the shelf. She threw one on like a coat, completely covering her back, and the second on the right way.

She took another, using it as a makeshift sack for her rifle and the supplies, and put on a white face mask.

Cracking the door, she peered into the hall. An officer was walking past the nurses' desk. She slipped out of the room and turned right, heading away from the cop.

Quickening her step, she shoved through a set of double doors and hustled down the corridor.

She glanced over her shoulder. The cop hadn't noticed her and was checking the rooms. Three more doors and he'd find his partner unconscious.

Charlie faced forward as she rounded a corner and slammed into a hard wall of muscle.

Aiden. Her throat loosened.

She hadn't heard any movement coming in her direction. His stealth never ceased to amaze her.

He was wearing scrubs over his clothes and carrying a gym bag that must've had his vest and rifle inside. "The cops have the employee entrance locked down," he said.

No. They had to get out of the medical center.

If they were arrested, no one would listen to them. Even Draper was ready to think the worst and he had known them for over a year, had witnessed firsthand their work ethic and integrity.

No one would believe anything they said, and Edgar would be tortured and killed.

Think. She had to think.

"There's another way, but we have to hurry," Aiden said, giving her a wild flash of hope.

He handed her a lab coat, scrub pants and a cap, then stuffed her makeshift sack into the gym bag.

They went down the hall as briskly and discreetly as they could, with her changing along the way. She ripped off the gowns, handed him her vest, which he stowed in the bag, and she put on the white coat.

As she finished shoving her legs into the pants and put on the cap, a nurse came through a set of double doors. If the woman hadn't been looking down at her cell phone, she would've caught Charlie in an awkward position that would've been difficult to explain.

Charlie pushed the balled-up hospital gowns into the trash, and they passed the nurse, who was still preoccupied with her phone.

Aiden led her through a mini maze of hallways. They moved with confidence, acting like busy people who were supposed to be there.

They strode past a small elevator toward an unguarded door.

"That elevator goes directly to the maternity ward. This is a separate entrance for people with newborns, so the babies aren't exposed to germs. I overheard a nurse escorting a family through here." Aiden winked at her.

Warm pride filled Charlie's chest. He was brilliant. She wanted to hug him tight and kiss him. On the cheek only and not all over, she had to remind herself.

She was so attracted to him that it scared her. Attracted

to the point where she worried that it distracted her on the job sometimes.

The moment they had first met, there'd been off-the-charts chemistry. Not a simple spark but a lightning bolt. And she knew he posed an indefinable threat. Whenever they'd got close to kissing or anything romantic, instinct cautioned her to keep away, the same sense of self-preservation that warned someone not to get too close to an open flame.

There was a line that she'd never cross. The problem was that the line with Aiden was drawn in sand, easily washed away by waves and redrawn. Sometimes it inched forward; sometimes it was pushed back. While knowing she couldn't have him made it worse.

The automatic door swooshed open. They stepped out together, breathed fresh air. The door sucked shut behind them.

"Now what?" Aiden asked.

"Leave that to me." Charlie gestured for him to follow her. "I'm going to hot-wire a car."

"What?" The surprise in his voice matched his expression. "Why am I just now learning that you even know *how* to hot-wire a car?"

She shrugged. "I guess it's the first time I've needed to do it." As an adult. "We'll need to find an older model." Those were easier. "Ten years at least, but the older the better."

"If we wander around, checking vehicles, we'll look like car thieves."

"We are car thieves." She'd never thought the day would come when she'd say such a thing, and definitely not to Aiden Yazzie, the most upstanding, principled man she knew.

There was a parking lot to the left, across a wide expanse of blank blacktop, in full view of several police officers. They rounded the corner to the left.

Ahead of them was the smaller parking lot for employees. A guy got out of a luxury sedan and hit the key fob, locking it. The lights flashed and he tossed the keys in the right pocket of his suit jacket. Looking frazzled, the man jogged toward an entrance, where one police officer was busy on his radio.

"Better idea," she said. "Head to that sedan. I'll meet you."

They separated. Aiden quickly disappeared among the other cars in the lot.

Charlie picked up her pace, putting herself in the man's path. As he was about to pass her, she bumped into him, slipping her hand into his pocket and grabbing the keys tight in her palm, without letting them make a sound.

"I'm so sorry," she said.

"No, excuse me." He gave her a hurried look-over, but kept going, none the wiser.

By the time Charlie had reached the car, the man had already cleared the cop and was in the medical center. She hit the key fob button. The car lit up inside, turn signals flashed once and the door locks clunked open. They climbed inside, and he threw the bag in the back.

She pushed down on the brake, pressed the start button, got the engine going and pulled out of the lot.

Charlie went west on the side street, at a speedy but not suicidal pace, as if they were late for an appointment, past a market and veterinarian and eateries. At Mission Gorge Road, she made a left, going south.

A *thwopp, thwopp, thwopp* sound had them both peering low through the windshield and up at the sky. A police helicopter was inbound, heading to the hospital.

Farther down the road, on the opposite side, a string of police cars raced north. Lights flashing. Sirens blaring.

At least ten squad cars flew past them.

The police would have the entire medical center locked down and under aerial surveillance within minutes.

They'd made it out in the nick of time.

"We need cash," Charlie said. They wouldn't be able to use credit cards since those left a digital trail anyone could follow. "Then we need to get a car that won't be reported stolen."

She drove to Seaport Village. A fourteen-acre waterfront complex of shopping, dining and entertainment. The meandering walkways and beautiful plazas attracted tons of tourists and locals. It also had one of the few banks in the city with ATMs inside that allowed up to a three-thousand-dollar cash withdrawal.

The police would eventually monitor the activity of their credit and debit cards, but for right now, the cops thought they were pinned down somewhere inside the hospital. On the off chance that they were already plugged into their financial transactions, it would be easy to hide in the crowd and disappear. It wasn't as if they were going to hang around the area waiting for the police to arrive.

She parked the sedan as close to the bank as she could while staying away from CCTV cameras. It was impossible to avoid all the cameras between the parking lot and the bank, but every little bit of prevention helped.

In case the car was reported stolen sooner rather than later, they decided to ditch it. Aiden grabbed the bag from the back. They hustled to the bank and both made withdrawals, not knowing how much money they might need.

Better to have too much than not enough. This was their one chance to get cash.

On the way out, she spotted the Green Line trolley pulling to a stop.

"It'll take us where we need to go." She pointed to it.

Aiden nodded and they ran, hopping on board just before it pulled off.

"Whose car are we taking that won't be reported stolen?" Aiden asked, whispering in her ear.

"Someone who won't miss it."

Nick McKenna. Fellow marshal and former lover, currently out of town visiting his girlfriend, Lori Carpenter, who happened to be in WITSEC. They'd fallen in love on a yearlong assignment where he'd protected her.

A solid, stand-up guy, Nick could be relied on in a pinch. At least Charlie hoped so, considering their baggage.

Before she joined the SOG and was assigned to San Diego, she'd been at the Omaha field office. Her work relationships there had got so ugly they'd become toxic. When a woman slept with multiple colleagues—it was a small town and choosing lovers from the work pool was pragmatic—she developed a reputation that a man never would've had to contend with.

San Diego was a fresh start. She'd been careful. Then one night after dinner and drinks, she'd wanted Aiden so badly she ached. But what she shared with him was the most important relationship in her life, and she wasn't going to spoil it acting on an impulse that they'd regret.

So she'd taken the convenient bait of Nick's overtures and gone home with him.

A stronger woman, a better woman, a sober woman would've picked a random stranger. Someone anonymous. Someone disposable.

It had been fun, casual, easy, until she realized it had been a lie. Nick wasn't capable of emotionless sex. To him, none of it had been casual. Or easy.

"We're going to take Nick's truck," Charlie said.

A muscle jumped in Aiden's jaw. If she'd blinked, she would've missed it.

"What is it?" she asked as he straightened away from her. "What's wrong?"

Chapter Eight

Aiden reined in the sudden storm of emotions rolling through him, locked them up tight and washed his expression clean.

The day Charlie had been assigned as his partner and they'd shaken hands, the rush of endorphins was immediate, the attraction visceral. He'd been in a relationship at the time, but the more he got to know Charlie, slowly over time, the less he could silence the little voice whispering that she was *the one*.

So he'd broken it off with the other woman. Believing it was only a matter of time for him and Charlie until their point of happy confluence and they'd be together.

"What is it?" Charlie asked. "What's wrong?"

Every single detail from that night in the restaurant was burned into his memory. The flush on her cheeks from the alcohol. Candlelight on the table sparkling in her animated eyes. He'd put his palm on her thigh and she'd leaned into his touch, pressed her cheek to his. The way she'd smelled of wild summer flowers, the warm heat of her breath on his face. He'd caressed her jaw, her skin was delicate, soft, and every atom of his being screamed *kiss her*.

Then she'd straightened away from him, as if waking from a dream before he could, and gone to the restroom. He'd wrestled with his feelings and what to say, not wanting to still be stuck as just a *friend* in the morning.

Aiden wasn't interested in a brief fling with Charlie. He wanted forever.

But she'd never made it back to the table. Nick had found her at the bar, or she'd found him.

Either way, Aiden wouldn't think of the devastation.

He recalled happy things instead—riding a horse with the wind in his hair, making it through SOG training, the sound of his nieces and nephews laughing as they played—and pulled on a soft grin.

"Nothing's wrong," he said, doing his darnedest to sound laissez-faire. "It's smart." And it was. "Nick won't miss his car while he's curled up in bed for a week with Lori." Aiden watched, waited to see if an ember of jealousy sparked in her.

Charlie didn't bat a lash. "My thoughts exactly."

He wasn't sure which hurt more. The fact she'd slept with someone in the office, his friend Mr. Dark-and-Stormy with that carved-in-stone jaw, or that it had meant so little to her.

Nick was everything Aiden wasn't. A super serious loner, choosing a scowl over a smile. Hotheaded and impulsive to a fault. In many ways, Nick was like Charlie.

Aiden thought the fling would've lasted two nights, two weeks at most.

It'd gone on for two months.

Two months of dinner and drinks and public displays of foreplay. Two months of watching Nick's infatuation grow while Charlie maintained her "touch, but don't feel" approach, guarding her heart like the gold reserve at Fort Knox, and Aiden played man-trapped-in-the-freaking-middle.

Sixty-five days of torture.

Charlie had been blind to the pain it caused Aiden. She still was. In her defense, he worked very hard to blind her.

She wasn't property that he owned. They were friends, close as family. She had a right to sleep with whomever she chose without a guilt trip, without pettiness, without judgment on his part.

Aiden only wished she had chosen him.

They got off the trolley in the Gaslamp Quarter, two blocks from Nick's apartment building. The urban center was the heartbeat of the city.

Aiden preferred his tranquil condo overlooking the water. There he had peace of mind and the quiet to reflect.

Whereas Nick enjoyed the hubbub with energy always circulating, always something to do to keep him from thinking about life. Perhaps that was why things had lasted so long between Nick and Charlie. They'd been objects in constant motion bouncing between work, activities down at the Seaport, entertainment here in the Gaslamp Quarter, which turned into a playground for adults after dark, and then off to the bedroom.

Pushing it from his mind, Aiden followed Charlie into the residential parking garage. They walked to Nick's designated spot and found his Dodge Ram.

"Can you break in without smashing a window?" Aiden asked her.

"No need." She dropped to the ground by the front wheel on the driver's side and felt around for something. "Bingo."

Charlie stood, holding a magnetic key box. Inside was an extra fob.

Aiden had no idea it was there. Nick was like a Boy Scout, always prepared, but it was salt in the wound realizing that his buddy and his best friend—the woman he loved—knew things about each other outside the bedroom that Aiden didn't.

The stab of longing and jealousy in him was sharp.

No way was he delving toward things inside the bedroom.

Aiden tossed the bag in the back. They stripped off the scrubs and he got behind the wheel, firing up the fully gassed truck.

They took I-8 East. The first step was to get out the city, then the state.

"We need to find Albatross," Charlie said. "Finish what we started."

It was their duty to save him, if they could, but it went deeper now. "As well as clear our names. Everyone believes we're guilty because of this alleged eyewitness. I can't wrap my head around it."

"Pretty convenient, isn't it?"

"Too convenient. Too tidy." The whole thing reeked.

"Do you still have the hit man's burner phone?" Charlie asked.

"Sure do."

"Can I have it?"

Aiden dug in the pocket of his jeans and handed it to her. "What are you thinking?"

"We need to know who is accusing us, but we'll need a little assistance to find out."

"Draper won't lift a finger to help us, and no one else in the office is going to be inclined to stick their neck out. Not with this kind of heat. If Draper found out, he'd tank their career."

"There's one person who might help us." Charlie shifted in her seat, turning to him. "Nick."

Aiden was quiet for a long moment. Shame swept through him as he remembered the resentment that he'd held against Nick during those two agonizing months.

"On vacation, he can help from a distance," Charlie added. "He hates Draper just as much as we do, probably more, and is already planning to transfer to another office. I think he's our best chance to get some answers."

The reasoning was solid. Unable to find fault with it, Aiden nodded. "Call him."

"Maybe the request would be better received if it came from you."

Nick had moved on; he was no longer hurt by the way Charlie had treated him, and he was in love with Lori. Even better, the one thing his buddy couldn't resist was a woman in trouble.

"You call him," Aiden said. "Nick has a serious savior complex." Maybe Nick thought he could save Charlie from a loveless, lonely life. But Nick didn't understand that she didn't need to be rescued. Charlie had to be the hero in her own story. Fear was her dragon to slay. Love was her choice to make. No one could do it for her. "It's a big ask, but he won't say no to you. Trust me."

"What's his number?"

"You don't have it memorized?" Aiden asked, keeping his tone light, teasing.

A hint of a smile played over her lips, her eyes deadly serious. "The only number I have memorized is yours."

That was music to his ears. Aiden rattled off Nick's number.

"I hope he answers, since it'll be an unknown number," Charlie said.

He hoped Nick wasn't too busy making love to Lori with his phone shut off. Nick had only landed in Phoenix today. It'd been weeks since he'd seen Lori, and he must've missed her something awful.

Aiden was happy his friend had finally found happiness.

Charlie dialed and waited with the phone to her ear. Nick must've answered, because she put the call on speaker. "It's me, Charlie. Aiden and I are in a world of trouble. We need your help."

"What do you need?" Nick asked, without a beat of hesitation.

The man was a good friend and a great marshal.

Charlie explained the details of the situation. "According to Draper, the eyewitness is making a formal statement. We need to know who it is. Figure out a motive. Maybe discredit the person."

"I know Albatross," Nick said. "I was the one who got

him settled in San Diego and helped him with his transition. I might reach out to someone in our office for information, claiming I saw it on the news. I also have a reliable contact in the SDPD."

"Since you knew the guy and you're familiar with his history, do you remember anyone who might've had a grievance against him?" Charlie asked. "Or anything odd about his case that stood out?"

"As a matter of fact, yeah. The US attorney's office was livid at first. They were expecting information on one mobster they'd been going after. Some guy in New Orleans—uh, I can't recall the name. Anyway, Albatross had been working closely with him, was even engaged to his sister, I think, but in the end, Albatross gave them nothing on the target. Instead, he turned over evidence on two other big fish. Two convictions versus one, so the US attorney's office accepted it and made the deal."

"That's helpful, Nick," Aiden said. "More than you know. Thanks for helping us. We really appreciate it, brother."

"No problem. You'd do the same for me. When I get something, should I call this number?" Nick asked.

"Yeah, this number." Charlie lowered her head and her voice went soft. "Thanks, Nick. And hey…the way things ended between us, I, uh, I—"

"There's no need to apologize. It doesn't matter anymore," Nick said. "It was a long time ago, and I found what I was looking for with Lori. We're getting married."

A strange tension blasted off Charlie as she sat back in the seat.

Things had broken off badly between Nick and her.

Nick had ended the fling once he realized he'd never be anything more than entertainment for her, a diversion, a toy, and Charlie had lost it because Nick had beaten her to the punch. But no matter how ugly the breakup, Nick had defended her against others in the office who had snide, unkind things to say about her, and he had even broken one marshal's jaw.

Hotheaded and impulsive, but Aiden respected the heck out of Nick for it.

"Okay. Thanks. We appreciate the help." Charlie disconnected.

That wall of hers went up, like an iron curtain drawn between them, and Aiden felt lost. She hadn't cared about Nick, not romantically, but something troubled her.

"Does it bother you that he's getting married?" Aiden asked. "You're not jealous, are you?"

"Of course not." The stark sincerity in her voice relieved him. "It's just that... Nothing." She shook her head. "It's stupid."

"Nothing you have to say is stupid. What is it?" He glanced over at her.

There was a glimmer of pain in her eyes—just a flash like lightning in the darkness—and then it was gone. "The only reason I let it last so long with Nick was that I thought he was like me. That hooking up was enough. That he believed happily-ever-after was a crock," she said, a cutting edge to her voice. The normal confidence she carried faltered. "He pushed for me to spend the night, leave stuff in a drawer. And I thought it was about him needing to control a woman who refused to be controlled. Turns out that he really does want the lifelong commitment, house with white picket fence, two-point-five kids."

Sounded pretty good. Aiden wanted to get married, settle down, have kids, build a home like his parents had. Only problem was he couldn't envision it with anyone other than Charlie.

"What's wrong with wanting that?" Aiden reached for her hand and took it in his.

She flinched and he closed his fingers more firmly around hers, expecting her initial reaction.

"For every nine out of ten people who want it, are drawn to it, one isn't. Or can't have it. For every nine out of ten who run toward the dream, one is stuck with reality. I guess I'm that one." She pulled her hand away from his, shifting in her seat, and cleared her throat. "Do you think the men who attacked us are going to take Edgar to New Orleans?"

Aiden's head spun as he tried to keep up with Charlie's dodge-and-evade maneuvers.

There were times such as now, when she'd give an inch and he wanted to press for a mile through that thicket of thorn bushes surrounding her, needing to delve deeper so badly regardless of the injuries he suffered. But he'd get better results beating his head against a wall than taking a battering ram to her heart.

In the wake of his silence, she said, "504. That's the area code of the number that texted the hit men. New Orleans, right?"

Her emotions were compartmentalized and controlled to the point of strangling. She radiated a distance that was part of her core. She wore that cold bravado like armor.

One of the things Nick had grumbled to Aiden about Charlie was the lack of closeness. Nothing physical that wasn't foreplay, culminating in cool, no-nonsense sex. No hugs. No kisses beyond flirting. No postcoital cuddling. No sharing of anything of substance.

Nick's complaints had left Aiden mystified.

In those quiet moments between Aiden and Charlie, when an intimacy was tangible and a physical kind seemed possible, she shared bits of her childhood, glimpses of her soul. There was no doubt in Aiden's mind that hidden behind her cold reserve, she had an inner fire that raged, burned so hot that it would scald.

Sadness leaked through him at the absence of tenderness and affection in her life. He ached to give her the emotional warmth and security she deserved, to feed her heart and soul.

He gripped the steering wheel harder with both hands and took a deep breath. "Yeah, that's the area code for New Orleans. The hit on Albatross feels personal, with the offer of extra money to bring him in alive so he could be tortured. With the involvement of the mobster's sister and the fact that Edgar had worked closely with that guy, I'd say it's our best lead." The only thing they had to go on.

"It would be impossible for them to fly there with a hostage. They'll have to drive. How long do you think it'd take them to get there?"

Aiden had mapped out the drive from San Diego to Camp Beauregard in Pineville, Louisiana. Twenty-four-hour trip that he could make in two days, if he took the job. Tack on an extra four hours to get to New Orleans.

"I'd estimate twenty-eight hours," he said. "They'd drive straight through in shifts, only stopping when absolutely necessary for gas, food. Maybe twenty-nine hours if we're lucky."

"We need to beat them there, be ready once they arrive and find Albatross before they kill him. But with the head start they have on us, the only way to do that is to fly."

"Have you forgotten we're wanted? They'll be on the lookout for us at airports."

"I agree that trying to fly from any airport in California would be suicide." Charlie stretched, rolling her shoulders, and Aiden could hear the wheels spinning in her head. "Didn't you mention that on the reservation there are independent Navajo-controlled airports?"

"Yeah, so?" he asked, not liking where this was headed.

"So, your father is an important man."

Aiden's dad was the chief of a tribal council. He was essentially a governor with executive power, and the council had legislative power.

The position was one of great respect and influence.

"If you called him," Charlie said, "and explained the situation, don't you think he'd get someone to do him a favor?

Get us on a flight to New Orleans. With our weapons. No IDs needed. No questions asked. He would gladly help."

Without a doubt, his father would help any of his children in need, but Aiden would never ask such a thing of him. Charlie should've known better than to suggest it, but her upbringing was so different. Aiden's family was large and tight-knit. Honor and respect and principles were as important as love.

Charlie didn't speak to her mother anymore for some reason and only exchanged a few hollow pleasantries with her sister around the holidays. She'd never been taught the value of family, the sanctity of such a bond. All she knew was the anger, the fear and loneliness from not having it. He understood that was the reason she held herself at such a distance, but he was no longer sure she'd ever let him in on the other side of her wall.

"No," Aiden said, shaking his head to emphasize his point.

"Why not? It'd be easy."

"The easy way isn't always the right one. I won't ask my father. You don't use family like that. Not if you care about them. This is our problem. I won't drag him into this."

"Your family is off-limits, but it's fine for us to get Nick involved? He might only be getting us information, but we're also making him complicit. He's aiding and abetting us. I guess that double standard sits fine with you."

The hypocrisy of it twisted through Aiden's chest. Charlie's point was valid.

Growing up, he'd worshipped his father. He'd been taught to protect his family at all costs.

Nick understood the stakes, the risks, and knew that if the shoe was on the other foot, he could rely on them to stick their necks out the same way for him. Nick could've said *no*, whereas Aiden's father wouldn't have a choice. His dad would be compelled to help.

There was a fundamental difference that he couldn't put into words.

Folding her arms, Charlie looked out the window and dropped the issue.

A heavy silence filled the confines of the cab, almost consuming them in its enormity.

Aiden flipped on the radio and tuned in low background noise. He upped the speed a bit, keeping it under the limit. They didn't come this far to get stopped for a traffic ticket.

For a hundred miles they drove east toward the mountains and the Arizona border without talking. There'd never been the need to force chitchat between them. It always flowed. The quiet moments were natural, not awkward and uncomfortable as it was now.

Her stomach growled, but she said nothing.

He saw a billboard for a shopping mall and restaurants. They both had bloodstains on their jeans. Most people might overlook it, but a keen eye would find it suspicious. If they figured out a way to fly, they couldn't go through an airport looking like this.

Taking the off-ramp, he pulled into Yuma, five miles across the Arizona state line. First, he stopped for gas, making sure to keep his face turned away from the cameras.

Then he found the mall, which wasn't hard. It was a sprawling, palm-tree-studded outdoor complex with plenty of stores to choose from, dining options and a theater.

He parked at a department store. "We should get fresh clothes," he said.

"Good idea."

Inside, Charlie headed to the women's section and he went to the men's.

Under normal circumstances he'd gravitate toward the sales, but efficiency was his focus. They needed to get in and out. He browsed quickly and found a replacement pair of jeans. Dark wash. Perfect size in a brand he was familiar with. Fifty bucks. His shirt was in good condition, but after smelling under his arms, he searched for something new. He grabbed a moisture-wicking crew T-shirt that had the stretch and fit he preferred, navy instead of black, and a long-sleeve button-up shirt to wear open and hide the bandage on his arm.

He changed in the cubicle, trashed his old stuff and took the tags to the checkout. Near the register, he saw a ball cap and grabbed it, too. His total was a hundred and twenty dollars.

It took them ten minutes to meet back up. Charlie wore slim-fitting jeans that looked great on her and a V-neck T-shirt in light gray that hugged her curves and flat stomach. She'd also added a cotton warm-up jacket.

"Hungry?" he asked.

"Starving."

In-N-Out Burger was a close walk and the food would take no time. They ate inside, their backs to a wall, away from cameras and other people.

Charlie took a bite and moaned. "This is the best burger ever."

Digging in, he had to agree. After the day they'd had and three hours hauling butt to get out of California, they were both famished, and almost anything would've tasted good, but the thick patty and cheese and grease hit the spot.

"You never did tell me where you learned how to hot-wire a car and pick pockets," he said.

"In a group home. The place was like a jail, with white concrete walls and bedrooms that resembled cells. They even had rules against hugging because it violated the no-physical-contact policy. Some of the girls in there were on the road to becoming criminals. I picked up those skills from troubled kids, to pass the time, for fun. Other things I had to learn to survive. Like how to fight. To make sure that if I let the other girl get back up, I taught her a lesson first so she'd never touch me again. It wasn't an easy place to grow up. But in there I figured out how to turn my anxiety into anger, channel it into something useful."

He knew about her mom's drug problem and Charlie's

time in foster care, but he'd thought it had been a brief stint. "How long were you in the system?"

"My sister and I bounced in and out from elementary to high school."

Her most impressionable years had been spent in an institutionalized environment with child welfare monitors instead of loving parents. His heart sank. It pained him to imagine it.

"Why didn't you ever tell me all of this?" He opened his water bottle and took a long draw.

She shrugged. "I guess I don't like thinking about it. All of your childhood stories are wonderful."

"That's not true." He'd shared his tough lessons and disappointments. The racism and stereotypes he had to endure outside of Navajo Nation. His world wasn't sunshine and rainbows every second of the day.

"Okay, you're right. That's not fair. But I don't really have any happy stories. With the stuff I learned in the group home, being in that environment, I could've just as easily ended up like my sister instead of…" Charlie lowered her burger, her gaze darting around. "I have an idea. I know how to get us on the plane. I'll be right back."

She wiped her mouth with a napkin and went up to a male employee mopping the floor.

A young guy in his early twenties. Laughter flowed back and forth. Then he wrote something down on a piece of paper and handed it to her.

Charlie waved bye to the kid and came back to the table. "Let's go."

They grabbed their burgers and drinks and got into the truck.

"We need to go here." She handed him the slip of paper.

"The Oasis. What is this?"

"The solution to our problem." A bright smile spread across her face, lighting up his heart. "Drive."

Chapter Nine

The atmosphere of the Windfall Casino on Fridays was an appealing balance of electric and calm. One of Big Bill's favorite things to do was stroll around undisturbed by anyone for a few minutes and take it in as a tourist might, but he could never shut off his managerial brain.

Dressed to the nines as usual, he wore a quiet dark suit, a perfectly laundered shirt, an elegant silk tie and gleaming black oxfords. First impressions mattered. He could intimidate a person, get inside their head and establish the pecking order simply with his attire, without uttering a word.

Bill walked through the main downstairs gambling room. It was filling up. By nine tonight, it would be packed.

He cast his gaze across the slots. Two-thirds of them were taken, a mix of men and women, most over forty, a relatively shabby bunch that'd stay planted well into the wee hours. The blackjack and craps tables and roulette wheel were in good use.

Bill had got his start in Las Vegas and risen through the ranks from croupier to pit boss to manager. Hustling was in his blood. He'd seized every opportunity to advance, even if it meant getting his hands dirty. *Bloody* would be more accurate. Notorious mobsters were responsible for making Vegas what it was today. Bugsy, Lansky, Luciano...

Those old-school greats had shaped Sin City. They'd given Bill the vision to one day go back home to New Orleans and open a casino of his own. Plunder an untapped market. Build a legacy for his family. With no children of his own, this would one day go to Tommy. He was as good a son as any who might have been his.

There were other casinos in the state on floating boats and at the horse-racing track with slots, but the Windfall—Big Bill's masterpiece—was the only land-based private casino with table games in the state. Louisiana law provided for fifteen riverboat licenses but only one land-based one. Plenty of others had applied, but Bill had shed a lot of blood and greased a lot of palms to make sure the Windfall won.

Now he had to fend off greedy interlopers like Vincenzo Romero, who coveted what Bill had built. They thought they could take it by putting a knee to his throat and applying pressure.

All because of Edgar.

Bitterness filled Bill's mouth. He had turned a down-on-his-luck accountant into the Money Magician, like turning polluted water into wine. Bill had even set him up with his younger sister, Irene, thinking they'd make a nice match.

And what did that dirty dog do?

Stabbed Bill in the back…and killed Irene on the way out the door.

Pain squeezed his heart, rage setting his blood on fire. For a moment, he shut his eyes in quiet misery. Bill had never imagined that Edgar was capable of murder, but he'd never underestimate him again.

Suffering was in store for that two-faced, double-dealing liar.

A comeuppance was due, and Bill was going to make sure Edgar got it. Slowly. Painfully. He'd make a list of Edgar's body parts to hurt and check it twice once that man was kneeling in front of him, begging for forgiveness.

Enzo strutted past the roulette wheel, wearing a two-thousand-dollar suit, shaking hands and kissing cheeks as if the

51 percent stake in the Windfall that Bill still owned was already his.

They were roughly the same age, had started making their mark about the same time, and both had ambition in spades. Enzo dyed his gray hairs and kept a trimmer physique, but the crucial difference was his deep familial connections in the syndicate supporting him.

A type of protection Bill lacked.

Bill had created this on his own, from nothing. Losing it because of Edgar, a man he'd protected, vouched for, had almost considered family…a man who'd killed Irene, was unconscionable.

Such a betrayal couldn't go unpunished.

Seething, Bill headed for the poker room.

Twenty tables open 24/7, offering Texas Hold'em, Omaha and seven-card stud for cash or tournament play.

Enzo slithered across Bill's path, intercepting him before he made it inside. "You're looking sharp as always."

"Good to see you making the rounds," Bill said, swallowing bile as he went through this nightly farce once again.

Given a choice, he'd sooner shove an ice pick in Enzo's heart than spout false pleasantries, but unfortunately, Bill's back was up against the wall and he had to endure this.

For now.

"We need to talk," Enzo said.

"It'll have to wait. I'm busy." Bill let his tone slide toward dismissive.

"Now," Enzo stated coldly, blocking Bill's path. "My office."

Any office was the last place they should talk. Didn't that fool know the radioactive level of scrutiny Bill was under? The FBI had bugs and agents throughout the casino. He'd wager there were federal eyes on them at that very moment. The feds had guys sitting in vans outside his restaurant and house and following him everywhere.

He wouldn't be surprised if whoever the special agent in charge was had a report detailing how often Bill went to the bathroom along with what kind of toilet paper he used.

"Let's have a drink later." Bill patted Enzo on the shoulder. "We'll talk then."

"Full operational control and seventy-five percent of the profits," Enzo said.

Bill chuckled, shoving his hands into his pockets. "I'll see you in hell before I give you seventy-five percent of my casino."

"Not the casino. The girls."

Alarm sent a chill down Bill's spine. Enzo was making a play for the lucrative sex trafficking ring.

"Not here," Bill whispered, glancing around to see if he spotted any of the agents in the vicinity. Between the lounges and displays, casinos were full of loiterers, which made spotting surveillance almost impossible. The feds always had at least two agents tracking him. Sometimes more. Whenever Bill caught one watching him, they quickly looked away.

Did they think avoiding eye contact would make them turn invisible?

It only made them look more suspicious.

A pretty lady with deep olive skin and thick, glossy hair from a Pantene commercial left the Texas Hold'em table and walked their way. She wore a revealing tank top, flashing more skin than a fed would, and slacks. He noted her shoes.

Sensible shoes a person could run in was one telltale of those agents on mobile surveillance.

This woman wore killer high heels and had no qualms meeting Bill's gaze.

"I offered to discuss it in my office. You declined. So we'll do it here," Enzo said, checking out the woman passing by. "I don't care who hears us. It doesn't endanger me. Only you. I don't have a vested interest. Yet." Enzo pulled on a smug grin that Bill wanted to slap off his arrogant face.

"The bosses are meeting in a week here in New Orleans to discuss your future."

Time was almost up. Bill needed Edgar and any incriminating information he had on the lot of them pronto. It was his only salvation.

"Look, I'm trying to help you." Enzo's smile widened like he wanted to devour the whole world. "Give them a reason to spare you. After all, we're friends."

"Like a viper and a mongoose are friends," Bill spit.

"Which one am I?"

You'll find out when I rip off your damn reptilian head with my teeth and dance on your cold-blooded corpse. Bill smiled back but said nothing.

Tommy strode over and gave Bill an affirmative nod, which meant one thing.

Devlin had Edgar.

If Bill wasn't standing in the middle of the casino in front of this dirtbag and didn't have bad knees, he would've jumped for joy and pumped his fists in the air. "I'll have something that I think the bosses will be much more interested in," Bill said, "but thanks for the offer."

He'd give the vultures Edgar's bruised and broken body to pick at and use whatever evidence that traitor had squirreled away for old-fashioned blackmail. Put them back in their places. Show 'em Big Bill was the boss once again ruling New Orleans.

"It better be good or it's your funeral." Enzo turned and left.

Bill took a cleansing breath and led his nephew to one of the four restaurants in the casino. They entered the busy, gleaming kitchen. He acknowledged the head chef and some of the underlings and went into the walk-in refrigerator, where sides of beef hung from the ceiling. Tommy closed the door behind him.

It was freezing in the tin icebox, but it was a safe space to talk freely.

"What did Enzo want?" Tommy asked.

"Seventy-five percent of the sex ring."

"Wow." Tommy rocked back on his heels. "They're really gunning for you."

Didn't Bill know it. But it was time for him to hit back. "Don't worry about it. I've got a plan."

"No offense, but I gotta worry." Tommy's breath fogged the cold air. "If they slit your throat, Uncle Bill, I'm going to bleed out with you."

The kid's concern was warranted, and Bill had an obligation to protect his sister's only son. "You spoke to Devlin?"

Tommy nodded, rubbing his hands together. "D got him. *Alive.* The boys just passed through Tucson. They'll reach the city in twenty-one hours, but D is flying back tomorrow. He got delayed in San Diego. When he gets back, he wants to meet face-to-face."

"You told him we'll do it at Avido's?" The casino wasn't an option and Bill's days of meeting in back alleys and cars were done. He was reduced to having conversations in meat lockers, for Pete's sake.

"Yeah. I told him," Tommy said. "He wants to arrange half the payment before his boys set foot in New Orleans with Edgar. The rest on delivery."

Bill blew into his cupped hands, starting to shiver. "Fine. Whatever he wants. As long as I get Edgar alive. And what about the evidence? Digital? Hard copies? Anything?"

Tommy shrugged. "D said he's working on it."

"What the hell is that supposed to mean?"

"He said he'd explain in person."

Bill was too damn cold to blow a fuse.

Nabbing Edgar was a major win. Bill would toss the other bosses a juicy Plinski bone to gnaw on, but he needed that evidence—in black and white, so to speak—to get out of this alive.

SOMETIMES ASSISTANT SPECIAL AGENT in Charge Ava Garcia strolled through the casino on one of her breaks or after duty, to play a hand of poker or have a meal.

She liked to change her shoes first. A woman walked differently depending on her footwear. Three-inch heels didn't scream federal agent but purred all-woman.

It helped her blend in, appear nonthreatening.

Garcia spent more time at the Windfall than she did at her apartment in the hopes she'd see something, overhear a nugget she could use to nail Big Bill Walsh to the wall.

Today she'd got that kernel, making all her free hours spent here worthwhile.

The other bosses in the syndicate were coming to New Orleans. That was huge.

Bill would have to meet with them, and he planned to offer them something they wanted more than his head on a pike.

She'd have to get extra agents and change out the vehicles Bill's people were familiar with. Anticipate how Big Bill would try to give them the slip.

No matter what, the FBI would also be in attendance.

Garcia watched Bill and his nephew leave the restaurant. They were rubbing their arms, looking chilled to the bone.

What were you two talking about in a meat locker?

Garcia left the casino, headed to her car in the parking garage and called her boss, Special Agent in Charge Bryan McCaffrey. "Sir, Garcia here. I'm going to need four more agents and to swap out vehicles as soon as possible."

AIDEN FOLLOWED THE directions Charlie gave him as she finished eating her burger.

Twenty minutes later, he turned off the highway and pulled into the cracked parking lot of the Oasis. Red *X*s blazed with the promise of scantily clad adult entertainment.

"Why on earth are we at a strip club and how is it going

to solve any of our problems?" Aiden usually trusted Charlie without question, but he looked at her like she was crazy.

"If I tell you, you won't like it."

"You're not going in there to strip, are you?" As soon as the words left his mouth, he regretted it, hearing how absurd it sounded. They didn't need money, but they were here for some unfathomable reason.

"Of course not. How is stripping going to help us?"

He threw his hands in the air and shrugged.

"Sit tight," she said, patting his leg. "I'll be back as soon as I can. Thirty minutes, tops."

Before he could protest about how this was a bad idea, whatever she was up to, Charlie was out of the truck and sauntering inside the Oasis.

Aiden left the vehicle running. No telling what Charlie was doing in there. Best for him to stay prepared for anything.

There were twelve cars in the lot on a Friday at three o'clock in the afternoon. Might be a payday for some.

A shame to blow it here. Then again, the women inside had to make a living, too.

Aiden stared at the red pulsing *X*s. An unspecified anxiety twisted through him. His thoughts raced.

Why couldn't he go inside with her? It was a gentlemen's club, after all. Why wouldn't he like her plan? Did it involve some dude rubbing his hands all over her?

"This is stupid," he muttered to himself. "I'll just go in there and see for myself."

No sooner had he cut the engine and taken out the key than Charlie came out, looking pleased as a cat that'd swallowed a canary.

She jumped in as he started the truck.

"Drive," she said.

He threw the truck in gear and turned onto the highway. "Talk. Now."

"Ta-da," she said, pulling two driver's licenses and a credit card out of her back pocket and holding them up next to each other. "You are now Rudy Benally and I'm Priscilla Johnson."

Aiden took one. Arizona State driver's license. The guy was forty, eight years older than Aiden, Native American, short black hair. Height five-ten, off by only two inches. Weight 180, lighter by twenty. But they didn't look enough alike to even appear related.

"Sorry I couldn't do better with yours. There were only two Native American guys inside to choose from."

Taking a glance at the other, he noticed a resemblance between Charlie and Priscilla. Blond hair. Blue eyes. Twenty-seven. Four years younger than Charlie. But time hadn't been kind and the woman in the photo looked older. Same height and weight. Priscilla was pretty while Charlie was gorgeous.

The credit card was in Priscilla's name.

"With your baseball cap," Charlie said, "this will work."

He gritted his teeth, not liking it, but he didn't have a better plan. "Did you pick-pocket all of that? As soon as the credit card is reported stolen, we're hosed."

"Ms. Johnson works there. She's a shrewd, resourceful businesswoman who was open to making a deal. I paid her to loan me her license and credit card. There's a thousand-dollar limit on the credit, so I gave her fifteen hundred, with the promise that I'd mail both back to her. For an extra two hundred, she was kind enough to help me separate Mr. Benally, a touchy-feely jerk and bad tipper, from his license. If it makes you happy, we can mail that back, too, since we have his address."

He heaved a big sigh. "Fine. We'll give it a go. But since we can't fly with firearms, we need to secure them."

"How far to Phoenix?"

"Two, maybe three hours," he said, tracking her thinking. Nick was there visiting Lori. They could park the truck at the airport and let him know where to pick it up. They'd also have more options of flights from the larger hub. "Phoenix it is."

Aiden took I-8 to I-10. Traffic in and out of a large city was always dicey, but with them only stopping once to use the restroom, they made great time.

At the Sky Harbor International Airport, they parked at the terminal and stowed their vests and firearms under a seat in the truck but hung on to their badges and comms devices.

Charlie also kept the gym bag.

"What else is in there?" Aiden asked.

"The supplies to stitch up your arm. They won't let us through security with everything, so I'll check the bag."

"Thanks," he said. "For thinking about it." That was what they did, took care of each other.

"No problem." She grabbed what was left of her soda and held it up. "In case we need a diversion when they check our IDs."

He locked the doors, placing the fob back in the key box, and had Charlie make sure no one was watching while he put it back under the carriage.

They walked directly to ticketing and checked the departure boards. A Delta flight to Baton Rouge. Ninety-minute drive. But it was boarding now. United had one leaving in forty minutes to New Orleans. A nonstop flight.

"Let's hope they have tickets," Aiden said.

The line at the ticket counter was short and moved quickly. A weary-looking woman of about sixty greeted them when it was their turn.

"We're hoping to get two seats on your last flight to New Orleans." Charlie placed the soda cup with plastic lid on the counter.

The woman clicked away on her keyboard. "I have a handful left. None together, unfortunately. But you'll have to hurry to make it."

"Sounds good," Aiden said, setting down Benally's license. "One bag to check."

"Thanks so much." Charlie handed over the ID and credit

card. "He just got a big promotion and I promised we'd go there to celebrate. My treat."

The woman lined the identification up in front of her and typed in their information, glancing between the cards and the screen, disinterested in their story, but Charlie kept talking.

"You've worked so hard. You deserve to have some fun." She wrapped her arm around his and put her head on his shoulder.

"*We* deserve some fun," he said, playing along as if they were a couple.

The woman swiped the credit card and took the bag. She typed some more, and the machine printed boarding cards. After attaching the baggage tag to their one checked item, she collated the tickets with the right licenses. "You two better hurry. Enjoy your trip and congratulations on your promotion," she said, handing them over.

Charlie picked up her soda with a smile. "Have a good evening."

They jogged to the checkpoint, where it was one person's sole job to verify a picture ID against the ticket. They got in place with the string of passengers and shuffled forward.

Loosening the plastic lid on her cup, Charlie adjusted it to sit on top instead of clicked down in place. Aiden lowered the bill of his cap.

Next in line, they were waved forward.

Charlie took his ticket and license, slipping them behind hers. They stepped up to the podium together, and she handed over everything to the fortysomething screener.

The man looked down at Priscilla's license and up at Charlie. Appearing satisfied, he scribbled a mark on the ticket and gave Charlie back hers.

Then the screener glanced at Benally's license.

As the middle-aged man's gaze lifted to Aiden, Charlie stepped to the side and tripped.

The lid of her cup flew off. Soda splashed on the floor, drawing everyone's attention.

"Darn it," she said. "I'm sorry about the mess. I really wanted to finish that, too."

"It's all right, miss. We'll get it cleaned up. You were going to have to toss that anyway before you got through security." He scribbled on Aiden's ticket and handed it to him along with the license and then gestured for them to move on. "Watch your step, please."

Clearing the rest of security was a breeze. They put their badges discreetly in the plastic tray along with their communication devices, the flash drive, shoes and the cell phone.

If they had been traveling on official business, they would have had their sidearms, gone to the head of the line and then through a side door.

As regular joes, they each took a turn in the security hoop, hands raised, boots off.

On the other side, they finished lacing up their boots and headed to the gate. It was fairly empty. The majority of passengers taking the flight had already boarded.

"Where are you seated?" she asked.

"Row twenty-three. Aisle. You?"

"Ten. Window. I'll talk to a flight attendant and see if she can get someone to switch."

The cell phone rang. Aiden took it out. "Nick's number."

"Good thing he called before we got on."

Their plane was going to land late in the Louis Armstrong Airport, after eleven.

He hit the answer button. "It's Aiden."

"Hey, man. I wish I was calling with better news."

Aiden met Charlie's gaze and shook his head. "Give me a sec." He took her elbow and steered her off into a corner, out of anyone else's earshot, and put the call on speaker. "Go ahead. We can both hear you."

Charlie paced in front of him, her hands on her hips.

"I've got details about the eyewitness," Nick said. "He was supposedly hiking at Mission Trail Park. As he was leaving, going south on Mission Gorge Road, headed back to a friend's house, where he was staying while on vacation, he claims he saw Yazzie shoot Torres and Killinger take out the cop."

"Vacation?" Aiden asked. "If he's not from San Diego, where does he live?"

"New Orleans," Nick said.

That jarred Charlie to a stop. "Are you kidding me?"

"Albatross is from New Orleans. You said yourself he has a powerful enemy there, a mobster who wants him dead," Aiden said. "Doesn't anyone find that the least bit suspicious?"

"The man has half a dozen powerful enemies from Houston to Biloxi. The eyewitness's friend, his reason for being in San Diego, checks out, and the time of his 911 call fits the time of the incident. So far his story is so airtight it can't breathe."

Charlie muttered a curse. "Albatross said the person who had the biggest ax to grind with him was a guy back home."

"Do you have proof? Or is it just hearsay? Speculation?" Nick sighed. "Listen, no one is going to take your word. Everyone believes the eyewitness lock, stock and barrel," Nick said with grim resignation. "From the police chief to Draper, who, by the way, has thrown you two to the wolves. It doesn't look good. The witness is hanging around San Diego for any follow-up questions and plans to leave tomorrow, seven p.m. flight back to New Orleans."

"What about the dead cop's body-worn camera?" Aiden asked.

"The BWC was no help. There was too much smoke and his car door obstructed most of the video. The audio does nothing to clear you. I'm sorry the news isn't better, but I'm rooting for you guys."

"We're being set up," Charlie said. "Why is everyone so

quick to dismiss our track record and believe this witness? What is he? A priest?"

"No. He's a cop."

Cold sweat broke out on Aiden's back. "Are you sure?"

"Yep. His police chief in the Fifth District attested to his honesty, integrity and astounding service record in SWAT."

The truth closed in on him. The fluidity of the men who had attacked them. Their precision. Their paramilitary approach. Their...*professionalism.*

They'd been ambushed by a special weapons and tactics team.

"This just keeps getting better and better," Charlie said.

"Do you have a name and address?" Aiden asked.

"Sure do. His name is Frank Devlin."

Chapter Ten

Everything Nick had told them played on a loop in Charlie's head during the three-hour flight. She and Aiden had to go up against a corrupt SWAT team.

Without backup.

Without weapons.

On the enemy's turf.

She cursed the hand they'd been dealt.

A flight attendant had managed to get Charlie and Aiden seats together, but they hadn't been able to risk discussing their predicament on the flight.

Her skin itched, and she couldn't wait to get off the aircraft and move.

The plane's touchdown was smooth and the taxi to the terminal was fast. The tiny chime sounded, the seat-belt light went out, and passengers leaped to their feet to disembark.

The plane emptied from the front, people moving in a steady single-file stream, funneling out row by row. Charlie and Aiden went out the door onto the Jetway. Muggy air and the stench of kerosene hit them, and they moved on into the Louis Armstrong Airport.

Thanks to their flight time plus the two-hour time-zone change, it was eleven thirty.

Nick had passed along Devlin's address. That was where they'd start.

They had to find the place on Rampart Street in the Seventh Ward, break in and search the dirty cop's home for anything that might help them.

Sounded simple enough, but in the pit of her stomach she knew better.

They went to the taxi line and slipped into the back seat of a sedan. Not as if they could take a cab to the cop's house.

"We need a car rental company," Aiden said.

"Which one?" the driver asked. "Enterprise? Avis?"

"No, none of those." Charlie shook her head. "Not one of the big brands or anything in the yellow pages. We want something away from the airport. Small. Discreet."

The driver flashed a lopsided grin. "I know just the spot."

Without asking questions, he drove them to a place fifteen minutes away. A lot with about twenty cars, located next to an auto salvage yard. There was a little shack situated between both properties, with two signs—Dan's Auto Wreckage and Dealing Dan's Car Rentals.

The driver honked twice.

A minute later, the door of the shack opened, and a man wearing a fedora stuck his head out and waved.

"You're good to go," the driver said.

Aiden peeled off a couple of twenties and took care of the cab fare, and then they walked to the shack.

"Looking to rent a car?" the older guy asked them.

Aiden nodded. "Yeah. Something with a navigation system. We don't know the city."

"Take a look at the five cars in the first row. Those have GPS. When you find something you like, give a holler. I'm Dealing Dan." He tipped his fedora to them and then disappeared back inside like he could've just as easily been called Shady Dan.

Bypassing the BMW and Mercedes-Benz, they looked at the Toyota, Honda and Chevy Impala. They needed something fast that would blend in and not call attention to them regardless of the neighborhood they might find themselves in.

"The Honda is out," Aiden said. "Too many scratches and dents."

"I don't like that bright cherry-apple red color of the Toyota," Charlie said. Too memorable when they wanted to be utterly forgettable.

Aiden agreed. "I guess we have a winner."

They walked to the shack and knocked on the door.

"Come on in." A comedy show played on a television behind the desk, where Dan had his feet up and hands resting on his big belly. "What'd you decide on?"

"The black Impala," Aiden said. "Is it reliable?"

"As reliable as it's going to get," Dan said, chuckling at the screen. "It's a 2005, one hundred and fifty thousand miles, new timing belt and tires. Runs smooth. Shouldn't give you any problems. How long will you need it?"

Aiden and Charlie exchanged a glance, an unspoken question passing between them. How long did Albatross have to live?

"Three days," Aiden said.

"At the most," Charlie added.

They did the deal using the licenses of Johnson and Benally, and Johnson's credit card. Charlie filled out the paperwork, listing a fake phone number and bogus address. So long as Dealing Dan got paid, Charlie suspected he wouldn't care too much if the information was made up.

Dan handed over the key. "Be sure to get some beignets from Café du Monde while you're here and try the coffee with chicory. Nothing else quite like it. Enjoy your time in New Orleans."

"One more thing," Charlie said. "Would it be safe to assume with you working out here at all hours by yourself that you're packing?"

Dan smiled. "Yeah, it would."

"Willing to sell us your gun?" she asked.

"No can do. But I can offer some nonlethal options." Dealing Dan pulled out a baseball bat and a crowbar and set them on the desk.

Neither were inconspicuous options, but they'd work under the cover of darkness.

"We'll take both," Aiden said.

At a significant upcharge, one hundred dollars bought them two weapons.

They climbed into the Chevy. The tints on the windows were a bit chipped and starting to bubble and the sagging seats creaked when they sat on them, but the engine turned over with no drama.

The address on Rampart Street was easy to find with the navigation system. The neighborhood had a bohemian vibe, colorful street murals, quirky boutiques and hip-looking restaurants.

Devlin's place was a small shotgun row house on a residential street with a driveway alongside. They parked two doors down across the street.

Charlie dug out two sets of plastic gloves from the box she'd taken from the hospital and handed some to Aiden. "So we don't leave any prints."

Putting them on, he said, "You really do have quite the criminal mind."

"What can I say? I'm a product of my environment."

"It's been useful." He put a hand on her shoulder and squeezed, filling her with warmth.

For the first time in her life, she wasn't ashamed or embarrassed about growing up in foster care and group homes. Even though Aiden had had a picture-perfect home with a loving mother and devoted father, he had a way of seeing her, accepting her, that made her feel valued and special.

They got out of the car, carrying their overpriced weapons, and crept around the long, narrow home. Red security storm doors were on the front and back, where there was also a small patio.

"Please tell me you learned how to pick a lock, too," Aiden said.

Charlie shrugged. "I did, but it's not like I have the right tools on me. We should try a window."

They did, but they were all locked.

"I'll have to break a windowpane," Aiden said.

That was when she noticed the aluminum sill. It was easily breakable. "No. Too risky. Someone could hear the glass breaking. I think I can jimmy it open."

She shoved the flat edge of the crowbar between the window and the sill. As she leveraged the pane up, Aiden pushed. The sash latch gave way and the window slid open.

He gave her a boost, with her foot on his palms, and she hoisted herself up the frame and climbed inside. Aiden followed behind her and they closed the window.

The houses on the street had historic charm on the outside, but inside, this one had been renovated with high-end finishes and stainless-steel appliances.

It was a straightforward two-bedroom, two-and-a-half-bath home. The living room flowed into the dining room and on to the kitchen.

They split up and searched the place. Aiden took the master bedroom and the other one set up as an office/guest room.

Charlie started in the kitchen. There was nothing hidden in the fridge or freezer. No false backs in the cupboards, no fake tins of coffee, nothing hidden in the jars of flour or sugar. No voids behind the wallboards.

Next, she checked the dining room and living room. No loose boards in the hardwood floor, no hollowed-out books. Nothing in the sofa cushions, either.

She blew out a frustrated breath and spun around to see what she might've missed.

On the wall in the dining room hung some pictures. Most of the photos were of one man surrounded by nature. *Frank Devlin.*

He knew their faces and names and now they knew his, too.

Early to midforties. Six-two. Athletic build. Rugged. A thick head of sandy brown hair. Eyes so intense they were chilling.

In one photo, Devlin held up a huge fish by a lake. Another was of him kneeling beside a dead deer in a meadow covered in mist. Two teenagers stood in front of a cabin in the next one. A boy with his arm around a younger girl's shoulders. They resembled one another. Brother and sister.

She stared at the last picture. Five men, smiling, standing together behind a bar. A backlit sign read The Merry Men.

Robin Hood's band of outlaws. Mighty brazen of them.

"I've got nothing," Aiden said, walking out of the office. "Not even a laptop. Any luck?"

"I think this is Devlin." She pulled out the cell phone and took a picture of the photo with the men. They looked like standard-issue tough guys: hardened, brawny, merciless beneath the smiles. Badges and guns on their hips. Devlin had his right hand on the shoulder of the man in the middle. "There's five of them here. But we were hit by a team of four. What if one of them stayed behind?"

"Only one way to find out. Are you up for a drink?"

"Always."

A 411 CALL GOT them the address. The parking lot of The Merry Men was almost full. Only a few spots left at the far end by a wall. The idea of getting blocked in didn't sit well with Aiden.

He parked across the street. "Stay here and keep it running."

"Come again?"

"One or more cops own that bar. That'll make it a *cop bar*."

She turned in her seat and faced him. "And?"

"Bars are already a weapons-rich environment with glasses, longneck beer bottles, even heavier wine bottles." You could club a person with one. "If they have pool tables, that'll mean pool cues."

Charlie's brow furrowed. "I have been in a bar. I'm familiar."

"But in *that* bar, most of the patrons are going to be packing heat, and we can't stroll in with a crowbar and baseball bat. We need answers about a dirty cop. Answers no one inside is going to willingly give. If the car is running, it'll be easier to make a quick getaway if push comes to shove."

Her frown deepened. "Why am I supposed to be the one left in the car? And if you give me 'it's an order' or 'I outrank you' crap, I think we'll have to arm wrestle for it."

He suppressed a chuckle. "I can take you in an arm wrestle."

"Not the way I play."

Which meant no rules. Winning by any means necessary. Would she throw a fist to his groin?

"Follow the order without giving me grief," he said, wanting to avoid an arm wrestle. "We can debate it later." If it came down to a fistfight, he'd rather be the only one getting his butt kicked. Spare her a beatdown from a bunch of cops.

"I have a better idea."

"Really?" He raised a suspicious brow. "What's that?"

She took off her jacket, tucked her short sleeves up into the body of her T-shirt, displaying her toned arms, and pulled the V-neck front down, showing off her ample cleavage.

He realized how she intended to play this, and it made his gut churn with a shocking possessiveness.

"You keep the car running while I drop a little bait and separate our prey from the herd." She fluffed her hair. "I'd kill for lipstick and a little mascara."

Aiden gritted his teeth, hating her impetuous plan from

start to finish. "You look better without it," he said without thinking. "Prettier."

Charlie's gaze flew to his as her jaw dropped a little.

He usually kept such comments to himself, not wanting to make her uncomfortable by reminding her that he saw her as an enticing woman.

Since he'd started speaking his mind, why stop there?

"You're a natural beauty, Charlie." He dared run his knuckle along the side of her face. "You'll have every guy in there drooling, wishing he could take you home tonight."

A slight flush stained her cheeks, and she gulped.

Maybe he'd been playing it too safe, not telling her, not showing her how much he desired her. Waiting for her to be ready. Sometimes a person had to be thrown into a sink-or-swim position.

He lowered his hand, cupping her neck. Her pulse throbbed against his palm. "Do me a favor and stay here. Don't make me watch you smile and flirt with some guy while he ogles you. Touches you." If he had to choose between that and a potential fistfight, bring on the brawl.

She wet her lips and clutched his wrist but didn't pull his hand away, turning him on bright as a bulb. Her eyes were luminous. Radiant with a hunger, a fire that drew him closer even though he knew he'd get burned.

The atmosphere in the car shifted, like the current in the air before a storm.

Her mouth opened, but before she could speak, he followed a foreign, reckless impulse and leaned over, pressing his lips to hers.

There was none of the cautious gentleness of a first kiss. No need to coax. No resistance given. All the desire that'd been kindling for four years ignited in hot bliss.

It was a long-overdue communion that touched him to the very core.

She arched up and let him in. As he sank into her warm

mouth, his hand slid up, cupping the back of her head. He devoured her, slowly, deeply, consuming and claiming. Every slick swipe of her tongue against his was liquid heat.

Holding her to him, he deepened the kiss as he found himself pushing her back in the seat.

A headiness enveloped him, seeping to every nerve fiber, but he forced himself to stop.

He pulled back, not wanting to ever let her go.

Her eyes fluttered open and he saw it—the evasiveness of her gaze, the set of her mouth, the stiffening of her posture, the crease in her brow. He'd cataloged every nuance of her body language, memorized every elusive emotion that passed across her face. She was retreating behind her wall.

His heart squeezed.

"If you don't want to watch, you should stay here and keep the car running." She hopped out, slammed the door and started crossing the street.

Aiden cut the engine and was hot on her heels. "Charlie!"

"What's the alternative? You get your face busted up, maybe a few broken ribs. No. Not on my watch." Stepping onto the sidewalk, she turned and faced him. "We should go in separately. If he's in there, I'll get him outside around back." Then she opened the door and disappeared inside.

Aiden scrubbed a hand over his face, hauling in a deep breath. That kiss. God, *that kiss* had been all-consuming. Set him ablaze, painting everything with a pall of red.

There was something he'd learned today, a lesson that had to be heeded.

Life could turn on a dime. His reputation and career hung in the balance. Circumstances kept shifting like grains of sand beneath their feet.

His love for Charlie was the one constant. In fact, it had got stronger since his tumble off the roof. Brought everything into high definition and surround sound.

He was done avoiding, making excuses, playing it safe. No more holding himself back.

SOG. Camp Beauregard. He had to tell her.

The secret he was keeping from her about the job offer was eating him up. The deadline to give an answer was next Friday. Eons away in light of what they were currently facing—

Finding Edgar and clearing their names.

Next Friday, he could be sitting in a jail cell, trying to explain how things had gone terribly wrong—or worse. And his biggest regret would be not telling Charlie how he felt about her.

He shoved the darkest thoughts from his mind. They'd get through this the way they did every other mission. As a team.

Aiden adjusted his ball cap and went into the bar.

It was wood-paneled, with taxidermied heads of deer, bobcats and gators protruding from the walls, and had a long line of taps that would've been a beer lover's dream come true. All the tables and booths were taken.

He grabbed the first seat he found near the door. Next to him was a tall guy, thin as a blade but wiry, with a gun and badge on his hip. Taking stock of his surroundings, Aiden counted ten more badges and guns in ten seconds. He spotted Charlie perched on a stool at the opposite end of the bar.

The guy from the picture, the one who'd been in the middle, was behind the bar, pouring her a drink and chatting her up. She sucked back the clear liquid in the shot glass and set it down.

The man poured her and himself another round. They clinked glasses and did the shot.

She worked fast.

Color Aiden unsurprised.

Not much of a beer drinker, he ordered a double bourbon, neat. A female bartender didn't waste time getting his order and was heavy-handed with the pour.

Aiden dropped a twenty on the bar. "Is that the owner?" He gestured to Mr. McChatty.

"*One* of the owners. Jeff Landau."

"How many others?"

She pointed to a picture hanging on the wall. The same as the one at Devlin's place. "Four. But Jeff is the only one here right now."

"Where are the rest?"

She shrugged. "Vacation. Hunting trip, I think."

"They all active over at the Fifth District?"

"Yeah, except Jeff. He retired a couple of years ago."

The dude sitting beside him gave Aiden the side-eye.

One too many questions asked. Got it. "Thanks," he said to the waitress and grabbed a handful of nuts from a bowl.

Watching the crowd through the mirror behind the bar, he estimated 75 percent of the patrons, including the man next to him, were cops. Either active or retired.

He nursed his bourbon while Charlie flirted and laughed and slammed back shots, throwing out stellar bait only a eunuch could resist.

A strange possessiveness roared through him. He'd never wanted any woman the way he wanted Charlie. In his bed, beneath him, above him, curled around him. In his life, beside him.

He put his jealousy in check as he'd done many times before, but the ache in his chest didn't go away. He'd dared showing her his feelings, asked her not to do this, and she'd done it anyway.

Charlie took another shot. He wasn't worried about her holding her liquor. She was able to drink a Russian under the table with his own vodka. He just didn't want to watch her throw herself at another man, even if it was playing a role.

In thirty grueling minutes, she had McChatty hooked.

Charlie stood, leaned over the bar, arching her back, projecting her breasts, her tight, round butt high in the air, and whispered in Jeff's ear.

The massive ball of tension inside Aiden burned hotter than a solar flare.

Every man in the vicinity checked her out, lust stamped on their faces, gleaming in their eyes. They were practically drooling. Aiden couldn't blame them. With no makeup, wearing jeans and a T-shirt, Charlie was stunning. Truly something to behold.

Jeff spoke to the other bartender for a second, and she responded with a nod and a sly smile. Then he led Charlie through a door outside to the back.

His muscles tightened, but he resisted the urge to jump up and leave right away. With his hand clenched in a fist on his thigh, he finished his drink. When the stopwatch in his head hit two minutes, he spun off his stool, yawned for good measure and went out the front.

As soon as the door closed, he forced himself to walk slow and easy, like time wasn't a factor, with his hands in his pockets, around the side of the building toward the back. A man running, especially one of color, drew unwanted attention and suspicion faster than one strolling along without a care in the world.

By the time he made his way to the dumpster, Charlie had Jeff pinned with his cheek pressed to the brick wall, his arm twisted behind his back at an angle meant to cause excruciating pain, with his pants down around his ankles.

From the blood on his face, she'd broken his nose first.

"Devlin and the others, who hired them?" she asked as Aiden came up alongside her.

"I don't know what you're talking about."

"She's got quite a temper," Aiden said, "and she's short on patience. I suggest you start talking."

"You're both making a big mistake. Messing with the wrong people."

Charlie gestured for Aiden to take over holding Jeff. He was more than happy to oblige.

After they swapped places, she snatched his right wrist and twisted until the knuckles were facing her. She grabbed his index finger. "The job in San Diego. Who hired him?"

Jeff called Charlie a bunch of foul names. In Aiden's experience, she wasn't going to respond well.

Without a word, she wrenched his finger back ninety degrees, snapping the first knuckle.

Jeff gasped and groaned in sheer shock and pain.

Impressive. He took it like a champ, without screaming.

"I tried to warn you," Aiden said.

"Tell us who or I break another and another until you won't be able to pour drinks with that hand, and then I'll move on to the other."

"Big Bill," he grunted.

They exchanged a glance. "Yeah, we're not from around here," Aiden said. "We're going to need a last name."

"Walsh. Big Bill Walsh."

"Why didn't you go with your buddies?" she asked.

"I busted my knee a couple of years ago. Forced retirement. I'm no good to them anymore out there like this."

"Why was Devlin hired for the job?"

She grabbed his middle finger when Jeff didn't immediately answer her question.

"Because Big Bill wants Edgar Plinski. The guy's a rat who killed his sister."

Aiden hadn't seen that coming. Most in WITSEC were some brand of criminal, but Edgar didn't seem the murdering kind. The Department of Justice was certainly unaware of the allegation. If it was true, he'd be out of the program, since the immunity deal that he'd been given didn't cover murder.

"Why is Big Bill offering so much money for any information Plinski might have in his possession?" Charlie asked, on a roll.

"Big Bill needs it. The other bosses are slowly squeezing him out. Enzo Romero already took half of his casino. It's only a matter of time before he ends up floating in the river. No fingertips. No dental records. That's if the FBI who've got him under surveillance don't arrest him first."

"Which casino?" Aiden asked.

"Which?" Jeff made it sound as if the answer should've been obvious. "The only real one in the city. Windfall."

"Hey!" someone called from the street. "What are you doing? Jeff? Is that you?"

"Time to go," Aiden said to Charlie.

Shots rang out as they took off down the alley.

Chapter Eleven

A second shot was fired somewhere behind them.

They rounded the corner, sprinted down the pavement and took another right turn, running side by side.

At the car, Aiden slid in behind the steering wheel and fired up the engine as Charlie dropped into the passenger seat. Without waiting for her to close the door, he swerved into traffic and peeled off down the street.

Pure adrenaline pumped in her blood and her head buzzed, but her thoughts circled around one thing.

Aiden Yazzie kissed me! Something she'd longed for and dreaded all at once.

And she had kissed him back. Without thinking, without choosing. It had been as necessary as breathing, and stopping hadn't even been a whisper in her head.

His sexy mouth, his hot tongue... When they'd touched hers, everything had trembled. Her lips, her limbs, her bones, her heart. She would've sworn that the car had shaken.

He'd kissed her so deeply that she couldn't tell where he ended and she began. She'd forgotten the rules, the boundaries, her name.

It was a good thing they'd been in a car parked on a city street. If they'd been anywhere remotely private, there would've been no stopping. The tension and touching would've grown hot and feverish, turning volcanic, until they were both ready to explode, their bodies demanding a release.

Arousing, erotic, enthrallingly rough images flooded her mind.

Crap. What the hell did this mean?

Did she really want to know?

Nope. Then she'd have to deal with it, which meant making a mess of things. Better to pretend it had never happened. Though it had, and she'd never forget it for as long as she lived.

"What's up?" Aiden asked.

"Huh?"

"You were shaking your head and then you were nodding at something."

"Oh, was I?" She cleared her throat, struggling for composure. "I was just thinking about bed. For sex. I mean sleep. For sleeping," she said again, emphasizing the word with her hand. "It's been a long day. I'm so exhausted that I'm delirious. I don't know what I'm saying. We need to find a hotel."

"Okay." He gave her a weird look. "Should be easy enough."

They chose a hotel on the outskirts of the French Quarter. A large, busy place with a heavy flow of tourists, but not surrounded by too much noise.

It was within walking distance of restaurants, shops of all kind and the Windfall Casino.

They parked in the hotel's garage. Aiden carried their one bag.

Walking up to the check-in desk, she realized they didn't have basic toiletries. Or pajamas. They'd have to sleep naked in the same room.

A hot rush of panic shot through her, stilling her.

Aiden's hand went to the small of her back and he ushered her forward.

The clerk welcomed them with a smile. "Good evening."

"We'd like to get a room," Aiden said.

"How many nights?"

Aiden looked at her and she shrugged. Edgar had been gone almost twelve hours. He had another sixty to live, tops, if he was lucky.

"Two nights," Aiden said. "A room away from the ice machine and near the stairs."

They didn't need the noise of the machine, or a reason for anyone to loiter near their room, and it was always good to be close to a second exit.

Charlie set the borrowed credit card on the counter.

"I'd prefer to leave cash to cover any incidentals," Aiden said, surprising her at first.

On the chance Priscilla Johnson decided to report it stolen, order a new one and keep the fifteen hundred without worrying about the bill, it could put them in an awkward situation. Not to mention it'd give the hotel a reason to call the police.

Cash was best.

"No problem," the clerk said. "For cash, we require two hundred and fifty dollars to cover any phone calls, the minibar and pay-per-view charges. If you order room service, you'll have to pay the waitstaff when they deliver it."

Aiden dug out enough bills from his wad of hundreds to cover the two-night stay plus incidentals. In return, the clerk handed them two key cards.

They swung by the mini-mart in the lobby, grabbed toiletries and got in the elevator.

She only meant to give Aiden's reflection in the shiny steel wall a quick glance, but her eyes lingered. On his strong jaw. His dark T-shirt stretched tight across his shoulders. His hard muscles. Those legs that looked incredible in a pair of shorts, sexier filling out jeans. Probably best with nothing on at all.

And man, he could kiss. She had wanted to lose herself in the confident, demanding way he'd owned her mouth with so much passion, melting her protective barrier of ice into a puddle of desire. If that was how he kissed, how did he do other things?

A sensation she couldn't name exploded through her. Stronger than lust. Animalistic and primitive. And she needed to shake it off quick.

With a ding, the elevator stopped, and the doors opened to the fourth floor. They found their room at the end of the hall. He opened the door, letting her in ahead of him.

She entered, taking in the spacious room, and froze.

There was one king-size bed.

"I can go change the room to a double," Aiden said.

Always the gentleman, never wanting to put her in a compromising position that other men would've orchestrated.

Deep down, she didn't know what she wanted. She'd fantasized about making love with Aiden more times than she could count on her fingers and toes combined. They were as close as two people could be without sleeping together. But in her experience, sex had a way of spoiling things. She'd do anything not to ruin their relationship.

Aiden was the only good thing in her life.

"Don't worry about it," she said. "I still have to stitch you up and it's almost three in the morning." They were both grown-ups and could handle sharing a bed.

Naked?

Maybe they'd have to sleep in their clothes.

"Why don't you shower first," Aiden said, and she nodded.

In the bathroom, she was relieved to find plush robes and slippers. The velvet-soft cotton would be much nicer to sleep in than her jeans.

Aiden knocked on the door. "Do you want me to order room service?"

I have one hell of an appetite. "No. I'm fine." She was starving, but it was her growing hunger for him that worried her. The last thing they needed was to lounge on the bed in robes, with nothing on beneath, eating and talking, having a drink from the minibar. It was a recipe for trouble. Hot, sweaty, naked trouble. "I'd rather hit the hay sooner, wake up earlier and have a monster-sized breakfast, if that's okay with you."

He didn't respond right away. Then he said, "All right."

She brushed her teeth and hurried through her shower, washing her hair. After towel-drying, she threw on her robe, tying the belt in a knot to prevent any mishaps, and went into the bedroom. She avoided eye contact with him and headed for the bag sitting on the dresser.

"Bathroom is all yours. As soon as you're done, I'll stitch you up and then we can go to *sleep*," she said, enunciating the last word slowly.

Although sex, not sleep, was at the forefront of her mind and her sensitive spots were in cahoots, ready for action. Ridiculous hormones.

It didn't help that she hadn't had sex in more months than she'd cared to admit.

"Sure," he said. The bathroom door shut behind him.

She relaxed, taking a breath.

On the other side of the TV, she noticed two empty protein shake containers. He must've gone back down to the mini-mart because he was starving, too.

Way to go, Killinger. Could you be any more selfish or paranoid?

She rummaged in the bag, took out the supplies, setting up on the desk beside a bright lamp, and put on latex gloves.

Aiden emerged from the bathroom. He stood in the doorway with a towel wrapped around his waist and another in his hand as he dried his hair, looking annoyingly delicious.

Her throat went bone-dry.

He crossed the room, shoved the chair out of the way and sat on the edge of the desk.

This wasn't the first time she'd seen his broad, muscled chest, those nicely formed pecs and washboard abs *completely bare*, but it was the first time she'd been close enough to stick her tongue out and lick every toned, sculpted muscle.

Perfection.

He was striking, had a sparkling energy that was warm, powerful, sexual. A magnetic presence that drew lesser objects into the heat of his sun.

Three minutes after they met and talked one-on-one, she would've dropped her panties for him, but he'd had a girlfriend at the time.

A saving grace that had allowed their friendship to blossom, given them a chance to become family. But looking at him now, butterflies fluttered in her belly. She had to squeeze her knees together to keep from spreading her legs apart.

She grabbed saline solution and the towel from his hand to catch the runoff. "Ready?"

Aiden gave a curt nod.

This was going to hurt him, and she hated that, but there was no way around it. Had to be done. She squeezed the saline into the wound to irrigate it and rinse off the last of the hemostatic powder.

When the liquid hit his skin, he gave a sharp hiss through gritted teeth.

"Sorry about that."

The wound went from oozing before the irrigation to bleeding in earnest.

She dabbed it with sterile gauze and covered the area with an anesthetic spray.

After giving the painkiller a minute to work, she held his arm, sutured his wound, giving him small, neat stitches, and then snipped the thread. She applied antibiotic ointment and put a self-adhesive gauze pad on to protect it.

"Finished," she said, tugging off the gloves and chucking them in the trash.

Thank goodness that was done.

Being so close to him, with all that bare skin exposed, and touching him had turned her insides molten. This was testing her sanity and tempting her in new ways.

She stepped around him to put away the supplies.

"Thank you." He caught her wrist and pulled her in between his legs.

As she leaned into his touch, her heart remembered the rule about keeping some physical distance with Aiden, but her libido seemed to have shredded the memo. She dragged her gaze down his sleek, tightly muscled torso to the unmistakable bulge tenting his towel.

How was that possible while getting stitches?

Then again, Aiden was the most remarkable man she knew.

Charlie looked up at him, her pulse beginning to race. Carnal images of them tangled up in bed together floated through her head.

Desire was etched on his handsome face, in the sexy grin on his full mouth. He exuded sex—raw, sheet-clenching sex—or standing this close to him, with his body on display and a bed a few stumbles behind her, simply made her think about all the ways they could pleasure each other.

For one night.

She pressed her palms to his smooth chest and wicked warmth spiraled through her. Touching him excited her; it was a heady intoxication, but she couldn't shake the wariness that came along with it. She was terrified to want this, terrified of how it'd change things.

He stroked her damp hair and caressed her face with the back of his hand. His eyes, glinting with sensual promise, blazed into hers, incinerating her doubts and fears one by one. She fought not to squirm while her thighs tingled and every cell in her body perked up.

She wanted to blame this craving to feel his skin on hers, this inexplicable draw to him, on the shots of vodka, on their near-death experiences.

But that was a lie too big even for her to swallow.

He wrapped his arm around her waist and brought her

flush against him. With the pad of his thumb he traced a searing path across her lips. The heat of contact had her melting faster than butter in a hot skillet.

His eyes were so dark and fathomless she could dive in and never find the bottom.

The air was thick and heavy, charged with an undeniable current like flammable gas. One lit match was all it would take for a total disaster.

Hell, static electricity might do it.

"I want you." His voice was husky and full of gravelly heat.

Sparks of arousal shivered along her nerves. As intense as their attraction was, there was understanding, too, a comfort in being known, and she had to protect that at all costs.

"I've had a lot to drink," she said. "If I don't remember this tomorrow, promise not to hold it against me."

Lies. Well, she did have a few shots, but she was far from toasted, and she'd remember every scintillating detail of being with this man. But they needed an out, a sort of parachute. Pull the rip cord and they'd land safely, nothing broken, and go back to normal.

His eyes narrowed, sending unease skittering down her spine. He studied her, and she met his measuring gaze, unblinkingly.

"So you'd only sleep with me if you could call it a slipup," he finally said, and she stilled at his tone, the gravity in his eyes. "Blame it on too much alcohol?"

"Yes. No. I don't know." Damn, he knew her too well. But he made it sound horrible and unforgivable. A betrayal of the worst kind. "You're curious about what it'd be like for us to have sex. I am, too, but once our curiosity is satisfied, we need to be able to go back to the way things were."

"Why do things need to go back? Why can't they move forward? As nature intended. I'm not curious about sleeping with you. I'm *interested* in *being* with you."

Her heart tripped into her throat as she felt the blood drain from her face. For a moment she didn't know what to say, silence swelling between them, but she gathered what wits she had left. "How many people have successful relationships in our office? How many are divorced, separated? How many in SOG, where we're constantly on call and have to drop everything to respond in six hours? This job, this lifestyle isn't conducive to matrimony or monogamy."

He dropped his hand from her face.

"The odds of anything romantic between us succeeding are bad enough," she added, her mind spinning, redirecting wherever she could that didn't lead to the painful truth. "If we became a couple it would muck up work."

"How?"

"At Albatross's house, you ordered me to take cover in the refrigerator while you took point and ran into the fray."

"I ordered you to protect him."

"Would you have done that if I were a man?"

"Yes! Because that's who I am. I can't help it. I'm not sexist, Charlie."

"What about at the bar? How you wanted me to stay in the car. Are you going to try and deny that, too?"

He blinked at her. "I'd never ask you to stop doing a job you're good at, one you love. Relationships are scary. They're a gamble. But I like our odds. I'd bet everything I have on us."

"What we have is special and I don't want to lose it. You're my—"

"Yeah, best friend. I know," he scoffed, looking away from her.

"No, you don't know. You're more than my best friend." She pressed a palm to his cheek, turning his head until their eyes met. "You're my only friend. You're my person." A tiny voice in the back of her head warned that she was getting in too deep, but she kept going. "The one I confide in, hang out with. You're my emergency contact, for God's sakes."

His whole face twisted in utter disappointment.

She let him go. "Come hell or high water," she said, stalking back and forth in front of him, "I've got your back and I know you've got mine. You're my family, Aiden. You're my..." She swallowed the word *partner*. In every way except sexual he was, but fear overwhelmed her, and she pulled the rip cord. "You're my brother." The necessary lie stung her tongue, but it was for the good of them both. "Maybe you should think of me as a sister."

In an explosive move, Aiden swooped forward with such forceful urgency it drove her feet back. This was bad, bad, bad. He cupped her face in his hands, bringing her pacing to an abrupt stop. Without warning or hesitation, he pulled her mouth to his and kissed her.

The instant their lips touched, her thoughts scattered and the lies were lost in a hot vortex of total oblivion.

There was no stopping the shocked moan that slipped from her on a wave of arousal that floored her like an express train. His tongue swept across the seam of her lips and delved inside. His fingers slid into her hair as he drew her even closer, his mouth hot and possessive against hers, claiming a deeper taste.

She threw her arms around his neck, her nipples tightening, her body burning with scalding need for him.

He spun her around, backing her up against the wall, and rocked into her, their bodies straining, melding in perfect harmony.

The hard ridge of his erection pressed into her abdomen. A yearning ache thrummed between her thighs. He caressed her breast through the soft cotton, dragged his thumb across her nipple, but it wasn't enough. She wanted more.

As if reading her dirty mind, he dived into her robe and cupped her sex, palming her. Stoking her arousal.

Guilty pleasure blindsided her. Her body throbbed with painful, wet need.

She couldn't stop herself from rubbing against the delicious pressure of his hand and didn't want to.

This was foolish. Reckless. That registered in some obsolete part of her brain, but the electricity crackling between them overrode her thoughts.

There was only hunger centered on this man. She wanted him more than she wanted to breathe. All of him. Inside her, deep and fast and hard and rough.

Blood thudded against her eardrums and pulsed in her groin. "More, more." The words spilled from her mouth in a rough whisper.

She was condemned to hell. The upside was the road was slippery and hopefully riddled with orgasms. If he kept this up, she'd have her first pretty soon.

His mouth left hers, gliding across her cheek, her jaw, to her carotid artery, where her pulse pounded wildly as she took ragged breaths, wanting to curl into him.

"I'm your brother, huh?" His voice, soft with menace, skated over her skin. "You sure as heck don't kiss me back like a sister."

Shock and hurt slapped her.

She very nearly picked up the gauntlet he threw down. But the one thing she was better at than fighting was running. And when your survival depended on it, you learned to run like the devil was chasing you.

"Out of all the excuses I imagined hearing from you, this one takes the cake," he said. Lust and anger etched his features into something dark and smoldering and dangerous. "Truly priceless. The worst part is, I think you're delusional enough to believe it." The harshness of his words stunned her heart, but she jerked out of his arms.

Her body mourned the loss of his male heat, his scorching touch.

"I'd give my right hand to get under your skin," he said, "to have you want me the way I want you. I've stood by for years, being there for you. Being *your person*. Loving you. Wanting you. I told myself that one day, when you were ready for a relationship, you would open your eyes to what was in front of you. Instead, you dated Nick. Not just a guy in the office, where I had to have it thrust in my face every damn day, but one of my friends. I had to hear about the details from both of you. Do you have any idea what that was like for me?"

After all he'd just said, the question was rhetorical, but he didn't let her off that easily.

"It gutted me, Charlie. And if by some chance the two of you had worked out, it would've broken my heart."

Guilt ripped her to pieces.

Aiden was twisting everything up inside of her into a giant choking knot.

"I wasn't serious about Nick." He was a friendly work associate that she passed her off-duty time with between the sheets. They'd hooked up until he started pushing to turn their superficial fun into a real relationship. She didn't do long-term with anyone. Living half a life wasn't so bad when the idea of anything else, anything more, seemed impossible, too far out of reach. "We didn't date. It was just sex. I never even stayed the night with him. He was a distraction." *From wanting you.* "I didn't sleep with him to hurt you."

"But you did hurt me!" The stricken look on his face was a knife in her chest. "Are you going to stand there and tell me that you didn't know how attracted I am to you? Are you going to deny that it's mutual?"

If she tried, a bolt of lightning would probably strike her. The intensity of their attraction was as strong as gravity. There were times when he'd give her a look that sent a current of raw desire racing under her skin, making her stomach dip and her breath grow shallow. Of course she knew.

Lowering her eyes, Charlie backed away.

"There's something I haven't told you." His voice grew

quiet. "I was offered a position at Camp Beauregard, as an instructor. I was torn about taking it because I was holding on to hope. About us. I think after we clear our names and go back, I'm going to accept the position."

Panic slithered up her spine and coiled in her gut. "No. No, no." A fierce longing shook her to the core. "You can't be serious." He wanted to leave her. "Why?"

"Because I can't keep pretending that this is platonic when it's anything but. My mind files away all these details about you. The way you move, your smile, the smell of you, that defiant way you hike your chin, the sexy hollow of your throat, the curve at the small of your back, creating a sick map of you. One that I see and want to touch that leads me back to you when I'm with someone else." Naked emotion passed over his carved features and he withered in front of her.

She stared at him, sad desperation flooding her veins.

"As long as I continue to be your person," he said, "I'll never be able to move on from you. It'd be impossible to fall in love with anyone else. I want to get married, have a family, children."

A sinkhole opened inside her, rattling her to the very foundation of her soul. *Children.* Something she'd never be able to give him or anyone else.

"I need all those things. I wanted them with you." He shook his head. "But I can see now that's never going to happen."

It was too much and not enough. "Aiden…"

He waited, the hope in his eyes glaring.

Tension swelled in the room around them. Her mouth opened, but no sound came out. She didn't know what to say to keep from losing him. The weight of that inevitability settled in her chest.

"Get some sleep," he snapped. "We've got a long day ahead of us." He stormed into the bathroom and shut the door.

Her heart hammered, her brain reeling.

The dread inside her shot to a higher pitch and her muscles turned to gelatin. Charlie sank down on the bed, trying to piece together what had started it all, how everything had spun out of her control. Her only answer—the kiss they'd shared earlier.

They'd opened Pandora's box back in the car when their lips had locked, and they'd tasted the passion burning between them.

A sudden realization struck her with such blunt force that it stole her breath. She was in love with Aiden. Not as a sister loved a brother, but as a woman loved a man.

And he was in love with her.

She'd been kidding herself all along that she could control this. What a fool she'd been.

Maybe she should tell him the truth. Why they couldn't be together. The real reason they'd never work.

A hurricane of conflicting emotions rioted inside her, making her eyes sting.

He'd stirred up a longing for something she couldn't have, to be someone that she couldn't—a mother...to be *his* in every sense of the word.

Her eyes watered, tears burning. She burned...ached for him. For the impossible.

Aiden threw open the bathroom door. He was dressed as he stomped out, not casting a single glance at her. "I need some air. I can't breathe."

Before she could utter a word, he was gone.

Chapter Twelve

His hands in fists at his sides, Aiden stormed out of the hotel as desire pounded through him. His straining erection was painful, and his head was a mess.

He was a complete wreck and Charlie was what he needed to fix it. She was like a drug, a habit he couldn't kick no matter the side effects or warnings or devastation.

Sleeping with her would've only made the addiction worse.

Aiden knew this and still he wanted her. Needed her. He was a lost man.

His lungs heaved with a foreign anger. Stalking down the street, he was furious. At himself. Not at her. It wasn't her fault any more than it was heroin's or meth's for a person needing that fix, again and again.

He never should've put her in that position back in the hotel room. Never should've thrown the job offer in her face that way.

It wasn't like him to be cruel. Even if she had been cruel first.

You're my brother. Maybe you should think of me as a sister.

A stab speared through his chest as he recalled her words. Her lies. It made him sick to his stomach.

He punched the air and swore under his breath, his mind, his body, every inch of him humming with the memory of kissing her, stroking her hot wetness between her thighs.

How good she'd felt, how receptive she'd been, turned on by him so quickly. How much he'd wanted to slip inside her and bury himself in her heart.

Madness whirled around in his head, a firestorm of pent-up sexual frustration consuming him. He was disgusted with himself for how he'd spoken to her. Touched her. A part of him felt as if he'd violated their friendship. The other part felt like he hadn't gone far enough.

What was wrong with him?

Aiden scrubbed his hand over his face. The musky scent of Charlie filled his nostrils, inflamed his blood. Stoked the madness swelling in his skull.

He should've washed his stupid hands, but he'd been fired up and in such a rush to get out of the hotel room that it was a miracle he'd taken the time to get dressed.

Desperate to shake himself free of this misery, he needed to focus on the trouble they were in, on finding a solution out of it. On anything except the always present chemistry between them. Chemistry that'd sparked the day they met.

A fresh clutch of pain tightened in his chest.

Stopping, he found himself standing in front of another hotel. He went inside and used the bathroom off the lobby, soaping up his hands twice and scrubbing them clean.

He threw away the paper towels and rubbed the outline of the flash drive in his pocket. They had no clue exactly what was on it. Finding out might give him some idea what their next step should be.

This situation wasn't going to fix itself, and dwelling on Charlie wasn't helping.

He walked up to the concierge desk as if he was a guest staying there. "Hi. Where's the business center?"

The clerk directed him to a comfy lounge with living room furniture, computers and printers. The lounge flowed into a twenty-four-hour coffee shop. Since it was communal space, the Wi-Fi was free, and he wasn't even asked for a room number to access the internet.

After he bought coffee and a premade packaged sandwich from the coffee bar, he settled in at one of the computers for a long haul. It'd take time to carefully sift through the drive. If they had any hope of winning this, they needed to know who they were going up against.

He had to concentrate on their current problem. Clearing their names, which also meant finding Edgar, alive.

Then he'd take the job as an instructor. Go to Camp Beauregard. *Rehab.* The only way to get over Charlie… Killinger. That was how he'd think of her from now on.

And she'd have to find a new emergency contact.

SITTING IN THE passenger's seat of the Crown Vic, Devlin sipped his hot coffee, grateful for the shades shielding his eyes from the early-morning light.

"That should do it," Detective Carol Jenkins said, switching off the recorder on the dash. "Thanks for answering all of my follow-up questions."

"No problem. I just want to help in any way I can. It's awful what those marshals did."

"Yeah." Detective Jenkins nodded. "It makes everyone in law enforcement look bad."

"The one thing I can't stand is a dirty cop. Or marshal, for that matter." He took another hit of much-needed caffeine, trying not to choke on his lies. At 7:00 a.m., his brain was still fuzzy, but deception came naturally to him. No effort or thought required. "Thank you for the lift to the airport and for understanding about me needing to catch an earlier flight."

"Of course. Who hasn't had a family emergency? I'm sorry to hear about your brother-in-law's heart attack."

When Jeff had called Devlin, hysterical, his brother-in-law had sounded as if he was going to have an actual coronary. Those marshals had some audacity to waltz into their place filled with cops and beat Jeff for information. At least they only broke his finger. They could've broken his arm.

The good news was his plan was working.

His worst-case scenario was Yazzie and Killinger being arrested. The flash drive seized. Stuff went missing from evidence rooms more often than civilians would imagine. Hell, if he could sneak out weapons and bricks of cocaine, he would've found a way to smuggle out a tiny thumb drive.

But luck was on his side. The best-case scenario was in play. The marshals were virtually bringing the drive to him. He owned that city.

Now that he knew they were there, he'd find them.

Smoke them out if necessary while Devlin's friend here in San Diego would tie up the loose end of the wife at Mission Medical.

"Detective, if you've got any other questions, I'm happy to answer them over the phone or even Skype."

She nodded, pulling up to the terminal. "What time does your plane land?"

"I'll be home by lunchtime. I'll take my sister out for a bite to eat, give her a break from the hospital." He'd have lunch all right, but not with his sister. His first stop would be Avido's, to ensure Big Bill made the initial payment.

"I wish I had a brother as thoughtful as you."

He shrugged. "I do what I can."

"I hope your brother-in-law gets out of ICU and recovers."

"Thanks. We're all fighters in my family." The strong survived. "I've got a good feeling that he's going to pull through."

IT WAS LATE morning by the time Aiden finished reviewing the evidence Edgar had hidden. After asking the concierge where he could buy a USB nearby, he dashed down a block and bought one. This city was great. Everything at his fingertips.

There was enough information on the drive to fill an encyclopedia. He copied about a chapter's worth to the new memory stick and printed some choice documents on Walsh and his hostile business partner, Romero, that, when put in the right hands, would send them to prison for a very long time.

On his way back to the hotel, Aiden swung by a restaurant. Grabbed breakfast sandwiches, beignets and coffee with chicory, black for *Killinger* and au lait for him.

He put his key card in the slot. The little green lights flashed, the lock released, and he opened their room door.

Charlie was dressed and on her feet, moving toward him before the door shut behind him. "Where have you been? Are you all right? I've been worried sick about you. I checked the business center and the front desk to see if you got your own room."

Good thing he'd used a computer at a different hotel. Otherwise he would've got sidetracked. He set the documents on the bed and handed her a coffee and a bag with her sandwich and half the order of beignets.

"What is this?" she asked, sounding bewildered.

"Breakfast and leverage," he said coolly, nodding to the pages.

She stared at him wide-eyed. "Where did you sleep?"

"Didn't. You?"

She shook her head, her eyes looking haunted.

He bit into a beignet. Warm and deep-fried and sweet, it hit the spot. He held up the pastry. "You should try one. You'll like it, Killinger."

She flinched at his use of her last name and grew overtly edgy.

If she wanted to play the he-was-her-brother game, he'd do her one better and play the they-were-only-partners game.

"We're going to get Albatross back," he said, trying to prevent things from getting unbearably awkward.

They were forced to be together, but he'd get his own room

or, to conserve their limited cash, at least switch to double beds. The more professional he kept their interaction, the easier it'd make things.

No compromising positions. No embarrassing confessions. No kissing. No touching.

Stick to business and the monumental task at hand.

"How?" she asked.

"Blackmail."

For the rest of the morning, they walked on eggshells around each other and avoided eye contact as he showed her the printouts and they hashed out a quasi plan.

They had to buy Edgar time and they had the power to do it. That was the easy part.

The rest would be tricky. There were too many variables beyond their control to know if it'd work. They had everything to lose, but it was their best chance. The key to success was proper redirection. Fortunately, Killinger was an expert at it and he was a quick learner.

He picked up the phone and dialed a number he'd written down last night.

The phone rang and was answered. "You've reached the FBI field office of New Orleans."

He listened to the automated menu and hit the number for the prompt that he wanted. As luck would have it, someone answered on a Saturday. "This is Agent Simmons. How can I help you?"

"Hello, I'm calling from the US Marshals office. I was wondering if Agent Bryan McCaffrey was in today," Aiden said, inquiring about the special agent in charge of the office, according to the website.

Most FBI field offices were open seven days a week and some of the larger ones worked around the clock. With a smaller office such as New Orleans, there was no telling if the boss would be in on a Saturday.

"Yes, sir. He is. May I ask what this call is regarding?"

"I had some questions following a hunch on a case I'm working and wanted to discuss something with him." Aiden didn't actually want to talk to McCaffrey; he'd called only to find out his schedule for the day. "On second thought, something just occurred to me. I think I should get some additional information first, get my ducks in a row before I bother him. How late is he going to be there today?"

"Well, he works from seven to seven."

"Is he just committed or going through a divorce?" Aiden asked, recalling that when Draper had been hired to take over the San Diego office, he had been going through a divorce and had worked twelve-to sixteen-hour days, as well.

"Both," the agent said. "Can I get your name to pass along to him? I'll give him a heads-up to expect a call later."

"Thank you." Aiden hung up and nodded to Charlie. "He'll be in. Let's go."

They left the hotel and scouted the area for a significant tourist site that drew a lot of foot traffic and offered multiple lines of sight.

Jackson Square was perfect. Fifteen-minute walk from the hotel. A wide-open space that could be watched from across the street at the outdoor Café du Monde.

Aiden purchased a postcard featuring the square from a shop, along with four envelopes and a pen. On the back of the postcard he wrote:

If you want the rest of the evidence, have the Assistant Special Agent in Charge who is building a case on Bill Walsh here, wearing a red hat and red shirt, standing next to the cluster of palm trees on the southwest corner of the Andrew Jackson statue. Noon. Sunday.

Aiden circled the specific tree on the card, silently thanking Jeff Landau for the tip that Big Bill was under federal surveillance. He put the postcard and two sheets from the pages that he'd printed out in an envelope, giving a tidbit of incriminating evidence on Walsh and Romero. Not enough for an arrest and conviction, just a taste to whet the appetite for more.

"They'll check for prints and get results in less than twenty-four hours," Charlie said.

"That's what I'm counting on. It'll save time when we make contact."

Charlie rubbed her hand across the envelope, getting her prints on it, as well. He addressed it to Bryan McCaffrey and marked it Extremely Urgent.

Then he put the flash drive with all the information in a padded envelope and made it out to the attorney general at the Department of Justice in Washington, DC. They couldn't risk hanging on to the drive when it was worth millions and could put half a dozen criminals behind bars.

The rest of the paperwork he divided between the last two envelopes. One labeled for Romero. The other for Walsh. Those two they'd deliver in person. The others had to be mailed.

New Orleans was such a convenient city. A courier service that guaranteed same-day delivery was located off Canal Street and was only a ten-minute jaunt on foot.

They sent the envelope to Special Agent McCaffrey with signature required for delivery. He'd get it no later than 4:00 p.m. that day. Twenty hours was plenty of time for McCaffrey to arrange things with his subordinate who was covering Walsh.

Next was the package to the attorney general. They'd mail it from the post office, priority but not overnight, since they didn't want it to arrive until Tuesday no later than close of business, when their hand would've been played.

By then, they'd either have Edgar, be in police custody or be dead.

No matter their outcome, Walsh, Romero and every other scumbag on that flash drive was going to prison.

"What if McCaffrey doesn't go for it?" she asked, her

cool, seemingly detached composure slipping. "What if an agent doesn't show tomorrow?"

"Chill out, Killinger." It would work. It had to. "Have a little faith."

What was the alternative? Expect the worst?

Not his style. He suspected that not only the agent covering Walsh would show but that the square would be swarming with federal agents tomorrow.

"We still don't know how to neutralize Devlin," she said. "He flies in tonight. He's going to find out that we're in town. If he doesn't already know."

Devlin was a wild card. A problem they didn't have a fix for yet. "Maybe we use the element of surprise. Get to him before he can cause any more trouble."

"How?" Aiden asked. "Nab him at the airport?"

They knew what flight he'd be on, seven o'clock from San Diego, and they knew what he looked like. Devlin wouldn't expect the preemptive strike. "Yeah, maybe."

One step at a time. First, they needed to deliver the other two envelopes. Throw out the bait and set the traps.

They walked to the casino in silence, resigned to their neutral corners, with the giant elephant wedged between them. She didn't seem to want to discuss it any more than he did.

Fine with him. *We just need to get through this and come out the other side.*

Carrying crowbars and baseball bats into the casino was a no-go. Even if they had guns, getting them inside would've been tough.

The Windfall was large and active and bristling with energy. Slot machines clinked off to one side. On the other, patrons gathered around card and craps tables and a roulette wheel. Shouted. Whooped. Cheered. Groaned. It was an overwhelming scene straight out of Vegas.

"Suggestions, Killinger?" he asked.

She stiffened and looked around. Her gaze was directed

at anything other than him. "I don't like the idea of an enclosed office surrounded by guards. There might be a better option. I'll ask."

They subtly slipped their earpieces in and Killinger fluffed her hair to cover hers. Aiden planned to keep his distance.

Killinger stopped a cocktail waitress who was carrying a tray of empty glasses. "Hey, I'm looking to catch Enzo Romero and Big Bill Walsh, discreetly," she said, the comms device allowing Aiden to hear everything. "To pass along some information. I'd prefer not to get trapped in a difficult position in an office behind a locked door, with some dude's hand shoved down my shirt, if you know what I mean."

The buxom waitress smiled. "Believe me, I get it. Enzo's right over there." She pointed to a man in a fancy suit in the poker room. "And Big Bill is at Avido's this time of day. But ask to see him at the bar, otherwise they'll send you to his office there."

"Thanks." Killinger handed her a hundred bucks. "How do I get to Avido's?"

The waitress gave directions and pocketed the easy cash.

"I count two bodyguards in Enzo's vicinity," Killinger said. "Give me his envelope. I'll get it to him without drawing too much attention. They won't see me as a threat."

He agreed and handed over the envelope. The contents would show Romero what type of damning information they had on him.

Killinger sauntered into the poker room and Aiden stayed across the walkway where he could keep an eye on her. She strode right up to Enzo Romero and proffered the sealed white envelope. "You're a very powerful man with a lot of influence and muscle, and I'm looking to make a deal. Help me get what I want and all the information I have is yours."

Enzo eyed her from head to toe, then opened the envelope and looked over the single page. His brows lifted. "What do you want?"

"Not money." She pulled on a smile smooth as cold butter. "I'll call you tomorrow with details."

Enzo reached into his suit jacket pocket, whipped out a card and handed it to her. "My private number. Can I buy you a drink?"

"Thank you." She took the card. "But it's a little early in the day for me." She turned and strutted out of the poker room.

Enzo signaled to one of his guards, who took off after Killinger.

In turn, Aiden was right behind him.

Killinger went to the ladies' room. The guard had the audacity to follow her inside. Aiden had no shame in joining the party.

He shoved through the door fast. As expected, the bodyguard turned and half stepped back, a fluid quarter circle.

Aiden threw a sharp left hook, catching him hard on the ear. The guy's head snapped sideways as Aiden was already launching a right uppercut that hit him under the chin.

The guard wobbled and swayed, staying on his feet. Killinger jumped up behind him and locked her elbow around his throat in a headlock.

Aiden could've been a referee in a ring, counting down the knockout.

Five seconds, and the bodyguard was out cold.

One baited hook had been dropped for Romero.

Time to cast an irresistible, shiny lure for Walsh.

Chapter Thirteen

Devlin shook Tommy's hand with a pat on the shoulder and strode to the small office in the back of Avido's.

Inside, Big Bill waved for him to come in. "Can I get you some lunch?" he asked, sprinkling salt on his chicken.

The food smelled wonderful and everything Devlin had ever eaten there had been tasty, but he wanted to get down to business. "I'm good." He took a seat in one of the leather chairs facing the desk.

Bill set the white porcelain shaker down and took a bite of his food. "What's the status?"

"Is this place clean?" Devlin asked, referring to listening devices. Bill's FBI problem was worse than an infestation of roaches.

"Yeah." Bill nodded. "Tommy swept it this morning."

"The boys are in Louisiana," Devlin said. "They checked in with me outside of Lake Charles. Your package can be delivered by five, if you'd like."

Bill leaned back in his chair, a satisfied grin tugging at his mouth. "I'd like that very much."

"Where?"

Without hesitation and with plenty of zeal, as if he'd given it a lot of thought, perhaps the only thing he'd thought of, Bill said, "Same place we bring the girls through."

The old port. Bill trafficked young women through on boats in shipping containers. The Coast Guard never went near it, the police were paid to steer clear, and the feds didn't have a clue Bill used it. A good spot for delivery and whatever else Bill had in store for the package.

"What about the information I need?" Bill cut another piece of chicken and chewed.

"There's a flash drive that supposedly has everything you could possibly want on it, but the package lost it. I'm working on getting it back."

"How in the hell are you going to do that?" Bill asked around the food in his mouth.

Devlin crossed his legs and folded his hands, letting his confidence shine through. He had this under control. "The flash drive is in New Orleans."

"I'm not tracking." Bill dropped his fork and wiped his mouth with a napkin. "Explain."

"Two marshals that were protecting the package have it. Aiden Yazzie and Charlotte Killinger. I framed them for the murder of one of their own and a local cop. Under the heat, they ran. I made sure to drop bread crumbs that led to me. They followed them and they're here. In New Orleans."

"How are you going to get the drive from them?"

"Leave that to me." One way or another, Devlin would get it and take care of them permanently. "I want the first payment. Three and a half million. Wired now to the same offshore account I used last time."

"Two million," Bill said flatly and took a long, hearty sip of his stout beer.

"Your math must be fuzzy. Seven million for the package alive. Half of seven is three and a half."

"Where's my proof of life?" Bill gestured dramatically around the office. "I have no doubt that you have him, but Edgar might've caught a stray bullet during the kidnapping and could be dead, for all I know. Two now. Five on delivery."

Devlin reached into his jacket pocket, past his holstered gun, took out a burner phone and dialed.

It rang twice. "What's up, D?" Tate asked. "We get paid?"

"We need proof of life. Send it now." Devlin disconnected. Eight seconds later, the phone buzzed. Devlin opened the text, bringing up a picture of the package.

His wrists and mouth were duct-taped, and he was wide-eyed with terror. A receipt from a gas station, with today's date and time stamp, was next to his head.

Devlin held up the phone, the picture facing out. He zoomed in on the receipt and then refocused on the package's horrified face.

Evil amusement lit up Bill's eyes as he flashed a Cheshire cat grin. "Three and a half million it is."

THEIR HALF-BAKED plan might get them both killed.

At least death would put her out of her misery, but the thought of anything bad happening to Aiden made Charlie physically ill. She could tolerate a lot, but not that.

She walked beside Aiden down quiet St. Philip Street in the heart of the French Quarter. The city was steeped in history, practically dripping with it. Nineteenth-century homes that lined the road resembled colorful dollhouses. The cheery, built-to-withstand-anything atmosphere was a stark contrast to their predicament and the current status of their friendship.

Charged silence stretched between them, prickling her nerves.

When she sidestepped a stray glass bottle as an excuse to move closer to Aiden, their hands brushed. He recoiled as if he couldn't bear the slightest physical contact with her and quickened his pace.

A cold shroud settled around her despite the sweltering temperature. With her stomach churning, she caught up and matched his stride.

She was a real mess, emotions running wild, and she couldn't let any of it show.

It was one bad thing after another. Losing a witness,

being framed for the murder of a colleague, no loyalty from a shameful boss, and now being on the run. Yet the distance from Aiden clung to her like a choking vine, tightening her throat, squeezing her chest and making it hard to breathe.

Finally, they reached Bourbon and turned left. The famous bustling street vibrated with crackling energy. The cacophony of laughter, conversations, jazz and rap music was an overwhelming relief.

They strode through the throng of people, looking for Avido's Restaurant, where they hoped to find Big Bill Walsh and survive the encounter.

Charlie hated fumbling her way through something on a wing and a prayer and unarmed.

At any rate, she wasn't stuck in this alone. She had Aiden. There wasn't a better person to have at her side if she was in trouble.

Even if he was still so angry at her that he hadn't looked at her since they'd left the hotel.

Not only had she deeply hurt him, but she'd also disappointed him.

If she could take back ever sleeping with Nick last year, she would. It had meant nothing to her, whereas Aiden meant everything. Not that it would change anything now.

A chasm had opened between them last night when he'd poured out his heart to her and she hadn't been fully forthcoming in return. All this time, she'd had him locked tight in the friend zone, never daring to jeopardize their precious bond by sleeping with him, and it had only pushed him away to the point he wanted to leave her. Take the job here in Louisiana, of all places, at Camp Beauregard.

It was like some twisted self-fulfilling prophecy.

There were some things that couldn't be fixed. Charlie feared that she and Aiden were one of them. If she lost him, it would do more than break her heart. It would devastate her.

The thought came with a knife-sharp pang, but she didn't break her stride.

She saw the sign for Avido's two doors down on the other side of the street. "There it is."

"I'd have to be blind to miss it," he said.

They couldn't walk into Big Bill's place like this—distracted and snapping at each other, their friendship fractured.

They needed to be the dynamic duo again if they were going to prevail with the deck stacked against them.

"Hey," she said, cupping his bare arm, stopping him from crossing the street. "We need to go in there as a united front."

He jerked away from her grasp. "We both want to clear our names and walk out alive. That's about as united as we're going to get. Look, I'm sorry I crossed the line and kissed you. Touched you like that. It was a mistake."

Her heart sank and her jaw dropped.

"Let's forget it ever happened," he continued, "and move on. Stay focused on the mission. Okay, Killinger?"

Inwardly she cringed so hard it hurt every time he called her by her last name. "Stop it. Stop calling me that." It was driving her insane.

"Why? It's your name."

"Aiden, I—"

The door to Avido's opened, drawing both their gazes.

Charlie's heart nearly stopped. Frank Devlin walked out along with another man, tall, thickset, with a shaved head. Both had the telltale bulges of holstered weapons under their arm.

The timing couldn't have been worse.

"He's supposed to be on a plane later tonight. Not here. Now," she said.

Aiden took her by the elbow and turned away, shoving through a group of singing drunk guys.

"Watch it, buddy," one of them said.

A surge of adrenaline made her body buzz. Charlie craned around for a quick glance back.

Devlin spotted them. He tapped the burly guy beside him, pointed at them and then launched across the street.

Charlie took off without saying a word to Aiden. There was no need. She knew he followed right on her heels.

No matter how disconnected they were personally, they had always been in sync professionally.

They ran, forcing their way through the dense weekend crowd.

Aiden snatched her hand and cut down the side street, Orleans, dragging her with him. Then they ran at a flat-out sprint. Keeping up with him wasn't an issue. She could run like hell. The muggy air seemed to thicken. Breath sawed in and out of her lungs. Her heartbeat and the thump of their boots pounding on the pavement filled her ears.

Devlin and his surprisingly fast cohort came charging after them.

They had to shake those two men.

Straight ahead was a fenced-in garden behind a three-steepled church with a statue of Jesus in the center of the lawn, His arms upraised. This was the time to say a prayer if she knew any. The garden would do them little good, since it was a wide-open space and provided no cover.

Neither Charlie nor Aiden knew the city, while Devlin had home-field advantage and the entire police force on his side.

Charlie and Aiden reached the corner, their breaths coming hard. Looked left. Looked right. Split-second decision made.

They bolted down Pirates Alley and threaded in between strolling pedestrians. To one side of the thoroughfare was a towering church. To the other, the Cabildo and a Technicolor melee of lime green shutters, garish blue doors and neon yellow walls in the bowels of the city—all screaming that they had no clue where to run.

At the gaping mouth of the alley was a milling crowd. With a little luck, they might blend in, disappear.

On instinct, they turned to the left in unison, without hesitation, toward the church. Charlie made a beeline for the doors, hand in hand with Aiden.

It was locked. On the sign, the St. Louis Cathedral didn't open until five on Saturday.

Aiden tugged her up against him into a pocket of shadows in an alcove. Her heart jackhammered in her chest. Her brain engaged. Professional awareness was in high gear. Her determination like a cold iron bar. But there was no ignoring the feel of him against her, every spot where they touched, each lick of friction as they pressed closer. He was so solid and heavy, warmth radiating from his muscles flexing under her palms.

She wanted to shut off that part of her brain that picked up those details but also commit the particulars to memory. How steady and calm he was. The world could be falling apart, and he'd still be rock-solid.

The taller, stocky guy pounded past the front of the cathedral as vacationers taking photos in the pedestrian-only plaza out front inadvertently helped shield them. It probably didn't occur to him to look at the entrance since he knew the church would be closed.

For once, not knowing the area worked in their favor.

The thin peal of bells rang out, calling to saints and sinners alike. A circus atmosphere pulsed around them—meandering tourists, mimes, artists, street musicians, magicians, living statues painted in silver and gold, palmists and tarot readers selling glimpses of the future.

She looked up at Aiden. Their eyes locked.

He pressed a palm to her cheek and something she couldn't define shone in his eyes. "Come on."

Staying there wasn't an option. With two men canvassing the area—one a cop—they'd eventually be spotted.

They made a break for it, dashing through Jackson Square, around the equestrian statue and past a row of iron benches with dividers. They narrowly avoided a collision with a group of teenage girls who were running up to a row of fortune-tellers.

Aiden looked back. The squeeze of his hand tightening on hers told Charlie what she needed to know. One of the men wasn't far behind. Or probably, both were close.

There was no outrunning them. No place to hide where they wouldn't be found.

They had to make a stand.

Surprise would help, but hesitation would be fatal.

On Decatur, they blew by the French Market and ducked into a restaurant.

"Hello," said the hostess. "How many—"

Aiden pointed toward the back. "We're meeting people."

They strode through the restaurant.

At the sound of the hostess's voice again, Charlie looked to the front. Devlin breezed inside while the other guy went around the building.

Aiden pushed into the kitchen. "We do it here," he said, echoing her thoughts.

"As good a place as any." It was great to be on the same page. "Get out now, or you'll be shot," Charlie said to the gawking cooking crew. She waved them toward the back door with all the fierceness the Marine Corps had instilled in her.

The cooks scattered and fled.

Aiden switched off the lights, grabbed a steel meat tenderizer from the counter and stood against the wall beside one of the swing doors to the dining room.

The only light in the room came from the small window in the door and the five burners going on the stove.

Charlie's gaze flew around for something she could use as a weapon. Before she found one, Devlin rushed into the kitchen. His gun with a silencer attached was already drawn and at the ready.

Menace radiated from him as he leveled the 9 mm at her. Aiden sprang from his position, smashing the steel mallet on Devlin's wrist and knocking the weapon from his grasp.

Charlie grabbed a metal bowl of flour and spun on her heel when the back door flew open and the stocky guy stormed in. She tossed the flour into his face, followed by the bowl. Metal struck flesh with a resounding clang.

In her periphery, Aiden was going blow for blow with Devlin. A flurry of punches and kicks issued back and forth.

Charlie seized a large rolling pin from a workstation and swung it like a bat. The wood smacked into the man's solar plexus.

A loud grunt whooshed from the guy's mouth as he doubled over.

She threw another whack to his head. And another. She planned to keep thrashing him until he was either knocked out cold or the rolling pin broke, whichever came first.

The man dropped to the floor like a wet noodle.

Devlin bulldozed into Aiden, lifting him from the floor and hurling him into a shelving unit. Produce went flying, tumbling to the floor.

Landing a wicked left hook, Aiden forced Devlin off him. The two tussled. Aiden got Devlin facedown over the counter, wrenching one of his arms behind his back.

Charlie rushed to help subdue him.

Aiden's gaze snapped up at her. "No! Stay back," he said, bringing her to a halt.

It was in that second, maybe two, when Aiden's focus slipped slightly, that Devlin reared his head up and back, smashing his skull into Aiden's face. Her partner stumbled, his arms flailing. Devlin spun, throwing an elbow propelled by the momentum of his full weight to Aiden's head, and was on him like a violent storm.

Charlie surged forward, hoisting the rolling pin high.

Pivoting with his arm extended horizontally, Devlin hit her hard across the cheek. The force of his elbow moving fast ahead of two hundred pounds of mean muscle sent her head twisting around, her body spiraling and knocked to the floor.

Her skull slammed against the cold tile. Her breath left her lungs.

"Charlie!" Aiden cried.

The scuffle between Devlin and Aiden was all she could hear.

Fear mingled with blood. It was bitter and coppery in her mouth. She fought through the haze, needing to move, needing to help Aiden.

Her blurry vision cleared, and Charlie rolled onto her hands and knees. She scrambled to find a gun, scouring the floor, searching under the prep table.

Where did it go?

She made it to her feet, gasped in horror. Devlin had an arm locked around Aiden's throat, but her partner kicked off the wall, propelling them both into the worktable at the center of the room, sending them crashing to the floor.

Aiden and Devlin were duking it out on the floor, rolling around in a death match. The blows were furious and fast. Aiden flipped him overhead, sending him hurtling against the stove.

As both men stood, Devlin's back was to Charlie. He reached behind into his jacket, going for the reserve weapon tucked in his waistband.

She snatched the pot of simmering water or broth from the fire and flung the piping hot liquid at him. Devlin howled and spun on her.

But Aiden threw a front kick that sent Devlin pitching to the side over the flames. The sleeve of his lightweight jacket caught fire. With a quick presence of mind, Devlin snatched a pitcher of water and doused the flames with a faint sizzle.

Charlie knocked the gun loose from his hand with the hot pan while he was distracted.

The Beretta clattered to the floor. Aiden grabbed it and leveled the barrel at Devlin, who stood gape-mouthed, manic anger burning in his eyes.

Following Aiden's hand signal to move toward the door, Charlie backed up and stepped over the unconscious guy sprawled on the floor spread-eagle. She slowed and picked up his suppressed .45 from the corner on the floor.

Devlin glared at them, his upper lip curling over his teeth, his eyes wild and furious. "This isn't over," he growled.

"It better be." Aiden came up beside her and they backed through the door one at a time, her first. "Because if it's not, I'll kill you. That's not a threat. That's a promise." He slammed the door shut.

They hustled down the alley behind the restaurant. Aiden scooped up a dirty paper bag from the ground, dumped the contents and stowed the two guns inside.

There was one thing Charlie had to know. "Why didn't you kill that bast—"

"It's not who we are and it's the last thing we need. To kill a cop, even if he's a dirty one. Every officer will turn this city upside down and inside out looking for us."

Aiden was right. There were multiple witnesses able to clearly identify them. They didn't need the extra heat. Things were sweltering as it was.

"Let's hope we don't regret leaving him alive."

DEVLIN WAS SEETHING. His body began to shake with the rage building inside him, overshadowing the pain from his burns. He whipped out his personal phone.

But not to dial 911.

He'd officially report the incident, portraying them as stalkers trying to silence him, and have an all-points bulletin put out on the marshals, but it'd take his brothers-in-blue twenty minutes to get there and start looking for Yazzie and Killinger.

A faster response was required.

He pulled up the French Quarter Task Force app. An enterprise initiated and funded by a billionaire who wanted to make the city safer, using a crowdsourcing approach to crime. The FQTF was a private police patrol that could be summoned via a mobile app. Its monumental success encouraged the Louisiana State Police and surrounding parishes to use it, too.

The screen displayed a digitized map of the Quarter. A grid of seventy-eight city blocks. Green arrows indicated a member of the armed squad—off-duty cops rolling around in matte black smart cars at all hours, with the ability to respond to a crime in progress in under two minutes.

He plugged in the address of the restaurant he was standing in. Prepared for this type of scenario, he next uploaded the photos of Yazzie and Killinger the SDPD had been kind enough to share with him and typed the notification:

Armed and dangerous fugitives wanted for the murder of two law enforcement officers just tried to kill a local cop. They're on foot. Apprehend with caution. $25,000 REWARD.

He hit Enter.

A red dot appeared on his location. Pictures of the marshals flashed on the screen.

Ten green arrows in the vicinity immediately reacted and began zigzagging through the streets forming a perimeter, searching for them. And every citizen who had the app loaded on their phone would receive the alert and could submit updates on the whereabouts of the fugitives if they spotted them.

The entire city would be on the lookout for Yazzie and Killinger.

Chapter Fourteen

All the pieces on the board shifted with Devlin's early arrival. They had to adjust accordingly.

"We need to check out of the hotel," Aiden said. Get back their money for the second night, grab the meager clothing they had, his shirt, her jacket and their *weapons*. "Find someplace new, off the beaten path."

There was no doubt in Aiden's mind that Devlin would put out an all-points bulletin on them and was probably calling it in at that very moment.

Ahead at the corner they approached, two women in their late thirties were chatting and laughing as they looked at something on one of their mobile devices. The phone buzzed and emitted the jarring, high-pitched tone of a public safety alert. Another phone in the vicinity, somewhere behind them, did the same.

The women stopped talking and stared at the phone.

One of them, a redhead, swiped up on her screen.

The other, a black woman with long braids, gasped. "Twenty-five grand."

Both women frantically looked around, spinning in circles.

The redhead hit her friend and pointed at Aiden and Charlie. "That's them."

Aiden's chest clutched. He and Charlie froze for an instant

and exchanged a glance. His mind raced to process what was happening, but there was no time to figure it out.

"That's them," the black woman said. "Report it."

The redhead started typing on her phone.

Charlie gestured to a massive open-air shopping complex that spanned several city blocks. They bolted across the street, skirting around vehicles.

A black smart car raced around the corner, lights flashing on top. Across the hood and side were the emblems of wings, a star and the words *FQ Task Force New Orleans Police Dept.*

Aiden and Charlie darted underneath the archway of the French Market as a second black task force car came zooming toward them from the other end of the street.

Rows of kiosks with vendors selling goods stretched out before them. They cut through the throng of shoppers, weaving their way around stands, hoping to blend in. Customers were absorbed in browsing and buying. Merchants focused on making sales.

The tawdry flea market was a veritable tourist trap, sitting at the edge of the Mississippi River, jam-packed with out-of-towners who didn't bat a lash at them.

Charlie spotted something, took his hand and led him to a bank of specialty shops. He didn't pull away. This was only about survival. Nothing more.

With his head on a swivel, looking for cops or anyone staring at them, he didn't understand what she was thinking until she pushed through the door of the store.

It was a costume shop.

"I'll wait out here." Not only to keep watch, but the store owner would be less likely to recognize or remember Charlie on her own if the proprietor had got the same notification.

Whatever alert the women across the street had received was about the two of them, together. So far, it didn't seem as if anyone in the market had noticed them. But that might not last much longer.

He glimpsed two cops working their way through the open-air enclave. More flashing lights stopped along the main street adjacent to the colonnade.

The seconds ticked down and his pulse kicked up.

Efficient as always, Charlie came out of the shop a minute later, carrying a bag. They pressed through the shopping colonnade, ducking into the first bathroom they came across—a unisex, single-occupancy room. She slipped on a short brown wig, tucking stray blond strands up inside, and a long-sleeve red shirt that transformed her into a stranger.

"Good work, Killinger," he said, her surname sliding from his lips before he could stop it.

This wasn't the time for him to deliberately rile her up by giving her the cold shoulder. To get through this, they had to act like a team, even if they weren't going to be partners for much longer.

To his surprise, she didn't roll her eyes or flinch or say anything at all. She dug into the bag and pulled out another hairpiece for him.

Charlie pulled the long black wig on Aiden. Her fingers caressed his forehead and cheeks as she straightened it, pulling errant strands from his face.

She took in a sharp breath, holding his gaze. Her piercing blue eyes were vibrant and inscrutable. It made his heart ache to look at her.

Then the ache deepened and spread when she cupped his jaw, rose on the balls of her feet and pressed her lips to his.

The kiss was soft, closed-mouth, but searing.

Relief flooded him and he hated her for it, because there was no escaping that, deep down, he never wanted to be separated from her.

She settled back on her feet and glared at him. "Don't ever

call me Killinger again." Then she threw a playful sucker punch to his gut.

Not hard enough to hurt, but a grunt escaped him nonetheless.

He glanced in the mirror. The straight shoulder-length hair reminded him of how he used to wear his own when he was much younger.

She handed him sunglasses, a green button-up that he threw over his T-shirt and a new ball cap since he'd lost his other one during the fight with Devlin.

They left the bathroom and headed for the closest exit.

The market was crawling with cops in every direction. If not for Charlie's quick thinking, there wouldn't have been any way for them to get out of the market without using violence.

Charlie linked her arm with his and they strolled by a police officer, making their way through the thick weekend crowd, beyond the souvenir stalls.

"Going back to the hotel is too risky," Charlie said. "We can't count on Dealing Dan not to report the car."

"Agreed."

Out on Decatur Street, a cab stopped right in front of a FQ Task Force police car and let out his passengers. The taxi light on the roof stayed illuminated. Charlie and Aiden got inside.

"Where to?" the driver asked.

"A motel," Charlie said. "Outside the French Quarter."

"Is a B and B okay?"

At B and Bs the owners chatted up their patrons, asked questions and shared stories. "No." Aiden shook his head. "A motel. We want privacy. Cheap. Clean. We don't need bells and whistles, but we do want outdoor access to the room."

The light-skinned black man eyed them in the rearview mirror. "I know you said no B and B, but if you're open to it, my aunt rents out a guest room above her garage to supplement her retirement. Outdoor access. Basic cable and Wi-Fi.

I can promise it's clean. And my aunt is good people. She won't get in your business."

Aiden looked at Charlie and she nodded. "How much?" he asked.

"Eighty bucks a night. Breakfast and dinner are included in the price if you want it. She makes a mean crawfish étouffée. Better than anything you'll get in most restaurants."

If Dealing Dan had reported the car they'd rented, then the cops would have the names of their fake IDs. An off-the-books rented room was just what they needed. "Sounds perfect," Aiden said.

"How many nights?"

Charlie shrugged. "One or two."

The driver made a call on his cell. "Aunt Henri, it's me. I've got a couple of boarders for a night or two. Nice couple, looking for privacy, so don't go talking their ear off. Okay?" He listened for a minute, then said, "See you in a little bit."

Staying at a garage apartment meant they'd no longer have access to a computer in a hotel's business center, and they needed toiletries, as well. "Before we go to your aunt's place, do you mind swinging by a couple of stores? We could use some supplies."

"Sure. There's a shopping center on the way."

The cabbie let them out in front of a supersize discount retailer that had chains everywhere. Two doors down was a huge sporting goods store that from the outside appeared to be a hunter's dream.

Aiden handed the driver enough to cover the fare. "Keep the meter running. We'll be less than fifteen minutes." They got out of the car, and he turned to Charlie, but scanned their surroundings. "Faster if we separate." Not to mention easier, too, after that kiss she'd given him. He could use a little distance to clear his head. "I'll grab a computer, burner phones and toiletries. From there," he said, gesturing to sporting goods, "we need ammo, holsters and anything else you think will be useful. How are you on cash?"

"Running low, but I should have enough."

After using close to a thousand, he had plenty left from the three he'd withdrawn. She'd spend more on gear than he would in the supercenter. He peeled off five $100 bills for her.

Once they cleared their names, the Department of Justice should reimburse them for work expenses. Being on the run added up quick. If they'd been penniless, they would have been in the lurch.

Charlie pocketed the cash, looking like she wanted to say something, but he was grateful when she turned without a word and left. Eventually, they'd have to talk, but he was content to put off the conversation for as long as possible.

Inside the sprawling megastore, Aiden first grabbed toiletries they might need, since it was closest, and then headed for electronics. On the way, he threw a roll of flat black duct tape into the cart.

He found an assortment of cheap laptops and chose one with 4GB RAM for under a hundred bucks. It wouldn't be the fastest or offer much in terms of storage, but that was fine. Stopping at a display of cell phones on clearance, he picked two. Both flip-style, no-frills, bare-bones devices that didn't have GPS, which would make them harder to track. Then he added a couple of phone chargers to his pile.

At the twelve-minute mark, Aiden climbed back into the car. No one had been in line at the register in electronics and checking out there had expedited things. Less than sixty seconds later, Charlie left the sporting goods store carrying a tactical black backpack that was stuffed with goodies.

"You two aren't going to be any trouble, are you?" the driver asked as he watched Charlie walk to the car.

Her long, confident, I-am-in-command stride was distinctive, hinted at someone in law enforcement or the military, or a cocky criminal. The tactical backpack hiked high on her shoulder didn't help the image.

"I assure you the last thing we want is trouble." Aiden removed his sunglasses so the cabbie could see his eyes and hopefully his sincerity. "Just privacy and a little peace and quiet for a couple of nights."

The man considered it, and by the time Charlie hopped in, he nodded.

It didn't take long before the cabbie stopped in the driveway of a modest house that was outside the French Quarter but within reasonable walking distance.

An older lady with a poof of short white curls who resembled the driver was waiting for them. She wore pearls, a pencil skirt and a kind smile.

Aiden paid the remaining taxi fare and for waiting while they shopped, and they all climbed out.

"This here is my aunt Henriette Bordelon," the driver said. "Everyone calls her Henri."

Aiden shook her extended hand. "I'm Rudy and this is Priscilla," he said as Charlie shook her hand, as well. "It's kind of you to let us stay here, ma'am."

"My pleasure." She smiled, but glanced down at their hands, noticing they didn't have any luggage, only shopping bags and the backpack. "I hope it's okay if I collect payment in advance."

"No problem." Aiden gave her two hundred dollars.

"This is too much." She tried to hand back several bills.

"Please, keep it," Aiden said. "We heard you're an incredible cook. Consider it a tip in advance."

"Very generous of you." She beamed. "Dinner will be ready by six, but I can keep it warm for you as late as eleven. That's when my last show goes off and I turn in. Breakfast can be served anytime, except tomorrow. I go to church on Sundays. So it'll have to be before eight. If you have any allergies just let me know."

"Wonderful," Charlie said, "and no allergies for either of us. We'll eat anything."

The cabbie took the key from his aunt. "I'll walk them up and show them the place. Save you the trip."

Aiden and Charlie followed him up the steep exterior staircase. The structure was a good ten yards behind the main house, which had blooming flowers in all the beds and a well-maintained lawn. The garage apartment was far enough back to give them ample privacy.

The driver unlocked the door and handed Aiden the key.

A decent-sized studio, the place was as advertised. Simple. Clean. A rudimentary kitchen outfitted with the basics, including a coffee maker and take-out menus from places that delivered. Towels in the bathroom along with bodywash and shampoo.

It was more than they could've asked for.

But there was only one queen-size bed.

"Henri's number and the password for the Wi-Fi are next to the phone. I'm Junior, by the way. If you need a ride anywhere, day or night, give me a holler. Here's my card." Smiling, he offered one that Charlie took. "I'll get out of your hair now."

Nodding his thanks, Aiden set the shopping bags down on the counter.

Junior hurried out the door like he was trying hard not to take up too much time or be too friendly.

Aiden appreciated it.

Once Junior had cleared the stairs and the car door slammed closed, Charlie said, "We never got the envelope to Walsh and I don't think it's a good idea to go back to the restaurant."

She emptied the backpack on the counter, setting out a Smith and Wesson M&P 9 mm, shoulder holsters, tactical knives, zip ties, extra clips, and ammo for the guns, which they had three of, including the ones they took from Devlin and his buddy.

In Louisiana, no state permit, driver's license, firearm registration or background check was required, and by the looks of the supplies, no magazine capacity restriction, either. He wasn't complaining. This was the perfect state if you were a gun enthusiast or an outlaw.

An expandable baton made of strong, durable seamless alloy steel rolled along the counter as she pulled out a few more items that looked more suited for camping than their needs.

Taking off the sunglasses and wig, Aiden sat on the bed and scratched his head. "If it wasn't Walsh who texted the hit men in San Diego, then it was one of his guys. Either way, he'd get a message if we sent one."

"Then let's do it."

Aiden tore open the sealed envelope and laid the documents on the bed. He snapped a picture of each and sent them to the New Orleans number in the phone along with a text.

We have the flash drive with hard evidence on you and your friends.

Want to trade? Or do you want to go to prison?

"That'll get Walsh's attention," Aiden said. No need to rush the *ask*. Walsh was willing to pay millions to torture Edgar. They had time to play their hand the proper way, but not much. "Now we wait." He glanced at the clock. "We've got a couple of hours until dinner. I'm going to get some shut-eye."

Charlie removed her wig and the tomato-red shirt. "Can we talk?"

"Nothing else to say. We covered it last night." He tugged off his boots and sighed in relief. "I've been pushing for over thirty hours and it's been a tough day. I just want to take a nap. We can talk over dinner if necessary. Okay?"

Charlie hung her head. "Sure." She went to the bathroom and closed the door.

The shower started.

Aiden lay down, facing a wall and nightstand, fully dressed, and stared at the clock. He knew he needed to sleep, but he was restless and edgy. Too amped up to close his eyes or to relax.

His thoughts were a whirlwind and his emotions were all over the place before Charlie had kissed him in the market, and at the moment, they threatened to call the shots, but he refused to let them mess with his head.

Flopping onto his back, he stared at the ceiling. The curtains were too thin. The room was too bright. The sun was too hot. The room was too stuffy.

He looked back at the clock on the nightstand. Charlie had been in there a long time. She'd taken five minutes last night and now had been in the bathroom for close to thirty.

It wasn't his business. She wasn't his business. If she wanted to spend three hours in the bathroom, that was her prerogative. *Have at it. Use all the hot water. I don't care.*

Going on close to an hour, he admitted he was getting worried. Tempted even to knock on the door and ask if she needed anything. But nope.

He. Would. Not.

Finally, the water stopped; movement in the bathroom. He rolled onto his side, ensuring his back would be to her when she came out.

The door opened. Aiden shut his eyes, stilled his body, pretending to be asleep.

Charlie padded around the foot of the bed. Based on the sound, she was barefoot.

The mattress sank as she sat and lay down. His pulse skyrocketed, but he forced himself to take slow, even breaths. Forced himself not to move beyond the rise and fall of his chest.

"Aiden? Are you awake?"

It crossed his mind not to respond, to keep feigning sleep, but pretending for years that he wasn't in love with her and that whomever she slept with didn't bother him had only made things worse—throwing gasoline on the fire that had torched their friendship.

"I'm up," he said, letting every drop of irritation that he felt leak into his tone.

The mattress shook as she scooted closer and clasped his arm. "Aiden. Please. Look at me."

But he couldn't. Listening was one thing, but he didn't have the strength to look at her and keep a rein on his emotions.

"I lied—" Charlie's voice was soft, quiet "—when I said I think of you as a brother."

Tell him something he didn't know.

"I'm sorry I slept with Nick," she said. "It wasn't fair to you."

No, it wasn't, but he was guilty of a far greater wrong by not telling her that he loved her and not telling Nick to back off.

"If I could undo it, I would," she said. "You don't have to worry about getting under my skin. You already are."

A flutter of hope beat inside him. Was she saying what he longed to hear?

Confessions were dangerous; they exposed a person, made them vulnerable.

Charlie would give him some *but*, some out, an excuse in the end to protect herself. He just had to wait for it.

"Please, look at me," she said, her tone soft. He didn't move, and she squeezed his arm. "Aiden...for me, home isn't a place or a house. It's you. You're home for me. I love you and I don't want to lose you."

His heart kicked hard in his chest. His first instinct was to look at her, make her say it again while meeting his eyes. But the expectation of disappointment inextricably tied to this miraculous admission from her made him sick. With sadness. With anger. With love.

Lovesick.

Wait for it.

Her voice grew brittle and her hand fell from his arm. "But…"

A lead weight dropped in the pit of his stomach. Everything inside him tensed. *Here it comes.*

"I can't give you happily-ever-after. A family. All the things your parents had. I can't have children." Her words stalled time, stilled the beating of his heart.

For a nanosecond.

He rolled over and faced her.

She was wrapped in a towel, stripped of all her defenses. Her gaze lifted to his, her eyes pink and her face flushed like she'd been crying in the shower. He read the misery and fear in her unguarded expression, saw the icy bravado melt, and he took her hand in his.

"I had endometriosis. Nothing worked to help, and I had to have a full hysterectomy. I know I'm damaged, and I don't mean just the surgery. You can have everything you want. A great wife. Kids. The kind of family your parents had. Big and loving and warm. But not with me," she said, her voice cracking. Tears leaked from her eyes, a pinch of pain between her brows, the strain of sorrow pursing her lips together.

He wiped at her tears with his thumb, slid his palm over her hair, his heart aching for her. For them both.

"I want you to have that," she said. "You deserve it. More than anyone that I know. Any woman would be lucky to have you and you'll make a fantastic dad one day. The absolute best."

Neither of them breathed for what seemed like an eternity.

"Why didn't you tell me?" he asked in a whisper.

"I tried. Once, when you took me home for your mom's funeral."

He remembered the moment she was talking about. They'd been sitting on the porch, watching his nieces and nephews play in the yard. He'd gone on and on about how much he wanted a big family—four or five kids. To be a good dad like his own father.

His sister had given Charlie her youngest to hold. Charlie held the baby close to her chest, rocking him. He'd imagined marrying her, how beautiful she'd be pregnant, her belly heavy and round, her face glowing, her holding a baby that was a little bit of him and a little bit of her one day on that very porch. He'd envisioned their life together, happy and playful and satisfied, side by side, growing gray and old together.

She'd turned so somber that he'd put his arm around her and waited. For her to share. That was what he did. Gave her space, showed her patience until it hurt. She'd put her head on his shoulder and he'd sensed she'd been close.

"That afternoon on the porch," he said. "But my brother asked me to go horseback riding. You insisted that I should, and I went with him."

Charlie nodded. More hot tears streamed down her cheeks.

He'd taken it as a sign of progress when she'd chosen to go home with him, that they were headed to the next level, but he realized he'd been wrong once he got back from riding with his brother. She'd left. Packed and taken a taxi to the airport. Given his family some excuse and had asked them to pass along the message that she'd see him back in San Diego.

He'd been shocked. Confused. Unbelievably hurt. Half tempted to run after her and demand an explanation like a lovesick fool, which he didn't want to be, and had chalked it up to Charlie being Charlie.

It all made sense now.

Aiden kissed her cheeks and wrapped his arm around her, bringing her in close. Held her tight, soothing her until she stopped crying. "I should've gone after you. To the airport. Made you talk to me and hashed it out then and there. It would've saved us so much time." So much grief.

"I'm sorry. You could've moved on sooner."

He pulled her deeper into his arms, cradled her head against his chest. "There is no moving on from you."

"Didn't you hear what I said?" She trembled against him and he held her tighter. "I can't give you a family. You want kids so badly."

"I want you more. You're my family. I love you, Charlie. The only future I want is one with you."

She shifted away, lifting her head. A tear slid down her cheek as she stared at him, lips parted. "No. You're supposed to understand. You're supposed to let me go."

"I'll never let you go. I'll always choose you."

"Aiden, I won't deny you—"

He stole her words with his mouth and kissed her.

Chapter Fifteen

His lips brushed over hers in a gentle, sweeping caress that made Charlie's heart turn over in her chest as he swallowed her objections. The kiss was raw and open and full of honesty.

She wanted Aiden to have the whole world. His greatest desires.

Not to choose her over having the family he wanted.

Aiden dragged his mouth across her cheek, slid his hands into her hair. "You're everything I've ever wanted, Charlie." He planted kisses along her throat to where her pulse pounded. "Let me love you." He nipped at the thundering beat in her neck. "Let me love you." The words sank into her, healing some gaping wound, and he repeated it like a mantra.

A demand.

A call from his soul to hers.

One she could no longer ignore, no longer refuse. Need unfurled inside her. A deep ache entangled with a much deeper longing to be with him in every way. To be his.

Warmth blossomed low in her belly, radiating through her.

His mouth turned insistent. Hungry. The kiss was long and wild. She glided her hands down his broad back and skimmed up again, taking his shirt with them. Her deft fingers undid the button on his jeans and lowered his zipper.

In a blink, he was off the bed, on his feet, and he made quick work of getting his jeans and boxer briefs off, tossing them to the floor.

Her jaw went slack at the sight of Aiden in all his naked glory. She'd never tire of seeing him, touching him, kissing this beautiful man, who, beyond reason and despite her numerous flaws, still loved her, wanted her.

Sitting up, she reached for him. He dropped back to the bed and shifted her onto his lap as he sat so she straddled him. She let her towel fall to the side, baring herself to his ardent gaze. He cupped her breast, thumbing the stiff peak as he watched her with a smoldering intensity.

Moaning under his touch, she took the hard, thick length of him in her hand. "I've wanted this for so long. To make love to you," she said, rocking against him. Dampness flooded the space between her legs, anticipation racing under her skin.

"You have no idea. I've wanted you since the day we met." His hand slid over her ribs, down her belly and lower to the apex of her thighs. "Knew we were inevitable." He groaned as he stroked between her folds, making her slick with desire.

As if he'd been studying her, preparing for this moment, he teased with expert fingers, used just the right amount of pressure, which sent an exquisite jolt of pleasure that left her throbbing with need for him.

The inevitability of their commingling, this communion shook her to the core.

Dropping his head to her breast, he sucked hard at a nipple, driving her crazy.

"Aiden." She made a tortured sound of pleading that she'd never imagined possible.

"Patience. You've rushed in the past with others," he said, proving once again how well he knew her. "Not with me. Not the first time, anyway. I need to savor this. You."

"Don't you want to devour me?"

"I intend to. Slowly. For hours." He kissed her with such fierce tenderness that a colony of butterflies took flight inside her on wings of fire.

She'd never been so aroused, so eager, felt so connected to another person.

Charlie didn't think he could get her any more excited or ready, but she couldn't have been more wrong. Exercising inhuman willpower, he made good on his promise. Savored her slowly. He explored every inch of her body from her scalp to the soles of her feet. Licked, tasted, nibbled and sucked, taking her to the brink with his clever tongue, only to deny her the ultimate gratification. Layered pleasure, letting it build and tighten, finally giving her a blinding climax with his head nuzzled between her thighs and his mouth on her.

Screaming his name, she shattered with the most uninhibited release of her life. Sensation thrummed along every nerve. But this wasn't her, wild and begging, writhing and loud.

Two could play the teasing game. It wasn't until she took him in her mouth and gifted him with a similar torture that he tossed her onto her back, flattening her against the mattress, and fully covered her in a motion of unparalleled grace.

She spread her legs wider in invitation.

Sliding his hand up to the back of her neck, he held her tight as he took her mouth and kissed her, deep and hard and wet. His first press into her was long and excruciatingly slow as though it brought him both pleasure and pain.

Which she understood. The friction relieved one kind of ache while making another deepen at the same time.

He rolled over, taking her with him, up into a sitting position. Her legs went around his waist, her hands to his shoulders. He held her hips, guiding her up and down the steely length of him. Pushing up on her knees for leverage, she pulsed with liquid heat, flowed with their building rhythm, matching his hunger and desperation.

"You're so beautiful," he said between ragged breaths. "You're perfect."

They took each other harder and faster, his mouth sensual

and sweet, his hands wild and possessive. Her heart brimmed with so much love—with the surety of his, bright as a star—that she cried. Happy tears.

Another shuddering release spilled through her. His arms locked around her waist and he drove her down, grinding roughly until he found his own.

In the past, at this point, once both parties had been physically satisfied, she would've said something callous and goading to establish distance and got the heck out of there.

Instead, when Aiden pulled her down beside him and wrapped his arms around her, she sank into it. Reveled in it.

The sun was fading, and it was nearly dark.

Snuggling with him, she was glad they'd made love slowly, so she'd always remember every caress, every whispered word of affection, each kiss and exhilarating breath of their first time.

First.

With many, many more to come.

Emotions barraged her. The world had changed.

Even she was different. Sort of. She wanted to be strong enough to handle this, brave enough. Aiden was right. It took courage to love.

"What are we supposed to do now?" she asked as a prickle of anxiety wormed to the surface. "Exchange BFFs bracelets? I guess it should say *lovers*. What does one put when your BFF is your lover?" Charlie pressed her lips together to stop the babbling redirection pouring out of her mouth. She had to be honest with him. Face her fears. "I don't know how to do this, a relationship, and I don't want to mess it up." Her stomach flip-flopped. She wanted it to work between them more than anything, but… "I'm scared."

"I know." He squeezed her arm and rubbed up and down. "We're going to keep doing the same thing that we have been. But we'll do it under one roof, sharing the same bed, only sleeping with each other. No bracelets."

She chuckled, her trepidation easing. "You make it sound so simple."

"Simple, yes. Easy, not always. But don't forget."

"What?"

He kissed her temple and tightened his embrace. "We're the dynamic duo. Together, we can do anything."

Next to Aiden, she felt invincible, like they could conquer the world. Maybe they could make a relationship work. Find happiness one day at a time.

The cell phone on the nightstand buzzed. A text came in.

Aiden reached over and grabbed the phone. He showed her the screen as he opened the message.

An orange jumpsuit wouldn't suit me. What do you want to trade?

"Even if Walsh agrees to give us Albatross, he'll never follow through and make good on it."

"We just have to buy Edgar time. Keep him safe until we can get to him."

Charlie nodded. "We should ask for money, too. To really sell it. Anyone corrupt would."

As GARCIA ILLEGALLY parked her car in a bus lane on Elk Place, her cell phone rang. She kept the sedan running, took out her mobile and noticed it was the office.

She was about to answer, but she spotted her confidential informant. Her CI abhorred working for the FBI. Most did. After getting busted and charged with drug possession and an intent to distribute, being an informant sounded better than jail, so here they were.

The girl was skittish, but careful. Garcia made their weekly meets as fast as possible to keep her at ease and lessen her exposure.

Whatever McCaffrey wanted would have to wait. She thumbed the reject icon.

The slim brunette pushed through the door of the Tulane University School of Social Work building. They rotated their meeting spot to a place she regularly continued to sell drugs to maintain her cover. The girl came up to the passenger's side of the car, and Garcia rolled down the automatic window.

Colette dug in her voluminous boho tote bag that had a colorful patchwork design and handed over the small six-by-six-inch box through the window. Inside was the special saltshaker that had been designed to match the others at Avido's and had a hidden recording device. The surveillance tool was voice-activated, with up to fifty hours of storage and battery life, and it didn't transmit a signal. Colette kept the saltshaker in the soundproof box in her purse, transporting it to and from the restaurant every day. It was only activated when she served Bill Walsh his lunch.

Garcia gave Colette the replacement device that she'd use for the next seven days.

The exchange was quick and fluid, and to anyone watching, it would look like a drug deal.

"You good?" Garcia asked.

Colette nodded. "Peachy."

Any other response meant something was wrong, like she was under duress or being followed or had been asked to hand over a fake recording. Anything seriously bad.

Colette walked off and Garcia drove in the opposite direction.

Instead of hitting the Windfall tonight, she would go home and start listening to the seven to fourteen hours of audio recording. Walsh was careful. Even in his office he tended to talk around things. But every week she hoped for another nugget while forgoing sleep.

Her phone rang again. This time she answered. "Garcia here."

"It's Jensen," said one of the guys on her surveillance team. "There's a lot of activity with Walsh. We just lost him. Something is up."

Garcia swore into the phone. "We need to find him. Do you have eyes on the nephew?"

"No. We lost him, too."

Going home and getting to slip off her shoes was out of the question. She was in for a late night, trying to track down Walsh and his sidekick Tommy Guillory.

She slapped the steering wheel. "I'm on my way."

"Also, call the boss. He's looking for you. It's urgent."

Garcia disconnected and dialed Special Agent McCaffrey. "Sorry I couldn't take your call a few minutes ago, sir. What's up?"

"I hope you're sitting down," her boss said.

"As a matter of fact, I am."

"Good. Because you're never going to believe this."

"Well, don't keep me in suspense."

"For starters, you're getting your extra agents tomorrow." *On a Sunday?*

"I've got three driving down in the morning from some of the resident field offices in Mississippi," McCaffrey added. "Pascagoula, Hattiesburg and Gulfport."

They were all within a two-hour drive, but that would've taken approval from the director up in Washington, DC, and coordination with the special agent in charge in Mississippi. "How in the world did you swing that?"

"You're going to need heavy backup for a meet tomorrow in Jackson Square at noon."

Chapter Sixteen

The bread truck came to a jerky stop. Big Bill caught hold of one of the steel racks lining the inside to steady himself.

Tommy killed the engine and opened the back doors. Bill climbed out and dusted himself off.

Going from the slightly sweet, yeasty aroma in the truck to the pungent, briny air at the old docks turned his stomach. This far down the river, there weren't any tourists taking in the sights. He took a few deep breaths, letting his nose adjust, and faced the warehouse.

He owned the building and the surrounding land under one of his subsidiaries. The property of each of his illicit businesses, the women and drugs, all fell under a different shell company to disguise the ownership from the feds. They couldn't very well put a place under surveillance and raid it if they didn't know it belonged to him.

Let them watch the Windfall and Avido's to their hearts' content. Didn't matter to him. They were both legit. But it did make traveling somewhat inconvenient at times such as now.

For the next couple of days, he had to steer clear of his house, the restaurant and the casino. He couldn't risk going back until he'd taken out his rage on Edgar and got some retribution.

Fortunately, Bill had a feeder coming in tonight with a new bunch of girls. The small container ship didn't attract as much attention as a larger vessel and it could navigate an older, smaller port. He'd oversee the off-loading of the girls, something Tommy usually took care of, and sleep in one of the passenger cabins once he tired himself out punishing Edgar.

The burner phone they'd used to stay in contact with the hit men from the bayou buzzed in his pocket. A response from those marshals.

It had to be them. They were the only ones in possession of the incriminating information that had been printed, photographed and sent to him. Bill wasn't sure what to make of them yet.

He'd hoped they would've thrown out a figure. Greed he understood, even appreciated. Everyone had a price, and once he'd learned theirs, he could be done with this.

Instead they wanted to trade.

But trade what?

Bill took out the phone and opened the text. For a moment, he was speechless with confusion.

Edgar Plinski. Alive. Unharmed. Plus $1M guarantees no copies of the drive are made.

What in the hell?

Bill read it again, shaking his head in disbelief. What cockamamie planet were these two marshals from? Was this some kind of joke?

Edgar could send him to prison just the same as the information on that flash drive.

Bill furiously typed back.

I need Plinski AND the contents of the drive. Name a new price $.

It took seconds for the phone to chime.

$2M + EDGAR PLINSKI. He's stayed quiet about you this long. We'll get him to keep his mouth shut. We need him to clear our names.

Grinding his molars, Bill kicked the truck tire. Another new message flashed. He stared at the screen.

Nonnegotiable!

Bill growled and shoved the phone back in his pocket.

Removing the delivery jacket and hat, Tommy asked, "What do they want, Uncle Bill?"

"The sun and the moon." They might as well ask for all the stars in the damn sky.

"Huh? What are you talking about?"

Bill shook his head at the kid. "They want," he said slowly, "what they can't have."

Why couldn't they ask for new identities? Help getting out of the country. Something reasonable.

Tommy hustled ahead of him, grabbed the door to the cavernous warehouse that was little more than a gutted-out shell and held it open.

Inside, Devlin and his crew were waiting. Along with a handful of Bill's guys, who'd keep watch over Edgar Plinski, doling out pain every hour on the hour once Bill was finished having his fun and he gave Tommy a go at him.

But he didn't see the traitor. "Where's that piece of filth?"

Devlin gestured to the van parked a few feet away. "You get the package once we've been paid."

"I'd like to throw in an extra hundred." *Grand* was implied. Devlin didn't get out of bed and put on his outlaw hat for less than ten thousand.

"What for?" Devlin asked.

"To kill those marshals." Bill's men were muscle, good

for run-of-the-mill protection and breaking kneecaps. This problem required a shrewd, ruthless predator.

"I need to find them first," Devlin said. "But don't worry. I will."

"No need to find them. They're going to come to me." Bill stuffed his hands in his pants pockets and rocked back on his heels, still fuming. "They texted. They want to trade. The flash drive for Edgar. Alive and unharmed so he can clear their names."

Devlin roared with dark laughter. The sound was spooky enough to give Satan himself the chills. "That's rich."

"Yes. It is. But not the least bit funny."

A smile ghosted across Devlin's lips as he rubbed the back of his head. "Those two have got a lot of grit."

"You almost sound as if you admire them," Bill said, disgusted.

"My father was a hunter. He taught me how to be a great one. To track something to the ends of the earth and kill it. First rule I learned was to respect dangerous things."

Bill huffed. He knew two plus two equaled four. Hell yeah, they were dangerous. That was why he wanted them dead. Respect wasn't a necessary part of his equation.

"I'd kill them for free," Devlin said. "For the sport of it. For payback. But we'll take the extra to fill our captain's pockets."

Their police chief was as crooked as they came. Loved being in front of the camera on the news, spinning manure into glitter, portraying his golden cops as shining examples.

Bill pulled out his other phone and made the call for the wire transfer. Three million six hundred thousand dollars.

"We're good," Tate said to Devlin a minute later, confirming receipt of the money.

Devlin nodded. "Give the man his package."

Tate opened the van door, hauled Edgar Plinski out onto his feet and dragged him over.

Pure satisfaction rushed through Bill's veins. Once the

traitor was in front of him, he ripped off the duct tape from his mouth, hoping it hurt. "I'm going to enjoy hearing you scream."

Edgar yelled and howled like a man in agony. Sweat and grime covered his reddening face. "I'll scream all you want. Please, Bill. Don't do this."

"You shouldn't have killed her." *Poor Irene.*

"It was an accident," Edgar said. "I—I loved her. Wanted her to go with me. But she tried to call you and I had to stop her. I didn't mean to kill her. I only hit her once."

Once across the back of her head with a solid bronze sculpture. Cracked her skull wide open and let her bleed to death.

That was the reason Edgar hadn't turned over evidence on Bill. If the FBI had arrested Bill, he would've told them about Irene's murder and Edgar's immunity would've been null and void. They would've been in prison together. Bill preferred to get his revenge as a free man.

"I've got a long list of things I'm going to do to you. Ways to make you suffer," Bill said. Then he thought about those marshals. *Alive. Unharmed.* "Damn it," Bill hissed and turned to Devlin. "They're going to ask me for proof that he's okay before they meet with me." They'd be fools not to. "But I've waited too long to put off making this one pay," he said, stabbing a finger in Edgar's direction.

"He just needs to *look* okay," Devlin said. "Plenty of options to bring him pain."

"Such as?" Everything Bill had planned was meant to scar and maim.

"Pull out some teeth. Start with the back ones. Rip off toenails. You could do waterboarding, one of my personal favorites. Or insects in a confinement box."

Edgar trembled, shaking his head, mouthing "No, no," dissolving into a pathetic heap as tears streamed down his face.

Good thing Bill had Devlin at his disposal to give him ideas. The man was a sadistic monster of the sickest kind.

"See. Plenty of options," Devlin said cheerfully. "Once we take care of the marshals, then you can really have at it with Edgar."

Grinning, Bill typed a response on the burner phone.

Let's trade. Midnight. Location to follow.

Then he hit Send on the text.

"Tommy," Bill said. "Make a list of the stuff we're going to need. I want to do it all, beginning with a pair of pliers."

Edgar started screaming again and Bill couldn't think of any sound in the world that had ever brought him more pleasure.

We say when. We say where. Or no deal.

Aiden sent the message and shut off the phone. The one thing they had to maintain control over was the rendezvous.

While eating the home-cooked dinner Henri had prepared for them, they sat on the bed in front of the laptop, strategizing their next step. Aiden had already got dressed to go down and get the food, sparing the older lady a trek up the steep flight.

"I think we should give Walsh a location for a fake meet," Charlie said. Wearing his long-sleeve button-up with the front open and revealing a tempting amount of skin, she shifted into a cross-legged position. "Catch them off guard early. Take the fight to them."

"But how? We don't know where they're holding Albatross."

"They're going to have him someplace Walsh completely controls. Somewhere contained, with no danger of him being seen. Not the casino and not the restaurant. His home is out of the question since the feds are watching him. Didn't you mention seeing deeds for other properties?"

"Yeah." Aiden brought up several documents that he'd pored over the night before. "Walsh is in some nasty business. Human trafficking, forcing the women to work in brothels, and he also has his hands in drugs. There are four properties that he's hiding under shell companies. Two are small apartment buildings, one-and two-bedroom units. All appear to be *leased*, but according to this, money is being laundered through there. I assume he's using those apartments for prostitution. If they're active, with a lot of traffic flowing in and out, Albatross won't be there."

"What about the other places?" Charlie finished her crawfish étouffée, scraping the plate clean with her fork.

It was a testament to Henri's cooking. Junior hadn't exaggerated about her culinary skills.

"There's an old processing plant in Metairie and a warehouse down by the docks. No documentation showing any income flowing through either."

"You think Walsh might be holding Albatross at one of those sites?"

"It's possible."

Charlie took a closer look at the paperwork. "We'll have to check them out to narrow it down."

"What you're proposing would require a lot of recon for just the two of us." Aiden ate the last spoonful of his dinner. "We might have to watch one location for a day or longer to be sure that Albatross is there, and we have multiple sites to cover. What if Devlin is holding him for Walsh somewhere else? Even if we did find him, we'd be seriously outnumbered and we're talking about the potential for a lot of bloodshed."

"That's a risk no matter what. I think we have to take the chance."

"If we hit them on their turf, even with the element of surprise, they'll have the advantage. They could use smoke against us again. We can't defeat thermal scopes or use flash bangs in return. We're operating on the shoestring budget and limited resources of street vigilantes."

Resting back on the wood headboard, she sighed. "The only other option is to set a legitimate meet in a public place, but civilians could get hurt. They could be used as human shields. If there's going to be loss of life, I'd prefer it to be the bad guys. We bought Albatross time. Walsh might still hurt him, but he'll be alive. We can do the recon."

Aiden shook his head. Albatross was worth three times more alive just so that he could be tortured. Walsh had a vendetta that he wasn't going to let slide. The odds of Eugene walking away uninjured were nil. "Alive, but in what condition after a day or two? In public, we can have the FBI there in advance waiting for him."

Charlie ran her fingers through his hair. "You're an eternal optimist and I love you for it, but we're fugitives. The FBI consider us a threat and are more likely to arrest us or shoot us before we can ensure Albatross is safe. And don't you think Walsh will send flunkies to check out any location we pick? Maybe even Devlin, who'd spot feds a mile away in a park or shopping mall. Walsh will never get out of the car, especially not with Albatross. We need to use the FBI as our final play."

Aiden ran his hands over his face, racking his brain. "There might be another way." He brought up the city of New Orleans on Google Maps. "What if we spend our time looking for the *right* public place, where we have more control over how everything plays out? Limit collateral damage. Terrain is everything."

Terrain and a lack of convergence led to General Custer's defeat. Why not Walsh's?

"Maybe," she said. "As they say, location is everything. It would mean the difference between success and incarceration or death."

"Controlling the terrain is possible, but Walsh has four highly trained SWAT officers working for him, plus however many thugs. We'd need to even the playing field. Reduce his forces."

Charlie shot him a confident, lopsided grin that was sexy as hell, and all he wanted to do was kiss her, but then he'd want to press down against the mattress, their limbs tangled, and work up a good sweat.

Restraint, he told himself.

"That's where Enzo Romero comes in," Charlie said.

"How so?" Aiden was skeptical about getting a second mobster involved, but Charlie had insisted they might be able to use him.

"The first year I was in a group home as a teenager, I was separated from my sister and surrounded by older, bigger, quite frankly tougher girls. There were two, Tasha and Judy. Both mean. Downright vicious. And they hated each other. Anyway, Tasha took this bracelet that Brit had made for me. I got my butt kicked trying to get it back. One day, someone messed up Judy's bed, went through all her stuff. I told her that it was Tasha."

"Did you do it?"

Charlie shook her head. "No, it was another girl who hated her. But I used it. When Tasha went for Judy, I went and got my bracelet back. We use Enzo to cause trouble that Big Bill can't ignore right before the meet. If Enzo is already squeezing Bill out, then what we want him to do should be more amusement than a chore."

"Divide and conquer."

"It's the only way to win." She moved their dishes, setting them on the nightstand.

"We need to make a list of places to scout tomorrow morning." He zoomed in on the map. "All within easy walking distance of Jackson Square. Then we should get some sleep.

We've got to get up early and tomorrow is going to be a long day."

"Do you want to make that list before or after?" Her mouth spread in a wicked hot smile that instantly heated his blood, igniting something inside him.

He closed the laptop and pulled her closer. "Definitely after."

Chapter Seventeen

Early-morning sun slashed through the opening in the curtains, banishing some of the shadows in the room. Charlie rolled over to find the bed empty, the room quiet and Aiden gone.

The aroma of fresh-brewed coffee wafted through the space. He knew that it was painful for her to operate in the morning without a cup of hot black java.

She ran her palm across the sheet, where he had slept snuggled up against her, and found the spot cold, as though he'd been gone awhile. Much longer than to dash out to get breakfast from Henri. Charlie buried her face in his pillow and smelled him on it.

The scent was comforting and made her ache for the feel of his warmth at her back, the weight of his arm draped over her.

They were neck-deep in a disaster, gambling everything on the choices and actions they made today, and she had never slept better in her entire life than she had last night with Aiden curled around her.

Home. Aiden was her home. Her constant that would never change. No matter how horribly the world fell apart, as long as they were together, she'd be able to deal with it.

Footsteps thudded up the exterior stairs. *Aiden.*

He unlocked the door and swept inside carrying two plates of food covered in aluminum foil. "Good morning. I have breakfast casserole with andouille sausage, eggs and potatoes, and bananas Foster French toast."

"Mmm. It smells delicious. If Aunt Henri keeps this up, we'll never want to leave."

He set the plates on the counter and unwrapped them.

"You were gone a long time." She slipped a shirt on and padded over to him. "Where were you?"

Leaning over, he cupped the back of her head and kissed her gently. Tenderly. "I went to Jackson Square to put things in position while it was still dark, before the FBI sets up."

"You should've woken me. I would've gone with you."

"It only required one of us to take care of it and I wanted to let you sleep."

He was amazing, beautiful, impossibly sweet and so much more than she deserved.

Rising on the balls of her feet, she threw her arm around his neck and kissed him again. "Thanks. But we should stick together."

He poured two cups of coffee and handed her one. "Hurry up and eat, then get dressed. Junior is waiting downstairs to give us a ride so we can check out locations."

She dug into the breakfast and silently sang Henri's praises.

"Which one of us is going to call Enzo and get him in play?" Aiden asked.

"You're better at sweet-talking than I am."

"Sweet won't work on him. I think he needs the way you talk."

Charlie shrugged. "If you think so."

Aiden picked up her jeans and pulled out the business card Enzo had given her with his personal cell number. He dialed using one of the new burners and put the call on speaker.

"Who is this?" Enzo snapped over the line.

"Someone looking to make a deal." She waited, letting

his brain wake up and register what she'd said. "If you want what I have on you, then you'll do what I say."

"Listen, sugar. You don't realize who you're speaking to. Nobody tells me what to do."

"Welcome to your new reality. Let's get something straight. I'm not your sugar, your babe or your sweetie." She kept her tone sharp as a switchblade. "I'm your guardian angel. If you're smart enough to want to stay out of prison, you'll do exactly as I say."

A breath of hesitation. "Go on."

"You're going to hit Big Bill where it'll hurt. His brothels. Where he processes his drugs. You're going to make it loud and ugly so Bill has to take notice. The strike happens at two thirty this afternoon. Don't be early. Don't be late."

"Are you trying to start a war?" Enzo asked. "I haven't been sanctioned to take that kind of action."

"Better to beg forgiveness than ask permission. Two thirty. Do this and Bill will no longer be a factor in New Orleans."

THE BELLS OF the St. Louis Cathedral finished clanging, marking the hour. Noon.

With a red hat on and matching T-shirt, Garcia stood in Jackson Square next to the tree marked on the postcard. It had multiple trunks and wasn't much taller than her five feet ten inches. The offbeat pulse of the French Quarter vibrated around the square.

Adrenaline was the only thing keeping her upright. She was exhausted from spending the night searching for Big Bill Walsh and Tommy Guillory, reviewing security footage of the casino and cross-referencing it with CCTV coverage. She'd only discerned that Walsh had sneaked out in the back of one of the delivery trucks at the casino. The normal schedule had been changed. Deliveries had been deliberately stacked to occur at the same time. The chaos had been too much for two agents to properly monitor.

Walsh and Guillory had slipped through their fingers. They were up to something and it wasn't good. She knew it deep down.

Every chance she had, she'd slogged through more of the audio recording from the restaurant, but there were four more hours to go and she still had no idea where Big Bill was squirreled away.

Garcia scanned her surroundings. Her agents had been in place, rotating positions for the past two hours in various disguises. A homeless man, shuffling around the square. A psychic seated at a small card table on the fringe. Jensen and the agent from Hattiesburg were camped out on a bench fifty feet away, pretending to be a couple, chatting and drinking coffee. The one from Pascagoula pushed a baby stroller with a doll inside and the other from Gulfport was dressed as a jogger, earbuds in, hanging around the vicinity.

A shiver slid down her spine and she sensed she was being watched. And not by one of her own. That spark of awareness every woman got when unwanted eyes were on her.

It was Aiden Yazzie and Charlotte Killinger. Garcia sensed it in her bones.

Their prints came back first thing this morning with a positive ID on both, and she'd picked up the alert notification that had gone through the FQ Task Force app, placing them in this area yesterday afternoon. None of it was coincidence.

Dirty marshals on the lam contacting the FBI was a first. Maybe they wanted to work out a plea deal in exchange for the evidence they had. Better to make arrangements to be taken into custody unharmed than catch an accidental bullet on the run.

Garcia and her people were prepared to apprehend them without incident. She kept her head on a swivel, surveying the area.

They were out there somewhere and could be in a dozen different places blending in. The Washington Artillery Park.

St. Louis Cathedral. Watching from a shop on St. Ann Street or St. Peter.

Garcia glanced at her watch. Two minutes past noon.

A cell phone rang, but it wasn't hers. The ringtone was the song "Bad Boys" by Inner Circle. Loud and close and designed to draw attention.

She followed the sound, tracking it to the palm tree with a cluster of trunks that had been circled on the postcard. The ringing cell phone had been duct-taped to the inner side of one of the trunks in the bunch near the fronds. She hopped up and ripped it off.

There was a flash drive taped to the phone.

She separated the drive and answered. "This is Assistant Special Agent in Charge Ava Garcia."

"I take it you know who I am," a smooth male voice said.

"You're Aiden Yazzie." She looked around, trying to pinpoint him or Killinger. "You know, this conversation would be easier to have face-to-face."

"I can see *your* face," he said in a friendly, conversational tone. "Do you have the drive?"

"I do. It would be best if you came out now, with your hands above your head. I promise no harm will come to either of you as long as you don't resist arrest."

"We're not turning ourselves in. Not until we've rescued the witness we lost."

Edgar Plinski. "You were the ones who gunned down fellow law enforcement officers and allowed Albatross to be taken." After reading the despicable details of the case, she'd found out the witness's code name.

"We're innocent," he said. "We were set up by the crew who ambushed us. They're crooked NOPD SWAT officers out of the Fifth District, hired by Bill Walsh. They're led by Frank Devlin."

Garcia knew the name. She'd suspected Devlin was dirty for a while, and when he turned out to be the only eyewitness accusing Yazzie and Killinger, it had struck her as fishy. Too convenient.

"If you dig," Yazzie said, "you'll find that Devlin and three other owners of The Merry Men bar were out of town Friday."

The FBI's top criminal investigative priority was public corruption. Any violations of federal law by public officials at the federal, state and local levels of government. She'd heard rumors about rotten apples in the Fifth District reaching the highest branches of power, but no one had been able to prove anything. One dead end after another. Sometimes literally, with witnesses having accidents or disappearing.

However, a fugitive's say-so wasn't going to cut the mustard. Even if Devlin and his buddies had been out of town, it wasn't proof. It was circumstantial at best.

"We've promised Walsh that he can have the flash drive you're holding," Yazzie said, "in exchange for giving us back Albatross, alive and unharmed."

Garcia scoffed. "And how do you see that playing out?"

"I foresee you using the information on the drive to put away Walsh and Enzo Romero. That evidence along with more has been sent to the DOJ. At the meet, Walsh will have his men try to kill us."

"What's to stop them from doing that?"

"Hopefully, you."

"Come again?"

"We're asking for your help. Call it interagency cooperation. The rendezvous will take place at three o'clock. In a public place that's less than one mile from where you're standing."

The FBI had achieved great success in combating corruption thanks in large part to working with other agencies on a federal, state, local and tribal law enforcement level, including the Department of Justice and by extension the US Marshals Service, but what Yazzie proposed was well outside of legal bounds.

"Give me the location now," Garcia said.

"I can't do that."

"Can't or won't?"

"Both."

Provided he was telling the truth, her people would be able to respond quickly if the location was less than a mile away, but she preferred going in early ahead of time. "If you truly want to cooperate with the FBI, you wouldn't stonewall. Full disclosure."

"Proof of our cooperation is on the flash drive you're holding."

"Why not share the site of the meet?"

"I'll give you six reasons. The vagrant, the two sitting on the bench chitchatting like they're a couple, the tarot reader in blue with sunglasses, jogger wearing track pants, woman pushing a stroller on your left. All six are yours. If I tell you where, you'll scare off Walsh. He and Devlin will spot your agents."

"Then how am I supposed to help you?"

"Keep the phone in your hand close. We'll call again from a different number when the time is right."

The call ended.

Slapping the flip phone closed, Garcia grunted in frustration and slid it into her pocket.

Jensen stared at her, waiting. When she shook her head that the marshals turning themselves in was a no-go, he came over. "Anything useful?"

"Maybe." *Hopefully.* "According to them, Walsh has Albatross. They claim they're innocent and are meeting Walsh to get their witness back. Supposedly this drive," she said, holding it up, "has everything we need to put away Walsh *and* Romero."

"Why would they give it to you when they could use it as leverage?"

Leverage? Hell, it was probably worth millions. "They say

they're innocent. That they were set up by the people who kidnapped Albatross."

"Do they know who?"

"Aiden Yazzie swears it was Frank Devlin and several other SWAT officers."

Jensen's brow furrowed and he looked down like something had occurred to him. "Devlin was at Avido's yesterday afternoon."

"What?" Garcia rocked back on her heels. "Why didn't you tell me?"

"He was there during regular business hours. It could've been just to eat, and once Walsh disappeared, finding him was our only focus."

Didn't it occur to Jensen that the two incidents could've been related?

If what Yazzie had told her was true, Devlin probably went to Avido's to coordinate payment and the drop-off of Albatross.

Garcia shoved the flash drive in Jensen's hand. "Have everyone stay close by for the next couple of hours and I want you to verify the contents of the drive." She turned and took off.

"Where are you going?" he called after her.

"To check the end of the recording from Avido's. See if we got the conversation."

Chapter Eighteen

After Bill had waited twenty-one hours, the burner phone on his side table in the small passenger cabin buzzed.

Audubon Aquarium. Send a picture of Edgar Plinski standing in front of the aquarium sign, Canal Street side, by three o'clock, or the deal is off. No Devlin.

Bill chuckled. The gumption of those marshals to think they could dictate to him. Bill would be crazy not to show up with Devlin, the most merciless monster on his payroll, to finish this.

With only thirty minutes to be at the aquarium, they needed to get going.

Stretching, he held his hands up and stared at the bloodstains under his nails. He should've worn gloves before he ripped out a few of Edgar's teeth.

Out of all the ways he'd tortured Edgar, for hours, none had brought Bill more than a modicum of the satisfaction that he sought.

He sighed but was comforted by the knowledge that soon the marshals would be dead, and Edgar would be his to do with as Bill pleased.

Then he'd work through his pain and grief with his fists.

Someone pounded on his cabin door. "Uncle Bill! Open up!"

Bill threw on his suit jacket, slicked back his hair and hit the lever, opening the door. "What is it?"

"Enzo. He's making a play."

"For the brothels?'

"No. For everything! His men are at both the apartment buildings, rounding up the girls, kicking out the johns, taking the money, and they're also at the processing plant. He's stealing our dope."

Had the whole world gone mad? An hour ago, Bill had been on the precipice of ruling New Orleans again. Now he was being threatened on all fronts.

"We've got to get over there and stop him," Tommy said.

"I can't. I have to head out for the meet." Bill left his room and walked with Tommy down the narrow corridor. "If I'm not there, I'll lose the drive."

"You're losing everything else right this minute."

Bill cursed the bad timing of things. Enzo must've noticed that he wasn't around and decided it was the perfect time to make his move. Damn vulture.

"You go handle it, Tommy." Bill knocked on Devlin's door and said, "It's time. We've got twenty-seven minutes. Grab Edgar and let's go."

"You want me to handle it?" Tommy asked, following Bill as he pushed through the outer door into the sunlight.

"Yeah, you. This will all be yours someday. You've got just as much of a stake in it as I do, and I trust you to deal with it." He clasped his nephew's shoulder and that seemed to calm him. "Take the boys with you."

"Are you sure? Who's gonna cover your back?"

"I've got Devlin and his crew. They're more than enough. After we're finished, I'll come help you get back what's ours."

WEARING THEIR WIGS and sunglasses, Charlie and Aiden leisurely finished their snack at the eatery, blending in. Once done, they strolled from the Café du Monde, where they'd observed Special Agent Garcia during their phone call, down by the river toward the Audubon Aquarium. They were both armed: tactical knives, suppressed firearms, and her telescoping baton was hooked to her belt loop and covered by her button-up shirt that she wore open over her tee.

If they could use nonlethal means, they would. Limiting collateral damage was a huge concern. They'd do everything in their power to protect innocent lives.

As they crossed through a playground, laughter from the kids playing there filled the air. Without meaning to, she looked over at the children whooshing down a slide.

She thought of the sacrifice Aiden was making by choosing to be with her.

The guilt she'd been trying so damn hard to ignore sank into her chest, an ache flaring sudden and sharp behind her breastbone.

But she had to shift focus, stay on target. On the mission. On getting Albatross back from those crooked cops who'd ambushed them, taken out their tires, sprayed paint on the windows, faked a bomb, used smoke and thermal scopes.

That fired her up, pushing the sadness aside.

Passing the sandbox, Charlie bent down, scooped up two healthy palmfuls of grains and put them into her pocket.

"What's that for?" Aiden asked, hiking the backpack up on his shoulder.

"To fight dirty." If given the chance. "Like them," she said, anger resonating in her voice.

"Don't worry. We're going to give them a dose of their own medicine."

They had a plan to do precisely that.

They entered the aquarium flashing the handstamp they'd received earlier when they'd paid and scoped out the place. Once again, the backpack hadn't been searched. Good thing, too, because Aiden had more than duct tape inside.

The main exhibits were emptying, as parents with kids and

others were making their way to the Entergy Giant Screen Theater. The IMAX theater was connected to and run by the aquarium but had a separate entrance outside.

The 3D larger-than-life movies explored nature, shown with the most advanced motion picture technology, and were a huge draw. They timed the meet to coincide around a show to reduce the number of civilians that would be inside the aquarium.

Aiden took her by the hand, leading her into the glass underwater tunnel of the Great Mayan Reef, which was set off to the side. No one entering the aquarium could see them. Surrounded by water that cast an azure glow over them and sea creatures from moray eels to stingrays swimming by, he backed her up against the glass wall and pressed his palm to her face. "Find a discreet spot outside to keep watch. I'll go set up and prepare upstairs."

The Amazon Rainforest Exhibit on the second floor was the best site to face Walsh. It was a contained area that was currently closed for repairs, and there were two ways to access it. One was farther down the corridor, beyond the Mayan Reef and to the stairs. The other, more obvious, route was through the main section of the aquarium to the stairs that led to the upper-floor exhibits.

"I don't like separating," Charlie said.

"Devlin might come. He'll use guerrilla tactics. If you keep watch outside, you can let me know who's headed my way."

"If I see Devlin—"

"Stay away from him."

She'd do whatever was necessary to cover Aiden's back. If Devlin showed, he'd have to go through her first before she gave him an opportunity to get the drop on her man. *Hers.*

"Devlin is dangerous," Aiden said, probably reading the bullheaded look in her eyes.

"So am I. You can't take on an entire team alone. We're

partners. Don't try and sideline me because I'm a woman or because you love me. We only win if we do it together."

Reluctantly, he said, "All right. But if you see Devlin, don't follow him. Come straight to the exhibit. We'll deal with him together."

She put her palm to his chest, stared into his deep brown eyes, finding her center. "Do you have any bad feelings?"

He nodded, his lips pressing tight like he didn't want to say more.

She wasn't going to push him. "Be careful."

"Always. You, too."

Charlie had no clue what was going to transpire once Walsh arrived in the next few minutes, but she'd promised herself to tell Aiden, every single day, what he meant to her. "I love you."

He lowered his head and kissed her, hard, quick. "See you soon." With that, he was off.

Taken aback, Charlie snatched his wrist and pulled him into the dim blue light. "Hey, Mr. Romantic, aren't you going to say it back?" Weren't couples supposed to do that? Exchange mushy sentiments before separating and running into danger.

"After," he said. The single, steely word was his promise to her that they'd get through this, that this wasn't their last chance to share what was in their hearts.

Oddly enough, it filled her with hope. "After." Another peck on the lips, and she let him leave.

She watched him take the entrance to the Rainforest Exhibit through the Mayan Reef and head past the sign that read Closed for Repairs.

Outside, she found a spot on a bench under a large shade tree, facing the river. The position gave her lines of sight to anyone approaching the entrance from the south or north and was partially concealed by a closed kiosk.

She put in her wireless earpiece. "One, two, can you hear me?" she said, doing a comms check.

"Loud and clear," Aiden responded. "I'm all set up. It's quiet in here. I think they moved the birds for whatever maintenance they're doing. Fish are still in the tank. Hey, did you know that a school of piranha can strip the flesh from a one-hundred-pound capybara in under a minute using razor-sharp teeth?"

"No, and neither did you until you read that on a sign."

Useless fact, but the viciousness made Charlie think she needed that same ferocious survival instinct.

She'd never had anything in her life as precious as Aiden's love. They had a chance at a future together, and she was going to fight like hell to keep it.

They needed a four-man team for this. Something Devlin had and they lacked. Hopefully, Enzo was doing his part. If an army of thugs showed up at the aquarium, they'd have to retreat and regroup.

At three o'clock sharp, a text came in. Charlie opened the attachment, finding a picture of Edgar Plinski at the south side of the aquarium, as they'd instructed.

Edgar was pale, with horror-filled eyes and puffy cheeks, looking as if he was on the verge of a breakdown. They must have put him through the wringer.

Charlie sent the exact location for the meet.

Amazon Rainforest Exhibit. Second level.

A man she recognized from Devlin's group photo approached from the east, alone, and went inside.

"Albatross is here, and a scout just entered, checking the place out. One of Devlin's."

"Roger," Aiden said. "I'll contact Garcia. Tell her to get over here ASAP."

Devlin's scout would do a thorough sweep, making sure

it was clear of feds and cops, and that nothing suspicious stood out.

By the time Garcia arrived, the meet would be underway, and it'd be too late.

The scout must've been satisfied, because a few minutes later, another goon appeared with his hand locked on Edgar's arm, dragging him toward the entrance.

Walsh followed at least ten paces behind them, carrying a briefcase and looking way too cocky, like this scenario was a foregone conclusion for him.

"Two SWAT operators and Albatross and Walsh are headed your way."

"Got it," Aiden said. "Don't rush in. Play it cool. Make sure there are no surprises coming up on my six."

"Okay." Tension rippled through Charlie, but she forced herself to appear relaxed, like a tourist enjoying the day.

Then everything changed.

From the corner of her eye, she saw them. Not a squad of armed thugs. Something worse.

Devlin and one of his buddies, lean and mean with a goatee, rounded the corner from the north side in a furious stride. They were out for blood.

She swore under her breath.

Stopping at the employee entrance, Devlin rang the bell and pounded on the door with a fist. A staff member opened the door.

Devlin flashed his badge, shoved the kid aside and bulldozed his way in along with the other guy.

A rush of dread, cold as liquid nitrogen, shot through her. "They're inside," Charlie said. "Devlin and another."

"Wait for Garcia. She's mobilizing. She'll be there in ten minutes. Stay outside."

Panic flipped to fury. Like hell she'd sit outside while they killed Aiden.

She had one advantage. With the wig, they didn't know

what she looked like. She could get close and do damage before they even realized it was her.

"You could be dead in ten minutes. I'm going after Devlin."

She'd do anything to protect Aiden, and everything in her power to keep them both alive.

An EERIE SPARK of awareness had trickled down Aiden's spine the minute he'd sent the text to Walsh about meeting at the aquarium. Someone was going to die today.

Now Charlie was rushing off to handle Devlin and one of his SWAT buddies alone.

And there wasn't a damn thing he could do about it. His chest squeezed with stark fear.

Impulsive, hotheaded, gorgeous woman! You better stay alive and not get hurt.

They'd waited too long, fought too hard, to lose each other.

She was smart. A fighter. A dirty fighter. Devlin had probably better watch out, he told himself, seeking a shred of solace.

One of the crooked cops wearing a ball cap entered the exhibit, scanning the area that was created to resemble the rainforest.

Aiden kicked the empty backpack at his feet out of his way.

Once the cop spotted Aiden standing on the Tree-Top Loop, a wooden bridge that connected two canopies with a small covered pavilion at one end, the cop moved to the bottom of the left staircase and stopped.

The position in the Tree-Top Loop gave Aiden enough camouflage from the pavilion to prevent him from being an easy target and a bird's-eye view of the entire exhibit, along with both exits.

Walsh sauntered in carrying a briefcase, with a smug

smile on his face. Behind him Albatross shuffled in, his head hung low.

The other dirty SWAT officer, who had outdated sideburns that Elvis wanted back, held a gun pressed to Edgar's temple.

"Here he is as promised, and the money." Walsh held up the briefcase and opened it, revealing bundles of cash. "Where's the flash drive?"

"Are you all right?" Aiden asked Edgar. "Did they hurt you?"

"He's walking and talking," Walsh said. "So he's fine."

Sweat trickled down the side of Aiden's face from the steamy jungle atmosphere as he raised an eyebrow. "Well, I haven't heard the talking part yet." For all he knew, they'd cut out the man's tongue.

"Tell him." Walsh poked Edgar in the cheek.

Wincing, Edgar recoiled. "I'm fine." His voice was low and hoarse, like he'd been screaming and lost it.

"I want a closer look at him before any exchange. Bring him up here." Aiden waved them up the right set of stairs.

As Edgar limped up the steps with Sideburns behind him, the other man set a foot on the left staircase.

"No." Aiden drew the suppressed Beretta he'd stolen from Devlin and pointed it at him. "You and Walsh stay there. Just them."

Edgar and Sideburns continued walking. The others stayed put.

Aiden backed up, drawing them in to where he wanted, without the gunman feeling crowded, threatened. Shifting to the side, Aiden guided them to move clockwise, ninety degrees. Right where the proverbial X marked the spot.

Sideburns held the back of Edgar's shirt collar with one hand and leveled the gun at his head with the other.

Looking over Edgar, Aiden noticed his eyes were bloodshot and swollen, and he kept swallowing in a weird way, like his mouth was sore. Hundreds of tiny red marks covered his face, throat, hands.

Were those bug bites?

Aiden had a plan to keep the conversation going until Garcia arrived. Edgar's current state was the perfect thing to pursue and draw things out, but every second he wasted stalling was one more second that Devlin had to kill Charlie.

"Where's the flash drive?" Walsh asked.

In his peripheral vision, Aiden caught the one wearing the ball cap slip his gun from his holster and creep up the left staircase, one slow step after another.

"Set the briefcase on the ground," Aiden said, tracking the progress of the one moving. By the time Walsh did as he was told, the other man reached the midway point on the stairs.

Precisely where Aiden wanted.

They were always going to try to close in around him. No warnings or threats were going to stop it, only delay it. So he had to prepare for the inevitable.

With the lush jungle environment, leafy tropical plants and verdant vegetation, it was easy to miss all the items that Aiden had hidden.

He let the guy take one more step. Then Aiden pulled the Smith & Wesson from his waistband with his left hand, aimed at the booby trap and pulled the trigger.

The portable fire extinguisher taped to a pole and concealed with palm fronds exploded in the guy's face. He shrieked and slipped backward down the stairs.

Aiden dropped to one knee—anticipating Sideburns would refocus the barrel of his gun away from Edgar's head toward the threat—and took aim in his direction. Edgar instinctively cowered, his hands covering his head, arms in front of his face as Aiden fired again.

With a loud *pop*, a second extinguisher exploded, sending a cloud of dry white chemicals bursting through the air around the pavilion.

Sideburns screamed, throwing an arm up to cover his face.

Aiden coughed from the particles in the air but had turned away to avoid getting any in his eyes. He reached out and pulled Edgar to the ground, getting him out of the way, and shoved him into the corner.

A bullet hit a nearby wooden post. Walsh was firing at them.

"Stay down, here," Aiden said to Edgar. Then he jumped up and threw a side kick into Sideburns's chest.

The blow drove the thug backward, the momentum carrying him over the rail of the pavilion into the piranha tank below.

Aiden launched himself down the right staircase, spraying a volley of suppressive fire from the 9 mm with the silencer.

If Walsh had gone left toward the stairs leading to the Mayan Reef, he would've got away without a scratch on him. Instead he ran in the direction in which he'd come, back toward the other exhibits on the second floor.

Aiden aimed and fired. Not at Walsh. And he was out of fire extinguishers. His bullet hit a cluster of paint ball grenades. The yellow liquid color sprayed in multiple directions, making the floor slick.

He could always count on Charlie to get creative in a pinch.

Running, Walsh couldn't get any traction in his fancy shoes and slipped around like he was trying to walk on ice.

Aiden punched him in the face, knocking Walsh to his butt, and kicked the gun from his hand.

A bullet struck a tree beside Aiden's head. The one in the ball cap had recovered, but the chemicals from the extinguisher had messed up his eyes. His aim was off.

Aiden returned fire.

The guy ducked and hit the stairs, going for Edgar. Heavy footfalls pounded up the right staircase, followed by more gunfire.

Leaping into action, Aiden rounded the corner and saw Edgar making a run for it across the wooden bridge and down the steps on the left side of the room. Aiden popped off a round, clipping the gunman in the leg.

The man dropped onto the stairs.

Staying on him, Aiden bounded up the steps, but the guy rolled onto his back. At that distance, a blind man could've shot him.

Aiden darted to the side at the right moment, avoiding a hot slug to the chest. He stilled and controlled the squeeze of the trigger. One shot to the wrist, forcing the man's fingers to open and drop the weapon. The guy howled, clutching his wounded arm.

Pulling out a zip tie, Aiden flipped the guy onto his stomach.

Edgar kept going. Darting down below, he scooped up the briefcase full of cash and took off running.

"Wait, Edgar!" Aiden called as he disappeared down the stairs toward the Mayan Reef.

Walsh was up on his feet, gun back in his hand, and hot on Edgar's heels.

Aiden yanked the man's arms behind his back and got his wrists and ankles restrained with zip ties. Then Aiden was up, on the move, again.

But as he ran down the stairs, he realized he had to make a choice.

Go after Edgar and Walsh. Or find Charlie.

Everything that they'd gone through—running from the law, taking on gangsters, going toe-to-toe with dirty SWAT officers to clear their names—would be in vain if they lost Edgar. Their careers, their future, would go down the drain.

His heart throbbed with immediate resolution. There was no choice.

CHARLIE FINALLY SPOTTED one of Devlin's men in the Gulf of Mexico Exhibit. The area was dimly lit so visitors could clearly see the seventeen-foot-deep, 400,000-gallon tank with sharks and other marine life, and a quarter-scale replica of an offshore oil rig.

The exhibit was stunning and at the same time alarming. Darkness shrouded the corners, black pockets like ominous voids. And there was still no sign of Devlin.

The man with the goatee was headed toward the Great Mayan Reef.

Was Devlin in front of them already, at the Amazon Rainforest Exhibit?

Or was he lurking somewhere behind her?

She took another furtive glance over her shoulder. Nothing but a family strolling toward a different exhibit in the opposite direction. Charlie pulled out her baton. The steel was well-balanced and heavy-duty.

The expandable rod would allow her to make physical contact while giving her a twenty-six-inch buffer zone. That might not be much, but when it came to a 200-pound man throwing a punch, those two feet of safety distance felt like ten.

She squeezed the rod in her hand, keeping her head on a swivel.

Timing the meet to coincide with the movie in the theater next door had worked. The place was fairly empty now compared to this morning, and the darkness seemed to have swelled as the number of people wearing bright-colored clothing dwindled.

The employee entrance opened in the middle of the aquarium. Devlin could be anywhere. She hoped she found him before he got to Aiden.

Goatee spotted something, picking up his pace as he reached into his jacket for his weapon.

With a quick flick of the wrist, the telescoping baton extended to full length. She swooped up behind him and whacked his gun arm twice, stopping him from drawing his weapon.

A couple in the vicinity gasped and ran for the exit.

Then Charlie went for the startled man's legs, hitting him behind the knees, bringing him to the floor. Hard.

He looked up at her, snarling. "You bit—"

Another strike to his face silenced him. She kicked him to the floor facedown and thrust her knee in the middle of his back.

Setting the baton on the floor, she pulled out zip ties and bound his wrists behind him.

"Charlie, where are you?" Aiden asked over comms.

She went to toggle her earpiece as a shocking blow to her head sent her spinning off the man and the black wig went flying. Charlie crashed into the wall.

A follow-up kick to her gut had her doubled over in pain.

Dazed, she swung out with a fist on pure instinct, but her attacker laid her on the floor with a leg sweep. As she sucked in for air, trying to breathe through the pain, he dropped on top of her, and she stared into Devlin's hateful eyes.

Her blood turned to ice, heartbeat thrumming sickeningly in her ears.

"Thought you could hunt me. That a wig would make you invisible. Like I couldn't draw you out." He cocked his fist, bringing his elbow way back, preparing to hurt her. Hurt her until there was only darkness.

She had to fight, act now. Charlie brought a knee up between his legs hard enough to jolt him forward and threw a punch up into his throat.

Then he was the one gasping.

He rolled off her, and she clambered to her feet.

Staggering away, she needed to get distance from him. She reached into her shirt to draw her weapon when a hand closed around her ankle. He yanked her back with such force that she had to throw out both hands in front of her to break the fall.

He was climbing on her, with her belly to the floor.

Facedown, she wouldn't stand a chance.

Charlie swung her elbow back and up, using the added rotation of her body to drive it hard into the side of Devlin's head. Her bone struck his face. He grunted and his weight lifted.

Without hesitation, she scrambled forward on her hands and knees. Pushed up from the floor to her feet.

Devlin growled. A shuffling sound told her that he was in motion behind her. A bullet bit into the wall near her head.

She bolted for the stairs. Her brain spun. Dread pooled in her stomach. Faster and faster she ran.

"Charlie!" Aiden's panicked voice in her ear reset her senses.

She spotted a sign that said Second Floor: Shark Discovery.

The new shark and stingray touch-pool exhibit was under construction. She grabbed the knob and jerked it. Locked. Her heart felt ready to explode in her chest.

"Don't go there. It's locked," Aiden said.

With a desperate curse, she drew her weapon.

Devlin pounded up the steps. His vile, evil energy was a force in itself, breathing down on her.

She shot the lock and kicked it open. Devlin charged toward her, taking aim. She threw the door wide open, punched holes into the other and ran into the construction zone.

Before she could get her bearings, he was barreling down on her.

She spun and fired but tripped on a cord and missed.

As he raised his gun, she was close enough to grab his right wrist and keep her head out of the line of fire, but he snatched her gun hand, as well.

They wrestled, struggling in a furious whirl to gain control or to break free. Both squeezing off shots, trying to nail the other with a bullet.

His gun clicked first. Empty.

Two more shots, and hers did the same.

The moment of decision froze between them, and their eyes locked.

One bloody lesson she'd learned in the group home as a teenager—hesitation could be fatal. Letting a fight unfold always gave your opponent the advantage.

She threw a headbutt to his face, slamming her skull down on the bridge of his nose, and nearly broke free of his hold. But he was tough. Unrelenting.

Devlin punched her, a quick jab that sent her to the floor and had blood pooling in her mouth.

Think! She inched away. Determination fired in her blood. *Think, or this man is going to kill you.*

She'd never given much thought to dying, had never spent much time wondering what came after. But right then, all she cared about was living and breathing and having a life with Aiden. She wasn't going to let this bastard take that away from her.

He stalked closer, violence etching harsh lines on his face.

Charlie shoved her hand in her pocket and gathered a handful of sand. *Hold*, she told herself. Pulse racing. Breath sawing from her mouth. *Wait for him to get closer.*

He reached down to grab her by the hair, and she threw the sand in his eyes.

Pitching away from her, he wiped at his face with his forearm.

She threw a boot heel to his groin.

Jumping to her feet, she drew the tactical knife from its sheath and lunged for him. The matte black blade slid into the sweet spot—the jugular notch right above the sternum.

A gurgling noise came from Devlin. He stumbled back, dropped to one knee as if still struggling to stand, to keep fighting out of sheer malice, but he toppled to the floor.

His lifeless eyes open. Blood pouring from his dead body on the floor.

She sucked in a deep breath and swallowed hard, her hands shaking. Her heart quivering.

Aiden stormed inside. His gaze fell to Devlin and lifted to her. The heated look in his eyes knocked her back a step. She saw the anger, the worry, the shadows of fear.

In a blink, he had her wrapped in his arms.

Relief rose like the sun inside her. They'd both survived. Together. She held him tight, pressed her cheek to his.

Then she remembered. Pulling away, she asked, "Where's Albatross?"

"He ran with the money. Walsh went after him."

She stared at him, her mouth hanging open. "Why aren't you chasing them?"

He ran his hand over her hair and caressed her jaw. "I had to make sure you were all right."

Shock left her speechless. The depth of his love was staggering. Blinding.

"You'll always come first," he said. "Before duty, before country. Before anything."

With a lump forming in her throat, she slid her hands up his chest and he enveloped her in his arms. She soaked in his warmth, his comfort. His love.

The distinct sound of helicopter blades cutting through the air outside quieted them.

They ran out of the room.

From the window, they saw a police helicopter hovering in the front of the aquarium.

They exchanged a glance and ran down the stairs, racing to the main entrance.

Beyond the doors, Walsh stood with his arm around Edgar's throat and a gun to his head. A hundred feet away, Special Agent Garcia had her weapon drawn alongside several other agents and had them surrounded.

Aiden took a step toward the doors with his gun raised.

"What are you doing?" Charlie grabbed his arm. "If you go out there, they might shoot you. They think we're fugitives."

Aiden considered what she'd said for a moment, pulled the cell from his pocket and called the burner he'd given Garcia.

What if she didn't answer?

She might not even be able to hear it with the helicopter overhead.

But Garcia patted her pocket and pulled out the phone.

"We're inside the aquarium," Aiden said. "We have a clean shot. But I need you to let us take it." He listened for a minute and hung up. "She's ordering everyone to hold their fire. The shot is ours."

Trepidation rippled through Charlie. It could be a trick, to get them to expose themselves, but Garcia wanted Walsh and to protect Albatross, a witness, as much as they did.

"I'll hold the door," Charlie said. "You take the shot."

Aiden was a better marksman. Not by much, but enough to wound Walsh and save Edgar's life. She couldn't guarantee the same. Shooting to kill was more her style.

They crept up to the entrance, waving back frightened employees, urging them to stay low.

Charlie grabbed a door handle, took a breath to stop nerves from rolling her stomach and waited for Aiden's signal.

With a two-handed grip for increased stability and accuracy, he raised the weapon, lining up his sights.

When he gave a sharp nod, she flung the door open.

Aiden squeezed the trigger once.

The bullet struck Walsh in the shoulder, causing the gun to jerk forward without discharging. Aiden fired again, hitting his hand. The weapon dropped to the ground.

FBI agents swept in and circled the two men.

Charlie and Aiden lowered their guns to the ground and

put their hands up behind their heads, assuming the standard position.

Cuffs were slapped on Walsh. "I'm going to tell them!" Walsh said. "About how you murdered my sister. Say goodbye to your immunity. I might be going to prison, but you'll be right there beside me!"

Edgar shuddered as agents took the briefcase and escorted him away.

"You can lower your hands," Garcia said, approaching them. "You've been cleared of charges."

"How?" Charlie and Aiden asked in unison.

"I've got Walsh and Devlin on tape. Devlin admitted to framing you. When I called your San Diego field office to let your boss, Will Draper, know, he informed me that Albatross's wife came out of her coma this morning. She told the police what really happened. Apparently, Draper had marshals providing protection for her around the clock, in case you two decided to…well." She stopped, not voicing the vile implication. "It was a good thing, too. A local cop tried to kill her."

"What?" Charlie asked.

"The cop was Devlin's buddy who'd provided his cover story for being out in San Diego."

Devlin was trying to tie up loose ends, including her and Aiden. Edgar Plinski was saved for last.

"Thank you for contacting our superior," Aiden said. "And for not shooting us."

Garcia smiled. "Glad I could help."

"What's going to happen to Albatross?" Charlie asked.

"We'll keep him safe in custody while we investigate Mr. Walsh's allegations. If they're true, Albatross will lose immunity and be sent to prison."

It made sense that he'd kept quiet about Walsh in order to protect himself from a murder charge.

"When are you going to get Enzo Romero?" Aiden asked.

"We heard he made a big power play today," Garcia said.

Charlie and Aiden exchanged a glance but said nothing.

"Thanks to the information you gave us," Garcia continued, "we're going to get a warrant and bring him in. After I get some rest."

"Thank you again for your help," Charlie said, shaking her hand.

Aiden did likewise. "There are four more inside. The dirty SWAT cops that ambushed us. Two are dead, including Devlin."

Garcia nodded. "This is proof that interagency cooperation works." She stepped past them inside.

"What now?" Charlie asked Aiden.

He circled his arm around her shoulders, and they started walking away from the hubbub of the scene. "Now we go back to our rented room in time for dinner. Henri's serving blue crab gumbo. We shower, make love and talk about my job offer at Camp Beauregard."

Being an instructor someday was always Aiden's goal. She couldn't give him children, but she could make sure he accepted his dream job. No way in the world would she take that away from him.

"There's nothing to talk about," Charlie said. "You're taking the job. End of discussion."

"Not so fast." He kissed her head. "If I take the job, we've got to talk about how to get you out there, too."

"Me?" She looked up at him, confused. "They're not going to make me an instructor and I'm not quitting."

He crushed his mouth down on hers, his palms sliding up and down her body, his strong arms pulling her against him so tightly she could scarcely breathe, and the worries swimming in her head dissolved.

Drawing his lips back, he smiled at her. "Where there's a will, there's a way, and when we're together, anything is possible. Have a little faith. In us."

Epilogue

The sun was setting, taking the natural light with it. Charlie grabbed another box from the back of the portable moving container that had been shipped from San Diego, and strode out into the steamy Louisiana air. The day had been long and hot and muggy, and the air-conditioning in their new house was on the fritz. An HVAC repairman wouldn't be able to come out for two days, and every time she turned around, it seemed like something else in the place had broken.

She'd be happier once the temperature dropped and Aiden came home from the Special Operations Group Tactical Center at Camp Beauregard.

Her new position there as a full-time SOG member assigned to one of the special teams didn't start for another two weeks. But she had a month of unused leave.

This was giving them a chance to settle in and find their baseline before his twelve-hour training days started and she deployed on a mission. Thankfully, Aiden hadn't fed into her worst fears and turned into a Neanderthal, demanding she not go out in the field without him. No, he was the best kind of man, a friend and partner. He trusted her to take care of herself.

Landing her a position so that they could be together had taken some finagling. Aiden told his supervisor that she was his fiancée, and since he didn't want to be a liar, he had popped the question.

For Charlie, she didn't need a ring or marriage or a piece of paper making things legal. She just needed Aiden. If going the traditional route kept them together, then she wasn't going to argue over a piece of jewelry and signing a license.

A car door slammed, and she spun around on the stairs leading up to the wraparound porch.

Aiden climbed out of his SUV with a bright smile on his face, and every single awful thing about the day melted away. As he hustled over to her, she set the box of dishes down on the porch. He reached out for her and she fell into his arms.

She kissed him, hungry and impatient. Ready to take his clothes off and lose herself in the feel of him. In his breath, the taste of him, the smell of him. While unpacking, she'd thought of nothing but undressing him and christening another room in the house.

To her surprise, she heard a motorcycle drawing closer. A single beam of light sliced through the trees lining the driveway, and a motorcycle coasted around the corner. Not one that was fast enough to race a Ducati, but it sure did look cool. And as bikes went, it was quiet on the gravel driveway. The guy parked behind Aiden's car, eased the kickstand in the down position and killed the engine.

"You didn't tell me we were having company," she said.

"It was a last-minute thing. I tried to call, but you didn't answer."

Her cell phone was in the kitchen on the counter, with music blasting. She must've been in the moving container when he called, and she hadn't thought to check for any missed messages.

The little things didn't come naturally, but Aiden cut her a lot of slack and encouraged her to do the same for herself.

They were in this together and would create rules that suited them. No need to talk of a wedding date until they were both ready. There wasn't even pressure to buy a dog.

But checking her phone for missed calls would have to be added to the list of rules.

The man took off his helmet and raked a hand through close-cropped light brown hair.

Clean-shaven with a streamlined, muscular physique and tattoos running the length of his arms, he had a thuggish vibe that spelled trouble. In Charlie's previous life, he would've been the perfect type for a one-night stand.

"Charlie, this is Horatio Haas. He works on one of the special teams."

"Please, call me Dutch," he said with an accent. Maybe from Chicago. He extended his hand.

Charlie shook it. "Why Dutch?" she asked.

"Why not when I've been saddled with a name like Horatio?" he said, and Charlie and Aiden both laughed. "In school, all the kids wanted to make fun of it, but once I started working out and calling myself Dutch, nobody tried to kick my butt."

He had a formidable presence. Not the kind of guy you'd want to mess with unless you wanted a broken jaw.

"I can see why you brought him by," Charlie said to Aiden.

"It's not just for my sparkling personality," Dutch said.

Aiden tightened his arm around her. "Your start date has been bumped up. You're replacing Dutch on the Fugitive Apprehension Response Team day after tomorrow."

Charlie was taken aback. Part of her was eager to get back to work, but the other part enjoyed these languid evenings with Aiden, neither of them on call, neither in any danger. "Why so suddenly?"

"I leave tomorrow," Dutch said. "Special assignment undercover. I've read the file on the high-priority asset, but I have some questions that the file can't answer. I was hoping you two could."

"What does that have to do with us?" Charlie asked.

"It's regarding the data breach in San Diego," Dutch said.

"We think we've found a way to possibly recover the Department of Justice hard drive that was stolen and prevent the sale of any more sensitive information. They want me to get close to the niece of the Los Chacales cartel leader. But I'll be working for your old boss, Will Draper. What can you tell me about him?"

Charlie rolled her eyes and blew out a harsh breath. "Nothing good. The only person Draper cares about is Draper. Rely on your own judgment, not his."

Aiden nodded. "This conversation is best done over drinks."

Lots and lots of drinks. "And dinner. I'm not much of a cook," Charlie said, "but I'm an expert at ordering good takeout."

"Were you told why you have to rush off so quickly?" Aiden asked.

"They said this is high priority and time sensitive. Apparently, there's a concern that the new identities of all the witnesses and the personal information of the marshals and their families in your region are going to be auctioned off to the highest bidder."

A chill ran down Charlie's spine. They knew the fallout of the data breach would far exceed Edgar Plinski, who was now in jail for the murder of Irene Guillory.

But no one would've imagined such sensitive information being auctioned off.

"Let's go inside. If there's anything we can tell you that might help you do your job, we're happy to share it," Charlie said, ushering Dutch in ahead of them.

She wrapped her arm around Aiden's waist, loving the feel of his immediate response to bring her closer, hold her tighter.

Their union was new and scary, but nothing had ever been more right. When they were together, the past didn't matter, the future was theirs to make of it whatever they wanted, and she was grateful for the present.

For the love and trust and respect between them that kept growing every day.

To some people, happiness was having a white picket fence, the marriage license and kids.

To Charlie, it was knowing that Aiden would kill to protect her and she would do the same for him. Come hell or high water, they had each other's back, and she wouldn't have it any other way.

Aiden kissed her, quick and sweet, but burning with desire. His fingers combed into her hair, locking her to him. Her heart thumped harder, filling with unfathomable joy. She'd never felt more loved or accepted in her life.

Here, with Aiden, she was safe. She was home.

* * * * *

For the love and trust and respect between them that kept growing day by day.

To some people happiness was finding a warm pocket where she had slipped inside, and tried...

To cherish. She knew now that Aidan would kill to protect her, and she would do the same for him. Come hell or high water they would have each other's backs, and she wouldn't have it any other way.

Aidan kissed her, quick and sweet, but not quite warm enough. His fingers tangled in her hair as he leaned in to him. Her changed maiden, filling with undisturbed joy. She'd never felt more loved or accepted in her life.

Here, with Aidan, she was safe. She was home.

* * * * *

COLTON 911: AGENT
BY HER SIDE

DEBORAH FLETCHER MELLO

To my agent, Pattie Steele-Perkins

You continue to push me to step outside my comfort zone.

Your encouragement has been the wind beneath my wings.

I soar because you make me believe I can. Thank you!

Chapter One

"Happy birthday, Special Agent Winston!"

FBI Special Agent Cooper Winston looked up from the files on his desk. "Thank you, Agent Miller," he said, tossing a smile at the regal black woman who stood in the doorway of his office. "I thought I'd done a good job of keeping that a secret."

She chuckled softly. "I think you're good. I just remembered that you and my youngest daughter share the same birthday. She turned thirty-four today, but don't tell her I told you that!"

Cooper gestured for her to enter, pointing her to an upholstered chair in front of his desk. He and Claire Miller had worked together since he'd been transferred from the FBI's main office in Detroit to Grand Rapids on Ionia Avenue. She had backed him up on his first case and they'd been good friends ever since. He couldn't imagine the resident agency without her bright personality keeping them all on their toes.

Cooper laughed. "Your secret is safe with me!"

"So, how old are you now?" the older woman questioned, eyeing him with a raised brow.

Cooper smiled a second time. "This year makes forty."

"A milestone birthday! We should be celebrating that with cake and champagne in the break room."

He shook his head and waved a hand. "That's what we're not going to do," he said. "You and I are going to keep this between us and remain good friends as we do."

A bright smile filled her dark face. "I understand completely. I'll be a year closer to retirement and my pension on my next birthday."

"How long have you been with the agency?"

"Twenty-six years next month."

"Wow! Now you've definitely earned that pension but you don't look anywhere close to qualifying for retirement. We might need to check your birth certificate," he said teasingly.

"Aren't you sweet! They say a woman shouldn't share her age, but when you consider the alternative, I'm proud to tell people I'm fifty-four, almost fifty-five years young."

"I'd be proud, too, if I looked as good!"

Claire laughed warmly. "So, how is that beautiful baby boy of yours?"

Cooper's smile widened. He reached for the framed photo on his desk, passing it to the woman. "Alfie is doing very well. He keeps me on my toes!"

"Isn't he precious! Look how big he's gotten! I swear, they grow up too fast."

"No one warns you about that when they're born."

She laughed. "No, they surely don't." She passed the image back to him. "I hear you caught the RevitaYou case! How's that going?"

Cooper nodded, pointing to the stack of files he'd been reviewing when she knocked on his door. "I did. And it's not. I could have used your expertise tracking down my bad guy but they tell me you're hunting down that serial killer."

"Bagged him earlier this morning. We caught him in the act and now I have a boatload of paperwork to d and a trial to help the DA prepare for before I catch another assignment."

"Nice work, Agent!"

"Thank you. I appreciate that. Especially coming from you. I'll get out of your hair," Claire said. "I just wanted to say hello and acknowledge your day."

"I really appreciate that. Thank you."

"You're one of the good ones, Cooper. Keep doing what you do!"

As Claire made her exit, Cooper turned back to the paperwork that was proving to be problematic. Despite the information in each of the file folders, he was no closer to finding the now infamous Wes Matthews than he'd been when the case was first dropped in his lap.

Wes Matthews had been the brain trust behind RevitaYou, a supplement that promised to be the fountain of youth for users and a pot of gold for investors. The drug itself had been created by renowned chemist Landon Street. Initial forensic tests showed that RevitaYou was chock-full of vitamins and minerals, but also tested positive for ricin, an extremely deadly poison.

Ricin was found naturally in castor beans. It could also be made from the waste material left over from processing castor oil. Street had discovered that the initial oil compound he created did wonders for smoothing wrinkles, but somewhere along the way, the self-professed healer became "the Toxic Scientist," as the media dubbed him, doing harm to those he claimed to want to help. He had purposely poisoned people. Multiple deaths had been attributed to RevitaYou and both Street and Matthews were now in the wind. But not before Wes Matthews had disappeared with millions from unsuspecting backers in a pyramid investment scheme. Now, finding both Matthews and Street was at the top of Cooper's to-do list.

He sighed, warm breath blowing past his lips. Frustration furrowed his thick brow. Since the start of this case he'd hit one dead end after another. Before Claire had walked into his office he'd been ready to fling the folders across the room. Now, he just needed to refocus, get back to work, and hope there were no more distractions.

"FBI TIP LINE. How can we help you?" Kiely Colton said. She did her best to keep her expression staid, although her disposition that day was less than stellar.

"Is this the tip line?" a woman questioned.

Kiely tempered her tone. "Yes, ma'am. You've reached the FBI tip line. How can we help you?" she repeated.

"If what I tell you gets someone arrested, will I get a reward?"

"That all depends on what you report, ma'am."

"Good, 'cause I know some things!"

"Well, let's start with your name. Who am I speaking with?"

"My name?"

"Yes, ma'am. I'll need your name and address and a good contact number to reach you in case one of our agents needs to speak with you further."

"Let me call you back. I need to check some things," the woman said as she disconnected the line.

Kiely rolled her eyes skyward. Most of the calls she'd taken that morning had gone similarly. Concerned citizens were more interested in reward money than helping to catch criminals. One man even had the audacity to insist they pay him in advance for information he didn't yet have, about a robbery that had never been reported.

Claire laughed. "It's like that most days. I think it's something in the water."

"Or a full moon," Kiely said with a chuckle.

"We appreciate you coming in to help out. Most of our agents are out in the field. If this keeps up we're going to have to hire additional staff."

"It's not a problem," Kiely answered. "I might be a freelance PI most of the time, but my motives are purely selfish if I'm honest with you."

"You still trying to find your foster brother?"

Kiely nodded. "Yeah. The last time any of us spoke to him he was scared and on the run. Getting him home is the surest way to keep him safe."

"I understand. Let us know if there is anything we can do to help."

Kiely gave the woman a wave as she replaced her headset and adjusted it against her ears. She worked for the family business, Colton Investigations. Her services were often utilized by the local police, the FBI and sometimes the CIA, because she had a reputation for always getting results. Kiely wasn't above circumventing the rules to get the job done. Because she was trusted and required no handholding, she was routinely invited into the FBI's inner sanctum and given privileges few others were granted.

For the moment, Kiely volunteering to answer the phones was all about helping Brody Higgins. Brody was family to her and her five siblings, ever since their father, Graham Colton, had taken him under his wing. Before then, Brody had been lost in the foster system. He'd been a smart kid with a string of misdemeanors who found himself in the wrong place at the wrong time. When he caught a murder charge for a crime he didn't commit, their father, a prominent Michigan district attorney, had declined to prosecute, taking him into their home instead. Love and family had turned Brody's life around...or until recently.

Now Brody was tangled up in the RevitaYou scandal and running from people intent on doing him harm.

Borrowing money from a loan shark to invest in RevitaYou then defaulting on that loan had made him a target. When Capital X, the predatory lending organization who'd fronted money to Brody had sent two goons to collect payment and he'd not been able to make good on his debt, they'd broken his fingers, promising to break more the next time they had to pay him a visit. Finding Wes Matthews, the charismatic criminal who'd drawn Brody into the whole mess, was a high priority for her. Kiely answered another call, and then a third and fourth. The tip line was suddenly flooded with incoming calls, pulling her attention from thoughts of Brody and Matthews.

Two hours, umpteen calls and only one credible tip later, and Kiely was ready to hang up her headset. Taking a quick glance down to the Apple Watch on her wrist, she realized it wasn't yet twelve noon. She needed to take a break and just as she pushed her chair from the desk, one last call rang for her attention. She sighed, pushing the button to answer the line.

"FBI tip line. How can we help you?"

A man's voice, deep and slightly muffled, sounded in her ear. "I have information about Wes Matthews, the Capital X and RevitaYou banker. I know where he is."

"Can you tell me your name, sir?" Kiely asked. She took a deep breath and held it. Goose bumps had risen on her arm after hearing Wes Matthews's name.

"No," the man said, his tone curt and short. "You just need to know that he's hiding out at Reeds Lake, off Lakeside Drive. There's a small, white cottage off the dirt road. He's there, but I don't know for how long."

"Sir, do you..." Kiely started, but a dial tone sounded in her ear, the caller disconnecting the call.

Kiely typed the information she'd received into the call screen, then jumped from her seat. Something about that tip registered on her radar and suddenly had her on edge. This was the one lead she planned to personally vet.

After conferring with one of the technicians she flung herself down the short length of corridor to the corner office with the door closed. Despite wanting to just take off, there were protocols Kiely still had to follow if she wanted to maintain a relationship with the FBI, and updating the agent handling the case was one of them. Unfortunately, the agent she needed to update was Cooper Winston, a man who riled her nerves more than most. He was way too straitlaced and slightly anal. She imagined he probably gave himself a headache due to always being so inflexible.

She knocked on the door but didn't wait to be welcomed inside. Kiely draped her frustration around her like a bold blanket. She couldn't begin to understand how such a handsome man could be so infuriating. And he was definitely handsome! His features were chiseled, looking like he'd been carved out of alabaster stone. With eyes that were oceanic blue and thick, reddish-blond hair combed back to tame the natural curl, he looked like a Celtic god. Or what Kiely imagined a Celtic deity should look like. Despite his good looks, he always seemed to take great joy in pushing her buttons and now his too-calm demeanor had her wanting to pull her hair out.

She moved further into his office and dropped down into the chair opposite him. She bit back the expletive on the tip of her tongue, instead focusing on the look he was giving her. There was something in his eyes that suddenly felt like a serious punch to her gut. Her stomach did a slight flip and she found it disconcerting, unable to explain it if she had to. She took a deep breath and held it, then blew it slowly past her lips, watching as he crossed his arms over his chest and leaned back against the metal desk.

As HIS DOOR flew open and Kiely Colton entered, Cooper looked up, his eyes widening in surprise at the sight of her. Although he had heard she was in the office volunteering her services, he hadn't expected to see her. The two had history and little of it had been positive. They'd butted heads often when Kiely circumvented the rules to work a case her own way. He worked by the books, moving from *A* to *Z* without skipping *E*, *F* and *G*. Kiely Colton acted like she didn't know how to count from one to one hundred, her mathematical manipulations all over the place to get the right answers. He found her tendency to leap before looking infuriating. She was reckless, was rarely a team player, or nice, and he knew that behavior could put others in harm's way.

"What's going on?" he said, resting his ink pen against the yellow-lined notepad he'd been writing on.

"We've got a lead on Wes Matthews. I'm going to go check it out."

Cooper stood. "No, you're not."

"Excuse me?"

As Kiely's incredulous expression exploded, Cooper noted confusion, frustration and a hint of hostility detonating in real time. He lifted a brow as she continued.

"Are you kidding me, right now? I need to…"

He cut her off, stalling the rant he felt coming. "Calm down, Ms. Colton, and tell me what you know."

"We're wasting time," she snapped.

"And you're still a civilian," he quipped. "So, please, take a breath, and update me! So, what do you have?" he asked, his tone even and inquisitive.

"We just got a tip that Wes Matthews is hiding out in a cabin on Reeds Lake. I asked one of your agents to get me a satellite image and I want to go check it out. This might be the break we've been looking for."

"I'm inclined to think your tip is a hoax. We've gotten credible information that says Matthews is in the Caribbean, well out of our jurisdiction. He'd be a fool to still be here in Grand Rapids."

"Then he's a fool. My gut is telling me that the caller might be credible and it's well worth checking out."

He shook his head. "I think it's a waste of time and resources."

"You do know that I don't need your permission to follow up on a lead, right? That this is just a courtesy? Obviously, if I lay eyes on him, I'll immediately call for backup." Kiely's tone was defiant and determined. She moved onto her feet. "Because I am going!"

No woman should be so lovely and so darn exasperating, Cooper thought as he stood watching her. He hated to admit it, but he had honestly tried to forget how attractive she was. But having her in his space had made that harder for him to do. She wore black denim. The matching pants and jacket were flattering to her petite frame. The white blouse beneath it was crisply ironed and an FBI visitor's badge hung from a lanyard around her neck. Her makeup was sparse, just a hint of eyeliner and clear lip gloss complementing her crystal-clear complexion. Bangs and a shoulder-length bob highlighted her lush brown hair.

Cooper found the pout on her face unnerving, stirring heat in places that he was finding difficult to ignore. He shook the sensation away, shifting his focus to the door behind her. Despite his conjecture, she was determined to do what she wanted, whether he agreed or not. And he didn't agree, believing she was headed out on another wild-goose chase.

"Fine," he snapped as she moved toward the exit. "But I'm going with you."

"Excuse you?" Kiely stopped short, turning around to give him a look. "I don't need a babysitter."

"That's not why I'm going. The FBI received a tip and an FBI agent will follow up on that tip. Chain of command and all that," he said, moving his hand in a dismissive gesture.

"That's a stretch, don't you think?"

"I think that you interfering could be considered dangerous. What if something happens? Like you see him and he gets away because you didn't have backup? I'd hate to charge you with obstructing my investigation. So, you will not go without me going with you. Give me ten minutes and we can head that way."

Kiely shook her head, her frustration knee-deep. "Fine," she finally snapped. "But I'll drive."

By THE TIME she was outside the office, standing at the bank of elevators, Kiely was not happy about the turn of events. She was very much a lone wolf when it came to the cases she investigated. Cooper's insistence that he join her was not sitting well and she felt like there would inevitably be a conflict with what she would need to do and what he would want her to do.

She watched him as he maneuvered around the office, moving from cubicle to cubicle. He dropped files onto desks and delegated orders. He had changed out of his black suit and was wearing khaki slacks and a dark blue nylon jacket with the prominent yellow FBI logo. She had always thought him attractive, but she hadn't realized just how gorgeous he really was. Because he *was* gorgeous. He was a tall powerhouse of defined muscle. His chiseled features and ginger-red hair made him model-pretty. His beard and mustache had been meticulously trimmed and his eyes were the most mesmerizing ocean blue.

As Kiely stared at him intently, his cell phone rang. He paused in the middle of the aisle and answered the call. The conversation was brief and clearly concerning. Kiely felt herself tense as the color drained from his face. He suddenly rushed toward where she stood, pushing past her as he hurried to the exit.

"What's wrong?" Kiely questioned, hurrying after him.

Cooper shot her a quick look. Resounding fear echoed in his voice as he answered, "My son Alfie is missing!"

Chapter Two

They were a few good minutes away from the preschool Cooper's young son attended. So, focused on getting there, Cooper seemed oblivious when Kiely slid into the passenger seat of his car. She said little to him, not even when he blew through three stop signs and barely stopped at the red light at the corner of Ionia and Fulton Streets. His frustration was palpable and growing exponentially. Kiely could only begin to imagine what he had to be feeling.

"Tell me about your son," she said softly, wanting to help center his focus.

Cooper told her he had chosen the Goodman Children's Center by default. Alfie had only been a few months old when he'd found the name of the day care and preschool in his late wife's papers. She had made a list of preschools shortly after discovering she was pregnant with their first child. The Goodman name had been circled in red at the very top of the page. "That was just like Sara, to make plans for our son before he was even born," Cooper shared with Kiely.

Sara had been his first love. They'd been the best of friends in college, both having an affinity for old movies and buttered popcorn tossed with M&M's candies. When their relationship became romantic it had surprised them both. One day they'd been bitterly debating the writings of William Faulkner and the next he was reading her John Keats as they fed each other strawberries slathered with whipped cream. Marriage had been a mere technicality, defining their relationship more so for others than themselves. From the moment they had claimed each other's hearts, nothing and no one could have kept them apart.

Sara had wanted children from the moment they said their vows. But getting pregnant hadn't been easy. There had been three miscarriages and both had given up hope, declaring themselves enough for each other. For a moment they had considered adoption but just days after completing the application, they discovered Sara was pregnant once again.

The pregnancy was immediately labeled high risk and his beautiful wife had been confined to their bed for the duration. By the start of her third trimester she'd made lists for everything. Lists for schools. Lists for doctors. Lists for everything she hoped for their baby.

Surprisingly, labor and delivery had been a breeze. Alfred Cooper Winston arrived in the wee hours of August first, bellowing at the top of his tiny lungs. Cooper's last memory of them together as a family, joyous and happy, was when they laid the newborn on his wife's chest and she introduced herself, and him, to their newborn son. Minutes later, little Alfie was snatched from his mother's arms and hurried off to the nursery as they rolled Sara to the operating room. The doctors were unable to stall the postpartum bleeding. Sara had died on the table, never able to hold her young son again.

Cooper struggled with the memory and to keep driving. He could see Kiely fighting back her own tears out of the corner of his eye. "It was a rough time for me," he said.

"I'm so sorry for your loss," Kiely answered.

Cooper shrugged his broad shoulders. "After that I had

to take care of Alfie and he became my entire world."
He choked back a sob and when Kiely reached out for
his hand, gently squeezing the back of his fingers, it
took every ounce of his fortitude to contain the tears that
pressed against his lashes. Her touch was consoling and
warm and there was comfort in her touch that he had not
expected.

COOPER TURNED IN the entrance gates, speeding past the
playground of sandboxes and swing sets. When he reached
the administration building and the parking lot, he pulled
into the fire lane and shut down his vehicle. A team of
local police cars lined the driveway, uniformed officers
milling around the grass and steps outside the entrance.

Kiely followed on his heels as he hurried into the building, flashing his federal badge at the officer who stood to
block his way. "It's my son who's missing!" he snapped.

"The parents are here," Kiely heard someone say into
a radio, the person on the other end responding with an
admonishment to let them enter. She tossed Cooper a look
but he seemed to not have heard the comment, blinded by
the emotion that had him in a vise grip.

The school's administrator met them at the door to the
office. "Mr. Winston, I am so sorry," she said. "We're
doing everything we can to…"

"What happened? Where's my son?" Cooper snapped
harshly.

The other woman repeated herself. "I'm so, so sorry!
He was outside for recess and someone just grabbed him."

"How did this person get on campus? And who was supposed to be watching my son?" Cooper's voice rose two
octaves, his emotion explosive. "I need answers. I want to
know who saw what happened!"

A plainclothes detective rushed to Cooper's side. He

held out his hand. "Agent Winston, my name is Detective Cranston. Will you come with me, please? We're reviewing the security tapes, and I need to know if you recognize anyone."

Kiely followed, standing at Cooper's elbow as they moved into the administrator's office. A team of police officers were all standing before a small video screen. Cooper pushed forward for a front row view.

There was no audio and the footage was grainy, but there was no missing the man standing outside by the gate that led into the toddler play area. He was dressed in a security guard's uniform and appeared to be on the job, wearing a ball cap, the brim pulled down low over his eyes. You couldn't see his face, but he was sizeable, with a beer gut and thick arms.

As the teacher and her assistant shuffled a group of eight kids from the play area back into the building, the man rushed forward and grabbed little Alfie. A dark sedan pulled up beside the two and just like that the child and the man were gone, the teacher screaming as she ran down the driveway after them.

"I tried to stop them," the young woman sobbed from across the room, where she sat talking to an officer. "I tried!"

"Does he look familiar to you, Agent?" Detective Cranston questioned, pausing the video on the image of the kidnapper.

Cooper shook his head. "No, I don't recognize him. But the uniform's off. The color is wrong. It's more army green. You can buy them at any military supply store. The security officers here wear a more military blue." Cooper sighed. "Do we know anything else?"

"No, sir," the detective said, "but we've issued an Amber Alert and all of my men are doing what we can to find your son. Right now, though, we need to ask you some questions." He gestured toward Kiely. "Another officer will speak with your wife."

Kiely shook her head. "I'm not his wife. I'm a private investigator."

The man narrowed his gaze and shot her a suspicious glance. "A private investigator?"

"Ms. Colton is partnered with the FBI on a case we're working," Cooper said, shifting his eyes back to the detective. "We were on another investigation when I got the call. Ms. Colton doesn't know my son."

The detective nodded. "Colton? We have a Sadie Colton working the case. She's an investigator. You're not related by chance, are you?"

Kiely said, "Sisters. Is Sadie here?"

He nodded. "Outside, I think."

Kiely pressed a warm palm against Cooper's forearm. "I'm going to go see what I can find out from my sister," she said, her voice dropping to a whisper meant only for his ears. "Are you going to be okay?"

"I'm not going to be okay until I get my son back," he muttered.

She locked gazes with Cooper. The look he gave her spoke volumes, the hurt in his heart monumental. He was clearly struggling to contain his emotion, wanting to rage and cry and still be strong for his son. Not wanting to be seen as weak to his colleagues. His concern for his child pulled at her heartstrings. Cooper the father wasn't nearly as hard and cold as Cooper the agent. His determination to find his son was impressive. She liked this Cooper a lot.

As they continued to stare into each other's eyes, it was a silent exchange that passed between them, words not needed. Kiely nodded her understanding. She squeezed his arm one last time.

"I'll be right back," she said softly.

Moving back to the parking lot, Kiely found her sister taking photos of tire tracks, the playground, and the landscape.

When Sadie looked up from what she was doing, she was surprised to see her. "Hey there! What are you doing here?"

"Working."

Sadie looked confused.

"Long story short, Agent Winston and I were headed to check on a lead when he got the call about his son. I tagged along to see if there was anything I could do to help."

Sadie nodded. A former police rookie turned crime-scene investigator, Sadie approached all her cases pragmatically. "This was brazen. Broad daylight, other children and staff right there. Whoever snatched the kid wanted to be seen." She pointed at the multitude of cameras positioned to capture everything that moved. "There was nothing haphazard about this. They were sending his father a message. Any idea who might have a vendetta against him?"

Kiely shook her head. "He's a stickler for the law. It could be anyone he's ever crossed paths with. And I have no doubt, that list is miles long."

"What case were you investigating?"

"The FBI got a lead on Wes Matthews's whereabouts. We were headed to check it out."

"I'll keep my fingers crossed. The sooner we get Matthews, the sooner we can get Brody home."

"We haven't talked in a while. Everything good with you?" Kiely asked.

Sadie tossed a look over her shoulder, making sure none of the other officers could hear her. "Tate wants to elope," she said casually.

The comment hit Kiely like a sledgehammer. Tate Greer was Sadie's fiancé. As far as Kiely was concerned, Tate was the product of bad sperm. He was egotistical and arrogant but deep down he was a coward who used others to make himself relevant. Everything about the man was a monumental red flag for the rest of the family. None of them were as charmed by him as their sister was. The two were like oil and water... snake oil and holy water, that is. But Tate had a viselike grip on her sister's heart. Kiely swallowed, slowly digesting the pronouncement. "Elope?"

Sadie nodded. "He wants us to sneak off to Las Vegas to get married."

"What happened to you two having a Christmas wedding?"

"Tate changed his mind."

"But you've always wanted a big wedding with bridesmaids and a ridiculous cake and a big white dress and all of us there with you. That's all you've ever talked about since we were all kids and you had a crush on Riley's friend Preston. Preston Richards with the Coke bottle glasses and that cowlick thing that always stuck up on his head. Remember?"

"I do, but Tate doesn't have any family and he thinks since we're going to be family that we should start our life together with it just being the two of us."

"You know how that sounds, right?"

"I think it's sweet! He's such a romantic and he just wants it to be a private celebration for the two of us and then we'll share it with everyone else afterward."

Nothing about it sounded romantic to Kiely. It sounded like Tate was trying to manipulate her sister. He tended to be overbearing and possessive. Because Sadie saw him with blinders on, Kiely found it best to say as little as possible about him when she could, not wanting to push her sister away and tighten the hold Tate had on her.

"What are you going to do?" Kiely questioned.

She made a mental note to call their other two sisters the first chance she got. An intervention was needed, she thought to herself. Sadie deserved so much better and Tate was not it. He professed to be in the import-export business but even that was questionable. Everything about Tate felt slimy, the man not having an ounce of substance equal to Sadie's intellect and compassion. But Sadie, who'd always been very much a late bloomer when it came to men and sex, apparently saw nothing but golden opportunities with the man.

"And don't tell anyone," Sadie said, seeming to read Kiely's mind. "I still don't know what I plan to do."

"As long as you don't plan to do anything before we have a chance to talk more," Kiely responded.

Movement by the school doors drew both their attention, cutting their conversation short. Cooper had stepped outside, pulling his cell phone to his ear as the door slammed closed behind him. He stepped away from the two officers standing guard. Something about his tense body language triggered Kiely's radar.

"I need to run," she said, tossing her sister a look. "I'll call you later."

"Is that the father?" Sadie asked, looking toward where Kiely was staring.

"Yeah."

Sadie hummed. "Interesting...very interesting."

Kiely cut her eye at her sibling. "Goodbye, Sadie!"

"Love you, too!"

THE IMAGE ON Cooper's cellphone screen read NO CALLER ID. Reception inside the school had been spotty and so he'd stepped outside. "Hello?"

"Is this Agent Winston?" Cooper didn't recognize the

female voice on the other end and the private number she was calling him on wasn't one he gave out readily. His anxiety level suddenly increased tenfold and he felt the knot in his midsection tighten.

"Who is this?" Cooper asked.

"I have your son. If you want to see him again, drop the search for Wes Matthews," she said.

"Who is this?" Cooper said, his voice rising as his pulse hammered. He could feel his pulse thumping loudly in his head, his heart about to burst from his chest.

"Drop the search," she repeated, "if you want your kid back." Then she hung up, disconnecting the call.

Cooper leaned forward, his hands on his knees. He could barely breathe and his vision blurred. He felt like he might vomit and suddenly he wanted to hit something. He turned and kicked the wooden handrail. Hard. When he'd dislodged one of the balusters, he stopped. He inhaled deeply and then again. He couldn't believe this was happening. That someone would go after his family to get to him. Keeping his son safe was the single most important responsibility he had, and suddenly he felt like he had failed. He had let Alfie down and he imagined his baby boy had to be petrified, not understanding what was going on. Cooper struggled not to rage. He needed a moment to collect himself and his thoughts to figure out what his next steps should be.

He suddenly slapped the smartphone against his leg just as Kiely reached his side. "Who was that?" she asked, as he stood up to stare at her.

"I don't know but she said she had Alfie and that I need to stop searching for Wes Matthews if I want him back."

"She actually mentioned Matthews?"

He nodded.

KIELY'S MIND WAS suddenly racing. First the FBI got a tip about where Matthews might be hiding out, and now this. She didn't believe in coincidences, and as the two stood staring at each other she realized he didn't either. He suddenly started texting fiercely, almost pounding the keys on his phone with his thumbs.

"It's a long shot," he said, "but I'll see if our techs can track this. But I'm betting it was a burner. There was no caller ID and the call barely lasted sixty seconds."

"I'll understand if you need to stay here, but I'm going to follow up on that tip. If someone doesn't want us to find Wes Matthews, then we need to find him. That may also help us find your son."

Cooper nodded. "I was thinking the same thing. But if anything happens here, Detective Cranston can call me. You're not going alone and if there's any chance that this could lead me to my son I want to be there."

There was a moment of hesitation as Kiely stared at him. Cooper the agent and Cooper the father were holding hands, both intent on finding his son. She admired his determination, reminded of her own father who would have moved mountains to protect her and her siblings. Knowing there would be no talking him out of it, Kiely nodded her agreement as Cooper dialed a number on his phone.

"Who are you calling?" she questioned.

"Something tells me we might need some help," he said.

Kiely met the intense look he was giving her. Having decided to press forward, he had determination emitting from his eyes. She had high regard for his devotion to his son and his job. A lesser man would have been brought to his knees. It moved her and she had greater respect for him.

She nodded again. "Backup is good," she said.

Chapter Three

An hour later Cooper had assembled an entire team. Grand Rapids Police Detective Emmanuel Iglesias and Lieutenant Tripp McKellar stood with them in the parking lot of a local Realtor's office located one mile from their target location: Matthews's alleged hideout on Reeds Lake. A ten-member SWAT team stood by, waiting for instructions.

"Kiely, have you met Lieutenant McKellar?" Emmanuel asked.

Kiely and Emmanuel had been acquainted for some time. Emmanuel was engaged to her twin sister. This was not their first time working together, and she appreciated having him by her side…but she'd never met Tripp.

"I don't believe I have," Kiely said. She extended her hand. "Kiely Colton. It's a pleasure."

"Kiely is Pippa's twin," said Emmanuel. "She's also a private investigator."

"The pleasure is all mine," Lieutenant McKellar responded. "Your reputation precedes you."

"Not sure if that's a good thing!" Kiely said with a nervous chuckle. She could only begin to imagine the stories her sister and Emmanuel might have told him about her, the two over exaggerating her antics.

Cooper looked from her to the other man. Kiely noticed

his jaw tighten slightly, as if their small talk was beginning to annoy him. "Everyone ready?" he asked.

There was an exchange of looks, the trio nodding their heads.

"More than ready," Kiely said. "Are you sure you want to do this?" She asked the question, concerned that him worrying about his son, he might not be as focused as they needed him to be.

"I'll be fine," Cooper answered. And for the most part he was, he thought. They didn't know how credible the tip was or if it would lead them to Alfie, but doing something felt better than sitting around waiting for others to report back to him. He gave her a nod of his head.

"Then let's do this," she said.

The four drove to the end of the dirt road and parked the black SUV. The SWAT team members followed. Exiting the vehicle, their plan was to walk the short distance to the home and execute a knock and enter once they assessed the situation. There had been no time for a search warrant, and no one wanted to risk violating anyone's rights and blowing the case. The SWAT team members would hold their position until needed.

The area was wooded, tall pine trees decorating the landscape and affording them a measure of cover. As they made their way to the small white cottage with the shuttered windows, Cooper gestured for Emmanuel to take one side and Tripp to take the other. When he motioned for Kiely to fall in behind him, she thought to argue but didn't.

Movement by the window caught her eye. A woman shuffled past once and then a second time in the opposite direction. All the windows were open, a slight breeze blowing their sheer white curtains aside. The sound of a child crying echoed through the air.

"Enough," the woman said, her loud tone filtering out

the kitchen window. "I said I'd get you a snack. You need to stop that damn crying."

Her brusque manner only made the child cry harder.

"It's Alfie," Cooper whispered.

He took a step and Kiely grabbed the back of his jacket. The look she gave him spoke volumes. She understood him wanting to rush in but they needed to proceed cautiously. They didn't want anyone to get hurt, most especially his little boy. Until they could assess who and how many persons were inside, they needed to stand down.

Cooper nodded his understanding, inhaling deeply to quell his anxiety. Moving swiftly, they approached the home prudently. Kiely took cover behind a tree as Cooper took the steps, his weapon drawn. Inside, the child suddenly cried out as if in pain. His little scream was gut-wrenching, even to Kiely. Evidently unable to contain himself a moment longer Cooper became less an agent and more a father as he rushed the door, Kiely covering his back.

Shots, fired from the inside and through the front entrance, sounded one after the other.

Bang!

Bang!

Bang!

All three shots splintered the wood door and hit Cooper square in the chest. The blow sent him backward down the stairs as Kiely screamed his name.

THE MOMENT WAS suddenly surreal. Shots were fired in the rear yard of the home. The child crying inside sounded hysterical. Kiely moved swiftly to the bottom of the steps to check on Cooper. Blood had begun to pool behind his head. She searched for a pulse and nodded at Lieutenant McKellar who knelt beside her. The lieutenant radioed for backup and an ambulance as Kiely continued up the steps and into the home.

Clearing the first two rooms, she rushed to the kitchen, arriving at the back door just as a woman dressed from head to toe in black jumped onto an older model Kawasaki motorcycle and took off through the line of pine trees. Emmanuel jumped into the back of a black SUV, the police in pursuit. Moving swiftly back into the house, Kiely found Alfie huddled in the bathtub, his little arms wrapped around his knees as he rocked back and forth. He was so tiny, she thought, and he looked fragile. Her heart burst, a wave of emotion flooding her spirit as she eyed him. She suddenly wanted to scoop him up into her arms and hug him like her mother use to hug her when she was afraid.

Kiely secured her weapon and held up her hands as if she were surrendering. She waved her fingers, doing jazz hands.

"Hi there," she said softly. "You must be Alfie."

His eyes widened at the mention of his name. But fear still emanated from his eyes.

Kiely knelt beside the tub, meeting the child at eye level. "Alfie, my name is Kiely. I'm a friend of your daddy. I'd like to be your friend, too."

The little boy's eyes were still locked on her. He pulled his thumb into his mouth and continued to rock.

She looked around the room. "This place isn't very nice, is it?" She made a funny face, wiggling her nose. "Would you like to come with me, Alfie?" she said.

There was a moment of hesitation as the child seemed to be considering his options and then he reached both arms out, standing to wrap them around her neck. Kiely blew a warm sigh of relief as she lifted him up into her arms and hugged him tightly. "That's a good baby." By the time Kiely reached the front door and the steps, little Alfie had fallen asleep on her shoulder.

She moved to the ambulance just as they lifted Cooper inside. "Is he okay?" she questioned. His eyes were closed and his breathing seemed labored. Not knowing the extent of his injuries, she could feel her fear rising swiftly, her heart beginning to beat rapidly. She wasn't sure if he was asleep, unconscious, or perched on the edge of his deathbed.

The EMS responder nodded. "He took a hard hit to the back of his head when he fell. He might have a concussion and he's definitely going to need stitches. And today was his lucky day. His vest caught the bullets. But he's going to feel that tomorrow and will probably be sore for a few days."

Kiely blew a soft sigh. She was flooded with a wave of relief at the good news. She tightened her hold on the little boy who would wake up needing his daddy, grateful that would be able to happen.

Stepping up into the ambulance Kiely reached for his hand. She leaned down to whisper into his ear. "Alfie's here, Cooper," she said. "We found him and he's safe."

His eyes fluttered open, closed, then opened a second time. He struggled to focus as he squeezed her fingers tightly. The faintest smile pulled at his lips. He reached a shaky hand out to touch his son, pressing his fingers to Alfie's back. Relief visibly flooded his body.

Cooper sputtered as he struggled to get his words out. "Don't...don't leave...don't leave him, Kiely. Please...don't leave him."

"He's safe," she answered. "I'm going with you both to the hospital so he can be checked out, but he's fine."

Cooper shook his head. His eyes were wide, a hint of desperation shimmering in the oceanic orbs. His grip on her fingers was almost crushing. "Promise…please! Don't let my son out of your sight," he implored.

Kiely nodded her head. "I promise," she said softly as she tightened her grip on the little boy. "I won't take my eyes off him."

ALFIE SLEPT SO soundly that Kiely wasn't sure if she should be nervous or not. He really was a cute little thing, she thought as she sat by the hospital crib staring down at him. He had a head of wavy blond hair, the chubbiest cheeks flushed a warm shade of pink, and his father's blue eyes. He smiled in his sleep, seeming to dream peacefully.

Dr. Mara Finley, the resident pediatrician at Butterworth Hospital, had decided to keep him overnight for observation, wanting to ensure that all was well with Alfie after his traumatic experience. He'd had a warm sponge bath, eaten grapes and spaghetti for supper, then had lay back in Kiely's lap as he watched an episode of some cartoon called *Peppa Pig* until he drifted back to sleep.

As promised, Kiely had not left his side since he'd been admitted. A nurse had been kind enough to give her an update on his father. Cooper had two cracked ribs, twelve stitches to close the gash in the back of his head and a confirmed concussion. According to her sources, he, too, was sleeping soundly.

Standing, she pulled a pale yellow blanket up over Alfie's shoulders. He'd kicked his covers off and the room had a chill. Continuing to watch him, his bottom lip quivering slightly, Kiely found herself awed by the turn of events. Of the women in her family, her sisters often joked that Kiely wouldn't know a maternal instinct if it stood up and slapped her. Growing up she had not been interested in playing with dolls and as an adult wasn't particularly fond of most children. In her mind, babies were like mini aliens and any place children gathered en masse was free birth control. It usually took less than an hour of them screaming and crying for her to dismiss the idea of kids in her life. Babysitting anyone's offspring had never been on her bucket list of things to do...before now.

She sat back in the pushback recliner, engaging the footrest as she lifted her legs and settled down for the night. She'd stay, she thought, only because she'd given Cooper her word. Tomorrow she'd have to rethink her plans to find Wes Matthews.

"Hi!"

"Hi!"

"Hi!"

The tiniest voice pierced her dreams and when Kiely opened one eye to see where it was coming from Alfie Winston was standing at the rail of the crib staring down at her.

When he saw that she was awake, the brightest smile pulled full and wide across his little face. "Hi!" he chirped again.

Kiely smiled and sat upright. "Good morning! How are you?" She stretched her arms out and then stood up, moving to the side of the crib. "You're looking good, kiddo!" She brushed a lock of curls from his eyes.

He bounced up and down. "Pan-pakes, peas?"

Kiely paused for a split second trying to ascertain what he was asking her. "Pancakes? You want pancakes?"

Alfie bounced again. "Peas! Pan-pakes!" he exclaimed, giggling excitedly.

"Pancakes are his favorite breakfast food." Cooper's voice suddenly came from the direction of the doorway. Kiely turned to look and saw a nurse pushing him in a wheelchair. "And he remembered to say please! I'm impressed."

Kiely turned toward him. "Good morning!"

"Dad-dy!" Alfie gushed, jumping up and down excitedly. "Dad-dy! Dad-dy!"

Cooper stood, moving to his son's side and lifting him into his arms. He kissed the child's cheek and hugged him to his broad chest. Alfie was still bobbing up and down, his infectious enthusiasm making them all laugh.

"Careful, Mr. Winston!" the nurse admonished. "You're not supposed to be lifting anything."

"Calm down, son. Daddy hurts!" Cooper said. He winced, as if pain was shooting through his torso.

"Maybe you should sit down," Kiely said, concern washing through her.

"That would probably be a good idea," the nurse said.

Cooper fell back into the seat Kiely had just vacated, settling Alfie against his lap. His son hugged him tightly.

"Looks like he missed you as much as you missed him," Kiely said, giggling softly.

"I definitely missed him," Cooper said, smiling. He kissed the child's cheek one more time.

"Dad-dy! Pan-pakes, peas?" Alfie repeated.

"I'll go to the nurses' station and call down to the cafeteria to see if we can do something about those pancakes," the nurse said. "Meanwhile, sir, please be careful."

"Thank you," Kiely said.

As the nurse exited the room, closing the door after herself, Kiely turned her attention back to Cooper. He was nuzzling his face into Alfie's hair, both of them calm and joyed to be back together. There was no denying the bond between them. Cooper the single father was clearly in love with the little boy now sitting in his lap, the wealth of his commitment to the child wholeheartedly evident. It felt slightly intrusive to be watching them so keenly but

Kiely was touched by the sight of them together, their relationship pulling at her heartstrings.

She excused herself from the room, moving into the bathroom to give them a quiet moment together. She also had to pee, her bladder feeling like it might explode. Relief came quickly and as she stood washing her hands and staring at her reflection in the mirror, she found herself curious about Cooper the man, wanting to know more about him. There was clearly a side to him that she didn't know well. A side that was far less stringent and definitely more relaxed. That man seemed extremely interesting!

She pulled a hand through the length of her hair and pinched her cheeks for a hint of color to warm her face. Not that she was vain, but it didn't hurt to not look like she'd been through a torrential storm, she thought, especially since she needed a shower and wasn't feeling quite so fresh.

As she moved back into the room, Alfie gave her another bright smile and Kiely smiled back. When he suddenly reached out his arms toward her, she was surprised.

"Down!" the little boy said.

Jumping from Cooper's lap, Alfie ran to her, wrapping himself around her legs in a quick hug. He reached his arms up again, imploring her to lift him.

"What's up, buddy?" Kiely said as she reached down to pick him up.

Alfie leaned his head against her shoulder and began to play with the gold chain around her neck.

"He really likes you," Cooper said. There was no missing the slight surprise in his tone.

Kiely laughed. "As opposed to his father not liking me?"

"Who said I didn't like you?"

Kiely shrugged her shoulders. "We haven't always seen eye to eye."

"If I didn't like you, I would never have asked you to take responsibility for my son."

The look he gave her was suddenly unsettling, so Kiely changed the subject. "So, did the doctors say when you can go home?" she asked.

"Not yet, but I'm hoping we'll be out of here by this afternoon."

Before Kiely could respond, her cell phone vibrated in her pocket. She gestured for Cooper to give her a minute, shifting Alfie against her hip as she answered the call. Holding the child was so natural that it barely registered on her radar that she was maneuvering him and her phone at the same time. It was as easy as walking and chewing gum.

"Hello?"

COOPER SWALLOWED HARD, his stomach doing a slight flip as he watched Kiely standing there with his son in her arms. The boy was clearly comfortable with her and he had never before seen Alfie respond to any woman so affectionately. Not that he had introduced many women into his son's life. He had not made time or effort for any relationship since Sara's death. Cooper truly didn't believe that he would ever again love another woman as much as he had loved his late wife. He had convinced himself that it would only be him and Alfie together until Alfie left to go find his way in the world.

The conversation was quick and when he heard Kiely express her gratitude to Lieutenant McKellar, he shook himself from the reverie he'd fallen into, shifting his gaze back to her face.

"Thank you," Kiely was saying. "We appreciate that." As she disconnected the call Alfie pulled her cell phone from her hands, then kicked his legs to be put down.

Kiely laughed. "Where are you going with my phone, buddy?"

Cooper shook his head. "He loves a telephone. Doesn't have a clue how to use one, but he loves to play with it."

"He's really a good baby," she said. "Not that I have a lot of experience with them. But he's quiet and he doesn't cry a lot."

"Trust me." Cooper laughed. "He has his moments."

Kiely shifted the conversation a second time. "That was McKellar on the phone. He's on his way here to update us. I told him we'd be here in Alfie's room. I hope that's okay?"

"That's fine. Let's hope he has some good news for us."

An awkward silence descended upon the room as they both sat watching Alfie. He was pushing buttons on Kiely's smartphone, enamored each time the screen changed. As they watched Alfie, he realized they were also watching each other, stealing glances when they thought the other wasn't looking. Pancakes arrived minutes later and Kiely helped feed the little boy as Cooper sat and watched. The child's excitement over his pancake and syrup made her laugh. He ate with gusto, then polished off a handful of grapes and drank a container of milk.

"Does he always eat like this?" Kiely questioned.

Cooper laughed heartily. "He inherited my appetite."

The knock on the door pulled them both from the moment.

"Come in," Cooper said.

Tripp poked his head into the room, looking from one to the other. "Good morning! I hope I'm not interrupting?"

"Not at all. Come on in." Cooper gestured for the man to enter. He reached out his arm to shake Tripp's hand.

"You definitely look better than you did yesterday. How are you feeling?" Tripp asked.

Cooper nodded. "Like I was hit by a bus."

"Three direct hits from a .45, I imagine you would. Thank God you were wearing your vest!"

"We get any leads?"

"Nothing. My guys lost the driver almost immediately. That road she took through the woods became too narrow for the chase car about five miles in. We're searching traffic cameras now to see if we can figure out where she came out and where she went from there."

"What about the house?" Cooper asked.

"We swept the entire cabin and came up empty. A few partial fingerprints that came back with nothing. But what I can tell you is that Wes Matthews is the legal owner of the property. He purchased the house last year through one of the shell companies that the FBI had tied back to him previously. The neighbors say no one has ever lived there."

Kiely summarized the timeline that they did know. "So, we get an anonymous tip telling us where we might find Matthews hiding out. As that call is coming in someone snatches Alfie, then they contact you to insist you stop looking for Matthews. We discover Alfie and one of his kidnappers at the location we were told we'd find Matthews. And Matthews is still out there in the wind somewhere."

Kiely and Cooper exchanged a look, their gazes lingering for a brief moment.

"We still have more questions than answers," Cooper finally said.

"My men are still on it and I'll update you as soon as we get something," Tripp added.

"Thank you."

"Under the circumstances, we're going to keep you

under surveillance for a few days. Until we can figure out who took your son, we can't be certain you're safe. We've posted an officer outside your door and there'll be a car in front of your home."

"I appreciate that," Cooper said with a nod, "but it really isn't necessary. I'm sure we'll be fine."

"The city of Grand Rapids insists," Tripp concluded.

For a moment Cooper thought to argue and then he looked at Alfie who had eased next to Kiely, holding onto her arm with a tight grip. His eyes were wide, something like fear shimmering in the blue orbs. His son was vulnerable and his kidnapping yesterday proved Cooper couldn't always protect him. There were going to be times he needed help. This might very well be one of those times, he thought as he pondered the ramifications of every bad thing that could possibly happen. He took a deep breath before responding. "Thank you," he said finally.

Tripp gave him an understanding nod. "Let me know if we can do anything else to help."

"Just stay on the case," Cooper concluded. "I really want to get this guy!"

Tripp shook his hand one last time. He winked an eye at Kiely who gave him a wave and then he made his exit.

Cooper looked from her to the door and back. Was Tripp flirting with her, he wondered. Was she enjoying the attention from the other man? And why was it suddenly bothering him? He shook the thoughts away, turning back as Kiely wiped syrup from Alfie's face and hands.

Another knock on the door turned all three heads. Doctors Mara Finley and Joshua Camp entered together.

"They told me I'd find you here," Dr. Camp said. He extended his hand to shake Cooper's, then introduced himself to Kiely. He was a small man with a very large mustache and a bald head. He had a booming voice that seemed to fill the room. "This must be Alfie!" he said as he leaned down to the little boy's level and gave him a high five.

"I should probably step out," Kiely said, her voice dropping as she gave Cooper a look.

He shook his head. "No, it's fine. I'd like you to stay. Please."

Dr. Finley had moved to Alfie's side. She ran a hand across his brow. "I think Alfie's ready to go home. All his tests came back fine. He slept well through the night and from this empty plate, I see he's eating well."

"He's definitely eating well." Kiely chuckled.

"How's Dad feeling?" Dr. Camp questioned. He was pressing a stethoscope to Cooper's back and chest, listening to his breath sounds.

"Ready to go home, too!"

"And we can make that happen but I need you to understand that home is where you're going to need to stay. It's going to be at least six weeks before you can go back to work."

"Six weeks!" Cooper's eyes widened, his mind beginning to race as he considered how he could make that work. He still had a case to solve and his son to care for. Recuperating would come with some challenges he wasn't quite prepared for.

The doctor nodded. "A minimum of six weeks and that's if you do everything I tell you to do to the letter. Do you have family close who can help?"

Cooper shook his head. "It's just me and Alfie. My dad lives in Boca Raton with his sister. If I need him to come he will, but I'll be able to work it out."

The doctor looked toward Kiely for a split second as he continued to talk. "Your treatment is going to be a combination of rest, pain management and breathing exercises. Rest being crucial which is why I asked about help. Not only will it reduce the pain, but it'll allow your body to navigate the healing process. You should get up and walk around but don't push yourself. No lifting anything over ten pounds. No contact sports. No high-impact activities. And no golf."

"No golf!"

"Your swinging will cause you excruciating pain."

"Do you play golf?" Kiely questioned.

Cooper shook his head and laughed. "No."

She smiled. "So, what can he do?"

"Starting next week, and let me repeat that, next week, you can return to low-impact activities. Light housework, and simple errands, but nothing that involves any heavy lifting or physical exertion. So that means you can sit at your desk but you definitely can't go out in the field."

"Anything else, Doctor?" Cooper asked.

"You can also resume sexual activity. Just remember to take it easy. No swinging from the chandeliers or anything too strenuous."

"That shouldn't be a problem," Cooper muttered.

Cooper saw Kiely blush, and knew his face was as red as hers. Neither doctor seemed to notice as he focused his attention on Alfie.

"Then, sir, I think we should be able to release you this afternoon. Someone from respiratory therapy will be up to show you some breathing exercises. Deep breathing is important but it's going to be painful for a while. We don't want to risk you getting pneumonia or any other respiratory illness right now."

"Thank you, Doctor," Cooper said.

Dr. Finley gave Kiely a light pat on the back. "Make sure he continues to eat well. And in two weeks schedule an appointment with his pediatrician just to follow up. But

I don't think you're going to have any problems with this little guy. He's healthy and he's happy."

When both physicians were gone Cooper turned his attention to Kiely. "I'd like to enlist your services."

"Excuse me?"

"If anything happens, there's not much I'm going to be able to do. I need security for Alfie. And I'm going to need someone to help me with him. He likes you so it just makes sense."

"So, you want to hire me?"

"Or you could volunteer your services."

Kiely repeated herself. "So, you want to hire me?"

Cooper laughed. "If you're available? And we can continue to work on the case together remotely from my home. It would be a win-win situation for both of us."

Alfie suddenly squealed, something on the television evidently tickling his funny bone. His laugh was infectious, feeling like a thick explosion of happy billowing through the room. Without giving it a second thought, Kiely nodded her head. "Yes," she said. "I can do that!"

Chapter Four

"I am so confused!" Pippa Colton exclaimed. "So, now you're going to be a nanny?"

Kiely rolled her eyes skyward, throwing a pile of sweaters into the oversized suitcase she was packing. Once Alfie had fallen asleep for a nap, Cooper curled up in the hospital bed beside him, she'd come home to take a quick shower and pack a week's worth of clothes. She had a good hour before she had to be back at the hospital to pick up the two to take them home. She had more than enough time to go through her mail, set the DVR to record her favorite reality show, and drop her cat off at her sister's house. The long-haired Birman named Jim Morrison brushed against her leg as if he knew he was going on a trip and he was ready to leave.

"Keep up, Pip! I'm working with the FBI agent handling the RevitaYou case. He was injured, his son was kidnapped and rescued and now he needs someone to help him out to keep the kid safe."

"You hate kids, Kiely. How is that going to work?"

"I don't hate kids. I just don't like them much. But this one's sweet."

"I don't know about that. I don't know if I'd trust you with any kid of mine."

"Thanks for the vote of confidence!"

Pippa laughed. "Seriously! I don't think I've ever seen you with anyone's kid. I don't know if you'd be any good at it. Is this one walking and talking so he can at least scream for help in case you do something wrong?"

"I don't know why I called you."

"I'm sure you just wanted my sage advice. So how long is this gig?"

"Just a few weeks. I'm going to be staying at his house while he recovers."

"His house? What about his wife?"

"He doesn't have a wife. Little Alfie's mother died in childbirth."

"Oh, my goodness! That's so sad!"

"It really is," Kiely said dropping down against the side of her bed. She reached for her cell phone and took it off speaker, pulling the device to her ear. "I almost cried when he told me what happened."

"So, he's single?"

Kiely didn't bother to answer her twin. Instead, she changed the subject. "I saw Emmanuel yesterday. We worked a raid together."

"He told me. He said you almost got yourself killed."

"I didn't get shot. The FBI agent did."

"That's so not cool. That could've been you. This entire case is wreaking havoc on my nerves."

"Speaking of, have you heard anything more from Brody?" Kiely knew that if anyone would hear from their foster brother it would be Pippa. The two were close and Brody trusted her more than anyone else.

"No, and it's driving me crazy. I'm worried to death that he might be out there hurt, with no one to help him."

"He'll be okay," Kiely said, her tone consoling.

Pippa blew a heavy sigh. "I hope you're right."

Kiely changed the subject again, hoping to shift the

mood. "How are your wedding plans coming along? Have you and Emmanuel set a date?"

"They're coming. I think I want all my bridesmaids to wear pink."

"I'm not wearing pink, Pippa! Oh, hell no!"

"You'll wear pink for me."

Kiely groaned. "Only because we shared a womb. I wouldn't do it for anyone else."

KIELY HADN'T BEEN sure what to expect, but she was surprised by the sizable twenty-four-hundred square foot home in East Grand Rapids. The location was one of the most desired in the East Grand Rapids school system and proximity to downtown Gaslight Village. She imagined that it must have cost him a mint. He seemed to read her mind.

"We had two incomes when Sara and I purchased this house. It was her dream come true. We moved in just weeks before Alfie was born. I thought about moving after she died but I knew she wanted to raise our son here. The insurance money paid off the mortgage, so it only made sense to stay. I've been able to maintain it on my own since then."

Inside, the open floor design featured a large kitchen with a granite center island, slate appliances, a main floor master suite and bath, three additional extremely spacious bedrooms and an attached three-car garage. There was an expansive bonus room on the second floor and the home also had a full, finished basement with a private exit to the outside. The entire yard was fenced, there was a private back patio with a bricked-in grill and a meticulously landscaped lawn.

The decor was sparse and very masculine. The furniture was dark leather and except for the multitude of toys splayed around the rooms, there was little color. Alfie's room was the brightest spot in the home. The walls had been painted a lovely shade of mint green and white built-in bookcases and a desk decorated the space.

"Excuse the mess," Cooper said. "I wasn't expecting company, so I didn't clean up."

"It's fine," Kiely responded.

"I usually do make an effort to pick up the toys."

Kiely smiled. Alfie was toddling around the room, excited to be back in familiar space.

Cooper pointed to the Jack and Jill bathroom and the bedroom on the opposite side. "You're welcome to take the adjoining room there, or if you want, you can stay down in the basement. It's more private and has its own little kitchenette. The baby monitor is wired into the sound system through the whole house so you'd still be able to hear Alfie if he were up here and you were down there. You'd just have farther to walk."

"This will be fine," Kiely said as she moved through the bathroom and into the second bedroom. It was a very pretty space with a simple crocheted bedspread and matching pillows.

"I'll need to find the extra bedsheets and make up the bed," he said.

"You need to go lay down." Kiely shook her index finger at him. "The doctors told you to rest. With your permission, I'm sure I'll be able to find everything I need."

"I am tired," Cooper said. "And please, feel free to help yourself to anything that will make this easy for you."

"Thank you. Now go take a nap. Alfie and I will be fine. He and I are going to make dinner."

"He can be a handful," Cooper said. "I just want to warn you."

Kiely laughed. "So can I!"

COOPER TOSSED AND turned for almost thirty minutes. The pain pill he'd taken had relieved much of the hurt he'd been feeling but he couldn't turn his brain off long enough to relax and drift off to sleep. For the first fifteen minutes he'd listened to the baby monitor in the family room, eavesdropping on Kiely's conversation with his son.

She cooed and Alfie chattered back, the two seeming to have developed a language all their own. Then there'd been the rattle of pots and pans and the entire time Kiely talked to Alfie, even pausing now and again to ask him a question. There were many yes and no responses and an abundance of laughter that brought a smile to his face as he imagined the antics the duo were up to. After a few minutes he cut off his speaker and tried again to go to sleep, but he couldn't get Kiely off his mind.

As much as he knew about Kiely Colton, there was probably twice as much that he didn't know. And he knew much about her father. Graham Colton had been one of Michigan's best state district attorneys. He was respected in the community, and his legal expertise, commitment to fairness in justice, and his dedication to service made him one of the good guys. He and his wife Kathleen had been pillars of the community. Her philanthropic interests and dedication to their children had made her a role model for many women. Sadly, the two were killed in an automobile accident, hit by a drunk driver as they returned home from the Michigan Governor's Service Award ceremony where Graham Colton had been honored just hours earlier. The loss to the family and the community had been devastating.

Their eldest son, Riley, had been with the agency during that time and Cooper remembered well how he had pulled his siblings together to get them through that tragedy and keep them standing. His eventual resignation to open Colton Investigations had been a loss for the FBI.

Since then the Colton family had worked with the agency when help had been needed on other cases. Cases that had sometimes put him and Kiely at odds with one another. Now, here she was, in his home, caring for his son, and by default, him, too.

It probably would have been easier, Cooper thought, if she wasn't so darn beguiling. Kiely was a beauty and her carefree spirit gave him many reasons to pause. It had been some time since any woman had captured his attention. She had gotten under his skin, threatening to spread like wildfire and he wasn't sure how he felt about that. He struggled with what could have happened had she gone to check out that tip without him. If she had taken those bullets when things went left. The mere thought cut deep, reawakening feelings of loss he hadn't felt since his wife had died. Had anything happened to Kiely he would have been devastated.

He took a slow, deep breath, wincing as the sheer effort of doing so was painful. Closing his eyes, he thought briefly about going back to the family room to sit with his son and the woman who had his child equally captivated. He had questions he wanted to ask her. What was her favorite color? Her favorite food? Did she believe in monogamy? Was she dating anyone? Did she think he acted like a bumbling fool when he was in her presence?

He thought about her smile and the wisps of bangs that he always wanted to push out of her eyes. He thought about the way she sometimes stood with both hands in her back pockets, her tiny waist accentuating the fullness of her bustline. He imagined the feel of her in his arms. Wondered what she might taste like if he ever had opportunity to kiss her lips. Because he really wanted to kiss her lips and then just like that, Cooper felt himself drifting off into a deep sleep as Kiely walked through his dreams.

WHEN ALFIE WAS down for his own nap, Kiely stood in the doorway of Cooper's office. The wood-paneled space was reminiscent of an old English library with ceiling-high bookcases stretching across two walls. An oversized desk sat room center and a large globe decorated the corner. Stacks of manila folders covered the desktop, while Cooper's college degree, Quantico certification, numerous awards and accolades decorated one wall. The space was comfortable and she got the impression that Cooper spent far too much time in that one room.

There were a half-dozen pictures of Alfie. Newborn Alfie, Alfie at his baptism, the playground, taking his first steps and a formal portrait of Alfie and his daddy together. There was one single image of his late wife in a classic silver frame. The wedding photo of him and her together, the two looking hopeful and happy. She was a beautiful woman and Alfie had inherited her blond hair and wide smile. The rest of him was all Cooper. Their baby boy was a beautiful blending of their best physical attributes. Kiely lifted the image from the desktop and studied it intently before returning it to its resting spot. It was evident that Cooper had loved her immensely and that bond hadn't died with her.

Kiely turned her attention to the oversized corkboard that rested on the floor, leaning against the wall beside the desk. Cooper had laid out all the elements of the Re-vitaYou case. Images of the players, detailed sticky notes and pushpins covered the surface. Pulling up a chair, she took a seat and studied it carefully. Despite the details that they knew being very straightforward, they still had more questions than answers, no closer to putting all the pieces together and closing the case. Even her brother Griffin's fiancée, Abigail—who was also Wes Matthew's estranged daughter—knew nothing.

Clearly, Cooper brought work home with him and she had to wonder how often and how much. Was he a perpetual workaholic, ignoring family and friends during his off time? Was he compromising his relationship with his son, too often focused on bad guys who'd done bad things? Was quality time not necessarily quality because he couldn't let his day job go?

Kiely knew his type and she avoided them like the plague. Men who knew how to work hard but couldn't or wouldn't play hard, too. Men more concerned about their pension than passion, unable to configure the two together in their lives. Men much like her father. Kiely blew a soft sigh.

The renowned Graham Colton had been beloved by all. But his career had sometimes taken precedence over his family. So much so that he rarely noticed how unhappy her mother had been, or he hadn't cared. Sadly, Kiely would never know which. Her mother had sacrificed much for the man she loved, giving up her own dreams of being a social worker to support his career. She'd dedicated her life to her children and her husband, her devotion to them all undeniable.

The last years of their relationship had been strained at best. They were cordial to one another in the presence of others, but behind closed doors, they lived in separate bedrooms and barely spoke. Growing up, Kiely had thought their relationship was perfection, their love for each other so abundant that it sometimes felt unreal. Discovering that it was and watching them slowly unravel until they were a semblance of the fantasy Kiely had made them out to be, was why Kiely avoided any man wanting a serious relationship. Casual encounters and having friends with benefits worked well and she couldn't think of any reason to fix what wasn't broke.

She stole another glance at the photo of Cooper and his wife. Joy shimmered in his blue eyes, his adoration for the woman so abundant that it leapt out of the picture. Kiely had never known that kind of love and didn't imagine that she ever would. But she couldn't help but wonder what that might feel like.

COOPER WOKE WITH a start. For a moment he did not know where he was and he sat up abruptly. The pain through his torso was a swift reminder of where he was and what had happened. He had cursed. Loudly. Inhaling air deep into his lungs he took a moment to collect himself, then had thrown his legs over the side of the bed.

The house was quiet. Almost too quiet. When he checked the time, he discovered that he'd been sleeping for almost four hours and was surprised. It had been quite some time since he'd slept so soundly. Before Alfie had been born had probably been one of the last times. He moved into the master bathroom to splash cold water on his face and wipe the sleep from his eyes. After rinsing his mouth with mint-flavored mouthwash, he slipped on a pair of sweatpants. With one last glance in the full-length mirror that hung behind the door, he'd pulled his hand through his hair and eased out of the room.

Alfie's room was his first stop. His son was sleeping soundly, curled in fetal position beneath a flannel blanket. His favorite stuffed bunny and a plastic Tonka truck lay at the foot of the bed with him. The child snored, his mouth open as he sucked air in and blew it out. Cooper brushed his fingers across the kid's forehead. He too seemed to be more relaxed and at ease, sleeping sounder than Cooper remembered having seen him.

Both doors to the bathroom were open, the second bedroom dark. Peeking in to make sure Kiely wasn't there, he felt his stomach flip, concern washing over his spirt. He moved back to the crib, leaning to kiss his son's cheek before he tiptoed out of the room.

He found Kiely sitting in his office, evidently lost in thought. She sat staring into space and he wondered what might be going through her mind. She'd changed, wearing oversized cotton pajamas that swallowed her petite frame. She'd pulled her hair back into a ponytail and fuzzy slippers covered her feet.

He suddenly wondered if asking her to stay with him to help had been a good idea. Because he found himself wondering what it would be like to hold her hand, brush his lips against her cheek and maybe even claim her heart. Thoughts he hadn't entertained about any woman since Sara. Thoughts he had no business contemplating. He suddenly felt a hint of guilt pierce his heart and he shook himself from the trance he'd dropped into. He cleared his throat to draw her attention.

KIELY JUMPED AT the noise, drawing her hand to her chest. She had been so engrossed in her own thoughts that she'd forgotten where she was and what she needed to be doing. She hadn't even considered Cooper might be awake.

He stood in the doorway of the office staring at her and she suddenly felt like she might have been intruding on space where she had no business being. He was also standing there half-naked, wearing only a pair of gray sweatpants. His abs were nearly perfect, his muscles clearly defined. Spending time in a gym had served him well. Him bare-chested, in his bare feet was disconcerting and admittedly, she thought, sexy as hell.

She took a deep breath. "You scared me!"

He smiled. "Sorry about that. You were so focused I wasn't sure if I should interrupt."

"I hope you don't mind that I was in your office." She gestured toward the board. "I was just looking at everything you had on the case."

"No, it's fine. I don't mind at all. Consider this your home while you're here." He pushed both hands into the pockets of the sweats, moving the fabric to tighten around his pelvis.

Kiely tried not to stare. "So, are you hungry? I made dinner."

"You cook?"

"Why do you say that like you're surprised?"

"I am. You've never come across as that Susie homemaker type."

"I'm not, but I can cook. I'm much more than my overwhelming intellect and charming personality, Agent Winston."

Cooper laughed. "Well, I'm starved so let's see if you're any good at it."

Rising from her seat, Kiely moved through the door, brushing past him. "I'll have you know," she said as she shot him a sharp look, "I'm good at everything I do."

In the kitchen she unwrapped the plate that she had set aside for him and popped it into the microwave. Looking around, Cooper saw for the first time, that she had been busy while he slept. The toys that had been scattered around the space had all been put away. The pillows on the sofa had been fluffed and the carpet had been vacuumed. The kitchen was also spotless, the dishes washed and the counters clean.

"Wow!" he said. "You've been busy."

"I had some time after I put Alfie down for the night."

"I'm sorry I missed that," Cooper said. "You must think I'm a horrible father. My son gets kidnapped and I've barely had ten minutes for him since we got him back."

Kiely shrugged her shoulders. "Not really. Now, had you not been shot, I might feel differently." She gestured for him to take a seat at the counter as she set the plate down against the marble countertop.

The aroma of buttered noodles topped with thin slices of ribeye roast seasoned with fresh rosemary, thyme and garlic and a side of peas and carrots suddenly had Cooper salivating. He sat down, grabbed a fork and began to eat. After two bites he nearly purred. "Mmm! This is really good."

Kiely smiled, her lips lifting sweetly. "I told you I could cook."

"Did you have any problems getting my son to eat? He can be very picky. Or he's just tired of franks and beans, which is my specialty."

"Not at all. He ate a nice portion of the noodles, peas and carrots and probably one or two slices of meat. Then we had peaches and ice cream for dessert."

Cooper shook his head. "I'm starting to think I may have gotten the wrong kid back."

"Why would you say that?" Kiely asked, her eyes wide.

"Because Alfie has never been that agreeable about food."

"Alfie's never had my cooking before."

"We might have to keep you!" Cooper said before realizing what that might have sounded like.

Kiely gave him a look but said nothing, instead turning back to the microwave to wipe it down with a damp cloth.

"Out of idle curiosity where did you get the groceries from? It's been a minute since I last went shopping. That had been on my to-do list before Alfie was snatched."

"You do know there are places that will deliver, don't you? You never have to step foot in a grocery store ever again."

"Groceries?" He looked genuinely surprised.

Kiely laughed. She pulled open the refrigerator door. "Groceries," she responded. "And on a good day, you can get your order within an hour."

Cooper stared at the once-bare refrigerator that was now fully stocked. There was a gallon of fresh milk, a jug of orange juice, eggs, yogurt, an assortment of fresh vegetables and multiple snacks. The freezer was equally stocked and Cooper stared in awe.

"Remember what I said about keeping you?" he said. "I think I may have meant that!"

Kiely laughed.

After Cooper had finished his plate, literally licking it clean, she filled two bowls with a scoop of butter pecan ice cream and peaches that had been oven roasted and then tossed with cinnamon and sugar.

She climbed onto the cushioned stool beside him. Conversation between them flowed like water from a faucet. Kiely discovered his affinity for sweets and his dislike for green vegetables. She shared that she was not a fan of cottage cheese, but potato chips, the lightly salted wavy ones, were her Achilles' heel. They talked about their families. His mother had died years earlier from breast cancer and his father was living in a senior community in Florida. They video chatted weekly but Cooper hoped to take Alfie to visit his grandpop one day.

He offered his condolences for the losses of her parents and listened as she talked about how she and her siblings worked daily to honor their memories. She was close to her siblings and called them her best friends. He was an only child and slightly envious, not knowing what it was like to grow up with family so close. Cooper was impressed with how well-rounded she was, not at all as flighty and reckless as he had once thought.

ALMOST TWO HOURS and a second helping of dessert later, Kiely realized he wasn't wound as tightly as she'd initially thought and he had a keen sense of humor.

"I should head to bed," Kiely said, reaching for his empty plate.

Cooper stopped her, his fingers gently grazing the back of her hand. "I'll clear the dishes. You've done enough. Thank you."

"You're supposed to be resting."

"I don't think putting a plate in the dishwasher will hurt me."

"Well," Kiely said as she stood up, "if it does, don't say I didn't warn you."

He smiled. "I'll keep that in mind. Good night, Kiely."

Her eyes shimmered as she met his stare. Her lips lifted in a bright smile. "Good night, Cooper."

KIELY STARED DOWN into the crib as she straightened the blanket around Alfie. She trailed a light hand against his back, patting him gently when he stirred. She found herself in awe of how peacefully he slept. He really was the sweetest little thing, she thought. Everything about him tugged at her heartstrings. She could only begin to imagine the fear Cooper had felt when he'd been missing because she knew that if anything were to happen to him now she'd be beside herself.

If she had to explain her sudden bond with the little boy she didn't know if she had the words. He had somehow wrangled a tight grip on her heart and she was feeling very protective of him. Maybe her sisters were wrong, Kiely thought, and her maternal instincts had simply been late to bloom.

She gave the baby monitor one last check to ensure it

was on and at full volume. Moving through the shared bathroom to the other bedroom she sat down on the edge of the bed. It had been a nice evening. She'd enjoyed her time with Cooper. He'd been easy to talk to and had even made her laugh a time or two. She liked him more than she had expected and liking Cooper Winston had never been part of her plans.

Slipping beneath the covers, Kiely settled down against the pillows. She pulled an arm up and over her head, her other hand playing with the buttons on her pajama top. She hoped that thoughts of Cooper weren't going to haunt her dreams, but she had a feeling she wasn't going to be able to get him out of her head anytime soon.

Chapter Five

The next morning when Cooper woke he was surprised by the late hour. He was also surprised that he had not heard Alfie because the youngster would usually have been crying for something to eat by now. Then he remembered he had turned off the baby monitor and his heart dropped into the pit of his stomach.

Jumping from the bed he made quick work of his morning routine and headed straight for the nursery. He found the crib empty and for a moment he panicked, hurrying toward the family room.

Alfie and Kiely were together. She sat cross-legged and they were playing a game of peekaboo. The toddler ran in circles around her as she pretended to cover her eyes and then surprise him over and over again. The little boy exploded with laughter every time she uncovered her eyes and said *boo*.

"Good morning," Cooper said. He gave them a wave of his hand.

"Dad-dy!" Alfie rushed forward, throwing himself into Cooper's arms.

"Don't lift him!" Kiely admonished, though her words fell on deaf ears. She shook her head and smiled. Cooper knew he'd conveniently forgotten, or had chosen to ignore, his doctor's orders. But Alfie's smile was well worth it.

Cooper lifted his son up toward the ceiling and spun them both in a circle. He brought him close and kissed his face. "Good morning, Alfie!"

"Alfie playing with Ki-Ki!" the child responded. He pointed toward Kiely.

"We're still practicing my name," Kiely said with a soft giggle. "I think Ki-Ki might be it for now."

Cooper laughed. His son's delight was infectious, and the little boy was completely smitten with Kiely. Almost as smitten as he himself was if he were honest. Watching the two together tickled Cooper's spirit, sparking joy he hadn't felt in some time. "You two are up early."

"Actually, I think you might be late. In fact, I'm pretty sure of it. We've been up for a while."

He nodded. "I don't know if I can get used to this rest thing. And it's taking me a minute to get used to someone else being in the house taking care of Alfie. I panicked for a minute when he wasn't in his room."

Alfie kicked to be put down and ran back to Kiely. He threw his little arms around her neck and hugged her.

"Snack time!" she chimed as she stood up, Alfie still hanging onto her back as she grabbed his legs for a piggyback ride. "And breakfast for Daddy."

"Don't worry about me. I usually only have coffee."

"Don't you know that breakfast is the most important meal of the day? You need to be setting an example for your son."

"I barely have time to feed him in the mornings before it's time to head to day care."

"Let me guess, you work until the wee hours of the morning and then you barely get a decent night's sleep before you need to be up doing it all over again?"

"Ding! Ding! Ding!" he said facetiously. "And you win the prize!"

Kiely laughed. "It's a good thing I'm here to help you figure out how to do better."

He gave her a wry smile but didn't respond.

"Come sit," Kiely commanded, pointing to an empty chair at the table. She placed Alfie into his booster seat and secured the safety straps.

By the time Cooper made it to the table to sit down, Kiely was placing bowls of freshly cut fruit on the table mats before him and Alfie. Alfie immediately grabbed an apple slice in one fist and two large red grapes in the other.

She moved back to the stovetop and turned on the burner. By the time Cooper was done with his fruit, she'd prepared him a croissant sandwich with honey-baked ham, a fried egg and melted brie. She placed his plate on the table with a cup of freshly brewed coffee and then her own.

The faintest sliver of melancholy swept over Cooper. He couldn't help but think how things might have been for him and Alfie had Sarah lived. How differently his son's life would be if his mother had been there to cut fruit for his breakfast and rock him to sleep at night. He shook the emotion away, turning his attention back to Kiely. "You didn't eat breakfast?"

She shrugged. "I wanted to wait for you. I cooked oatmeal for Alfie and fed him and then he and I played until you woke up."

"You cooked oatmeal? And Alfie ate it?"

"He loved it. It's one of my best recipes. You cook the oats and you can do them in the microwave or on the stovetop. After they're done you slowly stir in some egg whites for added protein. It also makes them super creamy. Then I add some coconut oil and cinnamon. Those are great immunity boosters and I'm told kids can never have too many. Then I top them with chocolate chips and raspberries, which Alfie loved. Sometimes when I make it I'll do nut butter or nuts, or toasted coconut and pineapple."

"That actually sounds pretty good and I'm not a fan of oatmeal."

"I'll make you some this week and you can give it a try," she said. "I'll have you eating healthy in no time."

Cooper held up the last bite of his ham and brie. "I imagine this isn't wholeheartedly healthy but it's very good."

"Thank you." She reached over to wipe Alfie's hands with a napkin. He'd eaten the last piece of cantaloupe from the bowl and the juice had run down his arm. She turned back to Cooper. "So, what's on your agenda today?"

"I need to get back to work. I need to solve this case."

Kiely nodded. "Well, first things first. You and Alfie need some quality daddy and son time. Why don't you read him a story or two while I clean up and then after you put him down for his nap, we can do some work so we can solve this case," she said, emphasizing the *we*.

Cooper gave her a bright smile, feeling amusement dance across his face. There was an edge to Kiely that he found exhilarating. There were moments of softness, too, that he saw when she engaged with Alfie. Then there was that take-charge, work-hard, no-nonsense side of her that didn't play. That side was commanding, demanding and quite engaging. "Yes, ma'am!" He lifted Alfie from his seat and nuzzled his cheek against his son's. "Kiely said it's story time, kiddo!"

Alfie threw his hands in the air and laughed. "Ki-Ki!"

AN HOUR OR so later when Cooper returned from putting Alfie down for his nap, his doorbell rang. He and Kiely exchanged a look.

"Were you expecting someone?" Kiely asked as she

moved to the cupboard and reached for the revolver that she had hidden behind a bag of sugar. She checked the chamber and slid it into the back waistband of her pants.

Cooper shook his head as he disappeared into his office. When he came back he was checking the chamber of his service weapon. Kiely watched him as he moved to the front door. After peering out through the peephole first, he took a step back then secured his gun in the waistband of his pants. He tossed her another look before pulling the door open. Tripp McKellar and Emmanuel Iglesias stood sheepishly on the other side.

"Good morning," Emmanuel said. "I hope this isn't a bad time?"

"Not at all," Cooper answered. "Come in." He stepped back to let both men enter the home.

"Hey, there!" Kiely greeted. She gave them a slight wave. "What brings the dynamic duo by this morning?"

Emmanuel's eyes widened at the sight of her. "Kiely! This is a surprise. I wasn't expecting to find you here," he said.

"On the job. Cooper needed help after he got out of the hospital," she answered.

He nodded. "Pippa didn't mention it."

"Bad Pippa," she said sarcastically.

Cooper laughed. "Kiely's been a big help, especially with Alfie."

Emmanuel eyed her with a raised brow and a smug smile. Kiely could already see him racing back to her sister to tattle as if she and Pippa didn't already share everything. She rolled her eyes skyward.

"Can I get you two a cup of coffee?" Kiely questioned, turning an about-face.

"No, thank you," Tripp answered. "We're not staying. I

wanted to check on your security detail outside and make sure everything was going okay."

"We also had some news to share," Emmanuel added.

"Good news, I hope," said Cooper. He gestured for the two of them to have a seat at the kitchen table.

Emmanuel shook his head. "It's Gunther Johnson. He's changed his mind about giving up the goods on Capital X."

"He's scared," Tripp said. "We think someone may have gotten to him."

Cooper shook his head. Kiely threw up her hands in frustration. Both were all too familiar with the career criminal. Gunther Johnson had been a hired enforcer for Capital X, the private loan operation whose seedy, underground lending operation preyed on borrowers with astronomical interest rates, substantial loan fees and shady collection practices. Known to respond with threats and violence if payments were missed, they had been on the law enforcement radar for some time.

Brody had borrowed fifty thousand dollars from Capital X to invest in RevitaYou. Wes Matthews had absconded with his money shortly after. When Brody was unable to make his repayment, Capital X had sent Gunther Johnson to break two of his fingers, promising to break two more if he didn't come up with the money he owed. Capital X's henchmen chasing him was the reason why Brody had disappeared.

Weeks earlier Pippa had helped with the sting operation to take down Capital X and its owners. Gunther Johnson had been caught in that sting but had been less than cooperative. Working out a deal with the district attorney, he'd finally agreed to give up the Capital X hierarchy and name who oversaw the operation. To now hear he was refusing to talk didn't sit well with any of them.

"We need that name," Cooper snapped, his irritation

clouding his good mood. "That name might get us closer to Wes Matthews."

"I spoke to the DA and he said he was going to contact you. I filled him in on the shooting so he said he was going to give you a day or two before he called," Tripp said.

"I'll call him as soon as we're done. I need to go see him," Cooper said, "to see how he plans to play this." He shot a quick glance in Kiely's direction, expecting a comment but none came.

"Just take care of yourself," Emmanuel said, rising. "We'll check back in with you and you know if you need anything all you have to do is call." He extended his hand to shake Cooper's.

"Thank you. I appreciate you guys stopping by."

"We're here if you need us," Tripp reiterated as they moved toward the door. "But I'm sure you're in good hands." He gestured with his head toward Kiely, winked his eye at her and smiled.

Kiely smiled and Cooper was ready for him to be gone. He looked at her and then Tripp and back at her. He took two steps to his right, as if moving to block Tripp's view of her.

"Yes," Cooper said. "I definitely am." He tossed a look over his shoulder.

Kiely laughed. And Cooper tightened his jaw, raising his brows. He practically threw the two men out the door, keeping his goodbyes short and swift.

"You're funny," she said.

"What?"

"I see how you act every time Tripp is around."

"I don't know what you're talking about." He double-checked the door lock one last time, feigning disinterest in her comment.

"If I didn't know better I'd think you were a little jealous," she said teasingly.

Cooper turned away from her, moving toward his office. "I don't get jealous."

She laughed again. "Not much you don't," she muttered under her breath.

He stopped in the doorway and it was on the tip of his tongue to ask if she were interested in the man, but he didn't. He didn't want to know the answer if by chance she said yes. He said instead, "I need to call the DA," and then he disappeared into the other room, closing the door behind himself.

Chapter Six

The next day, the Uber driver would not stop talking and his incessant drone was beginning to wear on Cooper's last good nerve. Using a ride-share service had not been his choice. He had wanted to drive himself to the district attorney's office. Kiely had no issues with him going but she'd been adamant about how he got there. Since she needed to watch Alfie and couldn't drive him herself, Uber had been her idea and he had acquiesced to stall the argument brewing between them. She'd issued a host of threats she promised to rain down on him had he gotten into his car to drive himself and none of them had been pretty.

Kiely Colton was spit and fire when she wanted to make a point and she'd had a few to make about him not following doctor's orders. Had this meeting not been important he would have crawled back into bed as she had wanted because he hurt. He hurt more than he wanted to admit—and he would never admit that to Kiely.

His first stop was the Kent County Prosecutor's Office. The district attorney of record was Eugene Beckwith. Eugene and Cooper had worked many cases together and he was highly respected amongst his peers. He rarely sugarcoated things and could often be bitterly blunt. Cooper appreciated that he always knew where the man stood on an issue.

Eugene rushed in his direction, visibly irritated. "It's good to see you, Agent Winston. I was surprised when you called. I got the impression you were going to be off your feet for a minute."

"I probably should be, but duty calls."

Eugene nodded. "Detective Iglesias said he updated you?"

"He did. Emmanuel indicated Gunther Johnson is recanting his earlier statements and wants to forfeit his deal with the state."

"That dirtbag is playing us. Personally, I don't think what he claims to know is as big as he wanted us to believe. Now he's got cold feet because he can't deliver. I know you need that information, but Johnson's looking at life in prison, no matter what he does. Whether or not we make that time comfortable for him doesn't much matter to me. Like I don't already have a dozen other cases to worry about. No one has time for this!"

"I agree, but we still need to try. I want to talk to him."

Eugene shrugged. "It's your time to waste. How soon are you looking?"

"I'd like to head over there right now."

"Give me a second to contact his attorney," the man said. He stepped away, pulling his cell phone to his ear. A few short minutes later he moved back to Cooper's side. He nodded. "You're good to go. His attorney will meet you at the jail in one hour."

Cooper and the man shook hands. "Thank you," Cooper said.

"I'd say good luck, but you'll need more than luck to deal with that con artist."

Cooper smirked. "I appreciate your faith in my abilities."

THE GRAND RAPIDS city jail was Cooper's second stop. The building at Monroe Center NW was a holding facility for the Grand Rapids Police Department and agencies within the judicial district of Kent County. Its proximity to the courthouse and the county clerk's office made for easy visits when needed.

When Cooper arrived, the jailer on duty took him directly to an interrogation room to wait. For twenty minutes he sat twiddling his thumbs, trying to decide how he planned to appeal to the criminal and sway his decision. When the defense attorney entered, looking slightly flustered, Cooper found himself whispering a quick prayer that this didn't prove to be harder than necessary.

The door swung open a second time and a guard walked Gunther Johnson into the room. Although Cooper had seen photos of the man—multiple mug shots, a high school yearbook image, and a picture captured on a nearby security camera when he'd been arrested—he was struck by Gunther's physique. He had a sizeable build, bald head and cold, ice-blue eyes. He was intimidating, looking like brute force beneath his ivory complexion.

Gunther gave his lawyer a narrow stare, then dropped heavily onto the wood chair. He leaned back in the seat as he shifted his gaze toward Cooper.

Cooper leaned forward in his own seat, folding his hands together atop the table. "Mr. Johnson, I'm FBI Agent Cooper Winston. I'm here to talk to you about your deal with the DA to give up the name of your Capital X associates."

"I'm not taking no deal. I told them that," he spat, annoyance furrowing his brow. "I changed my mind."

"May I ask why?"

"It's none of your business."

"Let me keep it real with you, Mr. Johnson. We need that name."

"And my client needs a safety net or that can't happen," the attorney interjected.

"I ain't talking!" Gunther reiterated, his lips forming a petulant pout like he was in kindergarten.

"The district attorney has been very generous with his offer to you."

"Is he going to let me off? Give me…what's that they call it…immunity…that's it…full immunity?"

"Be real, Mr. Johnson. The district attorney has an airtight case against you for murder, and I'm sure if the FBI does a little more digging we can probably link you to a few others. You'd be looking at the death penalty for certain, instead of a cushy life sentence."

"The death penalty?" Gunther shot his attorney a look. "You ain't said nothing about no death penalty!"

The man waved a dismissive hand. "Because the state of Michigan abolished capital punishment. He's just blowing smoke!"

Cooper smiled. "But Indiana and Ohio do and I'm sure it won't take much to tie you to Capital X customers in both states. Let me see," Cooper said as he flipped open the manila folder in front of him.

He continued. "Paul Phelps, a resident of Gary, Indiana, found dead with four fingers missing. Regina Leslie, also a resident of Gary. Jon Tucker of Columbus, Ohio. They all borrowed money from Capital X. They all had problems repaying. And what else do they have in common? You. You traveled to both states around the time of their murders. That sounds like a death penalty case to me. Crossing state lines means an interagency investigation."

"You said no death penalty!" Gunther shouted at his attorney, although he was staring at Cooper.

Cooper smirked. "Well, now I'm saying I'm sure my office will have no qualms pushing a death penalty agenda for the time you've wasted yanking our chain!" He slammed the file folder closed.

"He will kill me if I tell!"

"Who, Mr. Johnson?"

"You can't protect me!" He was shouting, still visibly agitated.

The guard by the door took a step forward. Cooper held up his hand to stall him.

"Yes, we can," Cooper said. "The DA laid out a plan that would guarantee your protection. He's agreed to protecting your identity and sending you to a prison facility where you wouldn't be recognized."

"And my television?"

"If he promised you that, he'll honor it. But you have to do what you promised to do."

Gunther leaned over to whisper into his attorney's ear. The two men whispered back and forth for a few good minutes before Gunther turned back to Cooper. "I'm just not sure."

Cooper stood up. "You have twenty-four hours, Mr. Johnson, or the DA's offer is off the table and then I promise to personally make your life a living hell." He gave the attorney one last look. "Twenty-four hours and that's being very generous."

THE UBER RIDE back put Cooper smack dab in the middle of evening traffic. The driver was regaling him with a story about his bachelor party antics in Brazil, where every woman with a tan and a bikini apparently wanted him. The man was hardly ready for marriage, Cooper thought. Marriage required a commitment of time and thought that few were prepared for. Marriage was about shared space and goals and sometimes stepping back from your own dreams for someone else to fly. He'd been there and done that, albeit not as well as he probably should have.

He had never been able to apologize to Sara for sometimes being selfish and self-absorbed. He often thought about the apology she had deserved from him when a case or a client had his full attention and she had felt taken for granted. Parenting Alfie had taught him much about himself. He hadn't been the man his wife had deserved but he was determined to be a better man for his son.

They were stopped at a light and Casanova Junior was still going on about some blonde with big boobs. Cooper stared out the window, his thoughts on Alfie, and on Kiely. He was still in awe of how quickly Alfie had become attached to the woman. To see them together one would think she'd been in his short little life since forever, Kiely mothering him as if he were her own. He also had to wonder what would happen when the time came for Kiely to leave them. How would Alfie handle her not being there. Because they couldn't keep her around indefinitely. No matter how much he suddenly found himself wanting to.

KIELY KNEW SHE was butchering the words to the lullaby that she was singing, but Alfie didn't seem to mind. She held him in her arms, his head resting on her chest, his little legs wrapped around her waist. She rocked him from side to side and he was slowly drifting off to sleep.

Her voice was a loud whisper as she sang. "The other night dear, as I lay sleeping, I dreamt I held you, up in my arms. But when I woke, dear, I was mistaken, so hmm hmmm hmm hmmm and cried."

She kissed his little forehead as his eyes finally closed, his little body relaxing against her. "You are my sunshine, my only sunshine. You make me happy when skies are gray! You'll never know dear, how much I love you. Please don't take my sunshine away."

She hummed for a few more minutes until she was certain he was sound asleep. Then she laid him gently in his crib. Everything about Alfie was joy. Kiely still couldn't fathom how quickly he'd captured a huge chunk of her heart. She was loving every minute of her time with the child. When Alfie had wakened from his afternoon nap Cooper was already headed to his meeting. She'd devoted the entire afternoon to the little boy's entertainment. They'd played hokey pokey, pick-up sticks, rolled a ball, played with slime, had two snacks, a bubble bath and now he was past the point of exhaustion. Admittedly, so was she. Kiely was quickly discovering that kids required an abundance of energy she had not anticipated.

She was still staring down at the little boy when she heard Cooper arrive home. She turned to see him watching her from the doorway. He moved into the room to stand beside her. She was only slightly startled when his arm brushed against her shoulder.

"Hey! I didn't hear you come in!"

"I haven't been here long. I stopped to chat with Officer Parnell. He's watching the house tonight. He said things have been quiet since he came on duty."

"It's been very uneventful."

"How long has Alfie been asleep?"

"About thirty minutes. He's just the sweetest angel when he's sleeping."

Cooper smiled. "He really is!"

Folding her arms across her chest Kiely bumped his side with her hip. "Hungry?"

"I could eat."

"Good. I'm starved and I waited to eat with you."

"You didn't have to wait!"

"I know that." She bumped his side a second time as she turned to exit the room.

"Do I have time to take a quick shower?"

Kiely nodded. "We're eating salmon. I'll put it in the oven when I hear the water shut off."

He gently tapped her arm. "Thank you, Kiely."

KIELY PULLED THE orange and honey-glazed salmon from the oven. The dining table had been set for two and she was ready to eat. She plated their meals and set the food on the table. Dinner was the salmon, a mushroom and spinach salad, rice pilaf, and a whipped chocolate mousse for dessert.

When another ten minutes passed and there was no sign of Cooper, Kiely eased her way down the hallway to his bedroom door. The door was cracked open and peeking through she saw Cooper standing in the center of the room. He wore a pair of boxer briefs, nothing more. His skin was flushed from the shower's hot water. He stood slathering his body with lotion, his hands gliding across his torso and up and down his limbs. Her eyes widened at the sight of him. He was a beautiful specimen of manhood and Kiely gasped, feeling heat course straight through her feminine spirit. She took two steps back, and one very big inhale of air, and then she called his name.

"Cooper? Dinner's ready!"

"Coming!" Cooper called back.

As Kiely moved back down the hallway, the bedroom door swung open and Cooper hurried after her. He had slipped on another pair of sweatpants and a T-shirt with the FBI logo on his chest.

"Sorry about that," Cooper said. "Emmanuel called to say Gunther Johnson is ready to talk."

"That's great! I guess you ignoring the doctor's orders was worth it," Kiely said, an air of attitude in her tone.

Cooper laughed. "Are you really going to give me a hard time about leaving?"

"Would I do something like that?" Kiely responded as she pulled her hand to her chest and batted her lashes at him.

"You have jokes!" He pulled the chair out for her and they both sat down to eat.

"How do you feel?" Kiely questioned.

"Better, now."

"So, will you have to go back tomorrow?"

"I don't think so, but we'll see. I'll know more in the morning."

"I'm just glad you convinced him to talk."

There was an awkward silence that suddenly settled over the table.

Kiely's gaze narrowed as she studied his expression. "What?"

Cooper lifted his eyes to hers. "I bluffed. I told him I had information that could possibly get him the death penalty." He gave her a blow-by-blow of his conversation with Gunther.

"And he fell for it?"

Cooper nodded. "It would seem so if he's ready to talk."

"Sounds like you might need to do some serious investigating. Clearly, he's been involved in some things we don't even know about yet."

"That's what I was thinking, too!"

"Well, if he talks, then the lie was well worth it. Sometimes you have to do whatever you have to do."

COOPER PROCESSED HER COMMENT. Skirting the rules by lying to get information wasn't something he ever did and he found himself feeling out of sorts about his actions. Although what he'd done was well within the scope of the law, it went against his personal moral code. He also found it interesting that Kiely hadn't blinked an eye, not at all bothered by what he had done.

"I've been thinking about Alfie's kidnapping. Going through all the players we know to try and figure out who could have done it," Kiely said.

"Well, we know a man snatched him. So, he and that woman at the cabin were working together."

Kiely nodded. "And both are somehow affiliated with Wes Matthews."

"What about family? There's his daughter, Abigail."

"It's certainly not her. Abigail and my brother Griffin are an item. She barely knows her father. Her mother left her father when she was a child. It was Abigail who helped uncover the ricin in RevitaYou. She wants to see him caught more than anyone."

"So, refresh my memory. Griffin is the attorney?"

"Yes. He specializes in adoption law."

"But he's not the only attorney in the family. Right?"

"That's right. My sister Victoria is a JAG paralegal and my twin sister Pippa is also a lawyer."

"Interesting."

"Why interesting?"

"It just is. But we digress." He took a sip of his wine and then refilled his crystal goblet. "So, we can eliminate Wes's daughter Abigail. And you said her mother is deceased, right? So, who else is there in his life that would want to protect him?"

Kiely shrugged. "Abigail said her father has dated a few women that she knows about."

Kiely leaned back in her seat. "What I find interesting is that the kidnapper called you specifically. And that she took Alfie. When you consider all the agencies working this case, all looking for Matthews in some form or fashion, why did she single you out to contact? Why your son? It makes me question if maybe she has some personal connection to you."

"I'm at a loss as to who it could be," Cooper said after a minute of contemplation.

Kiely continued. "I also keep thinking about the tip that came in over that hotline. Someone knew Wes Matthews had a connection to that property."

"Do you think they knew about my baby being there?"

"Good question. Wish I had an answer for you. Hopefully the info Gunther gives you will lead us all farther along on this case."

Kiely rose from the table and began to clear the dishes.

"Let me help with that," Cooper said as he lifted his own plate from the table. "Dinner was excellent tonight, by the way."

"Thank you."

She brushed against him as they passed each other. Heat blossomed between them like the sweetest breeze. "Excuse me," she muttered.

"No problem." Cooper moved to the sink and began to wash the dishes. He tossed a dry towel in her direction. "So, did you and Alfie have a good day?" Cooper asked, changing the subject.

"We had a great day," Kiely answered.

"May I ask you a personal question?" Cooper asked.

"I guess that depends on how personal the question is," Kiely said with a soft giggle. "But ask away."

"I was just wondering why you never married. Why don't you have any kids? You're so good with them. I would think that you would want to have children of your own."

Kiely laughed, the wealth of it gut deep.

"Why is that so funny?" Cooper questioned.

"Because I really have never had a lot of experience with kids. In fact, I never imagined myself having children. My sisters have always said that I don't have any maternal instincts whatsoever."

"Well, obviously your sisters got that wrong! You really are a natural."

"I'll be honest. It's really surprised me how much I enjoy taking care of Alfie. He's definitely a handful but I adore him."

"Well, I appreciate just how good you are with him."

"Have you ever thought about remarrying?" Kiely asked casually. "I mean, has there been anyone in your life that would be a great mother figure for Alfie?"

Cooper shrugged. "I've not dated much since my wife died." He gave her a quick look.

"I don't date much either," Kiely said. "Colton Investigations keeps me busy."

"So, you put work before everything else, too."

"I have. But my time with Alfie, and with you, has me rethinking what my future should look like. And don't get me wrong, I have a great life. But I've been happier these past two days than I've been in a very long while."

She gave him a slight smile, her demure expression hitting Cooper like a gut punch he wasn't expecting. He bit down against his bottom lip. His body's reaction was purely carnal, a rise of nature suddenly twitching for attention. He felt heat flush his cheeks. Kiely turned to put the dishes back into the cupboard, apparently pretending not to notice, as he turned his back to her, needing to adjust himself in his pants.

"Well," he said as he turned back. He reached for another bottle of wine, pulled two clean glasses from the rack, and poured. He passed one glass to her, then extended his in a mock toast. "Here's to embarrassing myself," he said as he clinked his glass against hers.

Kiely laughed. "That sounds very personal."

Cooper took a large swig of his drink.

"You do know you're not supposed to mix your pain pills with alcohol, right?"

"I won't tell if you don't."

"Cooper Winston, you know better!"

He shrugged. "I think you're rubbing off on me. I'm wanting to take more risks than usual."

"So, try skydiving. It's so much safer!"

He laughed, his joy rising abundantly. He was suddenly staring into her eyes as she watched him, the coy look on her face giving him pause. He rested his glass on the counter and took a step closer to her. Kiely's eyes widened, her lips parting ever so slightly. Her perfume wafted to his nostrils and her body heat felt like the sweetest caress as it rose with a vengeance between them. He found himself staring at her mouth, wondering what she might taste like, suddenly wanting to kiss her lips, to tease her with his tongue as he held her in his arms. He wanted her like a thirsty man did water.

"Kiely, with everything going on this may not be the right time," he started, "but I really like..."

Before Cooper could finish his statement, the room suddenly shook, something exploding outside. The loud boom was followed by a whooshing sound and the noise of shattering glass as the windows shook.

Instinctively, Cooper reached for Kiely, pulling her to the floor as he wrapped his arms protectively around her. The smell of sulfur dioxide hit their noses, pungent and thick, followed by Alfie's mournful wail.

"You okay?" Cooper asked, his hands clutching Kiely's shoulders as he looked her up and down.

She nodded. "I need to get Alfie," she said as she jumped up, racing down the hallway. "You check outside!"

Cooper went for his weapon, checking the chamber as he moved to the front door. Before he could pull it open, a second explosion blew a hole where the entrance was, knocking him backwards into the wall. He scampered back onto his feet. He screamed Kiely's and Alfie's names.

"We're okay!" she screamed back as Alfie cried hysterically. "Are you okay?"

"Stay inside!" Cooper responded. He moved back to the entrance and peered outside. Across the street the police patrol car was an amalgamation of burned metal, fire and smoke. His own car was nothing but melted shrapnel and Kiely's vehicle, parked behind his, was also engulfed in flames.

Moving to the middle of the yard he looked up the street and then down. His neighbors were peeking out their windows, some beginning to come out of their homes to see what had happened. In the distance, the faint sound of sirens could be heard rushing toward them. He looked toward the police vehicle a second time and his stomach pitched, bile rising into his throat. He bent forward at the waist, fighting not to vomit.

"Agent Winston!" A voice called his name from the side of the house.

Cooper turned abruptly, his weapon raised. He dropped it just as quickly. "Officer Parnell, thank God!" Cooper exclaimed. He rushed to meet the man, throwing his arms around him in a bear hug. Relief flooded his spirit, easing the knot that had tightened in his belly. "I was afraid you were still in that car."

"No, sir. Thank the good Lord! I thought I saw someone moving along the side of your home and I'd gotten out to investigate. That second blast knocked me on my ass, but I'm okay. Backup is already on the way. You good, sir?"

Cooper glanced toward the front door of his home. Kiely stood in the entrance, Alfie clutched tightly to her. She gave him a nod of her head as she pressed her lips to his son's forehead. "We're good," he said, shifting his gaze back to the other man.

The cell phone in Cooper's pocket suddenly rang. He pulled it to his ear, exasperation in his voice. "Hello?"

"You won't be so lucky next time," the woman on the other end spat. Cooper recognized her voice. It was the same woman who'd called after Alfie had been taken. "Who is this?" he snapped.

"Stop looking for Wes Matthews or I won't miss the next time," she said and then she disconnected the call.

Cooper tightened his fist around the device. Whoever she was, this latest rogue move had gotten his full attention. It was only by the grace of God that there had been no serious casualties. But she had now hit him twice. Hard. If he hadn't been certain before, he was now. He would have to change his tactics to catch this woman. Playing by the rules didn't apply when it came to his son and his home. He hurried back to Kiely's side. "Our kidnapper is now an arsonist," he said. "And that was a murder attempt. Parnell got lucky."

Her eyes widened as she reflected on what could have happened to them all. "We got lucky, too," she interjected. "She doesn't plan on stopping, does she?"

"No, which is why we need to find her and find her fast."

Chapter Seven

Thirty minutes after the explosion Grand Rapids police officials had cordoned off Cooper's street, firemen had put out the flames, and agents from the FBI district office were assessing the damage. Investigative teams from each agency were processing the scene and asking questions. Cooper's home had become command central, uniformed officers and suited agents walking in and out of the open door.

Alfie was wide-eyed and curious, trying to comprehend all the excitement. He clung to Kiely as if his life depended on it. She, Cooper and Officer Parnell had each relayed their memory of the event multiple times. One of Cooper's neighbors reported seeing a figure dressed all in black cutting through her yard on a motorcycle.

Emmanuel, Tripp and Agent Claire Miller arrived like the cavalry, each barking orders. Kiely was feeding Alfie orange slices as Cooper filled them in on the phone call.

"We're trying to trace it now!" Tripp said.

Claire shrugged. "If it's a burner, you won't get anything."

"Anything on the traffic cams?" Cooper asked.

"Nothing," Emmanuel said, shaking his head.

"Who is this woman?" Cooper snapped, tossing his hands up in frustration.

"We will get her," Claire said. "For now, though, I think you should stay at the safe house." She looked at Cooper. "We have that one spot you used for your witness protection case last year. It hasn't been put back into available inventory yet. Your stay will be off the books so if this woman is somehow affiliated with the agency she won't be able to find you through us. The only people who will know where you are will be me, Lieutenant Tripp and anyone you choose to tell."

"You don't think she's with the FBI, do you?" Kiely questioned.

Claire shrugged her narrow shoulders. "FBI, CIA, local law enforcement, mercenary training, who knows. She just seems to be good at what she does, so until we figure out who she is, we can't be too careful. I'd rather we be safe now than sorry later."

Cooper nodded. "That'll work."

"We'll make arrangements for your transportation."

"I can help with that," Tripp said. He began punching a message into his smartphone.

"A safe house?" Kiely looked concerned. "I can't just up and disappear," she said. "The case... My work..."

"You can work remotely," Claire volunteered. "It's a state-of-the-art facility with secure Wi-Fi and all the perks of a five-star hotel. You won't even know you're being protected."

Cooper eased over to her side, leaning to whisper in her ear. "I will understand if you don't want to do this, Kiely. I need to make sure Alfie is safe, but this is not your problem. She's after me, not you."

"Do you not *want* me to go with you?" Kiely whispered back. Her eyes skated back and forth across his face, as if searching for something that had yet to be defined or spoken.

He leaned closer, his hand resting against her waist. "I *need* you to go with me," he said. "And I want you to *want* to come."

Kiely nodded her head, her cheek brushing gently against his. Alfie giggled, reaching for his father. Lifting the child from her arms, Cooper gave her a caressing smile and nuzzled his face into the boy's neck.

KIELY WAS IN the master bedroom packing a suitcase for Cooper and Alfie when Sadie and Pippa barged into the room. The sisters all gave each other a look.

Pippa moved swiftly to her twin sister's side, punched her in the arm and then threw her arms around Kiely's shoulders. "You scared the hell out of me!" she exclaimed.

Kiely laughed as she hugged her sister back. When they finally let go, she rubbed the bruise rising against her skin. "Ouch! That hurt."

"You deserved it."

"I swear! Does that fiancé of yours tell you everything?"

"Emmanuel didn't tell me this."

"Well, how did…" Kiely started.

Sadie waved a hand. "Guilty! Lieutenant McKellar called me in."

"You're investigating?"

Sadie shook her head. "Transport. I'm taking you and your new family to the FBI safe house. He and Agent Miller thought you'd feel better about going if one of us took you."

"Well, isn't that special," Kiely said. "All we need now is Vikki to show up!"

"Don't think we didn't call her," Sadie said. "She didn't answer her phone. She was in court today on a case. But I'm sure we'll hear from her later."

"So, this is where you've been *working*!" Pippa said.

She sat down on the edge of the bed and began rifling through the suitcase her sister was packing. "And I assume these belong to your *employer*?" She held up a pair of black boxer briefs.

"Why are you packing for him?" Sadie questioned. "Are things like that between you two now, or is something wrong with his hands?"

Kiely rolled her eyes. "Someone tried to blow him up tonight. I'm just being helpful. Besides, Agent Miller is rushing us to get out of here and he's trying to tie up strings out there. It just made sense for me to help."

"You haven't slept with him, have you?" Pippa questioned.

"I have not slept with him."

Pippa's gaze narrowed. She gave her sister a smile. "But you want to!" she said excitedly.

Kiely held up her index finger. "Shh! Don't let him hear you!"

"I told you she liked him!" Sadie interjected.

There was a knock on the door. When Cooper opened it to peer inside, Alfie came running in, throwing himself at Kiely.

"Ki-Ki!" the little boy exclaimed as she swept him up into her arms. He gave the two sisters a look, staring at Pippa for a good few minutes. The family genes were strong and although she and her sister were fraternal twins they still bore a strong resemblance to one another.

"This is Alfie," Kiely said, making the introductions. "And this is his father, Cooper Winston. Cooper, this is Philippa, my twin, and my sister Sadie."

"It's a pleasure to meet you both," Cooper said. "I wish it was under better circumstances."

"Please, call me Pippa, and the pleasure is mine."

"Nice meeting you," Sadie added. "Isn't this sweet baby just a little doll! Hello there!"

Alfie was still staring at the two. He finally lifted his hand in a slight wave. "Hi! My name Alfie!" he said as he patted his chest proudly.

"Hi, Alfie," Pippa said, teasing his chubby cheek.

"I didn't mean to interrupt, but we need to get going," Cooper said. "I came to see if you needed any help. And I really appreciate you helping me out."

"I'm ready," Kiely answered. She snatched his undergarment from her sister's hand and tossed it back into the suitcase. "We're all packed."

KIELY APPRECIATED HER sisters not giving her a hard time, although she knew it would only be a matter of time before they did. The ride to the safe house was taking them through some heavily wooded areas as they headed about an hour's ride out of the Grand Rapids city limits.

Alfie sat in Kiely's lap, her seat belt wrapped securely around them both. His car seat had been collateral damage in the explosion, nothing but a blob of melted plastic. Sadie had promised to bring another when she came back to check on them.

Sadie drove, she and Pippa sitting in the front. Kiely and Cooper sat in the back with the baby. Nestled shoulder to shoulder the nearness of him gave her an abundance of comfort. His concern for her well-being had been admirable. She appreciated him wanting her opinion and asking her thoughts on what they should do and how they should proceed. His concerns had mirrored her own and he'd had no reservations expressing them.

Pippa tossed her a look from the front seat, her smile slightly smug. Kiely rolled her eyes and her twin laughed.

"You look good with a baby in your arms," Pippa said.

Sadie chuckled. "And a man by your side."

"She does," Cooper answered, a wide grin across his face.

Kiely sat up straighter, adjusting the hold she had around Alfie. He'd fallen back to sleep before they'd passed the first stop light and had been slumbering comfortably the entire ride. "My sisters can't wait to have kids," Kiely said. "And Sadie's fiancé has vowed to impregnate her the minute she says I do."

Pippa laughed. "Tate would impregnate her now if he thought our brothers wouldn't kill him. Because they would kill him!"

Sadie scoffed. "Let's not bore Agent Winston with our family drama, please."

Kiely laughed, Cooper chuckling with them. She leaned her head against his shoulder and when she did, Cooper gave her knee a light squeeze.

The FBI safe house was a stunning log home nestled in a forest of mature sugar maple and red oak trees. It boasted a covered porch, large deck, landscaped firepit area and a walkout basement. As Cooper carried their luggage inside and checked that all was well before her sisters pulled off, Kiely was already planning excursions for the three of them when safety allowed.

"It looks very pretty," Sadie said. "I wouldn't mind being locked away up here with a handsome man."

"Any handsome man in particular?" Kiely asked.

"She definitely doesn't want to be stuck up here with Tate," Pippa muttered.

"Now you're just being mean," Sadie snapped.

"But honest," Kiely quipped.

"Do you need anything before we leave?" Sadie asked, annoyance creasing her brow.

Kiely shook her head. "It's all good. I think we'll be fine. I'll get a message to you if I do."

"You really do look good with that baby," Pippa said. "You look happy. Even relaxed and every time you look at his father your face lights up."

"Shut up, Pip!" Kiely snapped.

Her sisters laughed.

Kiely moved toward the entrance, Alfie in her arms and sound asleep against her shoulder. "I need to go lay him down," she said. "He's getting heavy."

"We're going to head back," Sadie said.

"Don't hurry off," Kiely said, just as Cooper came out the door.

"Are you two leaving?" he questioned. "Don't rush off."

Sadie nodded. "Yeah! We need to get back." She gave him a wave.

"If you let anything happen to our sister, we will come for you," Pippa said. She was pointing a finger at Cooper. "Trust and believe, we will come for you."

Cooper nodded. "I promise, I'll take good care of her."

"You better," Pippa admonished.

Kiely laughed. "Go away, Pip, and leave Cooper alone."

Pippa pressed her cheek to Kiely's. She trailed her hand against Alfie's back. "Be safe," she whispered, "and make sure he wears a condom!" Then she turned, her expression smug, leaving Kiely and Cooper standing side by side.

Kiely giggled, appreciating that for once, Pippa had gotten the last dig.

They watched as Sadie pulled the car back down the length of driveway and when they could no longer see the Suburban's rear lights, they turned to go into the house.

CLAIRE HAD MADE arrangements for everything they could possibly need. A crib had been placed in the bedroom directly across from the master, an assortment of toys filling one corner. Kiely laid Alfie down and covered him with a newly purchased blanket. He stirred as if he might wake and then rolled into fetal position, continuing to slumber peacefully.

After a quick, self-guided tour of the house and the fully stocked refrigerator and cupboard, Kiely dropped down onto the sectional sofa and pulled a quilt around her torso. After everything that had happened she was feeling slightly squirrelly. The magnitude of how bad things could have been had suddenly hit. It had her feeling vulnerable and uneasy, fear and frustration not sitting well with her spirit.

Cooper came up from the basement. "Everything's good. We can communicate over the secure server so you can stay in touch with your family." He stopped short. The expression on her face made him pause. "Kiely? Are you okay?"

She shook her head, waving a dismissive hand. Tears formed and she struggled not to let them fall. Closing her eyes, she took a deep breath and held it, counting from one to ten in her head. She felt her bottom lip quiver ever so slightly. Minutes passed before she spoke.

"Does that fireplace work?" Kiely asked, gesturing with her head toward the stone structure that took up half a wall.

"I'm sure with enough firewood and a match we can get her working. I'll get right on that," he said.

Minutes later a fire was roaring in the fireplace. Flames crackled in vibrant shades of red, orange and yellow. Kiely pulled her knees to her chest, wrapping her arms around her legs. Cooper dropped down onto the sectional, sliding up beside her. She lifted the blanket to share the covering and he eased gently against her, extending his legs out in front of him.

"Do you want to talk about it?" he asked, cutting a quick eye in her direction.

"It hit me that we could have been killed tonight. Thinking about it has me rethinking my entire life. The risks I take. The choices I sometimes make to get a job done. What I want going forward. What changes I may need to make. It's just a whole lot. There's so much going through my head right now I'm finding it a little overwhelming."

COOPER SIGHED. HE understood because he too had been lost in his head about what had happened. He also knew that he didn't have the answers to make things better for either of them. Reaching for her hand, he entwined her fingers with his own. Kiely leaned her head back against his shoulder and he leaned his head against hers.

The crackling of the fire, a clock that ticked loudly, and a slow drip from the kitchen faucet were the only sounds through the room. The warmth from the fire wafted through the space but there was the hint of a chill in the air. Comfort came as they settled into the sound of each other breathing.

The morning sunrise found them both sleeping soundly, still sitting side by side. Cooper cradled her body with his own, his arms wrapped protectively around her. The fire had died down hours earlier and they were snuggled close together beneath the quilted blanket they shared. It was bliss that he knew he would not soon forget.

Chapter Eight

Adjusting to their new surroundings was proving to be more of a challenge than either of them had anticipated. Alfie was temperamental and whiney from the moment he woke. Clearly, he was not having a good day. So maybe she wasn't the kid whisperer she'd dubbed herself, she thought as Alfie threw his third, or maybe fourth, tantrum of the day and it wasn't yet noon.

She stood with both hands on her hips as the little boy threw himself to the floor kicking and screaming. This time he'd wanted chocolates that he'd seen in a jar in the pantry. One hadn't been enough and now he wasn't at all happy with Kiely telling him he couldn't have any more. Kiely watched him like he was an alien creature let loose in the middle of the room.

Cooper laughed. "And you said he was an angel!"

"I think he's possessed," she said.

"Just ignore him. He'll tire himself out in a while."

Kiely shook her head. "I don't want him to hurt himself."

"He won't. Trust me. That kid knows exactly what he's doing. Right now he's playing on your feelings. Hoping you'll let him have that candy."

"Well, we're not going to do that. It's lunchtime anyway," she said as she stepped over the child and moved to the kitchen.

Alfie revved his screaming up a notch.

"Do you need help?" Cooper asked, moving into the kitchen with her.

She shook her head. "No. Thank you for offering though. We're having handmade pizza. There's a baking stone!" she said, a hint of excitement in her voice. She punched down the dough she'd made shortly after their pancake breakfast.

"I think I've gained ten pounds since you arrived."

Kiely laughed. "Well, it looks good on you."

Cooper gave her a warm smile. "I'm going to take the munchkin for a walk. Hopefully he'll be in a better mood when we get back. Once he goes down for his nap we need to get some work done."

Kiely watched as Cooper scooped Alfie up off the floor and into his jacket, mittens and boots. He'd finally stopped screaming but the look he gave Kiely said he wasn't quite ready to be her friend again anytime soon. As father and son headed out the door she blew a sigh of relief and savored the moment of quiet. She punched the pizza dough a second time.

Cooking calmed her and Kiely planned to cook until she felt like herself again. Lunch was personal pizzas topped with Swiss chard, sausage and fresh mozzarella. She thought about baking cookies to make amends to Alfie. Moving to the pantry she found enough ingredients to make a few chocolate chip treats.

An hour later the smells of chocolate and vanilla filled the space. When Cooper and Alfie came back through the door both paused in the doorway, taking deep breaths to inhale the scent.

Cooper hummed. "Mmm! Something smells good in here."

Alfie peeled out of his coat and came running to her. "Ki-Ki!"

Kiely leaned down to give him a hug.

"I sorry Ki-Ki. Me was a bad boy. Alfie will be good, okay?"

She hugged him a second time. "Thank you, Alfie."

"I lub you, Ki-Ki!" he exclaimed as he threw his arms around her neck and kissed her cheek.

Kiely blinked away a tear. "I love you, too, Alfie."

"I hungry, Ki-Ki!"

"You take Daddy and help him wash his hands and then you two come back to get lunch. Okay?"

Alfie nodded. "Wash you hands, Dad-dy! Wash you hands!" He turned and raced toward the bathroom.

"He and I had a very long conversation about that tantrum," Cooper said. He tapped Kiely's arm, the gesture kind and tender.

"Go wash your hands," she muttered as she swiped a tear away. "Before you both have me crying!"

COOPER GRABBED TWO more cookies and a glass of milk. Although he was stuffed from lunch, he just couldn't help himself. They were that good and Alfie had finally gone to sleep so that he could enjoy the dessert without having to share. He moved to the sofa, taking the seat across from Kiely.

"I made those for Alfie," she said. "I didn't want him to stay mad at me over that candy issue."

"I left him some."

"I'm going to have to send my sister a grocery list so I can make some more."

"People in protective custody don't usually cook gourmet meals."

"I'm treating this little adventure as a spa holiday of sorts."

Cooper smiled. "A working holiday, I hope. I could really use your help figuring out who this woman is. I'm coming up with blanks. Nothing makes any sense."

"Don't feel bad. I've been thinking about her all morning, too. I've eliminated more women from the suspect pool than I've been able to consider." Kiely sighed.

"I keep thinking about Abigail Matthews. You said you don't think she's involved, but do you think she might know something? Something that might make sense to us even if it doesn't make sense to her?"

"She doesn't, but maybe she'll remember something if we ask again. I doubt it but it won't hurt."

"Since you know her, I'm going to ask you to give her a call. She might be more inclined to open up and speak with you than with me. Meanwhile I'm going to see if forensics came up with anything from the explosion."

"Yes, sir," Kiely said as she gave him a salute.

Cooper shook his head, swallowing his last bite of cookie. "Beautiful and funny!"

"Damn right!" Kiely said as she rose from the table. "And it's a lethal combination."

KIELY REACHED OUT to Griffin before calling Abigail. It had taken her sisters less than twenty-four hours to fill their brothers in on what she'd been doing and all that had happened and now they wanted answers she wasn't yet interested in giving.

"So, Riley says this Cooper guy is good people. But he has a kid. Are you ready to do kids, Kiely? That's an important step, and I speak from experience," he said reminding her of what he and Abigail had gone through to adopt their foster child Maya.

"We're just friends, Griffin."

"That's not what Pippa said."

"Can I just talk to Abigail, please?"

"Don't change the subject, Kiely."

"I'm not. I'm trying to work and you want to discuss my personal life. And you know that is off limits."

"Maybe to strangers, not to family, right?" There was a hint of sarcasm in his tone that Kiely picked up on but ignored. Griffin sighed. "She should be home if you're planning to call her now. I just had lunch with her and Maya, and the baby was going down for a nap."

"I need to make time to come by and see my new niece. I promise to do that soon."

"Yes, you do and I'm going to hold you to that."

"Love you!"

"Stay safe, Kiely!"

Disconnecting the call, Kiely sat back in her chair, thinking about her big brother. Griffin had been adopted when he'd been eight years old and she'd been six. He'd been a foster kid first and much like Brody, their father had seen his potential, believing in him even when he was unsure. Both their parents had loved him like he was their own. But there had always been something holding Griffin back from feeling like he belonged...until recently. Like he was really a Colton and not just carrying the name by default. Since he'd met Abigail and Maya, he'd changed and opened up more.

Any time Griffin mentioned family he always sounded like he needed a pep talk. That he needed to be reminded that they loved him immensely and considered him kin, whether they were related by blood or not. But right then she didn't have time to coddle his feelings and sing him a rendition of "Kumbaya." It would have to wait until she saw him next in person. She engaged the secure phone line and dialed Abigail's number.

Abigail answered on the third ring. "Hello?"

"Abigail, hello! It's Kiely."

"Kiely, hey! How are you?"

"I'm well. Is this a good time to talk?"

"Can you hold on for a second? Just let me check on Maya. She's teething and it takes forever for her to fall asleep lately."

"That's not a problem at all." Kiely waited, listening to the silence on the other end.

Abigail came back to the phone quickly. "Sorry about that. She's out like a light! What can I do for you?"

"I had some questions about your father."

Abigail groaned. "You know he and I don't have a relationship, right? It's been a while since I last spoke with him."

"I do. But we're trying to identify a woman who's connected to him. Someone he may be close to. She would be very protective of him. A girlfriend or lover, maybe?"

"Wes really isn't the relationship type."

"Maybe the two had a short-term fling?"

"I don't know."

"This woman has more of an athletic frame and she rides a motorcycle."

Abigail paused, seeming to think about who might fit that description. "I'm sorry, Kiely," she finally said. "I don't ever remember seeing him with someone like that."

"When was the last time you saw your father?"

"It's been a few months. My birthday actually, so it was in June. He dropped off a birthday gift."

"Do you remember what you talked about?"

"Actually, I do. He said that he'd gotten a new investor that he was very excited about. In fact, he made a crude comment about her becoming my new stepmother if she dropped a few pounds! He was so infuriating! I started screaming at him and told him what a horrible person I thought he was and how much I hated him. He was genuinely perplexed, like he couldn't understand what the problem was. He left after that and I haven't seen him since."

"Do you know who the investor was that he was referring to?"

"Sorry, Kiely. Since I never heard anything about a marriage or an engagement I never gave it another thought. I figured he was just talking out the side of his neck or maybe this mystery woman hadn't lost those extra pounds," she said sarcastically.

Kiely could hear the disgust in Abigail's voice and scathing tone. She could also detect the hurt and frustration. Knowing Abigail and Wes had not had a relationship for years, Kiely thought of her own father and the abundance of love that he had showered down on her and her siblings. Kiely had been a daddy's girl, her father the first man she trusted. She couldn't begin to fathom what it had to be like for Abigail to have a father like Wes Matthews. The young woman had gone through a lot when people discovered the connection between the two. She'd been bullied, threatened, and attacked, despite discovering the ricin connection to RevitaYou and sounding the appropriate alarms. Others hadn't trusted her and wanted her to pay for her father's crimes, considering her guilty by virtue of her bloodline.

Recently, Abigail had been framed for a murder she didn't commit. Despite being completely exonerated, she had found that the allegations had threatened her custody and pending adoption of Maya. Griffin had come to her rescue, riding in like a knight on a white horse. His actions had solidified the bond between them. Watching their happily ever after unfold had been the stuff of romance novels.

"Abigail, I really appreciate you taking time to speak with me. You've been a big help."

"I haven't. Not really. I wish I could tell you more. I really want you to catch him."

"We will. Don't you worry. Drinks are on me the next time I see you!"

The baby suddenly cried in the background.

"And that would be Maya calling for my attention. I have to run."

"I understand. Talk to you soon," Kiely said as Abigail disconnected the call.

Kiely sat for a moment thinking about what Abigail had told her. She replayed the details of the case over in her head. The initial investigation into RevitaYou had found investors personally recruited by Wes Matthews. Those three had recouped their investment and then some, actually doubling their money. The investors that followed hadn't been so lucky.

It had been a typical pyramid scheme where money collected from newer victims was used to pay earlier victims, providing a veneer of legitimacy. All the victims were induced to recruit others, Wes Matthews promising them recruitment commissions for their efforts. It was fraud, plain and simple. By the time Brody had invested, it was too late. Soon after it was discovered that RevitaYou was actually killing patients. Landon Street, the chemist behind RevitaYou had disappeared and so had Wes Matthews, with close to a million dollars of other people's money. Now someone close to Matthews didn't want law enforcement to find him.

Why? Was it personal? What was her motive? Was she a lover wanting to be a ride or die for her man? Or was her motive about revenge? Was she a lover scorned who wanted to find him herself without interference? And what was her connection to Cooper? Why had she singled him out to torment? None of it made an ounce of sense and there were still too many pieces missing from the puzzle.

Kiely moved down the hall to peek in on Alfie. He was still sleeping soundly and she imagined his lengthy walk had worn his little body out. She also knew he'd be wide open when he did wake, needing lots of attention.

She headed down the carpeted steps to the lower level where Cooper was working on his laptop. He wore a black T-shirt that clearly defined his muscles. He really was quite a handsome man. He was staring intently, reading something on the computer screen and there was something about this that was very attractive. She almost hated interrupting him. Almost. "Are you busy?"

Cooper looked up and smiled at her. He shook his head. "Just reading my emails. What's up?"

Kiely moved to the chair beside him and sat down. "I just spoke to Abigail about her father."

"Was she able to give you anything?"

"Not really, but she did mention an investor Wes may have been involved with romantically. Do you have a list of those women who gave him money?"

"I do." Cooper pulled a manila folder from the corner of the desk and began fumbling through the large stack of papers inside. "Here we are," he said as he found what he was looking for. "There were three initially who made out well. Jane Rodriguez, Marley Runyon and Meghan Otis. And a few others after who all lost their money."

"What do you know about them?"

"These three were the first investors. Their stories were instrumental in helping to secure the other investors. They got their money back plus sizeable profits for their efforts. All three also appear on RevitaYou promotional material."

"Have you talked with any one of them?"

"Not personally. I believe other agents with our fraud

and cybercrimes divisions did." He punched keys on his keyboard, then nodded. "Agent Jeff Taylor spoke with all three and filed his report at the beginning of the investigation. Obviously, they didn't have any complaints. They made money on their deals."

"Can we look at all the female investors? I know of one, Ms. Blythe Kent. My brother Riley is engaged to her niece, Charlize. Ms. Kent invested almost fifty grand and lost it all. She's up there in age, though, so I know she's not hot rodding around on a motorcycle. I'd also like to figure out who Matthews might have been involved with besides Landon Street."

"You think that's who might be our kidnapper?"

"It might be a long shot but it's all we have right now. I just know whoever doesn't want him found has to be personally connected to him."

Cooper typed again. "Jane Rodriguez...she doubled her initial investment. She's sixty years old and a retired teacher." He turned the computer screen so Kiely could see her picture.

"I don't think it's her," she said. "She looks like someone's grandmother."

Cooper shook his head and typed again. "Marley Runyon also doubled her initial investment. She is newly married and very pregnant. I'd say by this recent social media post that she's close to eight months along."

"The woman on the motorcycle was definitely not pregnant."

"And lastly, we have Meghan Otis." Cooper paused, reading the screen.

"What?" Kiely asked. She shifted forward in her seat.

"Meghan Otis, thirty-five years old, former college track star. Worked as a bank teller and won one hundred and fifty thousand dollars in the lottery six months ago.

According to this she was instrumental in helping bring investors to RevitaYou and reportedly, she personally used the product."

"Any pictures?"

Cooper grinned. "Yes, check this out."

Meghan Otis was quite the selfie queen. There were hundreds of pictures of her on her social media accounts. Meghan working out. Meghan eating. Meghan hanging with friends. And a favorite for Kiely and Cooper, a picture of Meghan with her arms draped around Wes Matthews's neck.

"So did Matthews prey on Meghan because she had money?" Kiely questioned.

"That's highly probable. I wouldn't put anything past Matthews."

"But what was in it for her? It looks like she had everything going for her. Smart, accomplished, financially independent. And she's pretty! Why would she even consider using RevitaYou? It wasn't like she needed it."

Cooper shrugged. "Who knows why women do what they do. I stopped trying to figure you and your kind out years ago."

Kiely laughed. "My kind? You have some nerve!"

Cooper shrugged a second time, pushing his broad shoulders toward the ceiling. "I'll put in a request for everything we can find about Meghan Otis."

"I'd like to go talk to her, too."

"Let's get the background information back first, and then we can figure that out."

Kiely looked down at her wristwatch. "Should we wake up Alfie? He's been asleep for almost two hours now."

"Give him a few more minutes. He did a lot of running when I took him for a walk."

"I just don't want him to be wide awake tonight because he slept so long this afternoon."

"I agree, but I don't think we'll have a problem."

An awkward silence danced between them, as she consciously tried to pretend that she wasn't feeling the rise of sexual tension that existed when they were in each other's presence. Kiely watched his mouth, thinking that kissing him would be the greatest joy. Both sat with clenched fists, struggling not to touch the other and desperate to shake away the fantasies that were coming all too frequently.

Kiely stood up abruptly. "I'm going to head back upstairs."

Cooper nodded. "I need to finish up some paperwork here. Then I need to call and see where we are with your friend Gunther."

"Not a problem. As soon as Alfie wakes up and has his snack, he and I are going to go outside to play in the leaves." Kiely was already at the bottom of the stairs. She gave him a wave and disappeared to the upper level of the home.

COOPER WAS SMILING, and he felt slightly foolish. He found himself fighting not to gush when he and Kiely were in a room together. She had a way of amusing him even when he was trying to be serious. There was something very special about Kiely Colton. She was sunshine in the midst of a storm. Her carefree spirit was like a breath of fresh air. She was light in a well of darkness. She was everything he had been missing in his life. He had vowed to never love again, but something about Kiely had him reconsidering that pledge. Something about her had him rethinking what love might look like in his future.

He appreciated her kindness toward his son. She was exceptionally good with the little boy and Alfie adored her.

Alfie, who was usually shy around other people, most especially women, had told Kiely that he had "lub" for her. His childlike admission had been sweet and joy-filled. Cooper suddenly wished he had the courage and wisdom of a two-year-old, so that he could tell Kiely he was falling in love with her, too.

Because what he was suddenly feeling for Kiely Colton felt very much like love. It was energizing and nourishing and made him want to be a better man. It left him happy and excited by the prospect of each new day. It was desire and passion and longing like he couldn't ever remember feeling. It had him feeling blessed.

Cooper rose from his seat and shook out his arms and legs, anxious to shake away the tension that had spread through his body. He sat back down and reached for the phone. He'd missed a call from Lieutenant McKellar, who had left a message for him to call back as soon as he was able. When he didn't answer, Cooper left him a message.

He sat for a moment weighing his options; trying to determine what it was he needed and wanted to do. Reaching for his phone a second time, he dialed the district attorney's office. His secretary was all too happy to tell him that Eugene Beckwith was gone for the day. Leaving a second message for the man, Cooper wished her a good day and disconnected the line.

Cooper suddenly looked down to the notepad he'd been doodling on. A line of little hearts decorated the page, Kiely's name and his block printed in the center. Feeling foolish again, Cooper shook his head. He was grateful Kiely hadn't witnessed his adolescent behavior. Then again, he thought, maybe it was exactly what he needed to break the ice and open the conversation about what he was feeling. Tearing the top sheet of paper from the pad, he folded it in half and slid it into the back pocket of his jeans.

Chapter Nine

Kiely stood in the spray of hot water, allowing it to rain down over her shoulders. It trickled over her breasts and puddled beneath her feet. The body wash smelled of Japanese cherry blossoms, the delicate scent one of her favorites. She lathered herself from head to toe and then stood beneath the water to rinse it away. She was grateful for the moment, enjoying the quiet.

It had been a busy afternoon. Alfie had been on overload times ten. From the moment he'd woken from his nap, he had called her name over, and over again. Ki-Ki! Ki-Ki! Ki-Ki! It had sounded like a mantra for preschoolers. Being able to take the child outside to run and play had been a godsend. His energy was abundant and Kiely joked that if she could find a way to bottle and sell it, it would make them millions. Cooper had joined them and they had stomped through the woods, thrown leaves and hiked the trails behind the property. Alfie's laugh had been infectious and Kiely had had the best time.

Before they'd known it, it had been time for dinner. It had taken no time at all to toss the chicken she had marinated into the oven and to prepare a salad. Mashed garlic potatoes rounded out the meal. Both Cooper and Alfie had eaten heartily, the fresh air and outdoor activities triggering their appetites. Brownies topped with vanilla ice cream had been the perfect dessert. After his bath and thirty minutes of playing in the bubbles, Alfie had gone right to sleep. Once he was down for the night, Kiely had stolen a few minutes for herself, the hot shower feeling like heaven.

Her fingers and toes were shriveled when she finally stepped out of the glass enclosure and cut off the water. She felt like new money. Every muscle was relaxed and her skin was glowing. Her Japanese cherry blossom lotion was the last layer before a few spritzes of body spray. For ten minutes Kiely debated which pair of panties to wear and then she had to question why. This wasn't a date and she was acting like Cooper was taking her dining and dancing. Kiely was excited about spending time with him as if they hadn't just spent the entire day together. Feeling like a teen with her first crush, Kiely was struggling not to act like one.

Kiely dropped down against the corner of the bed, a heavy sigh blowing past her lips. There had been men in her life before Cooper. Men she had liked and men she was still friendly with. There were one or two who were friends with benefits, only calling on each other when there was no one else in their lives to satisfy those intimate urges. Calling on them when battery-powered Bob wasn't enough. But Kiely couldn't say that she had ever been in love with any man because she'd been fearful of failing herself the way she'd seen her parents fail each other. She didn't want to trust her heart and have her heart be disappointed. She didn't want to be her mother, putting a man first while losing herself in the process. Her life was simpler without a relationship and Kiely always chose simple when the opportunity presented itself. Men complicated things; her feelings, her time, her head. Men disrupted her flow and made her second-guess her own wants and dreams as she tried to navigate theirs. Keeping all men at arm's length, far from her heart, protected her.

But there was something about Cooper that had her letting her guard down. Something grounded and comfortable. Though she considered him a friend that something had her wanting more and imagining the possibilities had her completely discombobulated. Everything about their situation was foreign to her. Had anyone told her she'd be playing mommy and acting like a wife she would have told them they were lying. It surprised her how easily she had slid into the roles and how much she was enjoying them. Alfie had stolen her heart, but truth be told, so had his father.

COOPER WAS SITTING on the sectional, playing with the television remote. A second helping of brownie and ice cream sat in a bowl on the coffee table. He'd also opened a bottle of wine and had poured them both a glass. He stopped to stare as she moved toward him, his eyes skating up and down the length of her body. Awe painted his expression and Kiely suddenly liked how she saw herself in his eyes.

She pointed at his bowl. "Really, Cooper?"

"It's all your fault. You're an amazing cook and you keep making these incredible desserts to tempt me. What else can I do?"

Kiely laughed. She moved to the kitchen. Her laugh faded quickly. "That was the last brownie! How many have you eaten?"

"Just grab another spoon. I'll share!"

"Yes, you will," she said as she pulled a utensil from the drawer and moved back to the sectional to sit with him. She swiped two bites of brownie before she scooted up to sit beside him. "So, any news on Gunther?"

"Your boyfriend Tripp and I are playing phone tag. I'll try him again in the morning."

"My boyfriend Tripp? You're funny!"

"I saw how he was looking at you."

"And how was that?"

"The way he's always winking his eye at you and that smirk on his face. I'm sure I don't have to explain it to you."

"No," she said, shaking her head, "you really do."

"I can't explain it. It was just inappropriate."

"You really are funny! That man is not interested in me and I am not interested in him."

"You sure about that?"

Kiely changed the subject abruptly. "The night the bombs went off you were about to say something to me."

Cooper paused and his cheeks suddenly flushed a bright shade of red. "Was I? I don't recall…"

"You recall," Kiely laughed.

"Has anyone told you that you can be slightly intimidating?"

"I intimidate you?"

"No! Not me! But I'm sure…well…" He suddenly stammered and then he laughed.

Kiely giggled with him. "I can't believe you're tongue-tied."

Cooper tossed up his hands. "You do that to me."

"Do what?"

"You know what."

"How long are we going to play this game?"

"As long as it takes for me not to make a complete and total fool out of myself. I don't know how to do this anymore." He suddenly looked exasperated.

Kiely shifted her body closer, settling into his body heat. She hooked her arm through his and leaned her head on his shoulder. "Tell me what it was you were going to say before that madwoman on the motorcycle interrupted us."

Cooper sighed, a soft breath of air blowing past his lips. "Before we were so rudely blown out of the moment, I was trying to tell you how I was feeling."

"And how were you feeling?" Kiely asked.

COOPER HESITATED, TRYING to choose his words carefully. He cut his eye at her, holding his breath deep in his lungs. He suddenly felt completely out of his depth and he knew it showed.

Kiely spun her body around to face him, sitting with her legs crossed lotus style. "You like me, don't you?" She met his stare, a hint of mischief shimmering in her eyes.

Her expression made him smile. "Yeah, I do. I like you a lot."

She tapped his leg gently with her hand. "I like you, too, Cooper."

His smile pulled into a full grin. "You do?"

"Why does that surprise you?"

"Because I don't get the impression that there are too many people you actually like."

Kiely laughed. "So now you have jokes!"

Cooper laughed with her. He took another deep breath, his expression turning serious. "I know this whole situation with us has been awkward."

"It's been interesting. Maybe not ideal, but it's felt pretty darn special."

"That's one way to look at it."

Cooper reached for her hand and held it, studying her fingers. She had the hands of a piano player, he thought. Her fingers were long, her nails cut short and manicured with a light coat of pale pink polish.

"Are you interested in a relationship, Cooper?" Kiely

was eyeing him intently. Watching him as he was watching her.

"After Sara died, I'd sworn off any kind of relationship. I'd pretty much given up on love. But yeah, since you and I have been getting to know each other, I'm very interested in seeing where we can go from here. But can I be honest with you?"

"I would hope you wouldn't have to ask. I expect honesty, Cooper. I don't ever want to be lied to."

He gave her a nod of his head. "This scares me, Kiely. I was never any good at dating. And I'm sure if she were here, my wife would tell you that I wasn't great at marriage either. I just don't want you to move forward thinking I have a clue about how to do this."

"Well, the way I figure it, we can stress over it or we can just make it up as we go along. And I don't stress out over anything," Kiely said softly.

"You really are an amazing woman, Kiely Colton."

"Yes, I am, and you'll have to work hard to earn me."

Cooper chuckled. "I just knew you were going to be high maintenance!"

The conversation was suddenly interrupted as Alfie came scampering across the room in their direction. Kiely's eyes widened as she tossed Cooper a look. "Alfie! Are you okay?"

"Want my Ki-Ki!" he exclaimed as he climbed onto the sectional and into Kiely's lap. "Where you go, Ki-Ki?"

Kiely hugged him. "Kiely's right here, sweetie. Why are you awake?"

"Did he climb out of the crib?" Cooper said, still looking stunned.

"You didn't know he could climb out?"

"You mean this wasn't his first time?"

She laughed, giving Alfie a tickle. "Your daddy is so silly!"

Alfie giggled. "Silly, Dad-dy!"

Cooper leaned forward to kiss his son's cheek. And then he pressed his lips to Kiely's cheek, the kiss lingering until Alfie pushed him away.

"No kiss my Ki-Ki, Dad-dy. Dat *my* Ki-Ki!"

COOPER NOTICED HE and Kiely were working well together, playing easily off each other's strengths and weaknesses. This dynamic give-and-take allowed them to discover more about each other as they continued to research the case. The friendship that had blossomed was full and thick. Their time together felt as natural as breathing and both found themselves wishing that it would never have to end. Conversation was sometimes intense and sometimes nonsensical. Laughter was abundant as they realized they were more alike than they were different.

When Cooper and Tripp finally connected, the call coming in the early evening two days later, Kiely excused herself from the room, heading back upstairs to check on Alfie. They exchanged smiles and Cooper winked his eye at her.

"Only my boyfriend does that," she said smugly as she pointed to the phone and the call that was on hold.

Cooper laughed. "I deserved that!"

"Yes, you did."

She waved her hand at him. "I'll be upstairs with the baby," she said, disappearing from his sight.

Cooper reached for the telephone receiver. "Tripp, hello! Sorry to keep you holding."

"It's not a problem. I'm glad we've finally caught up with each other. There's a lot I need to fill you in on. You want the good news or the bad news?"

"It's like that?"

"Why don't I just start with the good news. We've got a name!" Tripp said excitedly.

"Gunther came through?"

"Not before asking for a down pillow and cashmere blanket to go with everything else he wanted."

"That guy's a real piece of work."

"That he is. I just emailed you the report. According to him, the man behind Capital X is named Tate Greer."

Cooper frowned. Tate Greer? The name was familiar but he wasn't sure where he'd heard it before. "What do we know about him?"

"That's it, right now. He's been running under the radar for a while. He's got no rap sheet. Not even a parking ticket. He's squeaky clean. Almost too clean."

"Are we sure the name's not an alias?"

"We're not sure of anything at the moment, but from everything Gunther told us, he's bad news: racketeering, fraud, embezzlement, solicitation and possibly a murder or two. He personally ordered the assault on Brody Higgins and all the others. I sent you Gunther's signed statement. Once he started talking we couldn't get him to shut up. He was crooning like a stuck canary."

Cooper had scrolled through a lengthy list of email messages and was printing off the documents that Tripp had sent. "This is good news. Good work, Lieutenant."

"Couldn't have done it without you, Agent. I don't know what you said to him, but he's not interested in ever seeing you again." Tripp laughed.

"What's the bad news?"

Tripp sighed. "We've had another death. The coroner is attributing it to the ricin-laced RevitaYou product. The mayor is on a rampage. He wants Landon Street caught and caught yesterday."

"Damn," Cooper cussed. He suddenly felt like he was

losing traction with the case. "I really need to get back
to my office," he said. "I'm limited in what I can do remotely."

"I get it," Tripp said. "But when you do come back
you're going to be able to hit the ground running. You'll
be well rested, healed and ready to kick ass. Meanwhile
just do what you can do. We'll keep you in the loop here
and call on you when we need you."

"Thank you," Cooper said, suddenly feeling bad about
the names he'd called the man in his head. He realized they
might actually be good friends one day and when that day
came, he looked forward to laughing with him about his
assumptions about Tripp and Kiely. "I'd like to buy you a
beer when we close this case."

"I'm going to hold you to that," Tripp said. He continued. "My office also sent you the forensics report from
the bombing at your property. It was a nondescript pipe
bomb. There was nothing about it that we could connect to
anyone already in our database. But we're not giving up."

"I appreciate that." And Cooper did, but it wasn't lost on
him that they were no closer to finding the woman who'd
taken his son than when they'd started. Which meant Alfie
was still at risk.

The two men agreed to talk again later in the week after
Cooper was able to read through all the reports. After disconnecting the call, he sat back in his seat, his mind racing. There was information he still needed and he began
making a list of orders for his team at the agency. Even
though he couldn't be there, he knew how to delegate well.

Finding Wes Matthews and his cohort Landon Street
was at the top of his to-do list. He added the unknown
woman who'd kidnapped Alfie and bombed his car. And
now there was Tate Greer. Something told him the three
men were connected. He needed to figure out how. And

his instincts were shouting that the woman who had taken his son was a lone wolf and not necessarily doing the bidding of any one man. So, what was her connection to him and why his son?

Alfie suddenly called him from the top of the stairs. "Dad-dy! Dad-dy!"

Cooper called back. "Yes, son? What's wrong, baby?"

"Me and Ki-Ki making cookies!" he exclaimed excitedly. The pitter-patter of his little feet running back to the kitchen echoed after him.

Cooper smiled. Alfie and Kiely were definitely a thing. He had high hopes that if all continued to go well, he and Kiely would be a thing, too.

HOURS LATER ALFIE was down for the night and he and Kiely were enjoying cups of hot chocolate laced with bourbon and the white chocolate cranberry cookies she and Alfie had made. This was quickly becoming his favorite time of day, when he and Kiely sat side by side, their conversation easy. Sometimes they talked and sometimes they didn't. This night Kiely was scrolling through her iPad reading recipes while he watched some Jimmy Kimmel special on the television.

"I had a good conversation with Tripp," Cooper said, when she finally laid the iPad down.

"That's good."

"The case is…"

"Let's not talk about the case. Not tonight. We've been working the case all day and I need to take a step back from it. Please."

Cooper met the look she was giving him with one of his own. He nodded. "That's fine."

"Did you take your meds?"

"No. I actually feel good. I haven't needed a pain pill all day."

"That's good. You may want to take one before you go to bed to ensure you rest well."

He shrugged. "Maybe."

"Wanna play a game?" Kiely questioned.

Cooper grinned. "A game?"

"Twenty questions. We ask each other ten questions and each has to be answered. No shirking off an answer because you don't like what was asked."

Cooper eyed her curiously. His gaze narrowed just a smidge. "Why does this feel like it's going to get me in trouble?"

"I guess that all depends on your answers," Kiely said with a warm laugh.

He sat upright. "Okay, I'm game to play."

"What's your favorite color?"

"My favorite color? My favorite color is green."

"Okay, your turn."

"What's your favorite color?"

"You can't ask the same question."

"Why not? I want to know the answer."

"I'm going to give you this one, but don't do it again. My favorite color is beige."

"That's a color?"

"Is that your next question?"

Cooper held his hands up as if he were surrendering. "Sorry about that. Your turn."

"Name three people, living or dead, that you'd like to have dinner with if you could."

Cooper paused, giving the question a moment of thought. "My mother, my grandmother and Midge."

"Who's Midge?"

"Midge was a rottweiler I had when I was a little boy.

She was my best friend for many years. We did everything together."

"Midge isn't a person."

"You didn't know Midge," he said, giving her a look.

"Okay," Kiely giggled. "But why not Sara? Wouldn't you want to see her again?"

"My wife?" Cooper shrugged, his gaze shifting off into the distance as he pondered the question. He turned his eyes back to her as he spoke. "One dinner wouldn't be enough time to apologize to her for being a crappy husband. It wouldn't be fair to her." He dropped the subject, contrition cloaking his expression. "Your turn," he said. "Who was the first boy you ever kissed?"

Amusement crossed Kiely's face. "His name was Steven. I don't remember his last name. We were in the third grade and he kissed me one day on the playground."

"What did you do?"

"I told my brother Riley and Riley punched him in the face."

"Ouch!"

"It wasn't pretty," she responded. "Why did you become an FBI agent?"

"I've always wanted to be in law enforcement since I was a kid. I thought being an agent with the FBI would be like an American James Bond adventure. I saw myself going undercover, with high-tech weapons and always catching the bad guys. At the time it looked like a great career path."

"And now?"

"There are no cool weapons, rarely do I get to go in the field, undercover or otherwise, and it's been a great career path."

Kiely gave him a smile.

"French fries or hash browns?" Cooper questioned.

"French fries. Are you good at oral sex?"

Cooper choked on the swallow of hot chocolate he had just sipped. He was laughing and coughing at the same time, a blush of color warming his cheeks. "Really, Kiely?"

Her brow was raised as she looked at him. "Just answer the question."

He shook his head. "I've never had any complaints, but with all things, I'm sure practice will make perfect." Kiely gestured for him to ask his next question. "How long was your last relationship?"

"I've never really done relationships, but if you want to get technical about it, then the last guy I dated lasted ten days."

"Who broke it off, you or him?"

"I get the next question. It's not your turn."

"It was a two-part question. It should be allowed."

"Well, it's not."

Cooper laughed. "Fine! Ask your question."

"Do you like being a father?"

"I love being a father. It has made me a better man. And yes, I would love to have more children one day."

"I didn't ask that," Kiely said.

"But you were going to. That was clearly a two-part question."

"What are you doing, making up the rules as you go along?"

"I'm playing the game!"

Kiely folded her arms across her chest. "Ask your question."

"Your last relationship, who broke up with whom?"

"I broke up with him. There was no point staying when I knew it wasn't going to work out." Kiely shifted her body, stretching her arms outward. "Cats or dogs?"

"Definitely dogs. Cats jump on the counters in the kitchen when you're not home. I'm not a big fan of cats."

"That is not true!"

"How do you know? Do you have a cat?"

"I just know. And yes, I do. His name is Jim Morrison."

Cooper blinked. "Jim Morrison?"

Kiely laughed. "Ask your last question, Agent McKellar."

"My last? I didn't get ten questions, did I? You said I'd get ten questions."

"If I counted those two, you have exceeded your ten questions."

"You're one tough cookie, Kiely Colton!"

"You better ask before you lose your turn." She eyed him with a raised brow, waiting.

Curling his lips in an indulgent smile, Cooper grinned at her. He leaned forward in his seat, the gesture feeling very conspiratorial as Kiely leaned with him. "May I kiss you?" His voice came out in a husky whisper.

Kiely's expression shifted, her eyes widening. Her smile blossomed, light shimmering in her eyes. "A kiss?"

"Do I need to repeat the question?"

"No, I heard you."

Cooper repeated himself. "So then, can... I...kiss... you?" he repeated.

"Yes," Kiely finally answered. "I was wondering what was taking you so long to get to it!"

Shifting his body toward her, Cooper eased his left arm around her waist and pulled her close. Kiely reached both arms around his neck as he leaned in against her. He brought his face near hers and then pulled back. He repeated the gesture a second time, coming so close that his warm breath blew gently against her lips. The third time his mouth connected with hers in the sweetest kiss Cooper had ever experienced. Her lips were like plush pillows, soft like satin and she tasted of chocolate and mint.

In that moment Cooper knew that he would never want to kiss any other woman ever again. He loved how Kiely melted into his arms and she felt like home. He would have sworn that he saw fireworks, flashes of light behind his eyes brilliantly celebrating the moment. His tongue tapped lightly against the line of her teeth waiting for her to allow him in. As their mouths danced beautifully together, Cooper felt like he'd reached the mystical harmonious valley of Shangri-La. Kiely's touch was sweeter than his favorite cookie, ice cream on a summer day, and the little nougat candies his mother would make for Christmas. In his arms, she was sunshine after a spring rain, the light at the end of a dark tunnel, and the answer to prayers he hadn't known he needed. That first kiss was everything and more.

Chapter Ten

Kiely was pleasantly exhausted the next morning. She and Cooper hadn't gone to bed until the wee hours of the morning. That first kiss had led to a second and then a third and before either knew it they were making out like teenagers in the back seat of his father's Ford automobile. The experience had been incredible.

Kissing Cooper had felt like a dream come true. His touch was gentle yet also commanding and slightly possessive. His hands had danced across her back and down the length of her torso with skillful precision. His heated fingertips had ignited currents of electricity through her body. He had taken her on a sensual journey of warm caresses and hot touches, the likes of which she had never experienced before. If she had to explain it to anyone she wouldn't have been able to find the words.

The moment had been interrupted when little Alfie had woken with a slight fever. It had taken a good hour to get him back to sleep and then they were both too exhausted to go back to making out. Alfie still wasn't feeling one hundred percent and had been moody most of the morning. While Cooper had gone downstairs to work, Kiely had rocked Alfie with a half-dozen storybooks, the child's song "Baby Shark" on constant rotation, and sips of apple ginger tea.

Alfie had finally gone down for a nap and Kiely was in the kitchen humming away when Cooper came back up the stairs.

She greeted him with a wide grin and an eye wink. "Hey, good-looking! What are you up to?"

"Something smells really good and I came to check out what you were into."

"I was just about to pull your lunch out of the oven. I made individual chicken pot pies."

Cooper tilted his head slightly, his look inquisitive. "Do I smell apples and cinnamon too?"

"That's tonight's dessert. Apple pie with a buttermilk and rosemary piecrust."

"Mmm!" Cooper hummed. "I can't wait! We'll have ice cream with that, right?"

Kiely laughed. "Does butter pecan work for you?"

"I swear I've gained at least twenty pounds since you came into my life. It's been the best twenty pounds I've ever had."

"As soon as the doctor gives you the all-clear we need to get you back in the gym. Are you a runner by chance?"

"I don't hate it, but it's not my favorite thing to do."

"Thank God!" Kiely exclaimed. "I despise running."

"What do you do to stay in shape?"

"Do I have to do something?"

Cooper laughed. "So, you want me to believe that you do nothing to maintain that great figure?"

"I was blessed with good genetics."

"I think I hate you. I really don't, but still!" He laughed.

"Come sit down and eat your lunch," Kiely commanded. "The pot pies are ready."

After plating the food, Kiely sat down at the table with him. The conversation was casual as they savored their lunch.

"I sent my sister a shopping list. She's going to come up tomorrow. Do you want her to bring you anything?" Kiely questioned.

Cooper suddenly sat forward. He dropped his fork against his plate. A light bulb had gone off in his head as a piece of the puzzle came together. "Your sister. What's her fiancé's name?" he asked.

Concern blessed Kiely's expression, the abrupt shift in Cooper's mood disconcerting. "Pippa? She's engaged to Emmanuel. Emmanuel Iglesias. Why?"

Cooper shook his head. "No, your sister, Sadie. Who's the boyfriend you and Pippa were giving her a hard time about on the ride up here?"

Kiely scowled. "Tate Greer. No one can stand him. He's a real creep."

"He's more than that," Cooper snapped as he suddenly stood and headed for the office downstairs. He called out over his shoulder. "Tate Greer is the mastermind behind Capital X. Gunther named him yesterday. The FBI has deemed him dangerous. He's been placed on our Most Wanted list."

For the briefest moment Kiely sat stunned. Her eyes had widened and heat flushed her face a deep shade of rising rage. Her mind began to race, her heartbeat on super speed. Fear was holding hands and doing a two-step with anger, the likes of which she hadn't felt in some time. She'd always known Tate Greer was scum. She never would have imagined that he was even lower, more like the fungus that fed on pond scum. She cussed, a lengthy stream of expletives blowing past her lips.

Dashing after him, Kiely followed Cooper downstairs, taking them two at a time. Her voice was an octave higher when she spoke. "I just talked with Sadie about an hour ago. She wanted my recipe for fettuccine carbonara. She's meeting Tate at his condo tonight for dinner. They've been thinking about eloping to Vegas and she's supposed to give him her answer."

"We need to stop her," Cooper said. "She's not safe. Call your brother. I'm going to call Agent Miller."

COOPER AND KIELY were both pacing the floor, anxiety levels at an all-time high. Alfie was still under the weather and Kiely held him close as she walked him back and forth. Her nervousness was doing very little to soothe the whining child's discomfort.

"It's going to be okay, Alfie. It's okay," she cooed.

The couple had spent the last few hours on the telephone, back and forth with Kiely's brother Riley and the FBI. Cooper had alerted his team and a plan was now in place to catch Tate Greer. The challenge for them, was being able to catch Tate and keep Sadie safe. Tipping him off could easily prove to be a detriment to her sister. And there was no way they could tell Sadie and trust that she wouldn't reveal their hand if her emotions got the best of her.

After much discussion it was decided to let Sadie proceed with her dinner plans. Shortly after six o'clock, Kiely would call her sister and say that she had an emergency. When Sadie exited the home to come to her aid there would be an FBI team waiting outside. Riley would also be there to ensure that Sadie was safe. When Sadie was out of harm's way the team could go in and apprehend Tate Greer. It sounded simple enough, but Kiely and Cooper both knew that anything could go wrong at any time.

Cooper was able to monitor his team's activity digitally, and the plan was that as soon as they were in place, Kiely would make the call. With the clock ticking Kiely's nerves were on overload. She hated that Sadie was in this position. Not following her instincts, and wanting her sister to be happy, Kiely hadn't vetted him as well as she should have. And she couldn't help but wonder if Tate's interest in Sadie had been purely selfish, if he'd been using her sister to keep a close eye on what was going on with the case. After reading the report on Tate, she knew that he was capable of anything. He wouldn't hesitate to use Sadie if it meant saving himself. And if he harmed her sister she didn't know what she would do.

"It's time," Cooper said, gesturing at her. He reached for Alfie, taking the child out of her arms. "Remember, it's okay if you let your anxiety show. Use it so that she knows you desperately need her."

Kiely gave him a nod as she moved to the desk to sit down. She had tried to not let him see her nervousness, but Cooper had picked up on it. She had no qualms about lying to her sister, but she didn't want to do anything that would put her family in harm's way. She took a deep breath then dialed her sister's number and waited for Sadie to answer.

"Hello?"

"Sadie, hey. It's me," Kiely responded.

"Hey, what's up? You calling to see if I executed the fettuccine correctly?"

"Are you alone or is Tate there with you?"

"He's in the shower, why? Are you okay, Kiely? You don't sound good."

"No, I really need your help. But you can't tell Tate."

"Does this have anything to do with Cooper and the kidnapping case?"

"Yes. I'm actually outside," Kiely said, the little white lie rolling easily off her tongue. "There's a black sedan parked across the street. Can you sneak out for a quick second and come see me? I can tell you everything then."

Kiely could almost see her sister moving to a front window to peer outside. She lied again, saying, "The FBI picked me up and brought me here. It's really important, Sadie! I really need to talk with you. But I don't want to involve Tate, so please don't tell him."

"Don't worry, he's still in the shower. I'll be right there. I'm on my way out."

"Thank you," Kiely said. For a split second she wanted to apologize to her sister. To say she was sorry for the dishonesty. But more than anything she needed to know Sadie was safe from the likes of Tate Greer. She was desperate for her sister to know what kind of man he truly was but since she couldn't say those words, she said the next best thing. "I love you, Sadie."

Sadie disconnected the call and when she did, Kiely began to count. The few short minutes it took for her sister to exit the house and scurry across the street to the car felt like forever. When her eldest brother's number showed up on the phone, Kiely snatched it quickly.

"Hello?"

"We've got her. She's safe," Riley answered.

Kiely could hear her sister in the background, her voice raised as she questioned what was going on. Sadie fussing was all she needed to let go of the breath she'd been holding tightly in her lungs. When she exhaled, letting it go, warm breath and apprehension gushed from her like air from a popped balloon.

"She wants to talk to you," Riley said as Kiely listened to him passing their sister his phone.

"Kiely, what the hell is this?" Sadie snapped. "Where are you?"

"I'm still at the safe house with Cooper and Alfie. I'm sorry I had to lie to you. But Riley will explain everything."

"Somebody had better explain something to me!" Sadie shouted.

Riley had taken his phone back. "Tell Agent Winston I'll call him back with an update once everything goes down."

"Thanks, Riley! Love you, big brother!"

The phone line went dead. Kiely sat there for a moment, allowing herself to process it all. She couldn't begin to imagine what Sadie had to be feeling right then. Discovering that Tate Greer wasn't the man her sister thought he was would break her heart. Tate's deception would surely steal Sadie's joy. Understanding the magnitude of that left a bitter taste in Kiely's mouth.

As if he had a sixth sense, Cooper read her mood. "If you need to leave, I understand. I'm sure your sister needs you right now."

Kiely shook her head. "I need to be here with you and Alfie. Until we find that woman, neither one of you is safe. My family will make sure Sadie is okay. Besides, I'm sure I'm the last person she wants to see right now. She needs someone to blame and I'll be it while she figures it all out. I know her well."

Kiely rose from her seat. She moved swiftly to Cooper's side and into his arms. He hugged her tightly as she breathed a sigh of relief. She felt safe against him and could have held onto him forever.

She pressed her hand to Alfie's cheek. With Sadie secure under her brother's protective umbrella, keeping the little boy safe was now her first priority. Her family was everything to her and as far as she was concerned Alfie and his father were now family to her, too.

"He's still warm," she said. "It's time for another dose of baby medicine."

"Why don't you take him up and get him settled. I'll be up as soon as I hear something."

Kiely nodded, then reached to kiss his lips. She eased Alfie against her chest. "Come on, precious. Come to Kiely."

HOURS LATER ALFIE'S fever had finally broken and he was sleeping comfortably. Kiely had tried to call her sister multiple times, but Sadie hadn't answered. Kiely had no doubt that Sadie was furious with her, needing someone other than Tate to blame. This too would pass, she thought. She thought about going back down to wait it out with Cooper, but he needed to focus and she needed a moment to herself.

When her phone rang, it surprised her. Recognizing Pippa's cell phone number, she answered it promptly.

"Hey, Pip!"

"Are you okay?" she asked.

Kiely felt her stomach flip. Since they'd been little girls they had always been oddly simpatico; one always knew when something was wrong with the other. Anytime Kiely was feeling blue, she trusted that Pippa would call like clockwork to check on her.

"I'm fine," Kiely answered.

"Don't lie, Kiely. I got that gut feeling that things were off with you."

Kiely sighed. "I'm just trying to work through some things. Have you spoken to Sadie?"

"She's here with me now. She's been bawling her eyes out since she got here."

"I hate that this has happened to her. But I'm glad that she knows the truth about Tate."

"We just need to make sure she knows we're here for her. She needs to feel supported and she'll get through it."

"I wish I was there."

"You just need to keep yourself safe. How are things with you and that handsome agent going?"

"Hold on," Kiely said. She moved down the hallway

toward her bedroom to ensure Cooper couldn't overhear her conversation. She paused in the doorway to peek in on Alfie before disappearing behind her closed door and dropping down to the bedside.

"Don't laugh at me, Pippa, but I think I'm falling for Cooper."

Pippa laughed. "You think?"

"Okay, I know. I love him, and it scares me to death!"

"Why? That's such a beautiful thing!"

"Because I've become Mom! It's the craziest thing, Pip, but all I want to do is take care of Cooper and Alfie. I feel like I've been transported back in time and discovered my inner June Cleaver," she said. "I don't even recognize myself anymore!"

"But are you happy?"

"Happier than I think I've ever been. But I'm sure Mom was happy, too, until she wasn't. I don't want to look back twenty years from now and regret that I gave up being a wild child for a man."

"Kiely, you've spent the majority of your adult life running toward danger in order to run from commitment to anything. Nothing has ever brought you true joy so that you would want to settle down and avoid always putting yourself at risk. This man and his son are bringing you joy. Embrace that! None of us knows what the future holds and change happens every day. Twenty years from now you may still be happier than you have ever been."

Kiely reflected on her sister's comment. "He kissed me," she said.

"Just kissed you?"

"We've been taking things slow."

"I'm thinking if you haven't been to bed with him already then this man is definitely the one."

"Why would you say that?"

"Because you have never had any qualms about sleeping with a man you were attracted to. Your hit-it and quit-it attitude has always concerned us. Because you've dated some really good guys, Kiely. Good guys that you tossed away like trash."

Kiely sighed.

The knock on the door pulled her from the reflections.

"Kiely?" Cooper called her name. She could hear the concern in his voice and it tugged at her heartstrings.

"I need to run," she said to Pippa. "Cooper is calling me. I'll check on Sadie tomorrow."

"Sadie will be fine. Vikki is on her way, and we'll take care of her. I may not come up there tomorrow as I planned. Will you be okay if I don't?"

"I'll be fine. Just take care of Sadie. Tell her I love her, please."

"We love you, too! And, please don't sabotage yourself trying to overthink this! Care for this man and know that it's okay if he feels the same."

Kiely stood up from the bedside and moved to the door, pulling it open. Cooper looked anxious, standing on the other side.

"Is everything okay?" he asked.

"I was just on the phone with Pippa. I wanted to check on Sadie. She's not answering any of my calls."

"I'm sorry."

"There's nothing for you to be sorry about. So, what's going on? Did your team complete their mission?"

Cooper shook his head, his expression dropping. "We lost him," he said.

"Lost him?" Her expression was incredulous, her eyes wide as saucers. "How the hell did they lose him?"

"We're still trying to figure that one out. They raided the townhouse and he wasn't there. The shower was still running but Tate was long gone. We're thinking he slipped out the back and managed to get past our men who were positioned there."

"Did Sadie say something to him before she left the house?"

"Not a word. Your brother says she was as surprised as they were."

"So that means he's on the run now, too." Kiely threw up her hands in frustration.

"It also means that Sadie might be in danger. Your brother has asked us to move her into protective custody."

"Well, she can come here and stay with us, right?"

"I already suggested that option, but Sadie refused. She says she just wants to be alone."

Tears misted Kiely's eyes and she batted her lashes so as not to cry. "She's devastated."

"Agent Miller will take her to another location first thing in the morning."

Kiely shook her head. "I can't believe this is happening," she said.

"There's more. I need to go back to Grand Rapids in the morning. I have a meeting with the mayor scheduled first thing and he wants to do a press conference."

"A press conference? Do you think that's wise?"

"I'll be fine and I won't do anything that will jeopardize you or Alfie's safety. But he's on a real tangent about us finding Landon Street and making sure the public is aware of the dangers of RevitaYou. Will you and Alfie be okay by yourselves for a few hours?"

"He and I will be just fine. I don't want you worrying about us."

Cooper pulled her into a deep hug and held on tightly. He kissed her forehead, his lips brushing gently against her skin. "I can't help but worry, Kiely. You two are the most important people in my life right now."

COOPER WASN'T SURE what to think. He was still fuming about that raid going bad; thinking that if he had been there on-site they would've captured Tate Greer. He hadn't planned to go back to Grand Rapids, but political pressure was bearing down on the FBI. What he hadn't told Kiely was that he also planned to participate in a second raid while he was in the city. A random tip had come in on the hotline with an address where the caller claimed Landon Street could be found. Landon Street's picture had been in the news for days. The Grand Rapids Police Department had even issued a reward for information about his whereabouts. A special line had been dedicated to accept the flood of calls that had followed.

Earlier in the investigation Cooper had spoken with Landon's half brother, Flynn Cruz-Street. With two tours of duty under his belt, Flynn now worked as military police at the Fort Rapids military base. In their brief conversation it was obvious that Flynn had once idolized his big brother. He had claimed they were now estranged, claiming not to know where Landon was but that he had since seen him twice around the city. Flynn had assured them that he would call if he spotted his sibling again and so far he had been true to his word. Flynn sounded anxious to find Landon himself, hoping to convince his brother to turn himself in. Despite Flynn's many assurances that he wanted to do what was right, Cooper wasn't sure that he truly trusted the man.

He needed to vet this new tip personally. He also knew that if he told Kiely, it would be an issue. She either wouldn't want him to go or she'd insist on going with him. Keeping her safe was now as important as keeping Alfie safe. He figured he would deal with the fallout after things were all said and done.

The rest of their evening had been relatively quiet. Kiely hadn't talked much, retiring to her bedroom early. Now he was missing her something crazy. After a hot shower he moved from the bathroom to the bedroom and climbed into his bed. He had checked on Alfie before his shower and his son seemed to be past the virus that had raised his temperature and put him in a sour mood. Cooper knew that his little boy would sleep soundly through the night.

He tossed and turned for another hour, unable to fall off to sleep. Cooper couldn't stop thinking about Kiely. There had been a sadness in her eyes, her sister's heartbreak fracturing her own. Knowing the siblings were close, it wasn't until he saw how hurt she was that he realized just how close.

Cooper would've done anything to take Kiely's pain from her. He couldn't begin to know how to console her. He just knew that he wanted to put a smile back on her face and make things well. Breaking this case would bring comfort to her and so many others.

The knock at his door surprised him. When Kiely pushed it open, easing into the room, that surprised him more. She wore a black tank top and matching panties. She'd pinned her hair up and a wisp of curls framed her face. Her skin was bare of makeup and her cheeks glowed. She was stunning. Stepping into the room Kiely turned to close and lock the door behind her. She moved to the nightstand and turned on the baby monitor.

"We need to hear Alfie in case he wakes up," she said softly.

Cooper nodded his agreement. Nervous energy exploded through his lower extremities. He suddenly wanted her more than he could have ever imagined. Throwing back the covers he gestured for her to climb in beside him. Kiely sat down on the mattress, lifted her legs and slid her body against his, her buttocks grazing his pelvis. As he covered them both with the blanket he wrapped his arms tightly around her, curling himself against her backside.

They lay together for a good while, trading easy caresses. Cooper pressed a damp kiss against Kiely's neck. Others followed, trailing over her shoulder. His touch was featherlight and he felt Kiely's entire body tremble. She grabbed his hand and pressed it to her breasts, which fit perfectly in the palms of his hands. Her nipples were rockhard and as he gently kneaded the soft flesh Kiely slowly rotated her buttocks against the sizeable bulge that had risen in his flannel pants. The two did a sensual dance, lying side by side, cradled sweetly against each other.

When Kiely turned in his arms, pressing her mouth to his, that kiss felt as mesmerizing as their first kiss. Her tongue did a voracious tango in his mouth, teasing past the line of his teeth to dance with his tongue. Her warm breath was minty, tasting like the mouthwash they both used. Kiely's hands skated against his chest, wound around his back and settled along the round of his backside.

His heart fluttered and blood surged through every vessel in his body. His muscles tightened and when she slid her hand past his waistband, wrapping her fingers around his male member, Cooper thought he would explode right then and there. Their loving became feverish, heat rising like a vengeance between them. They tore at each other's clothing, desperate to feel skin against skin.

Cooper pulled himself from her just long enough to reach a condom hidden in his wallet resting on the nightstand. He sheathed himself quickly. When he rolled above her, Kiely parted her legs widely and welcomed him in. That moment of intimate connection, as Cooper slid his body into hers, affirmed what both had been feeling. Love spiraled in brilliant shades of joy and delight. It was thick and abundant and all-consuming. The pleasure was one he never would have fathomed. It was sensual gratification and hedonistic decadence. It was bliss beyond his wildest dreams.

HOURS LATER, WHEN Kiely woke, Cooper was gone. She missed him, and that surprised her. She had never missed any man before. But now she was missing him, missing his touch, and the scent of his cologne that wafted from room to room. The night between them had been exquisite. It had been more than she could have ever imagined. She couldn't see herself ever being with any other man ever again. Cooper had claimed her, body and soul, and he had a grip on her heart that was irrefutable.

Movement out of the corner of her eye pulled at her attention. Alfie had crawled up on the bed and sat on the pillow beside her, calling her name. He patted her face and lifted one eyelid and then the other. "Mornin', Ki-Ki!"

"Good morning, Alfie!" She gave him a hug.

"Alfie cuddle with Ki-Ki," he said as he snuggled with her beneath the covers.

She reached for the television remote and found the local PBS affiliate, playing an episode of *Sesame Street*. Alfie was excited to see Big Bird skipping across the television screen that hung on the wall. His joyous laugh rang through the room. Kiely laughed with him. It was going to be that kind of day for the two of them.

Chapter Eleven

Cooper entered the FBI office like a man on a mission, a pep to his step. Claire Miller stepped into his office, her brows raised.

"Good morning, Agent Winston!"

"Agent Miller, it's good to see you!"

"It's good to see you, too! You're looking all spry this morning. I thought you were still out on medical leave?"

"Technically, I am, but the mayor wanted to tear me a new one this morning."

"He's been here twice this week looking for a victim. Personally, I would have stayed in my sickbed. No point in just giving him a target to kick."

"What can I say? I'm a glutton for punishment."

"I keep warning you, that martyr complex of yours is going to be your downfall."

Cooper laughed. "Hard head, soft ass, what can I say!"

"Seriously though, why are you here? I know good and well you haven't been approved to come back yet."

"We got a tip on Landon Street. I want to personally vet it."

"So, if you couldn't vet it remotely, that means you plan to go out in the field."

"Unless you tattle on me."

"I'm no snitch as long as I can ride shotgun. You might need backup and I'm a better shot than you are."

"You are never going to let me forget that, are you?"

"The truth sometimes hurts, my friend!"

Cooper nodded. "I'd appreciate your help in case things go left. If we can get this monster off the streets it'll be worth the hurt I'm going to feel later."

"You mean when Ms. Colton finds out what you're up to?"

He lifted his brows and deliberately widened his eyes. "I don't know what you're talking about."

Claire laughed. "I saw how you two were looking at each other. Now you come skipping into the office like it's Christmas Day and you got all the presents you wanted. Clearly, protective custody with a beautiful woman becomes you."

Cooper laughed with her. He felt himself blush. "Ms. Colton and I are just friends and she's been a great help to me."

"It's your lie, tell it any way you want to," Claire said matter-of-factly.

He shook his head, changing the subject. "I'm ready to roll when you are. Carter and Jones are coming with us."

"Give me ten and make sure you put on a vest. If you get shot again, Kiely will kill both of us."

Cooper laughed. "You got that right!"

After rounding up the team, doing a weapons check and making sure everyone was tactically equipped, it was Cooper riding shotgun as Claire drove to the College Avenue location in South Hills. The residence was a single-family, Tudor-style Craftsman in a meticulously maintained neighborhood. The property was currently owned by the bank, having been foreclosed on months earlier. Anyone living there did so without permission.

Their two black Suburbans pulled into the home's driveway. The grass was freshly cut, but the mailbox overflowed, envelopes and coupon flyers littering the porch. There was a Realtor's security box on the doorknob and a call to the listing agent gave them the code.

Two agents covered the back of the home and Cooper led the way through in. He announced them as he threw the front door open, his weapon raised. Claire banked left through the dining room and Cooper went right toward the kitchen. When the first floor was clear, Claire opened the door to the other agents who scaled the second floor.

It took no time at all to assess that the home was empty, no sign of life to be found. Cooper secured his weapon. His frustration was palpable, feeling like he'd wasted time they didn't necessarily have.

Agent Miller suddenly called his name. "You need to see this," she yelled from the lower level.

Cooper descended the steps to find a makeshift lab in the basement. Bunsen burners, glass beakers and vials of chemicals littered a folding table that sat in the center of the room. A small cot and a sleeping bag rested in a far corner and an oversized garbage container was filled with empty cola cans, Cracker Jack boxes, and Kashi granola containers.

"He was here," Claire said. "I've already called for a forensics team but I'm betting this is ricin," she said as they appraised a tray of powder and a jar of castor beans.

Cooper barked out orders. "Talk to the listing agent. I want a list of everyone who requested access to this house. Names, addresses, contact information. And I want to know everything you can find out about the agent on record. If they're not showing this house I want to know why. I want to know how Street was able to set up shop down here and go undetected. I also want a team on surveillance. If he comes back we better know it. And find out who's cutting the damn lawn! I want to know who's been maintaining the property."

A round of "yes, sirs" responded back.

Cooper headed back up the steps, following behind Claire who led the way.

"We'll get him. I'll make sure they go through this house with a fine-tooth comb," she was saying. "I'll keep you updated."

"I appreciate that. I hate we didn't get him this time."

"You know how this goes, Cooper. Sometimes it takes the extra effort for us to get to the rewards."

Cooper nodded. "I appreciate you, Agent Miller."

She smiled. "Your ride's waiting for you. Tell Kiely I said hello."

COOPER DOZED LIGHTLY as a junior agent drove him back to the safe house. What he hadn't gotten was a lot of sleep the night before and the memories of why had him grinning from ear to ear. Making love to Kiely had been an unexpected blessing and they'd made love multiple times before the sun rose. She'd been sound asleep when the car and driver had arrived to pick him up for his morning meeting with the mayor. Watching her he hadn't wanted to leave and now he was excited to get back to her and Alfie.

Making love to her had confirmed that she had his heart on lock. He couldn't begin to imagine what it might be like to not have her in his life and all he wanted to think about was what their future would look like. Between their sexual escapades they had talked about their dreams, their aspirations and their fears. He'd shared things with Kiely that he had never shared with anyone.

Kiely knew he was petrified of failing his son. Kiely knew he wanted to be a better man for Alfie than his own father had been for him. Kiely knew he struggled with balancing work and family. Kiely knew his heart more than anybody else. He had allowed himself to be vulnerable and he had let her in. The entire experience had been transformative, and the loneliness he had often felt was gone.

Kiely's fears mirrored his own. She'd told him that she worried about not being able to make true connections. She was afraid of the walls that she placed in relationships and around her heart. Kiely was scared that pushing people away would leave her alone in her old age. And Kiely had opened up and shared those fears with him. Kiely had let him into her heart and her head, trusting him with her secrets and her body.

Cooper had one regret. He had not shared the depths of what he was feeling. He hadn't been able to say those three words. They had vibrated loudly in his head, but he hadn't been able to speak them out loud. He found himself excited at the prospect of telling Kiely that he loved her.

When the car pulled into the driveway, Cooper barely said his goodbyes before jumping out and racing to the front door. He gave the agent a quick wave of his hand and moved inside, locking the door securely behind him.

"Daddy's home!" he yelled.

"Daddy's home!" Kiely responded as she and Alfie came to greet him.

Alfie clapped his hands excitedly. "Dad-dy! Dad-dy! Alfie played outside. And me painted a picture. Then me cooked dinner with my Ki-Ki!" He took a breath and laughed, tossing up his hands gleefully.

Cooper scooped the child up into his arms. "Oh my! It sounds like you and Kiely had a day!"

Kiely pressed her palm to his chest and reached to kiss his lips. "How was your day?"

"It wasn't nearly as eventful as your day sounds."

"We had a great day. Are you hungry?"

Cooper nodded. "I am but I thought I would give you a break and spend some time with Alfie before we put him down to bed."

Kiely smiled. "He's missed you."

"Did you miss me?"

She kissed him again. "As soon as Alfie goes to sleep, I'll show you how much I missed you!"

ALFIE TODDLED HAPPILY around the small bedroom showing Cooper the toys that he was most enamored with. The two chattered like old men, mumbling nonsensically and laughing at everything. It wasn't lost on Cooper that times like this with his son were priceless and he had missed too many hours consumed by a case when he should have been focused on his child. He promised Alfie to do better. It was barely thirty minutes later when the little boy fell asleep in his lap. They had been reading Alfie's favorite book for the fourth time.

After tucking him in his bed, Cooper moved to the master bedroom to grab a quick shower. By the time he finished, changing into sweats and a T-shirt, Kiely was putting their dinner on the table.

"Something smells really good," he said.

"Lasagna with ground sausage and turkey and my mother's marinara sauce."

"You really love to cook, don't you?"

"I do," Kiely answered. "More than I realized."

She stood in the kitchen tossing a salad in a wooden salad bowl. Cooper eased behind her and kissed her neck. She turned her head to meet his lips, his mouth lingering against hers. Fighting the urge to lay her across the kitchen counter and cover every inch of his maleness with the softness of her femininity, Cooper found himself struggling to maintain some self-control. He turned his back to her, reaching for a glass out of the cupboard to hide the rise of his erection.

"How did your meeting with the mayor go?" Kiely questioned, seeming oblivious to his situation.

Cooper shrugged, his shoulders jutting toward the ceiling. "He's not happy and he wants to make sure no one else is either. I was able to talk him out of a press conference though."

"I thought you would have been back earlier."

"I stopped by the office and then I went on a raid," he said, avoiding her eyes as the words came out of his mouth.

"Really, Cooper? Didn't the doctor tell you to stay out of the field for six weeks?"

"We got a tip on Landon Street. I couldn't let that go. You would have done the same thing."

"Yeah, I probably would have." She nodded. "So, anything come of it?"

"No, it was a bust. He wasn't there. But he had been there and he'd set up a lab. We're trying to figure out now what he was up to."

"I spoke to Sadie this morning."

"How's she doing?"

"She's sad. And she's still having a hard time believing that Tate's a criminal."

"I'm sorry about that."

"She'll be fine. Sadie's a smart woman. She has always dealt in fact. The evidence against him is substantial and she's been reading through it all."

Cooper nodded. "We'll find him, too." He finished the last bite of his lasagna. "Dinner was very good," he said.

"Dessert will be better."

"Should I even ask?"

They talked for some time, comparing notes and catching up. Cooper was fully engaged when Kiely shared Alfie's accomplishments. His son was becoming quite the acrobatic daredevil, climbing trees without a care in the world.

When the meal was done, he pointed her in the direction of the living room. "I'll do the dishes, you take a break."

"Are you sure?"

Cooper nodded. "I've got this."

Minutes later Kiely lay with her eyes closed, her relaxed body sprawled against the sectional cushions in wild abandon. Thoughts of Cooper danced behind her eyes. Her full breasts pushed against the cotton fabric of her silky T-shirt, and the slight curve of her buttocks peeked past the hemline of the matching shorts she wore.

Moving into the room Cooper stopped to watch her. He was enamored with the harmony that shadowed her expression. He took a deep breath and inhaled her beauty. Kiely was breathtaking and Cooper was suddenly consumed by the heat that rushed from one end of his body to the other. He shivered with longing, scarcely able to restrain himself. Her name caught in his throat as he whispered it into the warm air, the lilt of it resonating throughout the room.

Kiely rose up onto her elbows meeting his gaze. It suddenly felt like he'd lit a fire within her, causing her to melt like butter. She could feel the swell of her breathing mirroring his own, could feel herself beginning to perspire as she stared up at Cooper. Tiny beads of moisture were forming in the valley between her breasts and she was fearful that she might break out into a full sweat. Cooper crawled over her, hovering easily above the length of her body. The moment felt unreal, like a sweet dream that had blossomed from many years of fantasy. His lips skated across hers, his tongue anxious and probing. Heat pulsed with a vengeance through her most private place.

Pressing her palms to Cooper's chest, Kiely followed as he eased her back against the sofa, reclining his weight against her. The reality of the promises they had made to each other, his heart in exchange for hers, suddenly filled her abundantly. Kiely wrapped her arms around him, her hands racing the length of his broad back. His skin was warm, the rising heat of his body simmering beneath her fingertips.

Cooper whispered her name against her skin, blowing promises with every kiss that touched her. His caresses were like feathery lashes against her skin and made her nerve endings tingle with anticipation. He suddenly sat back on his haunches, lifting the bulk of his weight from her as he stared down into the depths of her eyes. She could feel his heart beating in perfect sync with hers. Her breathing was static, desire desperate for oxygen. Kiely pulled her hands through her hair, her back arching ever so slightly. His lips searched the length of her neck, probing at the lobe of her ear before falling back to her mouth.

He undressed her slowly, pulling at her top, and she lifted her arms high above her head. The feel of his hands as he reached to cup her breasts, his palms dancing across the hardened nipples, flooded her body with sensation. His touch fired energy in the top of her head straight down to her curled toes. When his mouth followed where his hands had led, it left her breathless. Cooper was in full control as he guided her in an erotic two-step across the cushions.

Cooper tasted every square inch of her body with his own. It was pleasure beyond his wildest imagination. Kiely was completely lost in the ecstasy, sensual pleasure like a trusted tour guide. Savoring the enormity of the moment, both knew they had reached a point of no return.

"I love you," Cooper whispered into her ear as they climaxed together. "I love you, Kiely Colton."

Kiely whispered back, "I love you, too."

KIELY FELT RESTED even though she had only gotten a few hours of sleep. She eased her body from the bed, taking care not to disturb Cooper. He lay flat on his stomach with his arms curled over his head and gripping the pillow, snoring softly. He wouldn't admit it, but she could tell the previous day had been more than he was ready to handle. He hurt and didn't want to say so. But she was learning how to read him and his many moods. She knew he needed rest and their late-night antics were proving to be a disruption.

It was still very early in the morning. With luck, she had another two hours before Alfie would wake seeking her attention. She wanted to use those two hours wisely. She was hoping that she'd see her twin later that day and she needed to send Pippa an updated shopping list before she arrived. She also wanted to check her email and answer her messages. Despite her best efforts to be a superhero, Kiely had let some of her business responsibilities slide. She also couldn't remember if she'd made her car loan payment.

Rising from the bedside she headed into the bathroom and turned on the shower. In no time at all the hot water was calling her name. As she stood in the flow she made a list of things to do in her head but was pleasantly surprised when Cooper suddenly joined her.

"Good morning! I hope I didn't wake you?"

"No," Cooper said. "I woke up, and you weren't there. I missed you."

"Join me?" she asked.

Stepping cautiously behind her, Cooper eased in, moving to stand beneath the water. The shower was oversized and they both fit in nicely. The spray was heated and comforting. Cooper pressed his hand to her back, massaging a bar of soap against her skin. Suddenly Kiely could focus on nothing but the heat from his fingertips radiating through her.

Cooper's touch was electric, burning with fierce intensity. He drew a slow trail across her shoulders, down the length of her arms, to the curve of her breasts. He continued past her belly button, and finally rested his hand teasingly against the flat of her stomach.

Kiely backed up and fit tightly against him, caressing him in a slow grind. Spinning in his arms her hands danced like butterflies over his chest and around to his broad back. Cooper pressed a kiss to her mouth, greedily sneaking his tongue past the line of her lips. The kiss was hard and deep and when Kiely finally pulled away she could barely breathe from the sheer beauty of it.

Kiely laughed softly, dropping her forehead against his chest. "If we keep this up we're going to drown in here. We're also not going to get anything accomplished."

Cooper pulled her hand to his lips and kissed the tips of her fingers. "We should spend the whole day in bed together."

"Good luck with that. I'm sure Alfie has other plans for our day today."

"Twenty questions," Cooper said. "What's your dream vacation destination?"

"Spain. I want to see La Sagrada Familia Church in Barcelona. How many stamps do you have in your passport?"

"About a dozen."

"Whoo! That's really good." They were still lathering each other, spreading soap suds with their fingertips. "Who's your favorite singer?"

"Tim McGraw."

"Country music! I'm very impressed."

"Why do you say it like that?"

"For some reason I took you for a Wayne Newton fan."

"I like Wayne Newton, too!"

Kiely rolled her eyes skyward. "Ask a question."

"What's wrong with Wayne Newton?"

She laughed. "Not a thing if that's what you like." She jumped when his fingers grazed her nether regions, his expression smug. "What's your most sensitive body part?" she said.

There was a moment of hesitation. Cooper shook his head. "No, it was my turn to ask a question."

"You did," Kiely responded. "What's wrong with Wayne Newton?" Her tone was mocking and they both laughed.

"That's not fair. That wasn't my question."

"You asked it. Now answer my question, what's your most sensitive body part?"

Cooper licked his lips as he considered his response.

"Oh, forget it!" Kiely exclaimed. "I already know the answer." She wrapped her fingers around his manhood and gave it a gentle squeeze.

Cooper inhaled swiftly. "That wasn't my answer," he said.

Kiely giggled. "I know!" And then she licked his nipple, sucking him gently.

Cooper jumped, gasping. He moaned. Loudly. "You really don't play fair," he managed to mutter.

"What's that old saying?" Kiely quipped. "All's fair in love and love."

Chapter Twelve

Cooper and Alfie played a rousing game of hide-and-seek that afternoon. Alfie loved hiding, popping out when he felt you were taking too long to find him. Kiely knew all of his favorite hiding spots, but Cooper was completely lost as he threw open closet doors and looked under the beds. He moved back into the family room, confusion washing over his face. Kiely laughed heartily and pointed to the ottoman in the center of the floor. The top to the storage unit was askew, and if you looked closely you could see the child peeking out at the two of them. His father shook his head.

"Kiely, I can't find Alfie. I don't know where he is," Cooper said loudly.

Alfie jumped from his hiding space. "Boo!" he yelled, laughing hysterically.

Cooper clutched his chest. "Alfie! There you are, son!" He lifted the boy into the air and spun him around. "You are such a good hider, Alfie."

Once his little feet were firmly planted back on the ground Alfie ran to Kiely's side. "Dad-dy no find me, Ki-Ki! Alfie hide good!"

"Yes, you did, precious!" She knelt down to give him a hug. "Do you want to color a picture now?"

"No! Alfie go hide!" he said as he turned, racing off in the other direction. "Find me, Dad-dy! Find me!"

Kiely laughed. "Go find him, Daddy. He'll be in the clothes hamper in the laundry room."

"Will he do this all day?"

"He will do it until you make him stop." She checked the time. "You're in luck. *Daniel Tiger's Neighborhood* starts in five minutes. Daniel Tiger is one of his favorites," she said.

"Daniel Tiger?"

Kiely laughed again. "Don't ask. It's one of his favorite shows."

"How do I not know this?" Cooper muttered.

"You better count. He doesn't like it when you don't count."

Cooper shook his head. "One, two, three, four…" He moved down the hallway toward the laundry room.

Kiely was enjoying their time together. Cooper had finally slowed down long enough to enjoy his time with Alfie. He was relaxed and happy. And so was she. The dynamics of their relationship had shifted substantially. Cooper loved her and she loved him. Now she understood how Pippa had felt when Emmanuel had stolen her heart. Love didn't hurt and instead of being afraid for the future it made you hopeful. Unlike how Sadie had acted with Tate, Kiely couldn't begin to imagine Cooper bullying or trying to control her. Love didn't throw harsh words or impose rigid rules on a person's dreams.

In the other room she could hear Cooper and Alfie laughing together excitedly. She knew that his father finding him had gone well and pure joy rang out in Alfie's giggles. Kiely moved to the pantry, studying the inventory that was waning substantially. They were low on snacks for Alfie and the supply of baking ingredients was almost nonexistent. She added flour and chocolate chips to her shopping list. Moving to the freezer she checked the frozen items and ticked off vegetables and ice cream on her list.

Minutes later she emailed the list to Pippa, excited that she was going to be able to see her sister later that afternoon. She missed her family. She missed her brothers being annoying. She missed the camaraderie and laughter that she shared with her sisters. She also missed her cat, Jim Morrison. She smiled, excited that she would soon be able to introduce Jim and Alfie, knowing the two would become fast friends.

Minutes later Cooper returned to the family room. "Finally!" he said as he dropped down onto the sectional sofa. "He's in our bed watching that Tiger kid show."

"Daniel Tiger is actually very educational," Kiely said. "You should watch it."

"I have a boatload of paperwork to get through. I need to head downstairs and see where we're at with the case."

"Do you need any help?"

"No, but thank you for offering. I need to file my report on the Landon Street debacle, and that won't take long."

"Well, if you don't need me, I think I'm going to make challah."

"You know how to make challah? From scratch?"

"Is there any other way to make challah?" she said with a wry laugh.

Cooper laughed with her. "Yeah! You let a bakery do it for you. Wealthy Street Bakery has some of the best I've ever eaten."

She smirked. "Their bread is good, but mine is better. I do like their cinnamon croissants, though."

"Townies! Those things are incredible!"

Alfie suddenly cried out, racing back into the room, tears streaming down his little face. He held his finger out, his wrist resting in the palm of his other hand.

"What's the matter, son?" Cooper questioned, moving toward the child.

Alfie snatched his hand from his father's reach, giving him a mean side-eye. He darted past him and rushed to Kiely. "Ki-Ki! Hurt my finger!" he cried.

"What am I?" Cooper exclaimed, "chopped liver? Did you see the look he just gave me?"

Kiely giggled. She brought herself to his eye level as Alfie bumped against her leg.

"My poor baby! Let Kiely see." Kiely inspected the appendage, declaring the small scratch minor. "It's going to be okay, Alfie. Do you want Kiely to kiss it or put a Band-Aid on it?"

"Alfie want a Band-Aid."

Kiely tickled him, making the little boy laugh. "Kiely's going to kiss that finger," she teased. She kissed the back of his hand then blew a strawberry against his palm. Alfie erupted in giggles.

"Snack, peas? Alfie want a snack, peas!"

In no time at all, a major meltdown had been avoided and Alfie was settled back in front of the television with a small bowl of popcorn and a juice pack.

"He really adores you," Cooper said.

"Does that bother you?" Kiely questioned. "Because I don't want you to think that I'm trying to take your place or replace his mother."

"Not at all. I'm glad he has you. I know how much you care for him," Cooper said. "May I ask you a question?"

"Of course," Kiely answered. "You know you can ask me anything."

"How do you see things once we go back to reality? When we return to our homes?"

Kiely paused. "I'm not sure. I've thought about it but I don't have a cut and dry answer."

Cooper took a seat at the kitchen table. "I've actually been thinking about that a lot. Trying to figure out how Alfie and I can keep you." His eyes smiled as he stared at her.

Kiely lifted her lips in a smile. "There's so much we have to figure out, because in all honesty, I don't know that I want to go back to being a full-time investigator. I've really come to love being a stay-at-home mom." There was a hint of nervousness that crossed her face as she made the admission.

Cooper's gaze skated across her face. He nodded his head. "We'll have to make some serious decisions about our future living arrangements."

"We're going to have to make some serious decisions about everything," Kiely responded.

Cooper crooked his fingers and beckoned her to his side. When she stood beside him, he pulled her down onto his lap, his arms wrapped tightly around her. "Kiely, you make me happier than I have been in a very long time. I don't want to lose you. And I don't want Alfie to lose what you and he have together. You've become as important to my son as you are to me. We will make this work."

He kissed her lips and tightened the hold he had around her torso. Kiely wrapped her arms around his neck and hugged him back. It suddenly felt like Christmas in July!

COOPER WAS STILL in the basement office and Alfie was down for his afternoon nap when Pippa arrived. The two sisters hugged tightly as Kiely welcomed her into the home.

"This is cute!" Pippa said, her gaze sweeping through the space. "The FBI do things with style!"

"It's comfortable."

"Where is everybody?" Pippa asked, her voice dropping an octave.

"Cooper's downstairs and Alfie's still sleeping."

"I guess you're going to have to help me with these bags then," Pippa said as she turned, heading back to the car.

Kiely slipped on her loafers and followed her sister. "What do we owe you?" she asked as Pippa handed her two oversized cloth bags filled to the brim with foodstuffs.

"Nothing. Cooper gave me his business credit card."

"When did you see Cooper?"

"He stopped by the other safe house to check on Sadie. We really like him!" she exclaimed. "You done good this time!"

"He never mentioned it," Kiely said, suddenly wondering what else Cooper had conveniently forgotten to tell her.

"I don't think it was a secret, Kiely. He was genuinely concerned about Sadie and he said that you were upset that you couldn't be there for her so he wanted to assure her everything would be alright. He also had questions for her about Tate and wanted to answer any questions she might have had. After he left she actually perked up a bit. She agrees that he's perfect for you!"

Kiely gave her sister a look. "He told me he loves me."

Pippa grinned. "And what did you say?"

"I told him I loved him, too!"

"Maybe we can have a double wedding!" Pippa said excitedly.

"I don't know if I want to get married," Kiely confessed. "Why do I need a sheet of paper to legitimize what we feel for each other?"

"Why are you always so contrary?"

"I'm not. I just don't think I need a license to tell me that I love him and he loves me and we want to spend our lives together."

"And how does Cooper feel about that?"

"We haven't had that conversation yet."

Pippa shook her head. "Well, you do keep things interesting."

Kiely laughed.

"I brought you a surprise," Kiely said. "Grab the box on the back seat."

Opening the rear passenger door to peer inside, Kiely's eyes widened. "You didn't?"

Pippa nodded. "I did. I figured you might need it right about now!"

Cooper suddenly called from the open door. "Hey there! Do you two need some help?"

"Yes!" Kiely yelled as he moved toward them. "I need you to get this box off the back seat and do not drop it."

Cooper laughed, eyeing the Greek to Go label on top of the large white bakery box. "What's this?"

Kiely grinned. "The best baklava cheesecake you will ever experience. Take it inside and put it carefully on the counter!"

Cooper carried the cake inside, his viselike grip on the box moving both women to laugh jovially. The twins were suddenly giddy with laughter.

"You put the coffee on," Pippa said. "I'll cut the cake."

Kiely laughed. "We have a Keurig brewer. The coffee will be done before you get the first slice on a plate."

Pippa moved ahead of her through the doorway.

Kiely suddenly came to an abrupt stop, cocking her head as she listened. They had become accustomed to the silence, anything stirring between the trees, chirping or squeaking as the wind blew. For a split second she thought she heard an engine running but just like that the sound disappeared. She set the two grocery bags against the landing and moved back down the steps to look around. Nothing caught her eye or seemed out of place. The trike

Alfie had ridden earlier was still resting where he'd left it and nothing moved beyond the line of trees bordering the home. Kiely took a deep breath and held it.

"Everything okay?" Cooper asked, standing in the doorway staring at her.

"I thought I heard something," she said.

He moved down the steps to stand beside her. His gaze followed hers, searching where she looked. "Do you still hear it?" he asked.

Kiely shook her head. "No. It was probably just the wind."

He nudged her shoulder. "Let's go inside," he said as they moved back up the stairs. He grabbed the two bags of groceries.

They both tossed one last look over their shoulders and then locked the door behind themselves.

ALFIE STOOD AN arm's length away from Pippa. He stared intently, playing a game of eye ping-pong as he shifted his gaze back and forth between her and Kiely.

"He is so funny," Pippa laughed.

"He's trying to figure out why you look like me," Kiely said.

"I know you two are fraternal twins, but you do look very much alike. I can just imagine he's having a hard time processing why," Cooper interjected.

Alfie moved back to Kiely's side, the look he gave Pippa moving them all to laugh. Kiely lifted him to her lap. She ran her fingers through his hair. Alfie reached for her fork, wanting another bite of the cake that she'd been coveting.

"I think we have another convert," Pippa said.

Cooper took his own bite, swirling the taste across his tongue. The New York style cheesecake made with Greek yogurt had a walnut and cinnamon baklava filling encased in filo dough and drizzled with honey. It was everything Kiely had asserted, the decadence unrivaled by any other cheesecake he'd ever eaten. "I can't blame him," he said. "This is so good!"

"There are rules about when we can and can't eat this cake," Pippa said.

Kiely nodded. "We only eat this cake once per month."

"Also, on holidays, stress days and for special celebrations."

"The third Friday of every month."

"And every other Tuesday."

The sisters laughed.

"So, pretty much any time you want. Is that what I'm understanding?" Cooper said.

"I like him. He's smart," Pippa teased.

Kiely tossed him a look. "I'm sure he has moments."

"Okay! On that note, I am officially out of my depth. Time to retire to the other side." Cooper stood up. "Alfie, do you want to go outside and play with Daddy?"

"Alfie go outside," the little boy said. He gave Kiely a hug before jumping from her lap.

"Can I have a hug, too?" Pippa asked.

Alfie's smile fell into a deep frown. "You not my Ki-Ki," he said.

The two women watched as he stomped past Pippa, moving to Cooper's side. When his father had his hand, he tossed Pippa a look over his shoulder.

"I think he just gave you a middle-finger salute," Kiely said.

"I don't think I got a full finger wave. More like a little finger," Pippa joked. "That kid is so darn cute! And look at you being all mommy-like! Who are you and what did you do with my twin sister?"

Laughter was loud and raucous. "I like this mommy gig. More than I thought I ever would."

"Clearly! I'll be honest. We all thought it was just a phase. That by the second day you would have been ready to pull your hair out, or Cooper would find his kid stuffed in a closet."

"It's definitely not a phase. I don't know if I want to continue doing PI work full time. I think I want to be a more of a stay-at-home mom. Is that crazy?"

Pippa shook her head. "Not really. The risk factor in both is about the same."

Kiely laughed. "You might be right about that."

COOPER STARED OUT over the backyard. Alfie was digging a hole with a large stick. He was playing happily, oblivious to anything the adults around him might have been going through. He found himself thinking about what Kiely might've heard earlier. The area was pretty remote and had been chosen for a reason. There was a team in close proximity if they were ever needed. Agents could be there before they hung up the line. Although it appeared they were alone and might be hampered without transportation, such was farthest from the truth. Cooper hadn't intended for them to be bait; he knew that if that woman came for him, or his son, again, he would be more than ready for her.

He would check later to see if any of the agents had been out in the woods patrolling the area. He knew they would occasionally check the property in stealth mode so as not to be seen. They were undoubtedly good at what they did; they had strict instructions to stay at least sixty yards from the house unless the family's safety required them to be closer. He also wanted to make sure they'd found no one else on the property who wasn't supposed to be there.

Lost in thought, Cooper was halfway up the steps when

he realized Alfie wasn't beside him. Turning abruptly, he tore after the child, a moment of panic sweeping through him. By the time Cooper reached the steps, Alfie was banging at the door calling for Kiely.

"Ki-Ki! Ki-Ki! Open da door, Ki-Ki! Got to go potty!"

When Kiely pulled the entrance open, Alfie tore past her, leaving Cooper standing there feeling slightly foolish.

"He ran off," Cooper said as she stared at him.

"He has to go potty," she said.

"Potty?"

"We're potty training. He likes to aim. You should know all about that. It's a boy thing."

Alfie screamed her name. "Ki-Ki!"

"That sounds like he may need help wiping," she said as she turned from the door. "That requires a little more than aim and shake."

Moving into the home Cooper gave Pippa a look, his confounded expression moving her to laugh. He shrugged his broad shoulders, feeling slightly discombobulated.

"Yeah," Pippa said. "It's like that sometimes!"

ONCE AGAIN THAT NIGHT, Kiely was wrapped around a pillow and Cooper was wrapped around her. Pippa had left earlier, having already called to say she was home safe and sound. Alfie had gone down after one last slice of cheesecake. He'd played hard and was sleeping harder.

"When I looked up and he was gone, I panicked," Cooper was saying.

"He's fast. You can take your eyes off him for a split second and he'll be a mile away. I've lost him a few times myself."

"You lost my son?"

"You lost your son."

He brushed his pelvis against her buttocks. "Well, I felt wholeheartedly inadequate and then when I found out he was potty training...when did that happen?"

"We've really just started and he's pretty much training himself."

"There's so much I don't know about my son. I feel like I need to make up for a lot of lost time. It's made me realize how much I've been focused on the agency and my job the last two years instead of focusing on Alfie."

"You're here now. And Alfie is an amazing child because you have been here. I'm sure that as he gets older you'll have to be more hands-on. You'll figure it out."

"We'll figure it out together, Ki-Ki!" Cooper said, imitating how his son called her name.

She turned in his arms and pressed a kiss to his chest. They talked for a good long while, defining how they saw their future together. They were conscious of the fact that everything they decided would impact Alfie either directly or indirectly, and that he had to be in the forefront of whatever choices they made for themselves.

It was after midnight when Cooper fell asleep, slumber claiming him first. Kiely started to drift off as she settled into his light snores. She was groggy, her eyes opening and then closing. She saw a shadow moving past the window and heard a branch snapping, startling her awake so she sat upright in the bed.

She tapped Cooper awake as she slid out of the bed.

"What's wrong?" he said, rubbing his eyes.

Kiely whispered. "Someone's outside," she said, pointing toward the bedroom window.

Cooper jumped from the bed, reaching for the lock box by the bedside. Punching in the security code he retrieved his service weapon and passed Kiely her gun.

They moved through the house swiftly. Kiely hurried to the sliding glass doors in the back and Cooper opened the front door. Both eased out at the same time. At the bottom of the steps Cooper turned to the right, sweeping from one side to the other as he eased toward the end of the house and the bedroom window. Kiely's steps mirrored his as she turned left, headed in the same direction.

As they both turned the corner, they were suddenly standing in the midst of a herd of white-tail deer, some so close that they could have reached out to pet them. There were at least sixty of them of assorted ages and sizes. The air around them was still, the quiet like a thick fog around them. Just the occasional snap of a branch beneath their hoofs. There was a full moon lighting the dark sky, the bright glow illuminating the landscape. It was surreal and so breathtakingly beautiful that Kiely heard herself gasp. Realizing the threat beneath the bedroom window was only Bambi and company out for their midnight stroll, she lowered her weapon first and then Cooper dropped his arm down to his side.

The deer had bristled, heads turning in their direction, ears lifted as they measured the degree of danger to them. A few were skittish, eyes watching them cautiously. Neither Kiely nor Cooper moved, so mesmerized by the moment that they had almost forgotten why they were standing outside in the middle of the night, oblivious to everything, even the chill in the air. Almost, but not quite, acutely aware that they weren't out of the woods and a potential threat to their lives was still very real.

Finding nothing significant after one final sweep of the property, Cooper slowly slid his weapon into the waistband of his pants. Kiely did the same thing. She held her breath when a small fawn brushed past her leg, curiosity larger than its fear. It was eerie to have them inch as close as they came, curious to know if the two were friend or foe. Kiely reached for Cooper's hand and moved closer to him. He wrapped his arms around her shoulders and held her as they stood in awe of the moment.

Chapter Thirteen

The next morning as they sat over a breakfast of freshly squeezed orange juice and egg casserole, Kiely said, "You were up early. Is everything okay?"

Cooper swallowed the bite of toast he'd just taken. "After last night I wanted to touch base with the backup team. Another agent and I took a walk around the property just to be safe."

"Did you find anything?"

He shook his head. "No. It was clear. Even the deer were gone."

Kiely blew a soft sigh. "Do you believe in God?" she asked, the question coming out of the blue.

Cooper nodded his head. "I do. I consider myself very spiritual, but it's been some time since I last went to church."

"Define some time."

"Sara's funeral was the last time the pastor saw me."

Kiely nodded. "I was just thinking that there was something very spiritual about our experience last night. Like God walked us into an inspiring moment to show us something magnificent."

Cooper sat back in his seat. He nodded. "I wish Alfie could have experienced that with us. If they come back we should wake him up."

"It really was spectacular. Standing there in your arms, watching them, felt so calming. I almost cried."

"Baby! Aww!"

"Almost. Don't get sappy on me, Cooper Winston."

"We were just having a moment and you ruined it."

Kiely laughed. "Your daddy has jokes, Alfie!"

Alfie giggled. "You funny, Dad-dy!"

Cooper tossed up his hands. "It looks like I am never going to win with you two."

"Nope!"

"What's on your agenda today?"

"Laundry. I've run out of underwear."

"It's not like you really need them," Cooper said, his voice dropping to a loud whisper.

"So have you," Kiely added.

He blinked. "I can see where that might be a problem for us."

"What do you have to do today?"

"I need to figure out how much longer we're going to be here."

"I was actually going to ask you that. Not that I'm complaining. I've enjoyed our time."

"I really do need to get back to work, and I imagine you want to do the same thing."

Kiely rose from her seat and reached for the dirty dishes to clear away the table. Although she had thought about their return, she hadn't truly been interested in committing to any particular day or time. "No," she finally said. "I really could care less about returning to the job. Obviously, I want to solve this case so my foster brother Brody can come home, but I'm not invested in the rest of it."

"How is your brother going to feel about that?"

"It's not my brother's life."

Cooper stole a quick glance down to his wristwatch.

"Let's put this conversation on hold until later. I have a conference call in thirty minutes and I need to go prepare." He stood up from the table and leaned to kiss her lips. Alfie, who was playing with his cereal, picking out the marshmallows to eat first, gave him a wave.

The video chat to Cooper began as scheduled. When he answered, the mayor's secretary announced the call and connected them. The mayor, Grand Rapids Police Chief Andrew Fox, Lieutenant Tripp McKellar and Detective Emmanuel Iglesias had all been patched through.

"Everybody know each other?" the mayor queried.

A collective round of *yeas* responded.

"Good, then I can dispense with the pleasantries," he snapped. "Where are we with this case? I've got people dying, the press is up my ass, and you all have no answers! Someone tell me something!"

Cooper chimed in first. "The FBI has gotten a few credible tips pointing us in the direction of Landon Street and Wes Matthews. Thus far they've continued to be one step ahead of us. The FBI continues to be committed to bringing them to justice."

"That just sounds like a load of double talk to me," the mayor said. "I need results!"

Police Chief Fox added his two cents. "I've got my best men and women on the case. We'll get these guys."

"We'll get these guys. We'll get these guys," the mayor said mockingly. "I'm tired of hearing we're going to get these guys and these guys are still out here killing people."

"I understand your frustration, Mayor," Cooper interjected. "We're equally frustrated. But I assure you, we are all giving a hundred and ten percent. There are a lot of players tied to this debacle and each of them have their own agenda which has made bringing them down difficult. But we're proud to say that we've arrested one of the

Capital X henchmen and he named all of his associates. We know who was behind Capital X and we have him on our radar. I believe his arrest is imminent."

"Is that something we can announce to the media? We need to give them something!"

"I can have our communications person write up a statement for you, sir."

"Get this done," the mayor snapped one last time. "Or I'll replace the whole damn lot of you!"

Cooper disconnected the call, his frustration palpable. Had the investigation been that easy, they would've been finished by now. The mayor didn't seem to understand that the criminals who didn't want to get caught were hampering him getting the results he wanted.

The rest of the day was nondescript. Cooper spent most of it on the lower level of the home working while Kiely sorted clothes and kept Alfie entertained. When he finally emerged from the dungeon, the two were playing a game of Simon Says. Alfie was having a hard time grasping the mechanics of the game, but his enthusiasm made up for his lack of skill.

He moved to the kitchen hoping to sneak a bite of ice cream and leftover cake before dinner. He wasn't surprised to find the cake missing and barely enough ice cream left to fill an eight-ounce cup.

"Really, Kiely? You ate the cheesecake?"

She laughed. "What makes you think I ate it?"

"It's just you and me, babe, and I didn't eat it."

"Alfie, who ate the cake?" Kiely questioned.

"Simon!" He threw up his hands with a loud cheer.

"Simon who?" Cooper questioned.

"Simon Says!"

Kiely laughed. "Dinner's almost ready, Cooper. And I made brownies for dessert."

"Brownies with those little chocolate chips?"

"Lots of chocolate chips."

"As long as I get the last one I'll forgive you for eating the cheesecake," Cooper said.

Kiely laughed again. "I did not eat the cheesecake!"

"Then who ate the cheesecake, Kiely? Did the deer sneak in and eat the cheesecake?"

"No, smart-ass! I hid the cheesecake so you could have the last slice. It's in the plastic container on the top shelf of the refrigerator. Now say sorry."

Cooper gave her a slight bow. "Okay, I might've stepped in that one. I'm sorry, Kiely. Thank you."

Laughter echoed around the room. As Cooper went for the cake, Kiely moved into the kitchen to finish the dinner preparations. She and Cooper traded a quick kiss as Alfie continued to run and play, making up his own game of hide-and-seek and Simon Says. The table was set and Kiely was waiting for the pot of water on the stove to boil to cook the pasta for their spaghetti dinner.

Suddenly an explosion shattered the sliding glass doors leading from the family room out to the rear deck. It knocked Kiely off her feet and she narrowly missed fracturing her head on the edge of the marble counter. Cooper held tight to an upper shelf in the pantry as the room vibrated, soup cans sliding onto the floor.

Kiely screamed. "Alfie! Alfie!" The little boy was nowhere to be seen. Kiely raced to the back bedrooms calling his name. She and Cooper met back in the living room. "I can't find Alfie."

"He was just here!" Cooper exclaimed. "Where did he go?"

"He's probably hiding," Kiely said. "He wanted to play hide-and-seek. I'll check the laundry basket," she said.

She raced back to the laundry room and when she didn't

find Alfie there, she ran back. As she moved into the space Cooper stood frozen, staring toward the shattered glass door. Her gaze shifted to where he stared, her eyes widening. Meghan Otis, the RevitaYou-taking selfie queen, stood amidst the debris of glass, metal fragments and wood slivers, pointing a gun at him. When she saw Kiely, she shifted the muzzle from him to her and back again.

She was taller than Kiely had imagined. Her body shape was athletic and she wore biker leathers; black pants, thick-heeled boots and a jacket.

"Both of you, sit down," she said calmly.

"Who are you?" Cooper questioned, though Kiely knew he already knew the answer. He and Kiely had seen numerous photos of her and he had stalked her social media accounts until he thought he knew her well. Meghan Otis, however, had finally caught up with them and now he had to get her talking.

Meghan didn't answer his question, saying instead, "I warned you, Agent! I told you to leave Wes Matthews alone. It really didn't have to be like this!" Meghan stepped back, to peer outside. It was almost as if she were waiting for someone. She turned back to them just as quickly.

The large automatic weapon in her hands was intimidating. Both Kiely and Cooper were unnerved by how calm she was, speaking as if she were only talking about the weather and her latest Pilates class. Cooper suddenly gave Kiely a slight nod and gestured with his eyes toward the storage ottoman. Kiely realized the top was moving ever so slightly and she knew Alfie was hiding inside. She suddenly needed their baby boy to not move. To stay safe from the madwoman with the large gun who'd already kidnapped him once before. She started talking out loud, trying to keep her voice calm. "I'm counting," she said. "Kiely's counting. One, two, three, four..."

The other woman turned to stare at her. Her eyes narrowed into thin slits and she frowned. "What are you doing? I told you to sit down and shut up!"

Kiely didn't respond, eyeing the woman cautiously. "What do you want?" she finally questioned.

She pointed the gun back at Cooper. "I told him. I told him to leave Wes alone. I told him and he wouldn't listen. I told him. Now, you all are going to have to pay. Where's the kid?"

"MEGHAN, WHY DON'T we talk about this?" Cooper said, his tone equally as calm.

"No!" the woman snapped. She began pacing the floor, muttering under her breath. "I told you what to do. I told you! Now look what you made me do," she ranted. Her voice rose and fell from a yell to a whisper. Meghan Otis appeared to be coming unhinged right before their eyes.

Cooper shot Kiely another look, the top to the ottoman beginning to quiver a second time. "Still counting," Kiely said. "Six, seven, eight…"

Meghan suddenly stopped staring directly at Kiely, turning her attention back to Cooper. "I said, where is he?"

"Where is who?"

"The little boy."

"What do you want, Meghan? How can we help you?" Cooper asked, trying to shift her focus again.

"I told you how to help me. I told you to leave Wes alone."

"You're in love with Wes, aren't you?" Kiely questioned. "Did he hurt you, Meghan?"

Megan stopped pacing once again, turning to stare at Kiely. "Yes, I do love him. And he loves me. Everything was perfect. We were so good together. We were making money. Living well." She shook the gun at Cooper. "And then he had to go and mess everything up!"

"How did he do that?" Kiely questioned. "How did Agent Winston mess things up?"

Meghan sighed, seeming relieved to be able to tell someone her story. To make sure they knew what had gotten her there and how she had found herself in the predicament she was in.

She began to talk. "Wes and I met at the bank where I used to work. I was a teller and he would come to my window and flirt with me. It was love at first sight." Meghan smiled at the memories. "One day he invited me to lunch. He was such a romantic! When he found out I'd recently come into some lottery money, he offered me the opportunity to invest in his business. Wes was quite the businessman!" Meghan exclaimed. "And the product was amazing! I used it myself and it worked wonders. I looked years younger. My skin was vibrant and the wrinkles practically faded overnight. My hair grew in thicker and I had the energy level of a woman half my age. In fact, I was able to drop twenty-five pounds that Wes thought I needed to lose. The weight just fell off! It was as if time turned back ten years."

"So, yeah," she continued, "I invested. Who wouldn't invest in something that was going to revolutionize the wellness industry! Sales were spectacular and then Wes asked me to partner with him. He said I was his good luck charm. I became his golden girl, recruiting others to come in and invest as well. The media keeps saying Wes scammed people out of their money, but he didn't do that. I made all my money back and then some. And I wasn't the only one."

Cooper shook his head. "Wes paid you back with the money he took from the investors who came after you, Meghan."

"No, he didn't," she snapped. "RevitaYou was doing well. The company was making tons of money. You don't know! I saw the books. I was there helping Wes build the brand." She stepped closer, shaking the gun in Cooper's face for emphasis.

She took a step back, inhaling deeply to calm her rage. She narrowed her gaze on Cooper. "You did that press conference. You called Wes a con man and a thief. You lied and told people the product was tainted. I'm proof there's nothing wrong with the product! Then you said you were going to bring Wes down and I couldn't let that happen. I have to protect Wes, no matter what it takes."

"So, you kidnapped my son."

"He was going to be my insurance policy. But then..." She hesitated, falling into thought. She began to slap the side of her leg with the gun, her frustration rising with a vengeance.

"I'm sorry," Cooper said.

"You're sorry!" Meghan spun toward the door and back to him a second time. "You're sorry? If you had been sorry you would have stopped. You got lucky when you rescued your kid and you didn't die when I shot you. But instead of walking away, you kept digging."

"So, you set those bombs off at my house?"

"I sent you a message," she snapped. She moved back to the door.

"Who made the bombs for you, Meghan?" Cooper questioned.

The woman gave him a look that spoke volumes, her disdain for him so intense that if looks could have killed, Cooper would have died a thousand deaths. "You can learn anything you want to learn with the internet," she quipped. She turned back to peer outside.

Cooper shot Kiely another look. Alfie had slid the ottoman top over enough to peek out. He stared at them, his eyes locked on Kiely's face. Kiely was smiling. She shook her head no and pulled her index finger to her lips for him to be quiet.

"Good boys do what they're told, right, Meghan," Kiely said loudly. "Good boys sit quiet as mice. Cooper, you need to be a good boy like Alfie. Alfie's a very good boy."

"Why are you talking?" Meghan yelled. "I told you to shut up!"

Alfie appeared to settle himself lower in the storage bin and Kiely knew the woman yelling had frightened him.

"Where's that kid? I'm not going to ask you again," she screamed, stomping back to stand in front of Cooper.

"Why do you want my son?" Cooper asked. "He doesn't have anything to do with this."

"You don't deserve him. You deserve to die. He's going to need someone to take care of him when that happens. I've been a good mother. I have a son. My Neil used to be such a sweet little boy. He turned eighteen and now he's worthless like his father. He says I'm crazy. He was supposed to help me. Now I can't even trust him. He tried to turn Wes in, you know! He called your office telling you where Wes was. I can't believe he would do that to me. I was a good mother and Wes never did anything to him! He's been trying to keep me and Wes apart since day one. Neil's just jealous."

Meghan seemed to fall into thought reflecting on her child. Cooper realized it was her son Neil who had called in the tip that had led them to the property where she had been holding Alfie.

"You don't have to do this, Meghan," Cooper said. He moved as if to stand up, holding both his hands high as if he were surrendering. "Just turn yourself in."

"Sit down," Meghan hissed. She turned the gun toward Kiely. "Or I will kill her."

Cooper eased back into his seat. He knew it would only be a matter of minutes before the cavalry would be coming. He knew the explosion had triggered his team and they were already circling the property. They just needed to keep her talking. "How did you find us?" he asked.

"You're really not that smart, Agent," Meghan answered. She gestured toward Kiely. "She led me right to you."

Cooper looked confused.

"I saw her in the store buying groceries. And I followed her. She led me right here to you."

Cooper nodded as understanding washed over him. Meghan had likely mistaken Pippa for her twin sister.

"And just so you know," Meghan continued, "she's not loyal. I saw her hugged up with that detective that you've been working with. Your girlfriend here has been lying to you. I would never do something like that to my Wes. I would ride or die for Wes Matthews."

"Where is Wes now?" Kiely questioned.

"Wouldn't you like to know! He's safe. That's all that matters. Wes is safe and you can't get to him." She suddenly reached into the back pocket of her pants and pulled out two plastic zip ties, tossing them both at Kiely. "Secure his hands and then do yours. Do it now!"

"It's okay," Cooper said, the comment meant for Alfie who was peeking out again. He held out his hands, his palms together, and Kiely secured the zip ties around his wrists.

"Make them tighter," Meghan snapped.

Kiely did as she was told, securing the zip ties even tighter. She pressed her fingers against the backs of Cooper's hands. Her touch was consoling. Her hands were steady, no fear reflected in her body language. He sat back down and she turned toward Meghan. "Now what?"

"Secure your wrists, that's what!"

"I can't do my own hands," Kiely said.

Frustration furrowed Meghan's brow. "You can and you will!" She took two fury-filled steps toward Kiely.

As she closed the distance between them, Kiely sprang into action. Meghan wasn't expecting the karate kick that landed in her chest. As she fell backward, Kiely slammed her a second time, dislodging the gun from her hands. When it fell to the floor Cooper lunged for it. Meghan scrambled to her feet faster than Kiely had anticipated. She also dove for the weapon, but Kiely blocked her. The two women were suddenly trading blows, each punch harder than the last. Going toe to toe, Meghan landed a blow that dropped Kiely to her knees.

At that moment, Alfie sprang out from the ottoman, tears streaming down his little face. He screamed Kiely's name, crying hysterically. "Ki-Ki! Ki-Ki!"

Meghan's eyes widened at the sight of him. It proved to be just enough of a distraction when Cooper reached the gun, took aim and fired.

Chapter Fourteen

Kiely sat on the front porch of the home rocking Alfie in her lap. It had been a good two hours since those shots were fired and the little boy was still traumatized. After being reassured that he'd been a very good boy to do what Kiely had wanted of him, he'd finally stopped crying, sitting quietly with his thumb in his mouth.

Inside, Meghan Otis was dead. The threat to Cooper and his family no longer existed. One piece of the larger puzzle had been found. Agents continued to traipse in and out of the house. They had finally breached the entrance just as Cooper had discharged that weapon. In the mayhem that followed Kiely had grabbed Alfie, using her body to shield him from any harm and the sight of the dead woman lying on the floor. Now, Kiely was ready to take him back to Grand Rapids and home.

Cooper stood in the doorway watching the two of them. Kiely had refused medical attention. "It's only a black eye," she had said. "It's not my first and it and the bruises will eventually go away."

"I just want to be…" he had started.

"Just make sure Alfie isn't injured," she said, interrupting his comment. "There was a lot of glass flying and that explosion may have hurt his eardrums."

He stuck his hands deep into the pockets of his pants.

Kiely had put herself in danger to protect his son, and him. During the commotion, he'd been petrified that anything could go horribly wrong and he could have lost her. His love for Kiely was corporeal. Thick, rich, nurturing. She'd become his lifeline. The air he needed to breathe. The sunshine that brightened each day. She loved him and he couldn't begin to fathom how he'd gotten so lucky. And most importantly, she loved his son as if Alfie were her own.

Watching her hold him in her lap, her arms protective vises to keep him safe from harm, the gentle reassurances whispered against the child's cheek, reaffirmed that fate had blessed him and his immensely. He had no intentions of letting karma take that from them.

He moved to where she sat and dropped down onto the top step beside her. Alfie tapped his arm with his foot.

"Hey," Kiely said softly. "How's it going in there?"

"They're almost done. But we're going to head out in a few minutes. I'm ready to go back home and I know you are, too. It's been a long day."

Kiely touched the bandage on his arm where he'd been cut by glass rolling on the floor. "What did the medic say about your ribs?"

"That I should take a few weeks off to heal."

Kiely laughed. "Where have I heard that before?"

Cooper wrapped an arm around her shoulder. "This isn't the most romantic time to ask you this question and I don't have a ring, but…" He moved to the step below them, dropping down onto one knee. "Will you marry me, Kiely Colton? Will you marry me and my son?"

Before Kiely could answer, another black sedan pulled in front of the home, coming to a screeching halt. Tripp, Emmanuel and Riley Colton exited the vehicle, rushing to where they sat.

Cooper shook hands with the trio.

"You all good?" Tripp questioned.

Cooper nodded. "We are."

"My guys just picked up Neil Otis for questioning. The kid is telling everything and he's given us full access to his mother's personal possessions. We might have another lead on Matthews."

"That's good work," Cooper said. He gestured to Grand Rapids' finest to follow him into the house. He leaned to kiss Kiely's cheek as he passed her.

Riley stood in front of her. His expression was intense as he debated whether to fuss at her or not.

"Hey, big brother," she said.

"Hey! You know you scared the hell out of me, right? Emmanuel called saying there had been a shooting and a woman had been killed. He didn't have any details and we knew you were up here alone."

"Sorry about that." She shifted Alfie against her lap and the child sat up straighter. He eyed Riley curiously, his gaze moving from the man's head to his toes.

"Who's this?" Riley asked. He gave Alfie a little poke with his index finger and the little boy giggled.

Kiely smiled a dazzling smile that lit up her face. "This is Alfie. He's mine. He's going to keep me!"

Riley nodded. "Okay. If it works for you, it works for me." He held out his hand. "Hey, kid! I'm Uncle Riley!"

Alfie smiled, pulling his thumb from his mouth. "Hi! My name Alfie!"

COOPER AND KIELY both knew that bringing a sense of normalcy back to their lives would be the best thing for Alfie. After a quick Happy Meal dinner at McDonald's, he had fallen asleep on the ride back to Grand Rapids. By the time Riley dropped them off at Cooper's home, the kid's power nap had him wide open. His excitement was infectious as he raced from room to room, exploring the repairs and renovations, happy to be back in familiar surroundings.

Riley and Cooper stood in conversation as Kiely assessed the contents of the refrigerator and cupboards. They needed a serious food delivery; Alfie was in want of milk and snacks.

"I'll touch base with Tripp in the morning to see where we're at with Neil Otis. My office can help run down any information he gets," Riley said.

"I appreciate that," Cooper said. "I'm officially on desk duty pending the agency's investigation of the shooting."

Riley shot a look in his sister's direction. Kiely was muttering under her breath, making lists and quietly fussing about all she needed to do. He shook his head. "What did you do to her?"

"Excuse me?" Cooper looked confused.

"She's being nice. It's like she's been transformed. You didn't work some sort of Stepford Wives thing on her, did you?"

Cooper laughed. "You probably know better than I that Kiely does exactly what Kiely wants to do."

"Yeah, I do."

"Your sister is an amazing woman. I've fallen in love with her. I asked her to marry me."

"You're moving fast, aren't you?"

Cooper shrugged. "I think when you know, you know."

Riley suddenly thought about the woman he would soon be marrying. Charlize was pregnant with his baby, and he had lost much time with her, fighting what he knew. He would never want Kiely to make that mistake if Cooper was the man for her. He extended his arm to shake Cooper's hand. "I'm sure my sisters have already threatened you," he said. "Just make sure you take care of Kiely. I would hate to see them hurt you."

"She's in good hands. I promise you, I will protect her with my life." The two men shook hands one last time.

Riley sauntered to the kitchen, reaching out his arms to give Kiely a hug. "Call me if you need anything," he said.

"Thank you," Kiely said. "We do need to talk soon. I want to make some changes."

"We all need to meet in the next day or so. Let's plan on talking then?"

Kiely nodded. "I love you, Riley."

Her brother winked his eye at her. "I love you more!"

"Bye, Wi-ley!" Alfie screamed from the other side of the room. He had stacked a pile of blocks, trying to build a fort.

Riley waved. "See you later, alligator!"

"After while, croc-dile!"

COOPER WAS HAPPY to be back in his own bed. He was even happier that Kiely lay beside him. They were both still wide awake, chatting easily as they made plans for their future. Earlier, shortly after Alfie had finally fallen to sleep for the night, Cooper had dropped onto his knee a second time to ask Kiely to be his wife. This time he produced his mother's engagement ring, a family heirloom that he'd inherited after she had passed. It was a meticulously hand-crafted vintage design band of solid fourteen-carat white gold with a stunning two-carat natural diamond and a trellis of diamonds cascading downward from either side.

After she had said yes, kissing him passionately, they had both called their families to give them the happy news.

"I want to hyphenate my name after we get married," Kiely was saying. "Kiely Colton-Winston. You don't have a problem with that, do you?"

"No, not at all."

"Because my father made me a Colton. That means something to me. I can't see myself ever letting that go. It's my identity, who I am. I'm the daughter of a Colton."

"Kiely, I respect that. I want you to carry my name, but I don't want you to lose your identity to do that. Colton-Winston works for me."

"Thank you. Also, I don't want a big wedding. Nothing extravagant. In fact, a civil ceremony down at Town Hall and maybe a reception in the backyard would suit me just fine. Just something very casual."

Cooper chucked. "Do you even want to wear a wedding gown?"

"Only if you insist."

He nodded. "It would be nice."

"Okay. Just for you." She lifted her lips to his and kissed him, then laid herself back down beside him. "Now, what requests do you have of me?"

"I want you to adopt Alfie. I want you to legally be his mother."

Kiely turned to eye him closely. "But... Sara..."

"Sara gave birth to him. And she died after. She will always be his mother. No one can take that from her or from him. And we will tell him about her. He will know the sacrifices she made for him to be here. But, you are the only mother he will ever know. You love him as if you had birthed him yourself. I want you and Alfie to have all the legal protections you would have if your name were on his birth certificate. I need to know that if, heaven forbid, anything ever happened to me that you will be there for Alfie. He has never been able to call anyone mommy. I want him to call you his mommy."

FOR THE FIRST TIME, in a very long time, Kiely wasn't able to hold back her tears. She cried. She cried like a baby herself. She cried to release the fear that had gripped her earlier. She cried for Meghan Otis who had loved a man unworthy of her heart. She cried for the woman's son and the pain he would now have to endure after the loss of his mother. She cried for Cooper who was trying to be a wall of strength for everyone else. She cried for Alfie and the innocence this case had tried to steal from him. She cried for Brody and all those people who'd been harmed by Wes Matthews, Landon Street and Tate Greer, and everyone else affiliated with this whole mess. And she cried for herself and the journey that had taken her far from what she imagined her life to be and had dropped her exactly where she was supposed to be.

Wiping at her eyes with the backs of her hands, she brushed her tears over her cheeks. Cooper wrapped her in his arms and held her until she was all cried out.

"I didn't mean to make you cry," Cooper said softly.

"These are happy tears," Kiely responded. "I love you so much. And I love Alfie. And I don't ever want to lose either one of you. Yes, I wouldn't hesitate to adopt him. I want to be his mother and your wife."

Kiely rolled above him, straddling her body over his. There was a long pause of silence as she stared into his eyes. When she leaned in, their lips met, barely brushing against each other before she pulled back from his touch.

Cooper eased his hands into the length of her hair and pulled her back to him. He captured her lips above his own and kissed her hard. His tongue invaded her mouth and they shared the most sensuous French kiss.

His hands wrapped around her waist, his fingers grazing the taut skin of her behind. He let go of her head and began to work the buttons on her flannel pajama top. His fingers were trembling as he undid each button, exposing her breasts. Cooper massaged one breast and then the other. As he lightly pinched and tweaked her nipples, a low moan escaped Kiely's throat.

Following suit, Kiely pulled at the string that held his pants closed and slipped her hands inside to tease the curl of pubic hair that nested his erection. Their lips met again as Cooper held her tightly to his body. He suddenly swept an arm around her waist and flipped her until her body was beneath his. He nibbled her earlobe, teasing her with his tongue. Kissing down the length of her neck, he licked and nipped at her skin, his pace slow as he explored each square inch of her.

Cooper glanced at her face. Kiely's eyes were closed and there was a beautiful smile on her face. When he sucked her nipple past his lips, she gasped. He moved from one to the other like a man starved, bringing each nipple to a peak. Cooper continued his ministrations, moving slowly down the length of her torso until he reached her feminine core.

Droplets of dew clung to the hair of her landing strip. Her sensual aroma had him brick hard, anticipation fueling the trail he left with his mouth. She squealed when he snaked his tongue into her. She spread herself open, her legs wide as he tasted her, feasting on the pinkness that lined her most private space.

He dipped and dabbled with his mouth, purposely avoiding the sensual nub as he built her up until she was desperate for release. She tasted sweet and when his tongue grazed her clit and he sucked the little nub into his mouth, Kiely arched her back and fisted the sheets beneath her.

Cooper whipped his tongue back and forth until she cried out and her juices flooded the bed beneath her buttocks. He eased himself between her legs, teasing the inner walls with his body. She met him stroke for stroke and then he felt her clench down and tighten her body around his as another orgasm ripped through her, followed closely by a third. A tear slid past her lashes as she clung to him, her nails digging into the flesh along his back. He pumped himself in and out, round and round, back and forth. When his own orgasm hit, Kiely exploded one more time, slipping sweetly with him into an erotic bliss.

The morning sunrise found them still wrapped around each other. When Kiely woke, Cooper had rolled over onto his back and she lay with half her body covering his. His morning erection beckoned for her attention. Cooper opened his eyes as she lifted herself back above him. He gasped as she plunged her body back down against his. She rotated her hips slowly against him as he reached both hands out to grasp her by the waist.

He gasped. "Good morning!"

"Good morning," she said, biting down against her bottom lip. "I thought I'd start your day off with a little dessert!"

"No wanna go to da school," Alfie said later that morning, stomping his foot at Kiely.

"Alfie, you have to go to school, precious. Your friends miss you!"

"Wanna stay wit' you, Ki-Ki!"

Cooper blew a soft sigh. Alfie had been fighting him at every step since he'd wakened. Kicking and screaming he hadn't wanted to brush his teeth, get dressed, comb his hair or eat his breakfast. Now he was adamant that he wasn't leaving the house.

Kiely sat down on the floor beside him, wrapping him in a hug. "I'll tell you what. We'll let Daddy go on to work and you and I will go to school together. I will take you to your class and when I'm done doing my work, I will come back and get you."

"Promise?"

"I promise."

"You back in two minutes, o-kay?"

Kiely smiled. "Two hours, okay?"

Alfie pondered for a moment. "O-kay." He gave his father the evil eye. "I go school wit' my Ki-Ki, Dad-dy."

Cooper laughed. "Okay, buddy!"

Alfie dashed toward the door to get his coat.

"I think it's official. He likes you more than he likes me."

Kiely laughed with him. "I have that effect on men. Especially short men who still occasionally need a diaper."

Cooper hugged and kissed her. "I should be jealous, but I get it. I like you more than I like me, too!"

"As you should," Kiely said teasingly. "Are you going into the office?"

He nodded. "I won't be there long though. All I can do is catch up on the reports and I need to sign my statement about what happened at the safe house. And since I'm technically still on medical leave, they're not going to let me stay long. What were you planning to do?"

"I'll drop Alfie off and then I need to go buy me a car. The FBI were very generous about replacing the one your suspect blew up."

"You're welcome."

She laughed. "How about I take you to lunch? I've got a taste for sushi."

Cooper frowned. "Yuck. Personally, I prefer my fish cooked."

"We're going to have to work on your palate. Meet me at Maru's on Cherry Street so I can start to school you."

"Twelve thirty?"

Kiely kissed him one last time. "Twelve thirty works for me. You ready, Alfie?"

"I going to school wit' Ki-Ki! Bye, Dad-dy! Lub you!"

Cooper laughed. "I think he's ready!"

Chapter Fifteen

Kiely had expected Alfie to put up a fuss when she dropped him off at the Goodman's Children Center. But he was excited when he saw his friends and the classroom teacher he called Miss Gee. All the children had hugged him, pulling him along to the play area and he had gone willingly once Kiely had assured him she'd be back to pick him up at the end of the day. As she exited the building the FBI agent assigned to keep an eye on Alfie gave her a nod, promising she had nothing to worry about. She didn't have the heart to tell him she would worry anyway.

The search for a new car took less than an hour. Kiely had known before she'd left the house where she was going and what she wanted. Someone from Cooper's office had already called Toyota of Grand Rapids and a young salesman named Glenn was overly excited when she stepped through the door. Forty-five minutes later, Kiely drove off the lot with a brand-new Highlander in a loud shade of red called Ruby Pearl. After a quick stop by the local Walmart to purchase a new car seat for Alfie, Kiely headed to see her sister.

Pippa was on the phone when Kiely knocked on her office door. She waved her in as she continued her call. Taking a seat Kiely watched her twin tear into someone who hadn't done his job. When she slammed the phone receiver down, Kiely knew she had swallowed the curse word that had been on the tip of her tongue.

"Welcome home," Pippa said. She paused to jot some notes onto a pad and when she dropped the blue ink pen she turned her full attention toward Kiely. "I hear you almost got yourself killed."

"It was touch and go there for a minute."

"The black eye is pretty."

"You should see the other guy!"

Pippa shook her head. "To what do I owe the honor?"

"Wedding dresses. Where's the best place to shop for one?"

Pippa laughed. And she wouldn't stop laughing. That hysterical laughter that only got worse when people stared or commented. When you couldn't catch your breath and it felt like the room might start to spin. Pippa laughed until tears began to roll down her face. Kiely wasn't amused.

"Why do you find that funny?"

Pippa gasped, sucking in air until she could breathe again. "Because a few days ago you were telling us you had no interest in being married. Or did you forget your 'why do I need a license to validate my relationship' speech?"

Kiely blinked. "Can't a girl change her mind?"

"You're killing me, Kiely!"

As she shrugged her shoulders, a smirky grin pulled across Kiely's face. "Give me a little credit, please. I'm here because Cooper and I would like to retain your services."

"Prenups?"

Kiely shook her head. "Adoption papers. Cooper wants me to legally adopt Alfie after we're married."

Pippa sat back in her seat, reservations simmering in her eyes. "That's a big step, Kiely. Maybe we should go back to wedding dresses. What color is your wedding party wearing? As your maid of honor, I think a mint green would be nice."

Kiely waved a dismissive hand at her sister, refocusing the conversation back on why she was there. "I love them both so much, Pippa. It just feels right. I can't imagine *not* being Alfie's mother now."

"I have to say, watching you with Alfie and Cooper reminded me so much of how Mom had been with all of us."

"So, you'll help?"

"You know I will! But have you considered asking Griffin? Adoption is his specialty."

"I did, but with everything he and Abigail have going on I didn't want to add to his load."

"You should still ask. I think he'd appreciate it. You know he sometimes thinks we leave him out of things when that's the last thing we're trying to do. Let him say no."

Kiely nodded. "I will, but do you have any advice?"

"Personally, I would make you wait one year to officially adopt. There's going to be a lot of adjustment for you and Cooper and most especially Alfie. For now, I'd suggest you two amend your wills first and put a custody plan in place should something happen to Cooper before that year is up. You also need to consider a plan for any biological children that you two may have together, if that's something you're considering."

"That should work. Cooper and I are having lunch later. I'll tell him what you said."

Pippa's phone rang. She glanced down to the caller ID. "I need to take this. But I will call you later and we can plan on going wedding dress shopping!"

Rising from her seat, Kiely laughed. "Thank you, Pip!"

COOPER SAT BACK in his chair, his hands folded together in his lap. He'd spent a good hour with the FBI psychologist, talking through everything that had happened. He hadn't wanted to admit that pulling the trigger and taking a woman's life had left him traumatized. Doing his job often came with regrets, but this one ran deep. Mental illness had driven Meghan Otis to do all she had done. If only her actions had not pushed them to a point of no return, helping her might have been possible.

But Cooper knew he couldn't live with second guessing his actions. Protecting his family would always be foremost in everything he did and he couldn't question choices made in the heat of a moment when they'd been in harm's way. Kiely had reminded him that talking things through would help him sleep at night. He would meet with the doctor again, for as long as he felt he needed help.

Shifting forward in his seat, he had gone through a dozen files catching up on every aspect of the case. They were getting closer to catching Wes Matthews, but they weren't there yet. The information they'd received from Neil Otis had been more than helpful. His mother had kept detailed records of her transactions with Wes. From bank accounts opened under an alias to properties purchased in the name of a shell company the FBI had been unaware of, they discovered more about Wes and his activities. He completed the paperwork to seize the bank accounts, successfully cutting Wes off from most of his money.

Claire knocked on his door. "How are you doing, Agent?"

Cooper nodded. "Still standing, Agent Miller. How are you doing today?"

"No complaints. I hear congratulations are in order."

Cooper laughed. "Who spilled the beans?"

"You know the Grand Rapids police department can't keep a secret!"

"Well, thank you," he said, shaking his head. "Kiely and I are very excited."

"I'm not going to hold you up. I just wanted to pop in and say hello and tell you how happy I am for you."

"I appreciate that. I was just reviewing the Neil Otis file and the information he provided."

"Have you talked to that kid?"

"No. Why?"

"I couldn't put my finger on it initially, but the more I thought I about it, I don't think he was totally honest with us about his part in all of this. It's a gut feeling. As a parent you always know when your kids are lying to your face but they think they're getting away with something. Because every kid is smarter than their parents are. I felt like he was lying through his teeth because he thinks he's smarter than the rest of us."

She took a deep breath. "Neil was more than happy to throw his mother under the bus. We heard sob stories about her mental health issues. How much he hated her boyfriend. He was a gold mine of information, no doubt. I mean, you read the report. But I wasn't happy about letting him go. We just didn't have anything to hold him on and he knew it. Personally, I think he's a powder keg waiting to explode."

"I appreciate you sharing that. Let me finish reading the file and maybe I'll drop by his home and have a chat with him myself."

"Good luck. Let me know if I can help."

Cooper gave her a nod as she exited the room. He reached for the file and flipped it open a second time. There was a picture of Neil Otis paper clipped to the inside of the folder. Although he was only eighteen years old, he looked substantially older. He had an acne problem and carried some excess weight. He was a diehard gamer, had already earned an associate degree in computer science, and worked part-time as a security guard for an industrial packing company. Cooper placed the photograph to the side but kept coming back to it as he continued to review the notes taken by his agents.

Minutes later, it clicked. He powered up his computer, then searched for an evidence folder. Inside the folder, he found the digital file he'd wanted. He played the video once and then again. After the seventh or eighth viewing he picked up his phone and dialed Claire's extension.

"Agent Winston, what's up?"

"Neil Otis participated in the kidnapping of my son. He snatched Alfie."

"Are you sure?"

"I'm positive. Pull up video #379475. It's the security tape from the school. It's him."

"I'll send a team to pick him up right now."

"I'm grabbing my vest. I'm going."

"You know you're on desk duty, right? You haven't been cleared yet."

"He snatched my son!"

"You already know the narrative. His mother made him do it."

"I'm going. I'll stay out of the way but I want to be there when they put the handcuffs on him. He terrorized my son!" Cooper's voice had risen two octaves.

"I can't approve that, Cooper. As your friend, I'm going to advise you to go home and hug your son. As your senior agent, I'm going to order you to stand down. We can't risk you jeopardizing the case. We want to see justice served. We can't risk losing him on a technicality."

Cooper threw his stapler across the room into the wall. He heaved a gust of air. "Fine," he said. "But I'm not happy about this. I'm not happy at all!"

KIELY PULLED UP into the driveway of her home. It felt like it had been a lifetime since she was last there. After much discussion she and Cooper had decided that she would rent her small cottage and move into the home with him and Alfie. Cooper wasn't keen on Jim Morrison coming along, having no experience with cats, but they both agreed that he might make a good companion for Alfie.

She hadn't planned to stop by the house but she had a few minutes before she was scheduled to meet Cooper. It had seemed like a good opportunity to assess all that needed to be done to prepare the house for rent. What she would take to integrate into his space, what she would leave, and what she would dole out to her siblings. She also needed to pack a second suitcase of clothes.

She didn't give much thought to the young man walking on the sidewalk in front of the property. Not until he called out to get her attention. He appeared to be young. Maybe in his late teens or early twenties. He wore a local high school's varsity sports jacket. It was ill fitting but she thought it might have more to do with the oversized sweatshirt he wore beneath it. He had bad skin, a raging case of acne across his cheeks and nose. As he moved toward her she bristled, her stance defensive, but she didn't necessarily consider him threatening. He simply appeared to be lost.

"Excuse me, ma'am? May I ask you a question, please?"

Kiely walked toward the back of her car. "Can I help you?"

"I apologize for the interruption, but my cell phone battery just died and I can't use my map feature to find Chambers Street. Do you by chance know how close I am?"

Kiely pointed right. "It's two blocks that way. You're actually very close."

"Thank you. I really appreciate that." He turned and moved to head in the direction Kiely had just pointed him to. He suddenly turned back toward her. "I'm sorry, may I ask you one more question, please?"

"Sure, what's up?"

"I really like your car. Are you happy with that model?"

Kiely narrowed her gaze ever so slightly. "My car?"

"Sorry, yeah. My father always said that if you are interested in purchasing something big, like a car, that you should ask people what they think of it when you see them driving one. He said the user of a product can tell you more about it than a salesman. I'm actually headed to Chambers Street to see a guy selling one. It's used. I know yours is newer but I thought I'd ask."

Kiely nodded. She took a step closer toward the young man. "I really like mine. I haven't had it long but right now I have no complaints."

He nodded at her. "Thank you! I really appreciate that. You have a good day now!"

Kiely turned to head into the house when she heard the young man suddenly rush up behind her. Before she could respond, a heavy arm moved around her neck and then the sharp sting of a taser rendered her unconscious.

COOPER HATED TO cancel lunch with Kiely but he was determined to see how things played out with Neil Otis. A team had been sent to escort him into the office and Cooper was waiting anxiously for them to return. When she didn't answer her phone, he sent her a quick text message.

Hate to do this but business calls. I'll explain later. Raincheck on lunch?

Cooper had been pacing the floors, moving from his office to the hotline call center and back. It was taking longer than necessary to hear from the team and he was starting to regret that he had not defied Claire and gone anyway.

Claire met him in the hallway as he was headed back toward his office. "Otis wasn't home. Two agents are going to sit on the house," she said. "They'll bring him in when he returns. Now go home. I will call you once we have him in custody."

"I think I'll wait," Cooper said. "This is personal."

"That's why you need to leave. It is personal and you're starting to be a problem."

Cooper stared her down and Claire stared back. She folded her arms across her chest and leaned against one hip.

"Fine. But please, call me."

Claire didn't bother to respond, stepping past him as she returned to her own office.

Thirty minutes later Cooper moved toward the elevators, headed home. He had managed to successfully clear off his desk, returning the last of his files to their proper place. He was trying to call Kiely for the third time when his cell phone rang, a call coming from Alfie's school. He was suddenly gripped with fear.

"Hello?"

"Hello, is this Mr. Winston?"

"Yes, it is. How may I help you?"

"Mr. Winston, this is Mrs. Glembocki. How are you, sir?"

"I'm well, thank you. Is everything okay with Alfie?"

"Yes, sir. Alfie is fine. But no one's come to pick him up. I understand you're just getting back to a routine and wondered if you had forgotten?"

"I'm sorry, my fiancée was supposed to pick him up."

"Your fiancée?"

"Kiely Colton. I added her to the approved pickup list."

"No one by that name has come to pick up Alfie."

"Thank you for calling, Mrs. Glembocki. I'm not sure what happened, but I'm on my way."

"Thank you, sir. We appreciate that."

After disconnecting the call, Cooper tried Kiely's number one more time. When it went right to voice mail, he began to worry. Kiely would never have forgotten Alfie.

Chapter Sixteen

When Kiely regained consciousness, she was chained to a dining room chair in her living room, and someone was puttering around in her kitchen. She tried to shake off her restraints but they wouldn't budge. She took a quick assessment of her surroundings. None of her personal possessions seemed to have been moved. A blanket rested on the floor at her feet. Her purse, cell phone, revolver and a bottle of RevitaYou rested on the coffee table. The high-definition television was on, a commercial for life insurance playing on the screen.

She turned to the clock on the wall. She knew Cooper would be looking for her. She'd been scheduled to pick up Alfie from school two hours earlier. She was certain that when she didn't arrive, he would send a search team to find her. The only thing that would delay him, she thought, was that she hadn't put visiting the house on her schedule.

"You're awake! I thought you were going to miss *Family Feud*." The young man who'd asked about her car stood in the doorway holding two TV dinners in his hands. "I really like that Steve Harvey! He's so funny!"

"Who are you?" Kiely asked. "And why are you doing this?"

"I'm sorry. Where are my manners? My name's Neil. Neil Otis."

"You're Meghan's son."

He nodded. "Steve's about to come on." He gestured with the two microwaved meals. "Would you like the Salisbury steak or the meat loaf? They both actually taste the same, if you want my opinion. Mom liked the steak better though."

"I'm not hungry. Thank you."

He shrugged. "I'll save you the steak. You can eat it later."

"Why are you doing this?"

"Let's watch Steve. We can talk later," he said, ignoring her question. He moved to the sofa and made himself comfortable, reclining back against the pillows.

Kiely struggled against her restraints a second time.

"You shouldn't do that," he said. "You might hurt yourself."

"I really need to know why you're doing this," Kiely persisted. "I don't know you."

"Yes, you do, Ms. Colton. Please don't think me a fool. I don't like that. My mother treated me like I was a fool."

"So, you know who I am?"

"I saw you at the school today. I know that you're Alfie's mom. Well, not his real mom but you act like it. You seem like a really good one, too."

"You've been watching me?"

"Of course. Well, my mother was. Sort of. You and Agent Winston. More him, than you. She really hated him."

"Is that why you're doing this? Because you hate him?"

"I don't hate anyone. Hate is not a healthy emotion."

"Then why?"

Neil seemed to ponder the question for a moment. "I don't know. I just wanted to talk to you. You had kind eyes."

"Neil, there are better ways to have a conversation with a person than kidnapping them."

"Where's your cat?" he asked, changing the subject. He pointed at the sisal-covered scratching post in the corner of the room.

"I gave her to a relative," she said.

"Your sister," he said, the statement more comment than question.

Kiely watched him keenly as he finished his meal. He lifted the paper tray to his mouth and licked it clean. When he was done, he carried it and the full tray of food back to the kitchen. "Just tell me when you're hungry," he said. "I'll heat it back up for you."

They sat together through two episodes of the *Feud*. Neil played along, pretending to be a member of the families he liked most.

"Family is very important. My mother didn't appreciate that. She treated me very badly. Mothers shouldn't treat their children badly."

"I'm sorry," Kiely said.

"Don't be. It's not your fault. My mother had emotional issues. She was very young when she had me. I don't think she knew who my father was until I was born. I think that's why she resented me. Her hatred for him is why she could never really love me."

Kiely took a breath. "I don't think that's true. Your mother told us she loved you very much."

"She told everyone that. Didn't make it true though."

He moved to the table and the bottle of RevitaYou. Taking two pills from the bottle, he popped them into his mouth and washed them down with a swallow of water.

Kiely's eyes widened. "Don't take those!" she shouted.

"Why not? These are the good ones."

"The good ones?"

"Yeah, the ones that work. Mom has cases in the basement. She swore by them."

"You need to turn those over to the police."

"No," he said, sounding like he was eight and not eighteen. "These are the ones that work!" he repeated.

Kiely's frustration level was steadily rising. She knew she was in trouble, no matter how mild-mannered Neil seemed. She just wasn't sure what his endgame was. Her cell phone suddenly vibrated against the table. Neil jumped up to see who was calling, annoyed when he saw Cooper's picture on the screen.

"He calls a lot."

"He'll be looking for me, Neil. A lot of people will be looking for me."

"No, they won't. I've been texting them. He thinks you're helping your sister with a problem. Your sister thinks you're in a meeting and can't talk. No one is missing you."

"My son is missing me."

Neil slammed a heavy fist against the table. He rose from his seat and stormed back into the kitchen. Minutes later, when he returned, so had his mild-mannered mood.

"I don't want you to talk about him."

"Why? He's just a baby!"

Neil winced, her words apparently off putting to him. "My mother kept saying that. He's a baby! Watch the baby! Be nice to the baby! Mother wanted to keep him. But I couldn't let her do that. I had to protect him."

"You need to let me go, Neil. This is ridiculous! You can't keep me hostage here forever."

"It's not forever."

"Then for how long?"

"You really need to eat," Neil said. He moved to the back of the sofa, rummaging on the floor. When he stood, he held a gas can in his hands and began to splash gasoline on the furniture and floor.

Kiely's eyes widened. "What are you doing? Why are you doing that?"

"Because you're a good mom now. I don't want you to be a bad mother. You'll go bad. All of you go bad. I have to stop you before that happens. I have to do it for the children."

ALFIE HAD FINALLY cried himself to sleep. He'd been devastated when Kiely hadn't picked him up. When she hadn't arrived by dinner, he'd been beside himself. It had taken Cooper forever to calm him down. Although Kiely hadn't answered Cooper's calls, she had texted him. Multiple times. She'd been apologetic about not showing to pick up Alfie, claiming an emergency with her sister was holding her up. But now his concern had increased tenfold. Something wasn't right and he regretted not following his first instinct.

Reaching for his cell phone, he read through the text messages a second time. Most of the responses were short and sweet. But short and sweet didn't feel like Kiely. He sent one last message.

Should we invite the deer to the wedding?

As he waited for her to respond, he paced the floor. He needed to find her. And something in his gut told him he needed to find her quick.

A reply message came back promptly.

I'd rather invite the kangaroos!

Cooper placed three phone calls. The first was to the FBI offices. The second call was to Lieutenant McKellar and the third was to Riley Colton.

"We're pinging her phone now to see if we can get a location on her. Can you check if any of your sisters have heard from her, please?" Cooper said.

"I'll call them now and I'll call you right back. Do you have any idea what's happened to her?"

"Not a clue," Cooper answered.

Cooper had just called the teenager down the street to come sit with Alfie when his phone rang, Claire on the other end.

"Hey, did they update you?" Cooper questioned.

"Yes," his friend answered. "But you're not going to believe this," she said. "We just got a DNA hit on three murders. The agency hadn't wanted to say they were the work of a serial killer, but the similarities in each case can't be ignored. Three young mothers with small children, all kidnapped, each burned alive in their homes. The last murder occurred one year ago."

"Why are you telling me this? I've never worked any of those cases."

"Because that DNA is the same as Neil Otis's. He's a perfect match and we still haven't been able to find him."

Something dark pitched through the pit of Cooper's stomach. He suddenly felt like the tuna fish sandwich he'd eaten for dinner might come back up. Pieces of a puzzle were falling into place through no effort of his and he wasn't liking the picture coming forward.

"And all the murders occurred in the victims' homes?" he asked.

"That's correct."

Panic swept through Cooper like a storm wind. He shouted into the receiver. "I need a team sent to Kiely Colton's house now! She's missing and if Neil Otis is your serial killer then she may be your next victim. I think he might have her there!"

THE SMELL OF gasoline was thick through the air. Kiely found it revolting. It was turning her stomach and giving her a vicious headache. Neil seemed oblivious to it as he sat watching an episode of *Thundercats*. He had abandoned all efforts at conversation, ignoring Kiely's admonishments for him to talk to her.

When the cartoon was over, he asked her one last time, if she wanted something to eat. "I can heat up your TV dinner if you're hungry. You really should have one last meal. All the others ate their last meal."

"The others? You've done this before, Neil?"

"Of course! There are so many children that need to be saved."

Kiely closed her eyes, the significance of what he intended feeling like a gut punch. She couldn't begin to fathom how she had come to be in this place. Or how Neil had become the way he was. A tear ran down her cheek. All she wanted was to get back to Cooper and Alfie.

"Was there anyone in your life who you loved, Neil, who you miss now?"

Neil's expression was cutting. "No," he said matter-of-factly. "Not really."

"Did you love your mother?"

"When I was small. Like your son's age. And I tried to be really good so that she would love me, but it never worked."

"Well, Alfie loves me, Neil. Alfie will miss me. If you do this, you are going to break his heart. You won't be saving him, you'll be hurting him."

Neil looked at her. "This hurt will go away and soon he won't even remember you. And when he does, all he'll remember is what a good mother you were. He'll never have to remember you turning on him. You really should thank me."

Kiely begged. "Please! Don't do this."

Neil moved to her side and patted her hand. "I can give you something if it'll make it easier. Mom had tranquilizers and pain pills stashed away. All kinds of stuff."

"Go to hell!" Kiely snapped.

Neil bristled. "See, it never fails," he shouted. "All of you go bad! Before you know it you'll be calling Alfie bad names and hitting him and you'll hurt his feelings and..." He became choked up, fighting not to cry. He gasped for air, then just like that collected himself.

"It's time!" he exclaimed, his singsong tone disconcerting.

"What do you mean? What are you going to do? Please don't do this, Neil! Please!"

Despite her best efforts to remain calm, panic had begun to set in. Kiely shook the chains harder, desperate to release herself. Panic suddenly became rage. Neil had disappeared to the second floor of her home, a second gasoline can in his hands. He rested the container at the bottom of the steps and then he moved to turn the television volume up higher.

He lit one match and then the entire book, tossing both to the floor behind the sofa. Flames suddenly shot skyward. He moved to Kiely's side one last time.

"It was very nice talking with you, Ms. Colton," he said, and then he walked calmly out the front door.

Chapter Seventeen

Cooper arrived at Kiely's house seconds after Claire and her team had descended on the property. The fire department was already on-site, fighting the barrage of flames that lit up the late-night sky. His heart dropped into the pit of his stomach and he raced toward the house screaming Kiely's name.

Someone from the fire department grabbed him by the shoulders and swung him back around, refusing to let him pass. There was a struggle of wills as the fireman ducked a punch he threw, Cooper determined to get inside the home.

Claire suddenly grabbed his arm, pulling at his attention. "Cooper, Kiely's okay! Kiely's fine!" she shouted above the noise of his screams.

Claire pointed to the EMS vehicle. "She suffered some smoke inhalation, but she's fine."

Tears were streaming down Cooper's face. He grabbed Claire and hugged her before tearing across the yard to the ambulance. Kiely lay on a gurney inside, an oxygen mask over her face. He jumped into the back of the vehicle and when she saw him, she ripped the mask off. Sitting upright Kiely stretched her arms out and clung tightly to him.

Cooper kissed her cheeks, her forehead, her nose, her lips. Kisses rained down on every square inch of her face and he refused to let her go until his nerves had calmed, his heart beating normally again.

"Are you okay? Did he hurt you?" Cooper questioned.

"I'm fine. Really. I'm okay."

"Her vitals are good," the technician said. "But we should transport her to the hospital to be examined."

"That's not necessary," Kiely said. "I feel fine. I'm not going to the hospital." She threw her legs over the side of the gurney and went to stand but felt light-headed and sat back down.

"You're going, Kiely."

"I really don't want to. It's not necessary."

"I'll meet you there," Cooper said, his tone commanding. "Let a doctor clear you and then we can go home to Alfie."

"Is he okay?"

"Pissed that you weren't in the kiss and go lane this afternoon."

"My poor baby!"

"He'll be very happy to see you."

Kiely hugged him one more time. She was shaking slightly, hoping no one noticed. But Cooper noticed and he was suddenly angry that someone had tried to hurt her. He kissed her cheek. "I'll be right behind you," he said.

Jumping out of the ambulance, he watched until it pulled off, sirens screaming. He turned, searching out Agent Miller. Claire stood by a government-issued vehicle, debriefing one of her agents. Spying Cooper, she met him halfway as he moved in her direction.

"Please, tell me we did not lose this monster."

"Nope, we got him." She pointed to the back seat of a police patrol car. Neil Otis was leaning against the window peering out at the burning house. He looked lost and completely enamored with the flames that were being extinguished. "He'd barely gotten out the front door when we took him down. Kiely was chained to a chair in the front room and two of our agents went in and carried her out."

"I owe them my gratitude."

"Thank them by getting Kiely and going home and please don't come back until you have medical clearance from an agency doctor. Spend some time with your family, *not* working. Is that clear, Agent?"

"Have a good night, Claire. And thank you!" He turned, hurrying back to his car.

Claire called his name.

"Yes?"

"Good work, Agent Winston!"

KIELY WAS SO ready to be done with the emergency room that she was sitting in the waiting room when Cooper arrived.

"What took you so long?"

"Why are you out here?"

"Do you always answer a question with a question?"

"Depends upon the question?"

"Do you love me?"

"Forever and always." Cooper captured her lips with his own. The kiss was tender and heated. When he finally let her go, he asked, "Have you been officially released?"

"If I say yes will you believe me?"

He chuckled. "And you give me a hard time."

Grabbing her hand, they made their way to the car and then home. Kiely called her brother to let him know she was safe and sound so that her family wouldn't be worrying about her. After a quick lecture, she was ready to be done with retelling what had happened to her.

"I feel sorry for him," Kiely said. "He's got serious issues."

"He's a psychopath."

"He thinks he's helping children."

"Well, thankfully he will never be able to hurt anyone else again."

Kiely sighed. She didn't have the energy to tell Cooper she was tired of this conversation. She wasn't much interested in solving anyone else's problems or putting herself in the path of danger. The only thing she wanted was to crawl into bed and forget that anything had happened. To ignore that Neil had disturbed her peace and left her feeling battered. She needed time to let it all go so that she could feel like herself again and not be afraid.

"Can we talk about this some other time?" she asked.

Cooper nodded. "Of course. Anything you want. You look tired."

"I just want to go to bed and I want you to just hold me."

He nodded again. "Baby, you can have anything you want."

THE FIRST THING Kiely did when they got back to Cooper's house was peek in on Alfie. He was sleeping soundly, his thumb in his mouth and his favorite blue blanket clutched in his fist. She brushed the hair off his forehead and leaned to give him a kiss.

She knew she smelled like smoke and she headed straight for a hot shower. She was grateful for Cooper giving her time alone to decompress and process everything that had happened. For a while there she didn't think there was enough soap and water or shampoo and conditioner to help her get the smell of fear off of her. She'd had many close calls over the years, but there had been something about this one that felt like dead weight on her shoulders, refusing to let go.

By the time Kiely had finished in the bathroom, Cooper was already showered and in bed. He'd used the bathroom in the spare bedroom, wanting her to take as much time as she needed. He understood that what she had just experienced was traumatizing and even the strongest person would have difficulties getting past it all.

She pulled a T-shirt from his top drawer and pulled it over her head. She slid into bed beside him and Cooper curled his body around hers. The nearness of him, the sound of his breathing, brought her joy that could not be verbalized. It just made her feel like all was well in the world. Back in Cooper's arms, Kiely felt like she'd found her way back home. The lights were on, a fire was burning in the fireplace and the smell of baking cookies filled the air.

"I love you," Kiely whispered. "I love you so much."

Cooper squeezed her gently. He threw his leg over hers and tightened the hold he had on her. He pressed a damp kiss against the back of her neck.

"Twenty questions," Kiely said. "What one place would you live if you didn't live in Grand Rapids?"

"Hawaii!"

"I like Hawaii! I could live there."

Cooper smiled. "Favorite flower?"

"Hydrangea. Favorite president?"

"Good question! I'd say… Jimmy Carter."

"Good answer!"

Cooper kept it going. "Last book you read."

"It was a mystery. *City of Saviors* by Rachel Howzell Hall."

"Not an author I know. Was it good?"

"I really liked it. Morning person or night person."

"Morning person."

"I'm more of a night person but I make it work when I have to."

Cooper hesitated, looking like he wasn't sure what to ask next.

"It's your turn," Kiely said to coax him along.

"Are you really okay, Kiely?"

She suddenly choked back a sob. "No," she said softly. "No, I'm not. But I will be. I'm home and I'm going to be just fine."

Cooper held her close for the rest of the night. He kneaded her shoulders and stroked her back. When she jumped in her sleep he whispered in her ear to soothe her. He would have done anything to ensure she was well.

KIELY WOKE THE next morning to Alfie tapping her face with the palm of his hand. Her mouth lifted in a warm smile but she didn't open her eyes. He tapped her a second time. She opened one eye and closed it again. His giggles were music to her ears and Alfie was giggling merrily.

He leaned to kiss her cheek. "Hi, Ki-Ki! You sleep?"

Kiely reached out to give him a tickle and Alfie erupted in laughter. "Do again! Do again!" he exclaimed, not wanting her to stop.

When Cooper came to check on the two of them they were cuddled together watching cartoons.

"Hey, buddy," Cooper said, "are you ready to go to school today?"

"No, Alfie stay home wit' Ki-Ki. No go school!"

"I propose we have family day," Kiely said.

"Family day? What's that?" Cooper asked.

"Daddy and Alfie and Kiely stay home together all day in bed watching cartoons."

"Yeah! Family day!" Alfie said excitedly.

Cooper laughed. "Does that mean we get to stay in our pajamas all day?"

"Pajamas all day, and we pop popcorn, and play

games!" Kiely said excitedly. "Maybe we'll even have a dance party!"

"And cartoons!" Alfie added.

Kiely gave the boy a little squeeze and another tickle.

"Well," Cooper said, "what would you two like to eat for breakfast?"

"I propose cereal with the marshmallows in it and we eat it right out of the box."

Alfie threw up his hands in agreement. "Cereal!"

"I'll have coffee with mine. Can I tempt you with a cup?"

"Alfie want milk," the little boy said firmly. "Just milk."

Kiely said, "One milk and one coffee would be appreciated. Thank you."

Breakfast was a big hit with Alfie, even with the spilled milk and cereal in the bed. They played games, watched cartoons, and spent the entire morning and afternoon together. Only once did Cooper try to answer his cell phone. After the dirty looks his son and Kiely gave him, he turned the device off and focused solely on the two of them.

Kiely made grilled cheese sandwiches, tomato soup and popped popcorn for lunch. Before putting Alfie down for a nap, the couple sat him down to talk about their plans.

"Alfie, how would you like Kiely to be your mommy?" Cooper questioned.

"Alfie mommy in hea-ben."

"Yes, she is. Your mommy Sara is in heaven," Cooper said. "But Kiely would like to be your *bonus* mommy, and Daddy *wants* Kiely to do that. How do you feel about that?"

"Alfie *lub* Ki-Ki!"

"So, you want to keep her?"

"Ki-Ki mine!"

"Yes, I am!" Kiely said.

Alfie jumped from his chair and took off running. They could hear him laughing in the other room.

"Why did I think having a serious conversation with a two-year-old was going to be easy?" Cooper said.

"It was."

"Are you sure? Because I'm not sure he got it."

Kiely smiled. "Trust me, he got it."

Minutes later Alfie came tearing back into the room with his stuffed rabbit. He shoved the toy in Kiely's direction. "Dis babbitt!"

"Hello, rabbit!"

He looked into the rabbit's face, poking it in the eyes. He climbed into Kiely's lap. "You Alfie mommy!"

"Yes, I am!"

"Alfie *lub* you Ki-Ki!" He wrapped his little arms around Kiely's neck and hugged her.

Kiely met the look Cooper was giving her. She grinned. "Told you!"

FAMILY DAY LASTED three whole days. By day four Alfie was excited to go back to school to play with his friends. Cooper headed to the office so Claire could yell at him about being there, and Kiely began to deal with the insurance company over the demise of her home and the loss of her property.

Someone from Cooper's office had retrieved her new car, depositing it in the empty parking space. She had driven by her house to assess the damage, but once she turned on the street she hadn't been able to stop. Passing by had been all she could manage and Cooper had agreed that had been more than enough. There was nothing inside that couldn't be replaced.

After making the turn at the corner Kiely headed to her brother's. Riley had called a meeting of Colton Investigations, insisting they all needed to be there. She knew he wanted to assess where they were with Brody's case, but it was also about the Colton siblings laying eyes on each other with everything that had been happening.

Traffic was light which made the ride easy and it took no time at all for Kiely to get to Grand Avenue, near the center of the historic Heritage Hill neighborhood. Riley lived in the family home where they'd grown up. The siblings had inherited the house after their parents' tragic deaths and operated Colton Investigations out of the rooms on the first floor. Deciding to make the locale CI headquarters had just made sense.

She pulled into the driveway and eased her car behind the house. Parking the vehicle behind Pippa's luxury sedan, she realized she wasn't the last to arrive. Their sister Vikki wasn't there yet either. That would take some of the heat off her when she walked in. Riley hated when they weren't on time.

She didn't bother to knock, throwing the door open and heading inside. Riley and Griffin were sitting at the kitchen table noshing on containers of Chinese food. Riley's German Shepherd, Pal, sat between them, her large head bobbing back and forth as she hoped one or the other would drop something to the hardwood floor.

"Hey," she said, greeting her brothers.

She rubbed Pal's head and the dog licked her hand in greeting.

Riley dropped the egg roll between his fingers onto his plate. He reached for a napkin. "I didn't know if you were coming. You never answered my text message. I was starting to worry."

Kiely shrugged. "Sorry about that. I had a lot going on."

"Cooper told us what happened and we saw the house."

She nodded. "It's totaled. I've lost everything, but I've

gained far more than I lost." She leaned to give Griffin a hug. "How are you?"

"Better than you apparently."

Kiely smiled. "If we can talk later, I need a favor. Cooper and I need an adoption attorney. I want to legally adopt his son Alfie."

Griffin was about to take a bite of his food, his fork stalling in midair. "I've clearly missed out on a lot!" he said, a hint of attitude in his tone.

"Not really," she said. "And if you have, I'm excited to catch you up."

He nodded. "You know I'll do whatever I can. Just let me know when you two want to schedule an appointment to meet."

Kiely leaned to kiss his cheek. "Where's everyone?"

"The girls are in the dining room. Are you hungry?" Riley said. "There's plenty of food. Just grab a paper plate and help yourself."

"I will," she said. "Let me go say hi to everyone first."

"Make it quick! Meeting starts in ten." Riley pulled his egg roll back to his mouth.

Kiely maneuvered her way through the home. As she entered the main area, Ashanti Silver, her favorite tech guru, jumped from her seat to greet her. Ashanti was one of her brother's first hires. Gorgeous, super smart and a wiz with a computer, she could back door her way past anyone's firewall and never be detected. She had helped Kiely get out of many situations, some business and some personal.

The woman threw her arms around Kiely in a bear hug. "Oh, my God! You're alive!"

Kiely laughed. "No one's killed me off yet! How are you?"

"I've got my heels and my health so I have no complaints," she said as she showed off the six-inch stilettos she was wearing. She tossed her long braids over her shoulder. "More importantly, I want to see that ring," she said as she waved her fingers at Kiely.

Kiely held out her hand. The two-carat diamond in the antique setting flattered her fingers.

"It's beautiful!" Ashanti hugged her a second time. "I'm so excited for you. Now, do you need me to run a background check on him?" she asked.

Kiely laughed. "I'm good. I appreciate you offering though."

"If you need me, just ask."

Kiely continued into the dining conference room. Pippa and Sadie sat at the oversized table thumbing through wedding gown magazines. Both women stood up to hug her.

"Why haven't you called anyone?" Pippa admonished. "I've left a dozen messages for you."

Kiely shrugged. "I needed some time."

"You're lucky Cooper's so good about keeping us all updated," Sadie quipped.

"You talked to Cooper?"

"We didn't talk to you!"

Kiely smiled. She would have to thank him later for looking out for her, she thought.

"Are you hungry?" Pippa asked. "I'll make you a plate if you want me to?"

Kiely shook her head. "I might get something after the meeting. I'm good for now."

Her sister tapped the empty seat beside her. "Sit down."

"We've taken up a donation for you," Sadie said.

"What kind of donation?"

"We all cleaned out our closets to collect some clothes for you. There are three large bags in the trunk of my car,"

Pippa interjected. "It should tide you over until you can start rebuilding your wardrobe."

Kiely laughed. "I hadn't even thought about it. I've spent the last three days in my pajamas."

"I bet that was cute," Sadie giggled.

"Cooper liked it," Kiely said with a smirk.

The conversation was interrupted when the brothers moved into the room. Riley took the seat at the head of the table. "Has anyone heard from Vikki?"

Gazes shifted back and forth and heads shook from side to side.

"I guess we'll start without her." Riley cleared his throat. "I think it's safe to say we are no farther along with this case than we were before. Still nothing solid on a location for Wes Matthews or Landon Street."

Kiely shared what she and Cooper had learned from Neil Otis. "Cooper has cut off much of Wes's bank access. Unless he has accounts that haven't been found yet, he'll be hurting for money sooner than later. That might be to our advantage. Cooper's office is still running down the leads Neil gave them."

"I feel like we're looking for a needle in a haystack," Pippa said. "Those two are cagey as hell!"

Kiely shot Sadie a quick look. "Cooper's also trying to find a connection between Matthews and Tate Greer. It looks like most of the victims who financed their investments in RevitaYou were referred to Capital X with guarantees of approved financing."

Riley nodded. "We'll see what we can find out on our end."

"Has anyone spoke to Brody recently?" Griffin asked. He looked directly at Pippa.

She shook her head. "Not a word. I don't know if we should be worried or not."

Everyone at the table went quiet, thinking about their surrogate brother and his predicament. The moment was suddenly interrupted when Vikki rushed into the room.

"Hello! Hello! Hello!" She moved around the table pressing her cheek to everyone else's.

"You're late," Riley admonished.

"And I can't stay. I just came for a quick lunch," she said. "We've had another RevitaYou death. A woman named Teri Emerson."

Riley cussed.

"Is she military?" Kiely questioned.

Vikki was a JAG paralegal for the U.S. Armed Forces assigned to Fort Rapids.

"Military wife," she answered. "Her husband is an army captain and he's on a rampage. He's looking for Landon Street and has vowed to kill him on sight. I've been assigned to investigate his threats. He's highly decorated and about to retire. I'm trying to keep this from blowing up even more."

"Understood," Riley said. "Do what you have to do."

"Is there anything I need to know, before I run out of here?" Vikki asked.

Riley threw up his hands in frustration. "No, there really isn't much we have to share."

Vikki nodded. She turned her attention toward Kiely. "Call me, please, and let me know what's going on with you. In fact, call and update me, if there is anything that comes out here that I need to know, too, please."

She gave her sister a hug, also grabbing her hand to look at her engagement ring. "Clearly, he has good taste!"

Laughter rang around the table as Victoria made her exit. She called out over her shoulder, "I'm taking an egg roll and the rest of the beef and peppers! I hope nobody wanted it."

Griffin laughed. "I guess if they did, it's too late."

Chapter Eighteen

Cooper stood in front of the burned-out shell that was once her home, waiting for her. While she had met with her siblings, he had taken the meeting with the insurance agent. She couldn't begin to tell him how much she appreciated his efforts. As she moved to his side, she felt herself begin to shake. She realized that even if the home had not burned, that returning to it would not have been easy.

Cooper immediately wrapped her in his arms and kissed her forehead. Kiely took a deep breath and held it for a brief moment before blowing it out slowly.

"How did your meeting go?" Cooper asked.

"It went really well," Kiely responded. And it had. After Vikki had made her exit, Kiely and her siblings had a conversation about her taking a step back from the business. She wanted to continue working on Brody's case until it was resolved, but didn't want to take on anything new. Her family had been super supportive. Riley, in particular, had let her know he would be there for her however she needed him to be. He promised not to call on her until she was ready.

"What did the insurance agent have to say?"

"Well, you won't be renting it anytime soon."

Kiely laughed. "So the agent has jokes like you have jokes."

"You had full coverage, so you have nothing to worry about. They'll be paying you fair market value for the house and for the land. When you're ready you can decide whether or not you want to rebuild or sell."

"I'm glad I don't have to make a decision anytime soon."

"Not until you're ready." He kissed her again.

"We have an hour before we have to pick up Alfie. Is there anything special you'd like to do?" He arched his eyebrows and gave her a look.

Kiely laughed. "Aren't you fresh!"

"We've never done an afternoon quickie."

"We might have to do that."

Cooper reached for her hand and entwined her fingers between his own.

"Twenty questions?"

"Ask away."

"Chicken or beef?"

"Beef, preferably grass fed. Birth control?"

Cooper looked confused. "Birth control?"

"Stop or keep taking it," she said teasingly.

He grinned. "Interesting! Stop or keep taking it? Hmm? I'd be happy either way. As long as you're happy with whatever decision you make for your body."

Kiely smiled and lifted her chin to reach his lips. She kissed him slowly, allowing her mouth to glide sweetly over his.

"Favorite girl names?"

"Good question! Emily, Allison and Grace are at the top of my list."

"I love Grace."

"Shaved or unshaved?"

"Are we talking a specific body part or body parts in general?" Cooper questioned.

Kiely shrugged her shoulders, a sly look on her face.

"Some parts shaved and some parts not shaved," he answered.

Kiely laughed and Cooper laughed with her. Joy blew with a quiet breeze that billowed around them. The temperature was beginning to drop and there was just a hint of a chill in the air. Kiely pressed herself against him and kissed his lips one more time.

"I have tinted windows," she said. "You ever get a quickie in the back seat of a new car?"

Cooper grinned. "No, but I think I'm about to."

Kiely turned and headed toward her new vehicle. Her hips swayed seductively from side to side. Cooper looked around quickly to see who might be watching and then he hurried after her. She climbed into the back seat and he followed. As he closed and locked the door, Kiely's delightful laugh danced sweetly with his.

* * * * *

COMING SOON!

We really hope you enjoyed reading this book. If you're looking for more romance, be sure to head to the shops when new books are available on

Thursday 15th October

To see which titles are coming soon, please visit
millsandboon.co.uk/nextmonth

MILLS & BOON

LET'S TALK

Romance

For exclusive extracts, competitions
and special offers, find us online:

f facebook.com/millsandboon

🐦 @MillsandBoon

📷 @MillsandBoonUK

Get in touch on 01413 063232

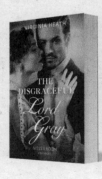  

MILLS & BOON

THE HEART OF ROMANCE

A ROMANCE FOR EVERY KIND OF READER

MODERN

Prepare to be swept off your feet by sophisticated, sexy and seductive heroes, in some of the world's most glamourous and romantic locations, where power and passion collide.
8 stories per month.

HISTORICAL

Escape with historical heroes from time gone by. Whether your passion is for wicked Regency Rakes, muscled Vikings or rugged Highlanders, awaken the romance of the past.
6 stories per month.

MEDICAL

Set your pulse racing with dedicated, delectable doctors in the high-pressure world of medicine, where emotions run high and passion, comfort and love are the best medicine.
6 stories per month.

True Love

Celebrate true love with tender stories of heartfelt romance, from the rush of falling in love to the joy a new baby can bring, and a focus on the emotional heart of a relationship.
8 stories per month.

Desire

Indulge in secrets and scandal, intense drama and plenty of sizzling hot action with powerful and passionate heroes who have it all: wealth, status, good looks…everything but the right woman.
6 stories per month.

HEROES

Experience all the excitement of a gripping thriller, with an intense romance at its heart. Resourceful, true-to-life women and strong, fearless men face danger and desire - a killer combination!
8 stories per month.

DARE

Sensual love stories featuring smart, sassy heroines you'd want as a best friend, and compelling intense heroes who are worthy of them.
4 stories per month.

To see which titles are coming soon, please visit

millsandboon.co.uk/nextmonth

JOIN US ON SOCIAL MEDIA!

Stay up to date with our latest releases, author news and gossip, special offers and discounts, and all the behind-the-scenes action from Mills & Boon...

 millsandboon

 millsandboonuk

 millsandboon

It might just be true love...

GET YOUR ROMANCE FIX!

MILLS & BOON
— *blog* —

Get the latest romance news, exclusive author interviews, story extracts and much more!

MILLS & BOON
MODERN
Power and Passion

Prepare to be swept off your feet by sophisticated, sexy and seductive heroes, in some of the world's most glamourous and romantic locations, where power and passion collide.

MILLS & BOON
DARE

Sexy. Passionate. Bold.

Sensual love stories featuring smart, sassy heroines you'd want as a best friend, and compelling intense heroes who are worthy of them.